A Tale Between Two Cities

Author: *Na An*

Translator: *Wu Ming*

Editor: *Qiao Xihua*

Remembering Publishing. USA

A Tale Between Two Cities
Author: Na An
Translator: Wu Ming
Editor: Qiao Xihua

ISBN：   978-1-68560-196-6   (Print)
              978-1-68560-197-3   (eBook)
LCCN：   2025 914723

September 2025, First Edition, First Printing

Remembering Publishing, LLC
RememPub@gmail.com

PREFACE

A Book that Tells a True Chinese Story

Xu Xin

A foreign writer recently criticized Chinese literature and art for having too many clichés. When discussing the way out for Chinese creation of literature and art, he emphasized that works must tell true Chinese stories. He expressed the basic law of artistic creation in ancient and modern times, both at home and abroad: truth is the life of art. I think the novel "Between Two Cities" is a book that truly tells a Chinese story.

The work truly describes the life of migrant workers in Guangdong at the turn of the century. The novel tells the story of a typical situation in Gongbei, a place bordering Macau under the "one country, two systems", where migrant workers hope to change their fate through cross-border marriage or acting as cross-border underground lovers. The protagonist Zheng Jianxin, in an awkward status, sticks to the moral high ground of universal values, creates life via her own hard work, and maintains the purity of love. The meticulous portrayal of her in terms of "ambition" and "emotion" has refinedly shaped Zheng Jianxin, a fresh artistic image that maintains dignity, fights against fate, and is deeply touching.

The "truth, goodness, and beauty" of art is based on "truth". While truly revealing the mental journey of Zheng Jianxin, Xu Zhuang, Lili and other migrant workers chewing the bitterness of the times, the author always runs through the thinking of "people" in real life, expresses the deepest desire of the disadvantaged groups for fair life, and is immersed in generous humanistic care, thus forming the artistic charm of the novel to impress and inspire readers with the desire towards upward and goodness.

I

In the picture of life in two cities, the author's descriptions of characters such as Lili, who has become a socialite, Bai Lang, a Taiwanese businessman who failed in investment, Chen Xiao, a corporate cadre who is confused about society and has a distorted personality, and Xu Zhuang, who insists on the principle of not destroying other people's marriages but waits hopelessly and attracts investment to change the poverty of his hometown, are all vivid.

The author reveals humor from time to time in the difficult days, which makes readers laugh in the heavy topic. In particular, the typical image of Liang Xiangyun, a special product of Macau society, pathological gambler, is very rare in the history of Chinese literature, adding an extremely vivid character portrait to the gallery of Chinese literary characters.

In addition, although the novel does not describe much about Chen Tianpeng, a patriotic old overseas Chinese, and Kuang Zhenzhu, a Macau businesswoman, together with the story of the Zhuhai Fisher Girl, it sets off the enthusiastic atmosphere of investment and construction in the Special Administrative Region. The description of the fate of Zheng Jianxin's father generation in his hometown and the sad love story of Zhong Wang, a Macau man, and Ali, a comb girl (a girl swears not to marry), expands the background of the novel and renders it a deep sense of historical weight.

The production and investment data of those labor-intensive small factories in the novel show the realism of the details of the novel. From this perspective, the author has a deep understanding of the "sweatshops" and "first pot of gold" in the early days of China's reform and opening up. This is rare in current literary works.

The social life of Zhuhai and Macau, which are two cities across the border but unified as one city, is rare. The work vividly shows this unique regional life and the impact of China's economic changes on the lives of people in the two cities, making the whole novel full of a strong and unique atmosphere of life.

The author personally experienced the reform and opening up of the Special Administrative Region and accumulated countless stories of ups and downs in his life, which prompted him to consciously embark on the road of realistic creation. Realism has made brilliant achievements in Chinese and even world literature and history. However, the road of realistic creation in China in the 20th century was full of thorns. Especially during the Cultural Revolution, starting from "class struggle" and "line struggle", the idealist "theme first" was advocated, and characters were fabricated, story plots were made up, and bold words were sought. It completely severed the connection between literature and people's lives and social practice, resulting in the falsification and formulaicization of literary and artistic works. It has not been completely eliminated to this day. Reviewing the past to learn new things, telling the real story of China, and taking the road of realism, I hope that this generation of writers and readers will keep a clear mind when welcoming the climax of the Chinese literary revival and building a magnificent building of a cultural power.

December 25, 2011
In Macau-Zhuhai

Xu Xin, researcher of the Cultural Affairs Bureau/Museum of the Macau Special Administrative Region, famous scholar in Macau, screenwriter of the 2011 Huabiao Award Movie "Xinghai" (Young Xian Xinghai). Mr. Xu has passed away. I would like to commemorate him here.

People are Running Around, What Are They Looking For?

Macau is a peninsula. If the mainland is a hand, it is a little fingertip extending from the palm. There are two bridges on the peninsula, connecting it with two outlying islands. Macau has an area of less than 30 square kilometers and a population of less than 500,000. But it is the earliest place where Chinese and Western cultures met and dialogued. When Hong Kong was still a barren land, it was already the busiest place for China's foreign trade. More than 400 years ago, Portugal exercised jurisdiction over it in the name of leasing land, until December 20, 1999, when China took back the sovereignty of Macau and implemented the "one country, two systems" policy, with Macau people governing Macau. It is still the world-famous Oriental gambling city and the colorful city that never sleeps.

On the mainland side, with the development of the Zhuhai Special Economic Zone, Zhuhai, a small border town, has become a prosperous city. Various industrial parks attract investors from home and abroad. In recent years, labor-intensive enterprises have gradually faded out, and technology companies, large-scale aerospace industries, and port industries have become increasingly popular.

Where the Macau Peninsula connects to the mainland, a gate is set up, which has become the dividing line between the two "worlds". The symbol of the Macau Gate is a Western Arc de Triomphe-style building with the words "1849" on the wall. The Zhuhai Gongbei Port Joint Inspection Building is a classical Chinese building with a large roof, solemn and majestic.

The left side of the building is the departure hall, and the right side is the arrival hall. In front of the building is an open square. Every day, 100,000 to 200,000 people leave and enter the country, men, women, young and old, in an endless stream. All kinds of people dress in various clothes: elegant, strange, sloppy...... Almost all of them are in a hurry: holding briefcases, pulling small trucks, carrying various luggage carts and large and small woven bags on their shoulders and in hands..... There are all kinds of pedestrians: excited, eager, looking around, sluggish, indescribable -- they are all running around, pursuing their own lives......

Life is life after all, and life is made up of people.

The prosperity of the city is a status. The city encompasses the complex desires of human nature, and desires shape the city.

Our protagonists walked in the crowd: Liang Xiangyun, Zheng Jianxin, Zhong Haicai, Lili, Xu Zhuang, Ahua, Lin Weihua, Zeng Sheng, Bai Lang......

Table of Contents

Port Square: The wife of Macau and the mistress of Zhuhai got into a fight

Zheng Jianxin, everyone called her Ajian, was a woman in her twenties. If she was not holding her child, she looked like she was in her early twenties. Slim with gentle appearance, oval face, slightly wide forehead, she was quiet and dignified. Her eyes and lip lines had clear contours, revealing a firm and tolerant character.

Every day at 7:30 she would send her child across the border from Zhuhai. Her son Huihui was six years old and studied in Macau. There was a group of children who went to school in Macau at the border, and they were his partners in crossing the border.

After walking through the square, in front of the departure hall, Zheng Jianxin straightened her son's school uniform again, tightened his shoelaces, and then hung the schoolbag on his back, kissed his forehead lovingly, and gently pushed him to the departure hall.

The child turned around, hugged her soft waist affectionately, and buried his head in her arms: "Mommy, running around like this every day is so tiring! I really want to go to school in Zhuhai and spend more time with Mommy!"

It was hard for the little child. After queuing up to pass the Chinese border inspection, walk a nearly 300-meter-long road to the Macau border inspection building, and then queue up for entry verification, enter Macau, and be greeted by the teachers of the "Supervision Center" (childcare center). Every day.

Gently stroking the back of her son's head, Zheng Jianxin's fair face showed a trace of helplessness: "Mommy wants it too, baby, you are from Macau, and you can go to school in Macau for free; the tuition in Zhuhai is very expensive, and Mommy can't afford it!"

Looking up at his mother's familiar expression, the child blinked and nodded sensibly: "I know!"

Whenever she saw her energetic son's smart little figure and his friends blending into the other side of the border, her pretty face would be filled with relief.

In the departure hall, the electronic boards of more than 20 channels displayed the words "Chinese Hong Kong and Macau Residents", "Chinese Mainland Residents", "Foreigners", "Chinese Taiwan Residents" and "Diplomatic Courtesies". The son and his friends lined up in a line with the "Chinese Hong Kong and Macau Residents" sign. After passing the border inspection counter, Huihui waved to his mother and soon disappeared in the crowd.

Turning to face Zhuhai, Zheng Jianxin's heart became as broad as the square in front of her. Her daily life was very fulfilling, but at this moment, she was actually a little confused. It was still early, and her steps slowed down involuntarily.

The flow of people in the west arrival hall was sparser. Most of those who rushed to enter Zhuhai through customs were housewives from Macau who came to buy vegetables. Among them, there were many "smugglers" -- Macau people called them "walking ghosts". Liang Xiangyun was obviously such a person.

She was over fifty years old, not tall, with a slightly hunched back, a thin face, a little nearsighted, wearing a blue-flowered white shirt, a silver plastic "hairpin" on her head, barefoot in a pair of dark blue plastic sandals.

Liang Xiangyun, like other Macau housewives, usually pulled a small cart for shopping, loaded two boxes of beverages and other items on the cart, and handed them to the grocery store near the customs ("semi-underground" purchasing point). She didn't say a word. She could earn more than 20 yuan for two boxes. After getting the money, she walked away silently.

Sometimes, people bring large quantities of goods to the Macau border, but they could not pass the customs due to quantity restrictions, such as clothes (customs stipulates that each person cannot carry more than 30 pieces). So those who do wholesale business ask these Macau "housewives" to take them through the customs. Once they pass the customs, they are handed over to the owner, and each piece was given one or two yuan, and high-end items such as high-end fashion, furs, and foreign wines were given more. Then these people went to Gongbei Vegetable Market to buy vegetables and daily necessities and return to their homes in Macau.

Between Shenzhen and Hong Kong, after passing the border, it is a mountainous area, and it takes a long time to take a train to the crowded urban area. This is not the case here. Zhuhai and Macau seem to be connected to become one big city. The port, which Macau people call it as Border Gate, is like a crossroads in the middle of a street. Unemployed housewives like Liang Xiangyun sometimes traveled five or six times a day, or even more than ten times, earning one or two hundred yuan to supplement their family expenses.

The only difference from the past was that she looked nervous today, her eyes were rolling around, which made her colleagues and the customs officers, who were already familiar with her, look at her a few more times.

"Zheng Jianxin! Zheng Jianxin!"

Zheng Jianxin, who was walking back slowly while thinking in the square, was startled by the scream with joy, hatred and pleasure. Before she could tell which direction the sound came from, her right arm was grabbed by someone in a burst of impatient footsteps, and the scream became a little deafening at the same time.

"Fifty thousand! Ajian, give me fifty thousand now, I will divorce my husband today, and you can apply for immigration to Macau!" Liang Xiangyun said in a clumsy but understandable Mandarin.

The incoherent words made Zheng Jianxin a little confused, but the old face in front of her made her understand what was going on in an instant. It can be seen that the two men wearing black round-necked sweatshirts behind Liang Xiangyun were the debt collectors of "big-eared

3

loan sharks" (loan sharks).

"Liang Xiangyun" Zheng Jianxin took a step back to get rid of the pull of her right arm, looking at the old woman in front of her with a vigilant face, "What do you want to do?"

The cold eyes made the other party weak all of a sudden. The woman looked back a little timidly, clasped her hands together, and begged in a voice several dozen degrees lower:

"I promise to do what I say, Ajian, I only want 50,000 yuan to divorce my husband. Can you give it to me now?"

Zheng Jianxin took another step back with disgust and disdain:

"What does it have to do with me if you lose money in gambling by borrowing usury?!"

Liang Xiangyun's embarrassed face immediately turned gray, her slightly hunched body trembled, and her begging voice even trembled a little: "I have a bad life. I lost 20,000 yuan the day before yesterday. You know, there is only a three-day interest-free period. After tonight, I have to pay double. If I can't pay it back, they can do anything. I know you have money, you......"

"I don't!"

Zheng Jianxin shook her head firmly and turned to leave. "Don't leave!" Liang Xiangyun grabbed her with both hands, turned to the two young men who already looked a little ugly and smiled coquettishly: "You two guys, wait a moment, I will pay you back. This woman owes me a lot of money......"

"Don't talk nonsense!" Zheng Jianxin shook her off again, "When did I owe you money?"

Then she turned around and left. Glancing at the people slowly gathering around to watch the fun, Liang Xiangyun saw that the two young men looked even uglier. She rolled her eyes and blinked a few times, stamped her feet, pointed at Zheng Jianxin and screamed even louder:

"You 'Canmei' (a derogatory term with the meaning of poverty and shabby)! You, a vixen who cheats on men, a shameless mistress, how many years have you been with my husband, ten or eight years? Tell me, how much money have you cheated from him? Tell me! I shoul have half of the money my husband earns, and you still dare to say that you don't owe me money? And, God knows what kind of tricks you, a vixen, have used. Even my daughter has been coaxed into submission by you. You have cheated a lot from her, right? Don't think I don't know!"

Zheng Jianxin lowered her head in anger.

People were pointing and whispering around: "It's the mistress who caused the trouble again......"

Zheng Jianxin was embarrassed by the commotion, and she lost control a little in embarrassment: "Who is your husband? Who seduced your husband? Don't talk nonsense!"

"Zhong Haicai!"

Liang Xiangyun was proud all of a sudden, "Zhong Haicai is my husband! We had a formal wedding. The marriage certificate is still in my house! You northern girl, vixen, you seduced my husband just to become a Macau resident?! A toad wants to become a phoenix, you are so beautiful......"

Looking at her short body but desperately holding her head high and chest out, and hearing her inappropriate words, more and more onlookers started to make a fuss. Some people who were afraid of no chaos in the world screamed and added fuel to the fire. For a while, various dialects intertwined and gathered, and one wave after another rushed Zheng Jianxin even more angry. In addition, Liang Xiangyun's sudden marriage declaration made her at a loss for a while.

"Nonsense!" Zheng Jianxin screamed hysterically, "Brother Zhong and I are the ones who got married legally. I......"

"Brother Zhong?" Liang Xiangyun sneered disdainfully, interrupting her with goosebumps all over her body, "How disgusting! Your own father is not even older than he, right? Shameless bitch, do you lack fatherly love or are you looking for a dad?"

The surrounding boos were everywhere, Zheng Jianxin's face flushed instantly, and she used her hands to pull back her thick shoulder-length hair, pointed at Liang Xiangyun and said "you, you, you" for a long time, but couldn't say a word again. In a hurry, she threw out a Cantonese curse, "You damn bitch!"

"What? You want to hit me? Am I afraid of you, a vixen?!" Liang Xiangyun was very proud of her achievements. She pulled the corner of her blue-flowered white shirt, glanced proudly at the countless spectators around her, stepped forward and slapped Zheng Jianxin's hand that was pointing at her. She wanted to seize the opportunity to expand her achievements. She wanted to defeat this woman who had suppressed her for several years. She knew that only by suppressing Zheng Jianxin mentally could she get the money she wanted.

Zhong Haicai had long been hopeless for her, but she wanted to prove to the people around her that she was a fighter who defended her marriage and family. The boos of the onlookers made the whole world become righteous. Zheng Jianxin, realizing that things were not going well, could only passively parry. But Liang Xiangyun became more and more courageous, cursing more and more viciously, pretending to chase and beat her madly, while she did not forget to ask for money to negotiate, whispering: "Give me money and I'll let you go......"

Just as Liang Xiangyun pushed Zheng Jianxin with all her strength, a pair of big hands stretched out from the side, held Liang Xiangyun, who was disheveled and looked like a mad woman, around the waist, and then shouted in a hoarse voice: "You are a dead gossip who only knows how to gamble, haven't you quarreled enough?!"

Zheng Jianxin was pushed hard by Liang Xiangyun, and she was already stumbling, and she could no longer control her body. With a scream, the back of her head hit the pillar heavily. She fell to the ground, and her head tilted and she fell, motionless.

The onlookers suddenly quieted down, and all their eyes were focused on Zheng Jianxin's graceful body, with different expressions on their faces.

"Ah...... bleeding!" The woman closest to Zheng Jianxin suddenly screamed.

The short and fat man who was still holding the crazy Liang Xiangyun threw her away. He was a little out of breath, and rushed to Zheng Jianxin's side and grabbed her hand. While checking the situation, he shouted anxiously: "Ajian, are you okay? Wake up......"

The onlookers immediately figured out the identity of this man. Everyone's eyes were on the beautiful Zheng Jianxin lying on the ground and the old man with bald head and swollen eyes. The strong contrast made the men on the scene full of envy and jealousy that could not be concealed and the women there full of disdain and contempt.

The onlookers were crowded. They didn't know each other at first, but in an instant they were whispering and chattering like old friends. Some said, he knew one of the two women; another said the younger one lived at a certain street corner...... In short, the words that were whispered one after another were summarized into one theme: "The wife and mistress are fighting!"

Liang Xiangyun, who was thrown away, finally calmed down a little. Looking at Zheng Jianxin lying motionless on the ground, she realized that she had caused a big disaster. However, her pitiful self-esteem made her unwilling to admit defeat. In addition, there were countless "supporters" around her. How could she let the victory go?

"Zhong Haicai, just help this vixen!" Liang Xiangyun roared again, but her trembling voice and wandering eyes made her look a little fierce. "If you don't give me money, don't blame me. I have someone in the police department in my hometown in mainland China. I will sue you for bigamy and put you in jail......"

"If Ajian has mishap, I will turn you into a concrete pillar and throw you into the sea tomorrow!" Zhong Haicai turned his head and glared at her, roaring in a deep voice.

Liang Xiangyun was startled and took a step back to look around for help. However, the onlookers saw that the situation developed beyond their expectations, and they also heard something strange from the conversation between the three people. They all lost their righteousness, shut up their mouths and avoided Liang Xiangyun's eyes, unwilling to get involved.

Although she did not get support, Liang Xiangyun was surprised to find that the two loan sharks who had been following her and waiting for her to pay back the money had disappeared. It made her feel greatly relieved.

"Disperse, disperse, what are you doing?" The patrol police in the square appeared. They dispersed the crowd, asked briefly about the cause, called an ambulance. Thus ended the farce.

There were constant sighs in the crowd: "It's all the mistress's fault!"

People were talking, and no one could tell whether it was true or false.

Zheng Jianxin's injuries were not serious. She woke up on her own as soon as the ambulance entered the hospital. After some examination, treatment and bandaging, she was fine. However, in case it should get worse, Zhong Haicai followed the doctor's advice and let her stay in the hospital for observation.

Outside the emergency room, Liang Xiangyun walked around restlessly. She no longer had any hope of getting the money. If Zheng Jianxin really had an injury, even if Zhong Haicai would not really turn her into a concrete pillar and throw her into the sea, she would be in jail.

Through the gap in the observation room, Liang Xiangyun saw that after Zheng Jianxin was bandaged, she was able to sit up halfway with the help of Zhong Haicai. Her face was a little pale, but her eyes were still clear. She patted her chest and breathed a sigh of relief: "Goddess bless, Goddess bless ......"

Liang Xiangyun clasped her hands together, murmured, looked at both sides of the corridor again and again, and then sneaked towards the door. No one knows whether her prayer was for Zheng Jianxin's safety, or to pray that she would not meet the two big-eared loan sharks again.

At noon, Zheng Jianxin took the fish soup with Zhong Haicai's help. But a pair of her doubtful eyes turned on his face from time to time. The man in front of her was already fifty-five or fifty-six years old, with clear forehead wrinkles, sparse hairs, and a few faint age spots on his sagging cheeks. Only his eyes still had some light. Years of working on the construction site, sun exposure and water exposure had made his skin dark and he looked older than his age.

Zheng Jianxin's heart skipped a beat. She pushed away Zhong Haicai's hand that was about to feed her again, glaring at him:

"Is what Liang Xiangyun said in the port square this morning true?"

"What?" Zhong Haicai was confused, putting down the tableware and wiping the soup that splashed on his body, "What's true?"

"She said she has a marriage certificate with you?"

Zheng Jianxin's eyes were sharp, and she didn't miss any changes in Zhong Haicai's expression.

"You believe her words?" Zhong Haicai stopped and frowned, "For money, what can she say?"

"But she said it as if it were true......" Zheng Jianxin continued to capture his expression with doubt, "If you dare to lie to me, do you know what the consequences will be?"

"No!" Zhong Haicai shook his head firmly, "We have been together for seven years, don't you know my background? I have a child with her, and we have never registered for marriage. If her words were true, she would have asked me for money to gamble every day in the past few years."

Zheng Jianxin saw that he really didn't look like a liar, and was confused.

2

Facing the foreign boss lady,
Zheng Jianxin shouted: I won't kneel

Seven years is not a long time, but it is enough to change many things, such as a city, a group of people, and a heart.

The story started from 1992, seven years before.

Zheng Jianxin had just come to Zhuhai from a small mountain village in Guizhou, from a place full of frogs and cicadas to a place full of bright lights and wine. She felt like she had gone from a bungalow to a skyscraper all of a sudden. She was a little overwhelmed and a little dizzy.

However, with the comfort and company of her fellow villager Lili and Lili's cousin Xu Zhuang, Zheng Jianxin quickly adapted to the environment. Through the introduction of another fellow villager Chen Xiao, she entered a joint venture electronics factory called Deyue.

"It's so annoying, going out of the ravine and into the ravine again!" Zheng Jianxin sighed. The boss was too stingy in calculating the cost and built the factory in a village-run industrial zone at the foot of a mountain in the far suburbs. Zheng Jianxin, who thought she had a strong body for work and could not be tired. But having worked for a week, her bones were about to fall apart. In order to make money, she gritted her teeth, telling herself: "Hang on, hang on!"

This factory had been in operation for more than ten years. It was a large workshop at best, like the handicraft workshops seen in the movies. Gradually, Zheng Jianxin learned that in the early days of the establishment of the special zone, people from Hong Kong and Macao took advantage of the policy. They could spend 300,000 to 500,000 yuan by one person, or several million yuan by a few people together, to open such labor-intensive small factories while enjoying various preferential policies. When the boss lady heard that the workers were complaining, she also complained: "You still have money to get, but I am losing money every month, and I may have to close down one day!"

Her words were not groundless. Labor-intensive industries, such as electronics, toys, and shoemaking, were moved from Europe and the United States to Japan, and then from Japan to Taiwan. The boss lady took over third-hand and fourth-hand orders from the Taiwanese, and the profit margin was often a few percent to 15 percent. If the payment for goods couldn't be received as scheduled, there was no money to advance the cost of raw materials. If some defective products were returned, it was not surprising to say that there would be a loss. Factories around were closed from time to time.

It was these factories scattered across the Pearl River Delta that absorbed thousands of migrant workers from other places like sponges absorbing water droplets. The factory stipulated that the working hours were twelve hours a day, from eight in the morning to ten at night, lunch time included. Zheng Jianxin's workstation was the first step in the workshop, stamping the product name code on the magnetic core, which was called "stamping".

The piecework wage for stamping was a quota system: one thousand stamps per hour, and the pay was one yuan and eighty cents. If the quota was not completed, the wage would be deducted. Zheng Jianxin's hands were fast, operating like a machine. She could barely complete the quota. The salary was nineteen yuan and eighty cents a day. Excluding one day off a week, working six days a week, a month wis four hundred and thirty-five yuan and twenty cents. The factory only counted overtime after ten o'clock in the evening. Overtime had an overtime pay of one yuan and a midnight snack allowance of one yuan to two yuan. Everyone was vying for overtime. Working four hours overtime until two o'clock in the morning could earn five yuan and twenty cents. A month meant one hundred and thirty-five yuan and twenty cents. Including wage and overtime pay, Zheng Jianxin's first month's pay was five hundred and seventy yuan and forty cents.

The factory dormitory cost 30 yuan per month which was deducted from the salary. The food was five yuan per day. The factory subsidized two yuan. The worker paid three yuan, which was 90 yuan a month deducted from salary. Zheng Jianxin received 450.40 yuan in cash. She was very excited. As her family needed to buy fertilizer, Zheng Jianxin immediately sent back 300 yuan. Zheng Jianxin's feeling of sweetness after suffering made her enjoy it very much.

Zheng Jianxin was a girl who could endure and be resilient. She didn't get enough sleep. She yawned from time to time at her workstation on the assembly line. She kept hitting her head and her mouth to wake herself up. At the end of the day, she felt dizzy and her face looked like an apple.

Another problem was the food. In her hometown, potatoes were the main food, baked potatoes and boiled potatoes. The factory provided three dishes and one soup. The main dish included two or three small pieces of meat or two small pieces of ribs stewed with potatoes or stewed lotus roots. The two side dishes were boiled vegetables and fried cucumbers, which were very small in quantity. Although the soup was called "seaweed egg drop soup" or "tomato egg drop soup", it was no different from plain water. A kitchen chef who worked part-time secretly told his co-worker Afang that the canteen of more than 100 workers only bought 100 yuan worth of vegetables at the market every day.

No wonder she felt hungry again not long after eating. Because of severe malnutrition, Zheng Jianxin's mouth always blistered and ulcered, and she hadn't had her period for two months.

Zheng Jianxin ignored all these. After all, she had more than ten "old heads" (100 yuan bills) in her pocket. When she invited Lili and two fellow villagers to eat at the food stall, she said with great ambition: I won't go back, I want to build my own career here.

Work, eat, sleep; work, eat, sleep.

The factory was more than ten kilometers away from the city, surrounded by sparse villages. At night, it was pitch black, with frogs and insects singing, and the clanging sounds from time to time in the factory building, which looked weird and lifeless.

Except for going out on Sundays, Zheng Jianxin, like other workers, spent all her time in the factory area, monotonous and repetitive, like a machine. Soon she was exhausted and lost her passion. She felt like a walking corpse, and realized that the working life in the prosperous world outside was not as beautiful as she thought when she was in her hometown.

The only surprise and nourishment was the sweet talk with Xu Zhuang on the phone. Only then did she feel that she was a flesh-and-blood person with emotions and desires.

Such days were repeated for more than half a year, and Zheng Jianxin's first disaster in the special zone happened.

The workers' dormitory was a four-story building. The first and second floors were for male workers and the third and fourth floors for females. The day before, the female workers' dormitory was locked at ten o'clock in the evening as usual. Zheng Jianxin and several female workers repeatedly pleaded with the administrator: there were still a few female workers who had not returned.

The boss lady flashed out and shouted angrily: "I knew they ran away! Let them come back but can't enter the dormitory, and sleep in the fields with wild men!"

The female workers' dormitory was very crowded. The door of the dormitory was locked every night and watched by guards. It was already annoying. Zheng Jianxin didn't know how she was so bold. She shouted to the boss lady: "We are human beings. This is not a pigpen or doghouse......"

The boss lady seemed reasonable in public and said considerately: "The female workers' dormitory is locked at night. Factories in Hong Kong and Shenzhen are like this to prevent men of questionable character from committing crimes and disturbing you girls. It's all for safety!"

In fact, the factory was afraid that the workers would go outside after work, get in touch with the outside world more, and become complicated in their thinking, or change jobs, or ask the factory for raise, improvement of treatment and other conditions. The owner only needs laborers, laborers that would work day in day out.

"You just treat us as living tools!" Zheng Jianxin couldn't stand such "courtesy".

Several females, unable to resist the instigation of their boyfriends, went to the town video hall to watch a movie. It was too late, and they shouted anxiously again and again. The manager was gloating in his heart, and just said slowly: "The boss lady took the key away!"

A few brave old female workers couldn't stand it anymore, and broke the iron chain of the lock with a hammer. The door opened, and the female workers in the whole dormitory cheered.

The hammer that broke the chain also hit the boss lady's heart, making her furious, losing the civilized elegance and rationality of Hong Kong people that she was often proud of. Her permed hair flashed black light, her face turned from gray to purple eggplant, and the loose muscles in her elbows shook. She rushed into the female workers' dormitory and ordered all the female workers to get out of bed and stand in the corridor immediately.

Many female workers were barefoot in pajamas, and they couldn't help shivering in the cold night of early spring.

The boss lady yelled: "Do you know how difficult it is for the company to get an order now? If the factory closes, you will all have to leave and have no food to eat, do you know that? Those who smashed the chains, stand up!"

After shouting three times, no one said anything. She wiped the sweat off her face and fiercely ordered all the female workers to kneel down and admit their blunders!

Zheng Jianxin and the other two females stood up and argued and would not kneel down.

The boss lady became more and more furious: "Either kneel down and admit your mistakes, or pack up and leave tomorrow!"

In the end, Zheng Jianxin and the other two chose the latter.

She couldn't figure out how things suddenly turned out like this. Although the factory didn't make her feel much belonging and the work didn't make her feel very happy, at least it was her first job outside the village. It was the first step for her to become independent and even give back to her parents and relatives. She silently accepted this environment and cherished it a little.

But......

Life in the countryside was poor, and it was also a struggle for money. It was the need for survival. After arriving in Guangdong, Zheng Jianxin heard and witnessed how people were madly chasing after money like flies to rotten meat in order to get a luxurious and noble life, and how they did not care about their dignity and personality in order to survive. Although her thoughts changed a little, she still could not accept it in her heart -- the domineering attitude built on money and the domineering attitude built on power.

"I won't kneel!" Zheng Jianxin's movements were slow and her eyes were blank, but she still uttered these words gently.

The next morning, Zheng Jianxin lay straight on the bed. She felt her body getting hotter and hotter, and she tossed and turned for a while before falling asleep again.

Where is this? There are so many people......

This house is so big, is it the palace? Are there so many people?

......

What is this, a table covered with green velvet in front of her? Is it the gambling table that she has seen on TV before?

Zheng Jianxin turned around with a little horror, and was a little panicked for a while: Why am I here?

Behind her, four men and women with rural looks and clothes complimented her with a smile: "Sister Jian, you are so amazing, you won millions in a short time......"

15

"Ha, let's continue." Zheng Jianxin signaled the dealer to deal the cards.

Flip the cards!

Zheng Jianxin won again. In the end, there was only a fat man who lost a lot of money playing against her.

The fat man took off his suit, untied his tie, and took out a silver revolver from his waist.

At this time, Lili appeared from nowhere and poked Zheng Jianxin from behind: "Ajian, go back!"

Zheng Jianxin shook her head slightly in response. The fat man's face was as bright as the moon: "Kneel down, beg me, be my woman!"

"Kneel?" Zheng Jianxin's eyes became wandering.

When she turned her head, the fat man disappeared, replaced by the factory's boss lady. She looked in her heart, and her eyes instantly regained clarity: "No kneeling! No kneeling! I won't kneel even if I die!"

Bang!

Blood flew past people around in a graceful arc.

"I lost!" Zheng Jianxin knelt down with weak legs.

When her knees were about to touch the ground, she stood up suddenly, holding the edge of the gambling table, and shouted: "I—will not—kneel!"

"Zheng Jianxin! Zheng Jianxin!"

Zheng Jianxin sat up with a "ah", and what came into her eyes was her mosquito net, her cup, and her woven bag that she had almost packed.

"I'm still in the dormitory? Was it just a dream?" Zheng Jianxin shook her head to make herself more awake. In the dream, it was the scene from Hong Kong and Western movies she had watched in the video room.

"Are you Zheng Jianxin?" The voice that had just awakened her sounded again.

Zheng Jianxin turned her head and saw a sturdy man standing in front of her, with a black baton hanging around his waist. His clothes revealed his identity as the security guard of the factory.

"Yes......" Zheng Jianxin was surprised to find that her mouth was dry and sweaty as soon as she opened her mouth. The word "yes" seemed to be spinning in her throat, and she couldn't spit it out clearly. She had no choice but to nod her head.

"You can leave, now!"

The security guard threw her ID card on the bed and turned away. According to the rules of the factories in this area, workers should surrender their ID cards to the factory after entering the factory and could get cards back when they left.

Zheng Jianxin's chaotic brain finally turned around, and she was speechless looking at her ID card.

According to the factory regulations, fired employees should leave the factory on the same day, even at night. According to Afang, the security guard came twice. The females pleaded for mercy. The security guard was also a worker. Seeing that she had a fever, it was difficult to drive her away. So he let her sleep until the afternoon.

"This is the fate of workers." Zheng Jianxin wanted to cry but had no tears.

The terrible thing was that she didn't have a fever earlier or later, but she had a fever at this time. Now she was weak all over. Where could she go? Whom could she rely on?

Afang, Aju and other females silently helped her pack her things, found antipyretic medicine for her to take, and helped her to the factory gate, wishing each other well and telling her to take care of herself. According to the factory regulations, workers could not leave the factory without the factory's pass. Therefore, they could not go with her out of the factory.

From this village-run industrial zone to the Shangchong bus station, it was four or five miles to walk along a small path. They were worried that Zheng Jianxin's weak body could not support it, but they could do nothing to help her, so they had to wave goodbye with tears.

Zheng Jianxin walked out of the factory gate. The construction site in the wilderness had just dug out a foundation pit. A gust of wind blew the moisture of the soil into her lungs, and she suddenly felt sober and relaxed.

The public telephone booth on the left side of the road was coated with a layer of dark orange outline in the afterglow of the setting sun. It was Wednesday, and 8 o'clock in the evening was the time to call Xu Zhuang. Now there was no need to wait, she would go directly to him.

Thinking of Xu Zhuang, her eyes lit up and her heart was much more comfortable. Zheng Jianxin still felt a little weak, a ball of hot air covered her whole body, breathing was difficult, as if she would fall down at any time. In order to support her body, she picked up a branch on the side of the road as a walking stick.

After walking a few steps, she couldn't help but laugh out loud, "Hasn't this become Sister Xianglin in Lu Xun's works?" "Am I really as pitiful as Sister Xianglin?" Thinking of this, she threw the stick far to the side of the road in anger, straightened her chest and looked forward.

She shouted "wow" and "wow", using this method to encourage herself, letting the big beads of sweat fall all the way on the dusty path.

3

The beautiful tenant in Gaosha Street -- Lili

For Zheng Jianxin, Xu Zhuang was still working for Hong Kong people on the boat, eating and living on the boat. His whereabouts were uncertain. Only by going to Gongbei to find Lili could she find Xu Zhuang. For now, she had to stay with her temporarily.

Lili was three years older than she, a fellow villager and former classmate, and Xu Zhuang's cousin. The two of them, together with Mingming, who had "bought" a house in Gongbei and opened a coffee shop, became the "golden phoenix" in the eyes of the mountain people because of their outstanding appearance and proud figure. From "Village Flower" to "School Flower" in middle school, and then to "Golden Flower" in the village, they had always been proud of it, and were praised as three beautiful red camellias.

Mingming was the first to go out to work, followed by Lili. When Lili was about to come out, her "fiancé" at home was afraid that she, the golden phoenix, would fall into someone else's nest and never return. He insisted on marrying her before letting her go. When Lili first arrived in Zhuhai to work in a shoe factory, her marriage was regarded as an entertaining gossip by her fellow villagers. They always teased her after dinner. While the girls were having fun, they always wanted to know from her the real feeling of close contact with men.

Zhuhai in March is humid and foggy, and the wet air is full of water. The streets and alleys always look like it has just rained, and the stone-paved sidewalks are sometimes covered with a layer of water. The warm breath of early spring mixed with the sea breeze hits people, blocking their sweat and making them sticky and uncomfortable.

Zheng Jianxin carried a woven bag on her right shoulder and held a blue plastic bucket. It was the standard luggage of a migrant worker. But the brand new small square brand-name handbag on her left shoulder seemed inconsistent with her identity as a migrant worker. It was bought by Xu Zhuang for her, a favorite gift for her.

Zheng Jianxin paid two yuan for the bus fare. When she arrived at Gongbei, there were only a few rays from the setting sun in the sky fighting against the increasingly dark night. The lights of thousands of houses began to write the prosperity of the city. The passing vehicles drew a line of light returning home.

There was still some distance from the port bus station to Lili's rental place. Walking in the crowd, Zheng Jianxin's body and face were sweating, soaking her clothes. The heavy sweating made her feel weaker and weaker, and the luggage on her back became heavier and heavier. However, the high fever began to subside, and her mind became clearer.

Zheng Jianxin recalled the scene when she just walked out of the mountain village: the mountain road was winding and undulating. She and several girls of the same age who were also eager for the prosperity of the coastal areas walked on the ground, chatting and laughing, leaving footprints one by one, and their young hearts followed the dust. She wanted to be with him, longing to lean on his warm and strong chest, and rest in his solid and gentle arms. —But until now, she had not allowed Xu Zhuang to touch her.

The place where Lili rented was called Gaosha Street. It used to be a border village that was almost as poor as Zheng Jianxin's hometown village. After Zhuhai became a special economic zone, the flow of people and materials in and out of Gongbei Port doubled, and the construction investment in Gongbei also increased rapidly. Hotels and office buildings had been built one after another. Gaosha Village had taken advantage of the right time, place and people. In a few years, it had changed from a desolate beach to a busy city in the city. Gaosha Village is no longer called a village, but a street.

The changes in the world are unpredictable.

Both sides of the street were full of rectangular multi-story buildings that were built not long before. They were close to each other, with windows facing each other, so close that you could hold each other's hands. These buildings were built by villagers who demolished old houses and divided them into small rooms for rent.

However, in Zheng Jianxin's eyes, these houses that had to install anti-theft nets on the bathroom air outlets looked like pigeon coops. The narrow sewer pipes were not draining smoothly, overflowing along the walls to the small streets, and emitting bursts of stench from time to time that were suffocating.

The stinky tofu tastes delicious (it smells bad but it tastes good). The cheap rental houses here were the foothold and starting point for outsiders to make a living. Whether they were college students, engineers, laborers, job seekers, or small and medium-sized foreign investors, they had to live here first, then make plans, and then move away, one after another. Those who had no development opportunities were stranded here.

Over the pass was Macau, which was beyond the border gate, people in the gambling city were gambling. People here were also "gambling", a saying runs: "South, North, East, West, make a fortune in Guangdong". People here were gambling with their lives. Whenever she walked down the small street, Zheng Jianxin felt a lot of emotion.

Lili's rental house was on the fourth floor of a building. Zheng Jianxin had been here twice and it was not difficult to find.

"Sister Lili......" Zheng Jianxin felt a bitter throat when she saw Lili opening the door.

Lili was slightly taller than Zheng Jianxin. As her name suggests, she was more beautiful after entering the city. There were a bunch of opened cosmetic boxes on the small table. She was holding an eyelash curler in her hand, and it could be seen that she was "decorating the storefront". Lili was very happy about the arrival of her good sister. But she immediately found that the other party looked depressed. In her nervousness, she saw the luggage on her back and in her hands. She asked in surprise: "Ajian, what's going on?" She was in her pajamas and let

Zheng Jianxin into the house, "Ah...... Come in first."

Putting down the things, Zheng Jianxin tilted her neck and drank two large glasses of water, then slowly recovered her breath, and said with a wry smile: "I was fired......"

"Fired?" Lili took the cigarette box and lit a cigarette. She knew Ajian. No matter how hard the work was, she would grit her teeth and do it silently. No matter how dirty the work was, she would do it seriously without complaining. She stood aloof from worldly affairs. It was easier for her to believe that she fired her boss on her own initiative. How could she be fired by the factory all of a sudden?

Zheng Jianxin nodded with regret and told the story again.

"F..k her mother!" Lili frowned and cursed the boss lady in Cantonese. She threw down the clip in her hand and jumped up. "The crows are all black everywhere in the world!" Lili seemed to remember something. She took two breaths and asked again, "Have you been paid?"

"The account was settled." Zheng Jianxin nodded, "The piecework was not completed and was deducted. The salary of more than 500 yuan was only 207.40 yuan. According to the factory rules, you could only collect it after a month."

"Isn't this just sending away beggars?!" Lili looked indignant. She exhaled a puff of smoke but sighed helplessly, "Does Chen Xiao know?"

"Chen Xiao?" Zheng Jianxin's mouth twitched slightly and shook her head.

"You bitch, you don't even give Chen Xiao a face (favor)?" Lili punched the mattress heavily, cursing the boss lady of the Deyue factory.

"Chen Xiao is not a local official. His father in Guangzhou is retired and he has no backing. How much face can he have?" Zheng Jianxin responded indifferently, "Forget it, let's not talk about it. It's better to rely on myself for everything. I'll stay here for two days, and move out when I find a place. Okay?"

She knew that this house was rented by a Hong Konger and was not a place to stay for a long time.

"Why should we sisters be polite to each other!" Lili patted her in a scolding manner, stood up and opened the simple wardrobe, rummaging through things while mumbling, "Well, to be honest, here the rich are the boss, not in our village where everyone is related to you. If you are asked to kneel, just kneel down. What's the big deal about lowering your head under someone else's roof? It won't cost you a penny. People in the mainland live here now, and it's not easy to find a good job...... I know you are talented and ambitious, and you are stubborn, but who would recognize a small person like us?"

"Alright, alright!" Zheng Jianxin was upset when she mentioned this, and shook her hand to interrupt Lili's words.

Among the three "Red Camellias", Zheng Jianxin was not the most beautiful, but the most stubborn.

"Okay, no more talking." Lili made a playful face to amuse Zheng Jianxin, and stuffed a towel and a piece of clothing into her hands, "You are sweaty, go take a shower first!"

Zheng Jianxin hummed and returned the towel to her: "I will use my own towel, and I will wear your clothes first." Lili pushed her to the bathroom with a giggle. The bathroom in the rental house had a small squat toilet and a shower head with a faucet hanging on the wall. After taking a shower, Zheng Jianxin felt refreshed all over, and her body temperature returned to normal. Except for being a little weak, there was nothing wrong with her. Looking at her body in the bathroom mirror, with big breasts, thin waist, round buttocks, and fair and rosy skin, Zheng Jianxin couldn't help feeling a little proud and a little shy. The mountains and rivers of her hometown had made her and Lili's natural beauty, and the unremitting labor since childhood had shaped a strong and beautiful body. "Home......" Zheng Jianxin collected her thoughts, sighed softly, and put on the denim skirt suit that Lili gave her.

The skirt had good texture, was soft and smooth, fit the skin but not tight, and was very comfortable to wear.

Zheng Jianxin saw Lili wearing this skirt, and she praised it with envy at that time. She didn't expect that she would use it to satisfy herself today.

Lili said that this dress was brought to her from Hong Kong by her "man" Zeng Sheng, and it cost more than 1,000 Hong Kong dollars.

"More than 1,000 yuan......" Zheng Jianxin hesitated for a long time at that time. She didn't know how much 1,000 Hong Kong dollars was in RMB, but she knew that Hong Kong dollars were more valuable than RMB.

After leaving the bathroom, Lili, who was painting on her face in front of the makeup mirror, turned her head and looked at her. Her eyes suddenly lit up: "Ajian, this dress really suits you. You are much prettier than I."

Zheng Jianxin pulled down the hem of her skirt that was higher than her knees unnaturally and replied shyly: "I am a little unaccustomed to it."

"Unaccustomed to beauty?" Lili waved her lipstick and made a fuss, "Oh my God, are you still a woman? I'm going to operate on your stubborn brain!"

She threw down her lipstick and jumped up, ripping off the elastic band that Zheng Jianxin tied her hair with, fiddling with it while scolding: "Zheng Jianxin, Zheng Jianxin, stop...... You are still the green fruit in the mountain valley of your hometown. This is Zhuhai, a special zone and an international city, you have to make some progress......"

"I miss home."

Zheng Jianxin said a few words, and Lili, who was excited to make her beautiful, calmed down. But it was only a moment, and she continued to be busy: "Can you go back like this? Are you embarrassed to go back? Your family is counting on you......"

Zheng Jianxin looked at her somewhat decadent face in the mirror in silence, and said after a while: "Where else can I go?"

"When the cart gets to the foot of the mountain, a way will be found." Lili patted her gently, "You retreat when you encounter a little difficulty, it's not your character, Zheng Jianxin."

Zheng Jianxin hummed, letting Lili toss on her head and face.

When the cart gets to the foot of the mountain, a way will be found. Since she lost the job, she had to change her face to face this city. Crisis is a turning point, isn't it?

Zheng Jianxin suddenly remembered her dream. When she told Lili about the gemstone ring and jade bracelet she wore in the dream, she found it funny and couldn't help laughing.

Lili didn't laugh, she looked at Zheng Jianxin dimly: "Good dream! Ajian, great fortune and honor!"

Zheng Jianxin pushed Lili and laughed: "You really took it seriously!" Then she grinned bitterly, this dream was a mockery of herself.

"Anyway, Ajian, you can dream of jewelry, which means you really have it in your heart; work hard and you will have it!" Lili said, which was what Zheng Jianxin was actually talking about herself. She could not hide her desire for money. Zheng Jianxin could see that her eyes were bright as if a canopy of flames was burning. Zheng Jianxin pushed her again: "Forget it, it's just a dream, don't talk about it!"

As the two of them comforted themselves, Lili picked up the hair dryer and comb neatly, and made a seaweed-like full and curly hairstyle for Zheng Jianxin in two or three strokes. This was a hairstyle popular among cute girls on the street. She also applied a thin layer of powder on her face to cover up the weakness of a minor illness, and her eyelashes were slightly curled up, which made her look a little playful.

Zheng Jianxin stood up and turned around, looking at herself in the mirror: a sweet and lovely puff sleeve T-shirt, paired with a torn and distressed denim skirt, a new image of pure elegance, lovely and charming. Zheng Jianxin was shy and happy, and couldn't help but give Lili a thumbs up: "You are really good!"

Lili was also very satisfied with her work, proudly raised her plump chest to accept the praise from her sister, but her little mouth teased: "Oh my...... I am asking for trouble. When I go out later, you will steal the limelight. How can I face people?!"

"You are going to die......" Zheng Jianxin shyly threw her on the bed, and the two of them started to play around with laughter.

After a while of making a fuss, Lili suddenly remembered something and sat up to check the watch. She jumped to the dressing table and quickly tidied up her messy temples while shouting, "Oh no, oh no, we're going to be late...... Jian, hurry up and get ready, let's go out."

"Where are we going?" Zheng Jianxin sat up with a puzzled look on her face, "We don't need to go shopping so early, right? I haven't eaten yet!"

"There's a dinner party later, let's go together, you can eat whatever you want. Oh...... I forgot. Your fever has just gone, you should replenish your nutrition......" Lili looked at her in the mirror and said.

"Dinner?" Zheng Jianxin shook her head, "I don't want to go."

"Why not?" Lili turned around and lectured, "More friends mean more ways, and they all hold some positions!"

After a pause, Lili put her face in front of Zheng Jianxin, blinked her watery eyes, and said seductively: "Maybe they can help you. It's for job. If one company doesn't work, go to another. The world is so big, there is always a place for us to stay!"

Zheng Jianxin opened Lili's shoe cabinet, tried on shoes, and had to wear Lili's shoes again. Fortunately, not only were their figures not much different, but their feet were almost the same size, so there would be no problem of whether they were suitable or not.

While looking for shoes in the drawers, Zheng Jianxin once again stared at the photo on the top of the cabinet. It was a group photo of her, Lili, Mingming, Xu Zhuang, and several friends from her hometown. She also had this photo, but there was no place to put it, so she kept it at the bottom of the luggage bag.

"Sister Lili, has Xu Zhuang been here these days?"

Zheng Jianxin finally spoke out the words that she had been holding back since she entered the room.

Lili burst into laughter, "I know you are here to ask about Xu Zhuang. Let's see how long you can hold it back. Finally speaking?"

Zheng Jianxin's face immediately flushed with a subtle blush.

Lili said, "He is hanging out with Hong Kong guys and hasn't come to see me, his cousin, for a long time."

"Oh......" Zheng Jianxin responded with a little disappointment.

Lili, who was finishing her makeup, turned her head and said, "He talks less when he meets people now, and his eyes are cold." Seeing that Zheng Jianxin was still looking at the photo and didn't pay attention to her, she didn't continue to talk. While she was talking, she sprayed the perfume on Zheng Jianxin and her neck, and Zheng Jianxin immediately felt the mist of perfume permeating her body.

Lili finally finished. She was dressed in a street-fashionable low-cut outfit: a sleeveless low-necked shirt with pink floral patterns on a black background, and a pair of loose yellow bloomers. This extremely simple outfit, due to the contrast of color and skin color, was gorgeous and highlighted her slim figure. She wore a silver necklace with glass flowers on her fair neck, and her low round neckline inadvertently revealed her sexy collarbone. Lili's unique dress fully demonstrated the mixed breath of femininity and straightforwardness.

Zheng Jianxin shouted: "Ah! Goddess!"

Before going out, Lili deliberately posed in front of the mirror, smoothing her long hair that showed her maturity and sweetness, and giggled with self-intoxication and self-admiration, as if she would not stop until she was charming to death.

"You narcissist, stop flirting!" Zheng Jianxin said jokingly with a disgusted look.

"I did it on purpose."

Lili wore dark brown high-heeled sandals and showed her bright red toenails to Zheng Jianxin. "You look like a lotus in clear water, and I will be a flaming red rose. Let's see who can attract more attention!"

Zheng Jianxin shook hers head, not wanting to pay attention to her, and just followed her out of the door.

After leaving the door, Zheng Jianxin found that it had been drizzling from the sky at some point. The raindrops flew on her face, and it was a bit chilly. The weather here was like this, after a period of heat, there would be some rain.

This little rain added a few traces of melancholy to her, and she was more eager to call Xu Zhuang.

Xu Zhuang's shipping route was from Hong Kong to Zhuhai Xiangzhou Port, and he arrived at the same time almost every day. When Zheng Jianxin first arrived in Zhuhai, Xu Zhuang found a way to save money when they talked over phone: every Wednesday night at 8:30, Zheng Jianxin would call the public telephone booth at the factory gate to the public telephone booth at the Xiangzhou Port Pier, or vice versa. If someone was unable to make or answer the call for some reason, they would call the next day and wait together at the same time.

Today happened to be Wednesday. Zheng Jianxin couldn't wait to call him. If Lili hadn't said that she had to go out for a dinner party, Zheng Jianxin would have rushed out without eating or drinking and found a phone booth to make a call.

Walking out of the street, Lili waved to stop a taxi.

"What's the hurry!" Zheng Jianxin went into the phone booth on the roadside.

Lili had to wave her hand and give up.

In the phone booth on the roadside, Zheng Jianxin dialed the familiar phone number over and over again, but the result was a long "beep, beep-beep" music and no one answered. Her mood changed from excited expectation to disappointment and frustration. Finally, she leaned against the phone booth with the microphone weakly, and her eyes were moist as she gently recited Xu Zhuang's name.

Lili looked at her good sister in the phone booth, her face was uncertain for a while, and finally she made up her mind to pat the door of the phone booth and pulled her out: "Let's hurry up, don't go too late and spoil the fun!"

Zheng Jianxin nodded with a pout, hung up the phone, and walked out reluctantly.

4

Xu Zhuang: The man who hit his forehead with three empty bottles in a row

Xu Zhuang, like his name, had a strong body, a stubborn personality, and was efficient. These merits made Lili's Hong Kong "man" Zeng Sheng admire him very much. He tried his best to make him work for him and taught him to read nautical charts and drive a motorboat. As long as it was time to call Zheng Jianxin, Xu Zhuang would put down his work no matter how busy he was, wait in the phone booth, and wait for the heart-pounding phone ring. In his mind, in this foreign land, besides being with Zheng Jianxin, there was nothing sweeter and more important than hearing her pleasant voice. Raindrops were floating in the sky, and the waves on the sea were much bigger than usual. The visibility was not good, and if he was not careful, he would hit the reef or other ships.

Relying on his familiarity with the waterway from daily trips, Xu Zhuang turned a blind eye to this and drove the boat at full speed. It was time to talk to Zheng Jianxin, and he couldn't let this happiness that he had been waiting for a week be blown away by the sea breeze and washed away by the waves.

He arrived at Xiangzhou Port. Braking, turning the hull, and docking, Xu Zhuang did it all in one go, with smooth movements without any delay.

The waves hit back, and the boat shook heavily. Zeng Sheng, who was leaning against the cabin door and admiring Xu Zhuang's series of movements, tilted his fat body and almost fell down. He was a little annoyed and scolded in poor Mandarin: "Damn handsome boy, are you crazy?"

"Sorry, boss, I have something to do! I'm in a hurry!"

29

Xu Zhuang jumped out of the cabin door and apologized while pulling the cable.

"Are you in a hurry to pick up a woman?" Zeng Sheng followed him out, smiling strangely, "No wonder you are so angry!"

"Boss is wise!" Xu Zhuang also laughed and gave Zeng Sheng a thumb up, ready to jump off the boat to tie the ropes.

"Young man, you should know how to be restrained." Zeng Sheng put on an experienced look, shook his bald head, and generously stuffed his newly bought "Nokia" mobile phone into Xu Zhuang's hand, "It's windy and rainy, don't run around, use this to make calls."

Xu Zhuang hesitated and looked at the mobile phone worth ten thousand yuan in his hand, and finally shook his head: "I'll call when I get ashore, so I don't have to pay for international long-distance calls and roaming."

After that, he returned the phone to Zeng Sheng and jumped onto the dock to tie the ropes.

Zeng Sheng was stunned. He looked at Xu Zhuang, who was wearing shorts and showing off his strong muscles, and shook his head and laughed, "I didn't think so much."

Xu Zhuang tied the rope, exhaled, and was about to walk towards the telephone booth in the port area. Zeng Sheng, who got off the boat, put his arm around his shoulder and whispered mysteriously, "Handsome boy, now you can drive the boat and are familiar with the route. I'll give you some urgent job to make money. -- Let's find a place to talk!"

"Okay, wait for me for a while." The telephone booth was a dozen meters ahead.

"No, I'm in a hurry. If you can't do it, I'll have to find someone else!" Zeng Sheng seemed to have changed into a different person. His face was cold and iron-colored, and his fierce look showed a bit of unconcealable irritation. He stretched out his arm to stop Xu Zhuang.

Xu Zhuang hesitated for a moment, looked in the direction of the telephone booth on the shore, looked up at the heavier rain, and nodded to Zeng Sheng: "Okay." He said to Zheng Jianxin in his heart apologetically, "Ajian, I'll find you at the factory after we finish talking!"

Zeng Sheng put his arm around Xu Zhuang's shoulders and said with a bit of contempt and a bit of pride: "That's right! With money, what kind of woman can't you want?!"

Xu Zhuang resisted the urge to elbow Zeng Sheng in the ribs, and retorted in a low voice: "I only want this woman in my life!"

"A great lover? No wonder you borrowed a year's salary to buy a brand-name handbag to please the beautiful woman, and even sold yourself to me!"

Zeng Sheng exaggeratedly stretched his arms, and then slapped Xu Zhuang on the shoulder again, "But think about it, if you want someone to live a good life, you also need money, right? Love is enough? Damn it!"

In order to buy a French brand-name handbag for Ajian, Xu Zhuang had to borrow money from Zeng Sheng. Zeng Sheng's eyes widened when he heard that he was going to borrow 20,000 yuan. Xu Zhuang made a face at the time, "I'll sell my body and pay you back as a long-term worker, isn't that enough?"

Xu Zhuang sighed secretly and once again resisted the urge to throw the fat hand off his shoulder.

When Xu Zhuang first arrived in Zhuhai, his cousin Lili had already been hanging out with Zeng Sheng. Coming from the mountains, he was a simple and honest young man, and he felt disgusted and angry about this. He intuitively thought that his cousin's fall was due to Zeng Sheng's seduction.

One day, when he learned that Zeng Sheng and his cousin had checked into a hotel room, he rushed into the hotel room and not only beat up the naked Zeng Sheng, but also slapped Lili in the face.

Ashamed of this, he hadn't seen or talked to his cousin again for more than two months.

Xu Zhuang thought that after this incident, his cousin would know shame and turn over a new leaf. But she ignored it all, quit her job, and moved into the house Zeng Sheng rented for her in Gongbei, openly becoming Zeng Sheng's full-time lover.

Xu Zhuang, who had fantasies, was beaten by the cruel reality for a long time. He couldn't eat well, couldn't sleep well, and became silent.

But he couldn't get angry anymore.

After being in Zhuhai for so long, the streets of Gongbei were full of temptations, just like the movies he had seen in his hometown: passing by a high-end hotel, with bright lights and wine, men dressed elegantly, and women showing their breasts, backs and thighs in the streets; in the large and clear glass windows, there were tempting desserts on the table, and people were sitting on the sofa, teasing and playing, with an air of rich men.

For the working people, the world was black and white and tasteless. Either toiling under the scorching sun, or running from the workshop to the dormitory, no matter where they went, they could not escape the steamer-like heat and humidity. Comfort and enjoyment were simply out of their reach.

When he saw his cousin Lili again, her yellow and tired face became bright and radiant, and her movements and behavior changed from the shyness of a rural girl to an elegant and confident one; with enough money in her pocket. She no longer had to worry about anything -- she could buy whatever she wanted and eat whatever she wanted, and she looked happy and joyful.

"Ah...... since she thinks it's good, then it's fine." Xu Zhuang shook his head, shook off the beautiful and simple image of his aunt - Lili's mother in his mind, and accepted this reality.

Zeng Sheng was not bad either. From time to time, he took them and his friends to high-end entertainment venues, to meet this "boss", that "bureau chief" and "section chief", and often invited them to eat seafood in a splendid hotel and drink foreign wine in an elegant western restaurant.

After going there many times, facing the white tablecloths, tall glasses, and fragrant napkins, Xu Zhuang slowly felt that he had become a person of status.

But this feeling and this life were all given by Zeng Sheng. Some people say that this society is full of debauchery and money, and Xu Zhuang had experienced these two aspects vividly.

Others can have money, why can't I? Xu Zhuang thought. When he saw Zeng Sheng, the bosses around Zeng Sheng, and the officials Zeng Sheng interacted with, Xu Zhuang gradually felt that this world was not prepared for hardworking workers and law-abiding people.

When Xu Zhuang first came to Zhuhai, he worked as a worker in a beverage factory. He was looking for piecework wages. The more he worked, the more money he could earn. Xu Zhuang had plenty of strength.

In the factory area, workers sorted out the bags of recycled empty bottles that were piled up like a small mountain and transported them to the bottle washing workshop. The job of Xu Zhuang and his co-workers was to "pick bottles." Pour the empty bottles out of the sacks, pick out 24 bottles, put them in a plastic box, seven boxes and five layers as a stack, and the forklift operator forked them away. The piecework wage for picking a stack of bottles was 2.975 yuan.

Under the scorching sun, Xu Zhuang and his team were shirtless. The skin that was scorched after a day was as thin as paper and rolled off with a light touch, revealing the tender flesh with blood streaks. Wearing a hat and tight work clothes could certainly protect against the sun. But picking up a pile of bottles would make them sweat all over. The sweat would flow down from their trouser legs like incontinence, soaking a large area of the ground.

Xu Zhuang picked up empty bottles for two months. One day, he threw his cowboy hat to the ground, stepped on it twice, picked up a bottle and slammed it against the wall, and shouted to the sky: "I quit!" He also shouted a Cantonese phrase he had just learned: "Wu Zuo Shuai Zai! (Don't be a useless person who is looked down upon by others)"

Zeng Sheng said that he was engaged in import and export trade.

Because he loved Lili, he liked Xu Zhuang. He was optimistic about Xu Zhuang and asked Xu Zhuang to follow him to do business and make a lot of money.

It is easier to reach the goal by walking the path others have walked, and it is easier to succeed by climbing up on the shoulders of others. Xu Zhuang agreed: do business! Okay, he followed him to do business.

But Xu Zhuang, who still had a grudge in his heart, didn't treat Zeng Sheng well, and sometimes even said something cold to him.

But the more he did this, the more Zeng Sheng liked him, saying that he was like himself when he was young -- honest, straightforward, and energetic, and a promising talent.

After using all his efforts and persuading Xu Zhuang to follow him, Zeng Sheng spared no effort to make him adapt to the life at sea, learn to read nautical charts, drive a motor boat, and become familiar with the waters of Hong Kong and Macao in the shortest possible time. Xu Zhuang lived up to his expectations and soon grew from a layman to a master of the tide.

In addition, for some reason, Zeng Sheng would take Xu Zhuang to an open-air bar on Lianhua Road every now and then, saying "work is for a better life, and rest is for a better work", while pointing at and commenting on the beautiful women passing by with bare backs and exposed breasts.

When Xu Zhuang saw someone who met his aesthetic requirements, he would also be filled with blood and his eyes would light up, and he would whistle mischievously to attract the attention of the beautiful women. But at this time, what he thought about most was Zheng Jianxin. When he thought of Ajian, he immediately restrained himself. He thought that if she wore such beautiful clothes, she would be more beautiful than all of them; if she wore such dazzling jewelry, she would be more eye-catching than all of them; if she drove such a valuable car, she would be more noble and confident than all of them.

Compared with Zheng Jianxin, these beautiful girls were nothing.

She was the person that Xu Zhuang loved and cared about the most.

He wanted to give her such a life and let her live in happiness all her life. At this moment, the inferiority complex of peasants and migrant workers that grew in his heart after he came to Zhuhai was driven away.

In his hometown, Xu Zhuang coaxed Zheng Jianxin: "There are many wastelands in Guangdong, and there is also gold. Look at my strong body, I will grab land and gold for you!"

Zheng Jianxin rolled her eyes at him and scolded: "You are so frivolous and make up nonsense!" However, Xu Zhuang's words were still like a spell, making Zheng Jianxin feel happy, shyly and obediently put her face against Xu Zhuang's chest. Soon she and him walked out of the mountains.

He vowed to work hard and make his lover proud of him.

Soon, he bought himself a cowboy hat. He wanted to be energetic and motivated himself to make a name for himself like a cowboy!

During the time he followed Zeng Sheng, he worked day and night. Loading and unloading goods, carrying sacks, and carrying wooden boxes, he never complained about the hardship and tiredness. In the end, he even suffered from lumbar vertebral protrusion but never cried out in pain, just to make more money.

When Zheng Jianxin was in the Gongbei public telephone booth, holding the microphone that no one answered and feeling sorry for himself, Zeng Sheng was holding Xu Zhuang's shoulders, waving his mobile phone and enthusiastically describing a bright future for him, passing by the Xiangzhou Port telephone booth.

Looking at the empty telephone booth, Xu Zhuang's eyes were tender, struggling, and sighing.

The rain stopped, and the salty sea breeze blew across the city.

The fire in the food stalls roared, and it was unclear whether it was responding to or fighting against the sea breeze. The smell of fireworks mixed with the aroma of meat made people's stomachs growl and made people salivate. In addition, the cheap price attracted many diners.

After a few glasses of Haizhu brand beer, Zeng Sheng continued the topic at the dock, "You will be the captain of the ship this time."

"What are you doing?" Xu Zhuang was a little surprised.

"I have other things to do and can't leave." Zeng Sheng's eyes flashed, "You have shown your ability during this period. Everyone has seen it. Who should I hand it over to if I don't hand it over to you? I will feel relieved if you do the job!"

He took out a small piece of paper with a map drawn on it from his jacket pocket, pointed it to Xu Zhuang bit by bit, and taught him to identify the location: "We are here. In Hong Kong, you just need to flash the flashlight three times and someone will come to you. Then load the goods, no need to say anything. "

"Why is it so mysterious?"

Xu Zhuang shook his head in confusion, put a duck's paw into his mouth, and just as he was about to chew it, he realized it and spit it out again, "You want me to do smuggling for you? Aren't you cheating me? I won't do it!"

"What is smuggling? Don't say it so badly! Otherwise, people will really think I'm an outlaw."

Zeng Sheng's eyes were shining like a thief, his mind turning around like abacus beads, and then he smiled with a fake smile on his face: "I have the approval document, and it will be my job to declare the goods. If this shipment is completed, I will give the boatman 100 and give you 500. How about it? You know I always value you. I will take you to Hong Kong to work in the future, 20,000 to 30,000 a month. After working hard for a year or two, you and your wife can live a good life! "

Xu Zhuang ignored his empty promises and looked at the two girls wearing suspenders at the table next to him, but his mind was spinning like a windmill.

Zeng Sheng saw this and bumped his shoulder with a strange laugh.

Xu Zhuang turned his head and looked cold, which made Zeng Sheng feel guilty: "Zhuang, what's wrong?"

Xu Zhuang pressed the back of Zeng Sheng's hand on the table with force, staring into Zeng Sheng's eyes: "You businessmen, half of your face is human, half of your face is ghost. You think I don't know your crooked intentions? I don't want the future, I want the present!"

After that, he pushed Zeng Sheng's palm away, pouted and said: "Don't make big promises to me, don't treat me as the ignorant country boy I used to be. I have been with you for a long time, don't I know that your so-called approval documents are all fake? It's just that I have been following you all the time, and you will bear the brunt when the sky falls, so I don't bother to care. But this time you want me to be your substitute...... hehe......"

Zeng Sheng was stunned at first, then calmly, patting Xu Zhuang's shoulder with a laugh: "I really didn't misjudge you. Since the topic has been brought up, I am not afraid to say it. It costs money to open a company, it costs money to support my family, it costs money to eat, drink and have fun, and it costs money to support your cousin's extravagant spending. If I don't make some money from the side way, where can I get so much money?! You northerners say it well: A man can't get rich without unexpected wealth, and a horse can't get fat without night grass. Taking some small risks in exchange for fine clothes and delicious food is cost-effective. We also rely on our own hands to work hard! Do you have a father who is a boss? No! ......"

Speaking of this, Zeng Sheng took a sip of wine, looked at Xu Zhuang's face which was no longer so angry, and continued to brainwash him with his eloquence: "Nowadays, except for those migrant workers who work hard for more than ten hours a day, how many people's income can be completely exposed to the sun? If you have money, you are the boss, who cares where your money comes from?"

Finally, Zeng Sheng comforted him again: "Don't worry, there will be no risk. You have been with me for so long, and it has been smooth sailing every time, right?! Think about it, with your cousin here, I am your brother-in-law, would I dare to push you into the fire pit? I don't want to die."

Zeng Sheng secretly glanced at Xu Zhuang, patted his chest slightly, and changed the angle to talk about "life", intending to educate Xu Zhuang again by provoking him.

"Life? Does gambling king Stanley Ho want to live?" Zeng Sheng set a goal and example for Xu Zhuang. "When Stanley Ho was 20 years old, he was escrowing a ship in Macau. There were typhoons, pirates, and Japanese at sea. He could be robbed and captured at any minute, but he braved machine gun bullets to protect the ship and the cargo." He stared at Xu Zhuang, "The boss likes this kind of people, so soon, the boss of the company called 'United Chang Company' gave Stanley Ho shares, and he has been prosperous since then!"

In order to show the authenticity of his knowledge, Zeng Sheng patted his forehead and said the name of the "United Chang Company" where Stanley Ho was at the time. Zeng Sheng acted as Xu Zhuang's godfather intentionally or unintentionally. He needed Xu Zhuang to be his loyal and dare-to-die warrior. Xu Zhuang looked at him, no longer moved by these empty sermons: "I want you to say something substantial!"

Zeng Sheng was stunned for a moment: "What substantial? Oh, you said money? Oh, you know, I also work for Lao Sai (boss)." After taking a sip of wine, he rolled his eyes and pretended to be happy, "I'll double your salary, two thousand, how about it? Two thousand for a trip, it's a lot."

Xu Zhuang still shook his head and stared at him closely: "I've been with you for five months, working hard every day. How much did you pay me? And what about the dividends you mentioned? I haven't even seen a shadow, and you still have the nerve to ask me to work for you? "

"This......" Zeng Sheng let out a heavy breath in disapproval, turning the wine glass in his hand and thinking for a long time, looking at Xu Zhuang's expression that he would definitely not give up if he didn't get an answer. In a hurry to find the captain on this urgent mission tonight, he had to bite the bullet. He slammed the table, and said resolutely, "I'll settle with you once you come back this time, and you won't lose a cent, okay?!"

"Really?" Xu Zhuang looked at him a little suspiciously.

"Really! I never treated you as an outsider." Zeng Sheng's mouth showed a hint of flattering smile, "We are brothers, the boat helps the water, and the water helps the boat!"

Zeng Sheng patted his shoulder again to give him confidence, then leaned close to his ear and whispered, "If...... I mean if you encounter a situation, you must not (never) stab me out......"

There was a row of empty wine bottles on the ground. Xu Zhuang's eyes were bloodshot. He burped, exhaled heavily, and stared at Zeng Sheng: "Boss Zeng, Mr. Zeng, if you cheat me again this time, don't blame me, Xu Zhuang, for turning against you! I will beat you up and make you crawl out of Zhuhai, do you believe it?"

Xu Zhuang's face turned from red to blue, and his two bloodshot eyes stared at Zeng Sheng, as if they were about to spit fire. Zeng Sheng was so scared that he didn't know what Xu Zhuang was going to do.

Xu Zhuang turned around suddenly, picked up three empty beer bottles on the ground with his left hand and put them on the table, saying: "You are my boss, I will beat myself in front of you first!"

As he said that, he raised the bottles above his head with both hands and smashed them on his forehead. The bottles broke one by one, and the fragments scattered in the air. The sea breeze blew them away for a long distance before stopping.

The people around were stunned.

Zeng Sheng's heart raced strongly when he saw this. He calmed down a little, and patted Xu Zhuang on the shoulder with a smile: "Why did you do this? It was fine just then!"

Zeng Sheng didn't smoke, so he lit a cigarette for Xu Zhuang. The humiliation and anger that Xu Zhuang had accumulated since he started working surged into his chest. He gently wiped his forehead with glass shards and shook his head in pain.

Zeng Sheng put away the lighter, lowered his head and pondered for a moment, and said sincerely: "You have to forgive me, I am also doing business for the boss......" He said with a trembling upper lip beard: "Brother, after running this errand, won't you be rich? With wages and dividends of more than 100,000 or 200,000 yuan, you can be considered a rich man. You can buy a suite in Zhuhai, 2,500 yuan per square meter, which is cheap! Living together with your little beauty, half of your life's ideals will be realized."

Xu Zhuang didn't respond to this "pie in the sky" talk. After a long time, he asked coldly: "When will I leave?" The voice was as fierce and tragic as the suicide squad.

"Now." Zeng Sheng became calm, looked at his watch and said softly.

"Now? So urgent?" Xu Zhuang wanted to go to the factory to see Ajian. He had calculated the time early. Ajian was working in the afternoon during this week and got off work at 12 o'clock in the evening. He could accompany Ajian to the stalls near the factory to eat her favorite spicy hot pot and talk about the pain of separation.

His wishful thinking did not work, and Xu Zhuang could not help feeling frustrated.

"Don't put on that bitter face."

Zeng Sheng, who was worldly-wise, knew what he was thinking and advised: "It's only one night, there are many good days in the future!"

Xu Zhuang said "hmm" in a muffled voice, thinking that it would not be too late to go to see Ajian tomorrow morning, and he could spend almost a day with her. By then, Zeng Sheng should give him all the money he deserved in the past six months, and he had to discuss with her how to spend it.

But then he thought, it would be the first time he led a team out on a ship, and it was obvious that Hong Kong was in a hurry. And Zeng Sheng's "preparation" was not as sufficient as before, so there must be risks. Let his cousin tell Ajian to let her rest assured.

"Let me use your cell phone." Xu Zhuang reached out and took Zeng Sheng's mobile phone to dial Lili's number. It rang for a long time but no one answered. He dialed several times and it was the same. He couldn't help but feel a little blocked in his heart. Finally, he had to send a message to inform her of the matter.

Zeng Sheng stopped talking and took out a heavy black thing from his handbag: "Satellite phone, dedicated to the sea. Take it just in case."

Xu Zhuang took it and said "hmm" again, feeling a little uneasy in his heart, as if it was an ominous sign.

5

Ajian met a Macau man who was more than 20 years older than her

After getting off the taxi and looking at the flashing sign on the roof of the restaurant, Zheng Jianxin suddenly woke up and pulled Lili and said, "Sister Lili, don't you have a mobile phone? Call Zeng Sheng to see if Azhuang is next to him. I have to tell him that I am not working in that factory anymore."

Lili said "Oh" and opened her Chanel handbag to search for it.

"Oh, Ajian, I forgot to bring it......"

"Sister Lili, what happened to you today?" Zheng Jianxin was disgusted by Lili spending so much time on makeup. It's just a meal, for a man, to please a man, not a festival!

In Zheng Jianxin's opinion, although mobile phones had become common, they were still not affordable for most people. They still had a strong symbolic meaning of status.

For Lili, it was the most important facade decoration. She even forgot to bring it. It seemed that she was really absent-minded. Zheng Jianxin scolded her in her heart.

After suffering multiple setbacks in one day, including unemployment, illness, and failed boyfriend's call, Zheng Jianxin went from being sensitive and suspicious to being somewhat angry.

"It's okay, what could have happened?" Isn't it just a small matter of calling Xu Zhuang? Lili felt that Zheng Jianxin's dissatisfaction was excessive, so she responded coyly, her face flushed a little, "I was just thinking about the dinner and forgot it in a hurry!"

"This dinner......" Zheng Jianxin wanted to say that eating a meal was nothing, but swallowed the words back when they came to her lips. Lili looked around like a thief and whispered to Zheng Jianxin: "I have a new boyfriend...... Well, do you understand? Don't tell anyone!"

"New boyfriend?" Zheng Jianxin asked suspiciously, "Aren't you with Zeng Sheng......"

"Shhhhh......" Lili quickly covered her mouth, "Zeng Sheng doesn't come here many times a month, who knows if he has women in Shenzhen or Huizhou?" Her face flushed with embarrassment, and she said the key point, "He can't pay me on time, and also I'm bored......"

Without waiting for Zheng Jianxin to answer, Lili pulled her towards the door of the restaurant: "Hurry up, don't keep them waiting......"

Zheng Jianxin pouted and followed Lili unwillingly. Through Lili's "frankness", Zheng Jianxin was amazed that the smell of copper coins and the breath of market butchers enveloped her so quickly, and became active cells in her body, and she became a stranger. When did she become such a person? Was it the extreme emptiness of spirit, the desire for money, or the instinct to have a man around?

Entering the restaurant, the flower carpet on the aisle and the exquisite decoration inside attracted Zheng Jianxin, who was in a state of excitement. When she was about to take a good look, she was pulled by Lili who turned a blind eye to it and went straight to the private room.

As soon as she entered the private room, Zheng Jianxin saw the huge crystal chandelier on the ceiling, which illuminated the whole room brightly. There were already several men sitting in the sofa on one side of the room, separated by a mahogany inlaid bamboo embroidery screen, and behind the screen, you could vaguely see a large round table covered with a pink tablecloth. The whole room looked luxurious and exquisite.

Zheng Jianxin was a little timid, as it was her first time to come to such a luxurious place.

"Don't be nervous. When you come a few more times and you'll be fine." Lili pinched her and said softly. Her towering breasts trembled gracefully with the frequency of her words.

The arrival of the two beauties delighted the men who were chatting.

The elegant man in his forties who stood up first stretched his two hands exaggeratedly and sighed with a loud smile: "Miss Lili, you are finally here. They are planning to put a knife to my neck and go to your house to look for you!"

"Nonsense. Don't I know what you are up to?!" Lili slapped his hands away and said with a giggle.

The man didn't care about it at all, and put down his hands, put them on the seam of his pants, and bowed deeply to Zheng Jianxin: "Hello, beautiful lady, my name is Bai Lang...... Ha, beautiful women always come on stage last!"

"Hello, I...... my name is Zheng Jianxin." Zheng Jianxin was a little unaccustomed to such communication, and was at a loss for a moment, not knowing what to do.

"Ajian, you're here too?" A voice from the side sounded, easing Zheng Jianxin's embarrassment.

"Oh, it's Chen Xiao, the great master!"

Lili saw the man's face clearly at a glance, glanced at Zheng Jianxin, and walked towards the sofa. "Why is the great master Chen free today? If you don't accompany your wife, won't you be afraid of your wife?"

Chen Xiao was short, thin, white-faced, wearing silver-framed glasses, and combing his hair neatly. He said with a smile: "Lili, I, Chen Xiao, have lived for more than 40 years, and it seems that I have never offended you. Why do you always make fun of me when we meet?" As he said that, he stood up, raised his hands to give the two women seats, and looked at Zheng Jianxin with a little hope, a little excitement, and a little apology.

Lili snorted: "You know everything, I'll settle the score with you later."

Chen Xiao smiled bitterly again and rubbed his hands subconsciously.

Bai Lang followed and said with a little surprise: "Mr. Chen, what a coincidence? Do you know each other?"

"We are from the same hometown." Chen Xiao was very grateful for the opportunity given by Bai Lang, "My family and Zheng Jianxin's family are old friends......"

"That's the best! It really proves the saying that people from the same family stick together! Today, all the wise men are here. This is God's will. God will help our project to succeed!" Such a small coincidence actually moved Bai Lang. He faced Chen Xiao with a touch of sincerity and humility.

Several men followed and smiled, and the atmosphere was very harmonious.

Everyone sat down, Lili leaned on Bai Lang elegantly, blinked at Zheng Jianxin, and introduced formally and concisely: "From Taiwan, Bai Lang, the big boss; from Macau, Zhong Haicai, the boss; this handsome guy is my brother, Macau Achang."

As she introduced, Zheng Jianxin shyly and restrainedly nodded and greeted each one, not daring to be as careless as Lili, for fear of losing etiquette.

Bai Lang stood up in response. He was tall and handsome, about 40 years old, with a handsome face and a pair of gold-rimmed glasses, which made him look a bit bookish. He wore a navy blue suit with thin white and blue stripes from the famous Italian brand Guinness. The suit was tailored very well.

He smiled and said, "My last name is Bai (white in Chinese), first name Lang. I'm sorry that I'm a little bit black. I'm not a big boss. I just came to the mainland to make a living!" His movements were natural and there was no sign of affectation.

Lili pulled the corner of Zheng Jianxin's clothes and whispered that Taiwanese people are very polite.

The man named Zhong Haicai on the other side of Bai Lang gave Zheng Jianxin a strong contrast: he looked to be in his 40s, with a dark complexion, sparse gray short hair around his bald head, a fleshy and slightly swollen face, and his head was held high, but his expression seemed to be unrrelaxed. What puzzled Zheng Jianxin the most was that although he was also wearing a suit and looked well-fitting, he always gave her the impression that these clothes were awkwardly put on him.

After hearing Lili's simple introduction, Zhong Haicai quickly added: "Boss Bai, he's amazing, a big boss from Taiwan! He runs a real estate company. Boss Bai wants to open eight rivers in the water village, build the Lanmeng Water Village Resort, and every family has a private dock......"

His Mandarin was even worse than Zeng Sheng's, and he was a little excited for some reason, so he stuttered, which made Zheng Jianxin feel weird.

"Boss Bai, when will you take us to your boat to have some fun?" Lili threw a wink, and shook Bai Lang's arm to flirt with him in a coquettish voice.

She knew the details of the Lanmeng Water Village Resort, and the current progress was only on the drawings. The reason why she was so exaggerating was to make this man happy. Once such a big project was successful, she would not be left out; even if the project was unsuccessful, it didn't matter if she had spent a few words. She would not be stingy with the words.

Bai Lang smiled and patted Lili's slender hands, then turned his gaze to Chen Xiao: "This depends on our great master Chen. As long as he says a few nice words and relaxes the policy, we can go on the boat and have fun in no time......"

He took out several copies of the "One-day Tour Plan for Lanmeng Water Village" from his briefcase and distributed them to Chen Xiao and others, and also gave one to Zheng Jianxin.

Then Bai Lang spoke seriously, just like a leader giving a report at a meeting: "The Lanmeng Water Village Time Sharing Resort is a pioneering effort to develop the tourism resources of the water village and promote the tourism industry. It will surely attract the attention of relevant units."

He paused for a moment and attracting everyone's attention. "We will organize a one-day yacht leisure tour in the water village in a timely manner, so that the members from Hong Kong, Macau and Guangzhou can appreciate the characteristics of the water village and the fun of appreciating the orchard, so as to understand the conception and actual construction of the resort, which can not only promote sales but also contact sales teams in various places......"

"Good, good," Zhong Haicai took the lead in applauding, his face full of joy, "Starting construction and making money at the same time, good! Good!"

Bai Lang had just told Chen Xiao about what he had begged Chen Xiao for. He asked him to talk to the town leaders through his acquaintances to let the project start first, and the land deposit would be paid later, and the yacht license should be obtained as soon as possible. Chen Xiao thought that the meat was in the pot, and the deposit would be paid sooner or later, so he generously agreed: "I'll give it a try."

Chen Xiao usually did not smile. At this time, he rubbed his hands, smiled, looked around at everyone, and attracted everyone's attention, then he continued seriously: "I am not a local official, but the superior unit has a lot of power, and friends sometimes give me some face. I will give it a try."

"Brother Chen is too modest. I am lucky to meet Mr. Chen today!" Bai Lang let go of Lili, stood up and motioned everyone to take a seat, "Your title is big enough -- deputy general manager of an overseas trading company, and the son of a high-ranking official, young and promising, the energy......haha, everyone is optimistic, Mr. Chen, young and promising!"

In fact, Chen Xiao was over 50. Bai Lang's excessive flattery made his face blush. Everyone agreed as they sat down, and Zhong Haicai even applauded.

"Come on, I wish Mr. Chen a prosperous career!" Bai Lang picked up the wine glass and circled it around, then said to Chen Xiao, "I'll drink first!"

Chen Xiao was obviously used to such compliments. He raised his glass and smiled without saying much politeness, but his eyes turned to

Zheng Jianxin who wanted to sit with Lili.

Following his gaze, everyone's eyes were focused on Zheng Jianxin. Zheng Jianxin's face immediately flushed, and the redness spread all the way to her white neck and chest, making her look delicate and lovely. Her two thick black eyebrows, dignified nose, and childish big and black eyes showed a kind of arrogant beauty.

Zheng Jianxin, who suddenly became the focus again, was at a loss. She blushed and looked down, not knowing what was wrong.

Everyone was amused by Zheng Jianxin's actions. Bai Lang pushed up his glasses frame on his nose with his index finger, and continued to use his eloquence to praise in a poetic tone: "Ah...... Miss Zheng is really the moon on August 15th, everyone is looking up to her!"

Life in Hong Kong, Macau and Taiwan is somewhat Westernized. It is a polite way for men to compliment women on their beauty, and they often blurt it out. Zheng Jianxin came from the mainland, and her first reaction was that these people had bad intentions, and then she instinctively rolled her eyes at them in self-defense, but she looked lovable.

"Yes, yes!" Zhong Haicai, who was sitting on the other side of Zheng Jianxin, immediately echoed Bai Lang, and the light in his eyes became stronger. He had just learned Mandarin not long ago, and "yes, yes" sounded like "die, die". Since Zheng Jianxin entered the room, his eyes were either lingering on her face or wandering around her, but everyone's attention was not on him, and no one had noticed it yet.

The words of Bai Lang and Zhong Haicai made the laughter in the room even louder. Achang even joked and made Zheng Jianxin sit next to Chen Xiao, so that the two "fellow villagers" could reunite.

Looking at Chen Xiao, Zhong Haicai's mouth twitched, his face was a little helpless and depressed, his eyes were still bright, but a little sharper.

The foreign wine bottle was opened. Zhong Haicai grabbed the foreign wine from the waiter, stood up and poured a full glass for Chen Xiao first, and smiled with a simple face: "Mr. Chen, come, this XO is good, it's a man's drink, more!"

Chen Xiao did not refuse, and talked and laughed freely while watching Zhong Haicai pour wine for everyone, and then raised his glass to toast each other. Zhong Haicai kept inviting everyone to eat. He specifically introduced the dishes to Zheng Jianxin: "You see, we Cantonese people often give dishes auspicious names...... You see, this dish is braised shark's fin, and the menu is called 'Hong Yin Zhan Chi'...... You see, this dish is abalone with abalone sauce, and the menu is called 'Bao You Ying Yu', oh, oh......"

Achang pulled him, "Boss, can you sit down and talk? You must be tired from speaking Mandarin!"

"Okay, okay, okay." Zhong Haicai wiped the sweat from his forehead with the paper towel on the table.

After three rounds of wine, the atmosphere changed from harmonious to warm, and the dishes were served. Everyone seemed to have known each other for many years and talked and ate and drank.

Chen Xiao saw that everyone's focus was no longer on him and Zheng Jianxin, so he turned to Zheng Jianxin beside him and whispered: "Ajian, Lili wanted to blame me, is it because of your work? Before you got here, the lay boss called me and kept apologizing. She said that she was so angry with the workers that she forgot that I introduced you to the company. She also asked if you want to go back. She would make you a squad leader......"

"Thank you, but no thanks." Zheng Jianxin shook her head and interrupted him, "No one can work in a factory run by a boss like her. A tree transplanted will die; a person relocated will live. Let's talk about it later!"

Chen Xiao was stunned for a moment, nodded and said: "Okay, as long as you can think it through. If you need any help from me, just ask."

Zheng Jianxin smiled without commenting, and the arrogant euphemism and cold submissiveness made Chen Xiao absent-minded for a long time.

Bai Lang seemed very excited, maybe he had drunk too much or something else. He swayed his body while holding up his wine glass and hummed "Only hard work can win" in Minnan dialect. His eyes behind

49

his gold-rimmed glasses would occasionally glance at Lili's half-exposed breasts. In the end, he even put a hand on Lili's shoulder, causing Lili to slap him coquettishly from time to time.

Achang on the side was not willing to be lonely, and he added fuel to the fire. He used the excuse of "helping" Lili get rid of Bai Lang's claws, but took the opportunity and held Lili's round shoulders.

Lili didn't care about this.

Zheng Jianxin was stunned for a while when she saw Lili playing with bees and butterflies like a fish playing in water.

Seeing Zheng Jianxin like this, Zhong Haicai blinked his swollen eyes, raised the goblet and shook it in front of her eyes: "What are you doing, pretty girl? Come on, have a sip, everyone is out to be happy, let's drink ours, ignore them!" He subconsciously pulled his right foot out of his sandals, raised his calf, stepped on the edge of the chair, and picked his toes with his right hand.

Zheng Jianxin was disgusted and surprised. Aren't people in Hong Kong and Macau rich and civilized? How could this be?

Out of politeness, she had to endure it and had to deal with him. She took another sip gently, and the hot feeling rushed into her throat again, as if it was about to burn, making her cough dryly a few times, and quickly picked up the water glass and poured ice water.

"Ah......you don't know how to drink?" Zhong Haicai, who had just raised his head to toast, quickly put down the wine glass, and tried to help in a panic, but didn't know what to do. Zheng Jianxin was disgusted with him and waved one hand. He had to maintain a weird half-sitting and half-standing posture, with an apologetic and caring face.

Lili noticed their situation, threw away the two gummy bears and came over. Seeing that Zheng Jianxin was fine, she raised her glass to Zhong Haicai and said, "Brother Zhong, my little sister is ignorant, please forgive me......"

"No, no, no, it's not her fault." Zhong Haicai waved his hand and said, "It's me to blame...... I didn't know Miss Zheng couldn't drink."

"I'm fine." Zheng Jianxin forced a smile to show that she was fine. Although she was not used to this kind of occasion for the first time, she knew that she couldn't spoil everyone's fun.

Lili nodded and raised her glass to Zhong Haicai again: "Brother Zhong, if you still want to drink, I'll accompany you! We won't go home until we're drunk today!"

"It's really my good Lili, a woman is as good as a man!" Seeing that everything was fine, Bai Lang tried to smooth things over again, and everyone laughed and cheered. The atmosphere became warm again.

"Brother Zhong, my little sister just lost her job and caught a cold. Her father is seriously ill and she is not in a good mood. You should be more considerate of her." Before returning to her seat, Lili took the opportunity to clink glasses and whispered to Zhong Haicai.

"Oh...... So that's how it is......" Zhong Haicai, who had gone through hard times, looked at Zheng Jianxin with a heavy heart, frowned and asked with sympathy: "Ajian, can I call you that? What disease does your father have?"

"Nothing." Zheng Jianxin bit her lip and didn't want to say more.

"Her father is a veteran," Lili, who was listening to their conversation, explained, "A few years ago, on the occasion of the August 1st, the county sent gifts and money to the town. When her father found out, he went to the town government to claim them. The town officials said that since he hadn't come to claim them for so long, they had already disposed them. Her father refused to accept the explanation and said that it was his own things and he had to ask for justice. He was pushed and fell during the argument and his lower leg was fractured."

Zhong Haicai was stunned, and subconsciously slapped his face with his palm, frowning and saying, "No one cares about this?"

Looking at Zheng Jianxin, who was about to cry, Chen Xiao smiled bitterly and said, "The mountains are high and the emperor is far away, who cares? I know this kind of thing better than anyone else, and we also want to help, but now that things have come to this, what else can we do?"

Hearing Chen Xiao's words, Zheng Jianxin bit her lips and pressed her teeth hard again, without saying a word, and without letting the tears flow out. In this society where everyone competes for power and wealth, many people are as small as a grain of sand and as weak as a blade of grass!

"What the hell! He is so miserable and pitiful......" Zhong Haicai sighed, raised his head and drank the wine in the glass.

"Uncle, I will drink with you." Zheng Jianxin suddenly raised her head and said to Zhong Haicai. "The Little Grass" was grateful to anyone, even if it was a little sympathy and help, even if it was a warm and caring word. In addition, she didn't want her own issues to make the atmosphere unpleasant.

Chen Xiao on the side was in a different mood. He frowned, looking very heavy, opened his mouth but said nothing in the end, a trace of embarrassment and shame flashed across his face, rubbed his hands, and thought to himself: "When and how can people live decently, especially the Zheng family!......"

"No more drinking," Zhong Haicai waved his hand and put down the wine glass, "Enough, I can't drink anymore!"

"I've had enough too." Bai Lang stood up with a burp, walked to Chen Xiao and said with an ambiguous smile: "Brother, do you want to go to 'exercise' and relax?"

While speaking, his body blocked the waiter's view and lightly put a swollen envelope into Chen Xiao's pocket.

Chen Xiao was still a disciplined and timid cadre, and hurriedly pushed Bai Lang's hand over: "No, no!"

He stood up again, "There are still some things to do at home, I'll go first, you all have fun!"

"Brother is really a good man who cares about his family!" Bai Lang laughed and waved to Zhong Haicai suggestively.

Zhong Haicai took out a bag with understanding. In the bag were two bottles of XO wine, the same as the one they had just drunk, and two exquisite cigar boxes the size of a palm.

Bai Lang handed the bag to Chen Xiao and said softly and kindly: "I know that you love wine and take care of your family. These two bottles are for you to have a few drinks with your wife, so as to add some fun to life." He took out the cigar box and opened it. Two rows of ten beautifully packaged cigars were displayed in front of everyone, and the air was immediately filled with a strange aroma. "This is what I bought when I traveled to Cuba. It is said that the quality is only a little lower than Castro's special products. I give it to you for my appreciation. I hope you will accept it!"

Chen Xiao couldn't decline the gift anymore, and quickly stood up with a smile: "Mr. Bai is so kind, I would be wrong to decline, but I feel ashamed to accept it! Okay, I'll leave first, call me if you need anything!" The last sentence seemed to be said to Lili and Zheng Jianxin.

"That's right, that's right! Wait for the good news!" Bai Lang couldn't help but smile when he heard him say that. He winked at Zhong Haicai and politely escorted him out of the room.

After sending Chen Xiao away, the dinner was over. Zhong Haicai called the waiter, took the bill and had a look. His hand trembled and he grinned: "One......"

He just said one word, as if he had realized something and shut his mouth. He glanced at Bai Lang, and immediately shook himself up, held his head high, took out a thick stack of Hong Kong dollars with one thousand yuan bills from the inner pocket of his suit, counted out twelve bills to the waiter, waved his fat hand and said loudly: "Keep the change!"

"Thank you, boss!" The two waiters were overjoyed and went out with a smile.

"More than ten thousand? So expensive?" Zheng Jianxin couldn't help but exclaim to Lili in a low voice.

Lili was used to it and explained in a low voice: "It's not expensive. A South Africa three-head abalone costs more than 900 yuan, plus we drank two bottles of XO, and Chen Xiao took two more bottles. How much is it?"

"It's my family's income for several years, isn't it expensive?" Zheng Jianxin muttered in her heart.

Bai Lang and Achang whispered something, and laughed from time to time.

Zhong Haicai seemed to be a little drunk, his loose cheeks were black with red, and red with bright. The Lanmeng Water Village project made him very happy!

Bai Lang promised to let him participate in the newly established Gaolu Real Estate Company and develop the Lanmeng Water Village Resort together. Judging from the current construction and development prospects of the Pearl River Delta, this was a project with unlimited "money". The lifelong dream of making a fortune was finally coming true when he was almost in his sixties!

Zhong Haicai was happy, very happy, and with the gradual intoxication, his steps were a little shaky.

He staggered to Zheng Jianxin, and just as he was trying to stand firm, his feet suddenly softened, his body tilted, and he was about to fall to the ground.

"Uncle, be careful!" Zheng Jianxin hurriedly stepped forward, supported his arm, and pulled out a chair for him to sit down.

"Nothing! Nothing!" Zhong Haicai's face was obviously excited and even agitated, and his eyes became brighter as he looked at Zheng Jianxin, "Thank you, you are so nice!" Zheng Jianxin smiled shyly at his gaze and took a step back.

"Oh......wait." Zhong Haicai seemed to remember something and called her. He took out the stack of Hong Kong dollars from his pocket, took out a few bills, and stuffed them into Zheng Jianxin's hand without counting them, "Take it!"

Zheng Jianxin was shocked by his sudden action and screamed "Ah", and quickly stuffed the money back: "I don't want it, uncle, have you drunk too much?"

"I'm not drunk." Zhong Haicai used both hands to forcefully stuff the money into her hand again, rolled up her five fingers, and said loudly: "I told you to take it, so take it!"

Zheng Jianxin held the money and looked at Lili for help.

"Ajian, just take it!" Lili chuckled, "Brother Zhong means well, don't refuse it!"

"Beautiful girl, just think of it as a Hong Bao (red envelope with money) given to you by Brother Zhong!" Achang didn't know the reason and helped on the side.

Zheng Jianxin had no choice but to look at Zhong Haicai's concerned eyes and took the money, saying: "Thanks. I will pay you back when I find a job and make money!"

"That's right, don't say you pay back......" Zhong Haicai nodded, hesitating a little bit, "If you can't find a job for the time being, first work with me, um...... deliver herbal tea to the construction site, twice a day, and I will pay you......"

"Okay." Zheng Jianxin didn't know the details of this person, and didn't discuss it with Lili, so she had to politely agree first.

"Thank you, Brother Zhong, for taking care of my sister!" Lili said with a smile.

"Miss Jianxin, Brother Zhong is alone, you'd better help him as an hourly worker, cook, clean up, etc......" Achang was teasing again, secretly winking at Zhong Haicai.

"Okay, no problem." Zheng Jianxin agreed readily, doing housework was originally her strong point.

"That's great." Zhong Haicai smiled so hard that his ears almost split.

"This is really a good opportunity for a drought-stricken seedling to get rain." Achang didn't expect Zheng Jianxin to agree so readily, and he was envious.

"You pretty boy, please behave yourself." Lili slapped Achang on the back of his head, "Ajian is my cousin's girlfriend!"

"Sister Lili, spare me......" Achang turned his head behind Bai Lang and pushed him into Lili's arms.

"The fire in the city gate will affect the fish in the pond (a Chinese idiom)......" Bailang's mouth was full of alcohol. Taking advantage of the alcohol, he rushed over without hesitation and held Lili who wanted to dodge. Lili shook her two white arms to break free, and said in dissatisfaction: "You stupid four-eyed man, you stinky Bai Lang, why are you so anxious?"

"The night is short, life is fleeting. How can I not be anxious?" Bai Lang had to concede and kissed her on the face, then let go of one hand, held her waist and walked to the door, laughing and shouting: "Let's go, 'Blue Dream' is a success!......"

"You're going to die!" Lili looked at Zheng Jianxin embarrassedly, took out a bunch of keys and threw them to her, "Ajian, go back to my place first. Have a good sleep tonight, and talk about it tomorrow......"

Zheng Jianxin looked at Lili's plump back and felt that she had added a bit of rough charm that teased men intentionally or unintentionally, but her originally bright eyes were now flashing with a frivolous smile. Zheng Jianxin sighed and shook her head gently......

6

Xu Zhuang, where are you

When the dinner party Zheng Jianxin attended ended, Xu Zhuang returned to the boat.

The boat was fully fueled. Zeng Sheng gave a few instructions to the other four boatmen who were temporarily recruited, and made an OK gesture to Xu Zhuang, signaling them to set sail. Zeng Sheng stood silently on the dock until the sound of the motor disappeared.

At nearly midnight, Xu Zhuang had already driven the boat to the sea of Cheung Chau. As Zeng Sheng said, he used a flashlight to shine three times at the speedboat cruising not far away.

The speedboat immediately responded: "Follow me!" The signal light ordered Xu Zhuang to follow, and then turned around and drifted into the depths of the night.

Xu Zhuang followed the speedboat around for a long time, and arrived at the receiving location at around one o'clock in the morning. It was a pump boat and a cargo ship, standing on the sea at midnight like a monster, the scene was mysterious and weird. Seeing Xu Zhuang's boat coming, the people on the pump boat flashed the flashlight in his face, and then did not say anything, just waved his hand, and the pump boat grunted and hoisted the two-meter square iron cabinets onto Xu Zhuang's boat.

It took more than 40 minutes to transfer the 36 iron cabinets. Xu Zhuang, who had been looking around nervously, finally breathed a sigh of relief and immediately ordered the boatman to start the boat.

"As long as we return to Zhuhai to unload the goods, everything will be fine. Oh my God, please don't let anything happen to me on the way back." Xu Zhuang felt a little uneasy again and prayed at the dark and gloomy night sky. He had been out to sea with Zeng Sheng several times before. Zeng Sheng always prepared a speedboat to accompany him, so that he could escape if there was a situation. This time, Zeng Sheng would not be able to go out to sea without a speedboat. If there should be a situation, he would be caught red-handed. Xu Zhuang was so angry that he cursed: "Damn you, Zeng Sheng, are our lives worthless?"

At almost three o'clock in the morning, Xu Zhuang's boat entered the Zhuhai Spider Sea. The boatman holding a night vision telescope on the top of the boat suddenly reported: "Boss, there are two boats in front of the right, what should we do?"

"Ship type, course and status?" Xu Zhuang's heart tightened. The boats that were still cruising in the border sea at this time were most likely the anti-smuggling ships that he least wanted to see now.

There was no radar on his boat, and he could not find ships with eyes. The telescope was just a better-than-nothing equipment, and it had basically no other use except to give him a little more time.

"If it is really anti-smuggling ship......" Xu Zhuang immediately turned the rudder to change the course, and his brain ran rapidly to think of countermeasures.

"Two steel ships, not big, not high, with no lights on, coming towards us, speeding up...... Damn it, they are outflanking us!" The boatman threw away the telescope and jumped down, holding the hatch and loudly asked Xu Zhuang, "Boss, what should we do?"

The other three boatmen also became nervous and quickly gathered in the cockpit to discuss countermeasures.

"Everyone moves. Raise the sail, release the talisman ball, and return to Hong Kong waters!" Xu Zhuang roared and pushed the throttle to the extreme.

Although the four boatmen were young, they were all experienced fishermen. Upon hearing this, they immediately divided the work: two raised the sail, and two took off a dozen huge copper buoys on the edge of the boat to give the fishing boat more buoyancy and speed. Fortunately, the sea breeze was strong at this time and the wind direction was right.

When the two anti-smuggling ships were about to catch up, Xu Zhuang's boat with the sail and buoys was racing at high speed. Xu Zhuang finally drove the boat into Hong Kong waters.

Seeing the two Guangdong Customs anti-smuggling boats turning back after cruising for a while, Xu Zhuang and the boatmen finally breathed a sigh of relief and laughed excitedly.

After a while of joy, Xu Zhuang directed the boat to the flood control dike while he was about to call Zeng Sheng to explain the situation and ask where to drive the boat next. Suddenly, the two Hong Kong police boats which had hidden in the gap of the flood control dike lit up their lights. "Oh no." The crew knew that it meant "surrender." Then a loud shout came from the loudspeaker:

"Attention, boats ahead, we are Hong Kong police, and now order you to stop and accept inspection......"

Xu Zhuang and the four boatmen were immediately so stunned that they had no reaction even when the strong searchlight was shining directly into their eyes. The thirty-six iron cabinets were all large and heavy. With such a short distance, it would be impossible for the five of them to push all of them into the sea to destroy the evidence before the other party arrived. Jump into the sea to escape? This place was far from the coast of Hong Kong, Macau, and Zhuhai. Unless they were Supermen, they would be drowned in the sea and eaten by fish.

Entering Zhuhai waters? No way! Hong Kong's anti-smuggling fast pursuit boat could reach a speed of 49 knots per hour. Not to mention whether it could cross the boundary before being caught. Even if it could escape, the two Guangdong Customs anti-smuggling boats may still be waiting for them.

When the time came, Xu Zhuang calmed down. He asked the boatman to pull down the sail and hoist the buoy, and he also reduced the throttle to slow down the boat, giving up the meaningless efforts for escaping.

Looking at the four boatmen who were nervous and even a little overwhelmed, Xu Zhuang ordered: "Let's surrender! Otherwise, whoever the flare falls on will become a dead meat.

After that, he smiled and waved his hand calmly: "It's okay. According to the rules, the responsibility for such things falls on the leader. If Zeng Sheng could not help us, I will take care of everything, and you will just be imprisoned for a few days and suffer a little."

"Boss!" The four boatmen were moved by his righteousness.

Xu Zhuang sighed secretly, and didn't expect that he was so unlucky that he was caught by the Hong Kong Marine Police the first time he led a team out to sea.

Thinking of Zeng Sheng's words that if he encountered an emergency, he must not expose him, Xu Zhuang's complaints about his selfishness deepened a little.

"Who is the captain?" Several armed marine police came on the boat and asked Xu Zhuang and the others. "Me!" Xu Zhuang stepped forward without hesitation.

Xu Zhuang could have completely denied it and insisted that "there was no captain on this boat, and his group was just rowing the boat", and maybe it wouldn't be a big deal. But he didn't know the seriousness of the consequences. Just because Zeng Sheng said that he was the captain, he really thought he was the captain.

Captain is a technical title. You have to take an exam to get the qualification and the Maritime Administration will issue you a captain's certificate. Xu Zhuang didn't know this, and Zeng Sheng couldn't tell Xu Zhuang about this.

Xu Zhuang thought that the "boss" was the captain, and he took on a lot of responsibilities. Of course, the police had reason to think that he was the "captain". The leading policeman looked at him a few times: "Are you from the mainland?"

"Yes," Xu Zhuang nodded. "Take out the captain's certificate?"

"No......no"

"Where's the fisherman's certificate?"

"No."

Looking at Xu Zhuang who kept shaking his head, the police also shook his head and ordered: "Open the box and check!" Xu Zhuang hesitated, looked at the several water police who immediately tightened their guns, and finally nodded. Pry open the iron cabinet, the label on the iron cabinet said it was made in Brazil. Inside were stacks of special refrigerated boxes, which were wrapped with frozen chicken feet, chicken wings and other things. —The total weight of the goods was 209.28 tons. "Does the cargo have the approval documents?" The leading water policeman asked again.

"I don't know." Xu Zhuang shook his head again, his heart sinking.

The policeman's face became stern, and he said in a routine manner: "Now we suspect you of smuggling, you are arrested!"

Xu Zhuang's heart sank to the bottom of the valley, and all he could see was Ajian's shadow and Ajian's angry and accusing eyes. At dawn, Xu Zhuang and the other four were taken to the police station for formal investigation and questioning. After asking a series of questions such as name, age, and address, the interrogating police repeated the quantity, grade, and value of the smuggled goods seized on the fishing boat, and then got to the point: "To whom are the goods to be delivered? What is the name of the company? Who is the boss?"

Xu Zhuang shook his head: "I only know that the boss's surname is Zeng, and he said he has the approval document. I'm just working for him, I don't know anything."

"Is there any contact information?"

"There is a phone number." Xu Zhuang hesitated and said, "He said to call him when the goods arrive at the destination -- it's a Hong Kong phone number."

As he said that, he wrote down Zeng Sheng's mobile phone number.

"You try it." The interrogating police took a look and pointed to the landline phone on the desk.

Xu Zhuang nodded, picked up the phone and dialed Zeng Sheng's mobile number, but it was turned off. He dialed again, but it was still turned off.

"Where is Zeng Sheng's home?" The policeman smiled as if he had expected it, and asked again.

Xu Zhuang shook his head again: "I don't know, I only know that he is from Hong Kong."

The policeman nodded, picked up the satellite phone that Zeng Sheng had given to Xu Zhuang and put in a plastic evidence bag on the table and shook it: "Is this what Zeng Sheng gave you?"

"Yes." Xu Zhuang was sensitive to the hidden meaning in his words.

"You've been cheated." The policeman looked at Xu Zhuang with a teasing smile and said leisurely, "Satellite phones have a geo-location function. Your boss can track the location of this phone and know where you are. Now that you have failed, he has of course disappeared."

"Ah......" Xu Zhuang screamed, "He is so vicious. I thought he was really so kind and gave it to me as a precaution."

"Do you remember anything now?" The policeman skillfully turned the pen in his hand, "For example, how to find you, the vicious old man......"

Thinking of his cousin Lili, Xu Zhuang lowered his head in frustration and buried it in his hands, shaking his head and said: "I don't know, I really don't know......"

"Then you just wait to go to court." The policeman sighed and began to pack up his things.

"Go to jail?" Xu Zhuang suddenly roared like an enraged lion: "No! No! I want to go back to Zhuhai! I want Ajian, Ajian!"

The four boatmen were so scared that they knelt down and begged for mercy: "Officer...... We are fishermen from Panyu. We only came out to find some work to earn money for our family during the fishing moratorium...... Please spare us, we only got a hundred yuan for this trip...... Please spare us!......"

7

The machete that Ajian used to sell sugarcane
was thrown into the sea by the urban management

Back to Lili's rented room, Zheng Jianxin saw the mobile phone on the dressing table at a glance and picked it up to check. Five missed calls, all from Zeng Sheng. There was also an unread text message: "Cousin, remember to tell Ajian that I'm going out tonight and I'll go to find her when I get ashore tomorrow."

"Going out tonight?" Zheng Jianxin frowned, feeling something was wrong, "Why are you so busy?" After thinking about it, she felt that it would be better to call Zeng Sheng to ask, because going out to sea at night was really worrying. When she called back, the system prompted that the other party's phone was turned off. She called again, but it was still the same. Zheng Jianxin stared at the phone blankly, feeling extremely disappointed.

Gongbei is close to the sea, and Gaosha Village is low in terrain. In this rainy season, the walls and floors of the house were wet. The bedding was also wet. Zheng Jianxin touched it with her hand and really didn't want to go to bed.

The aftereffects of the foreign wine and the fatigue accumulated throughout the day made her consciousness blurred. Zheng Jianxin had to climb onto the bed and wanted to fall asleep, but she tossed and turned, always half asleep. The room was poorly soundproofed, and noises came from the walls from time to time, waking her up time again. She opened her eyes several times, and faced the darkness with an unknown fear.

In the haze, the night rolled like the sea, and the boats instantly turned into snakes and rushed towards her. She was finally awakened by the fear and found herself covered with cold sweat.

She turned on the light and held the photo of her and Xu Zhuang on the table to her chest: "Brother Zhuang, where are you?" She closed her eyes and slowly fell asleep in such a hum.

The first thing Zheng Jianxin did when she woke up the next day was to call Zeng Sheng's mobile phone again, but it was still turned off.

There was no choice but to wait. Xu Zhuang, as he said in his message, would come to find her as soon as he got ashore. Even if he didn't know that she had been fired and went directly to the factory to find her, he would definitely come here as soon as he didn't see her.

Zheng Jianxin ate a few bites of the biscuits left on Lili's table and took a few sips of tap water. She decided not to go anywhere all day today and wait for Xu Zhuang here.

At noon, Lili came back and took Zheng Jianxin to the street. Through a real estate agency, she rented the cheapest underground (that is, the first floor) single room nearby. In order to facilitate the rental of houses, the owners here changed their three-bedroom and two-living room homes into five or six single rooms, each of which was less than ten square meters, with a bathroom of about one square meter and a kitchen of about one square meter. The room was equipped with beds and small tables sold at the flea market, and some even had air conditioners and televisions. The rent ranged from 300 to 1,000 yuan per month.

Zheng Jianxin rented a room with only one small bed, so she paid 350 yuan per month, two months' deposit and one month's rent, and Lili paid it for her. There were no windows in the room, and the landlord chiseled a hole high up for ventilation.

What was annoying was that there were a lot of posters on the door, "Drive away the Northeast fox, and return my good husband; drive away the Sichuan girl, and my husband will go home". This was the warning from a resentful woman to the single female tenants. There was also a small note: "A prostitute sells her body, and someone sells his power, who is the dirtiest?" This seemed to be a counterattack from an outsider, or it could be a complaint from a local frustrated person. Zheng Jianxin tore them all off.

On the wall of the room was a large colorful painting that could be seen everywhere in street shops: a Western couple playing in the water on the beach. Zheng Jianxin saved it, and the picture conveyed a sense of warmth, and it could also cover the dirt on the wall. In this way, Zheng Jianxin had a place to stay.

Moving luggage, cleaning, arranging the room...... After finishing the house work, it was late, and Xu Zhuang still didn't come. I called Zeng Sheng, but his phone was still turned off. She called the phone booth in Xiangzhou Port at the agreed time, but no one answered. She asked Lili, but she was also confused and didn't know the situation.

Zheng Jianxin's heart became more and more uneasy, always feeling that something bad had happened. In the next few days, there was still no news from Xu Zhuang. Zheng Jianxin asked Lili several times every day, but she didn't get any answers. Her mood became lower and lower day by day, and she even lost her appetite, and she became haggard.

Lili saw it with her eyes and was anxious in her heart. She was sure that Xu Zhuang had a trouble; but what was the matter, and how big was it? There was no way to know. She couldn't find Zeng Sheng to ask.

It was not until the morning of the fifth day that Lili came to tell her that Zeng Sheng had called her the night before and said that Xu Zhuang was very busy and might not be back for a while, so he told Ajian not to worry.

Zheng Jianxin, who believed it, was a little happy and kept asking for details, such as what Xu Zhuang was busy with, where he was, who he was with, etc.

Lili had difficulty to answer and finally told her: "Ajian, don't ask. Zeng Sheng just told me that he was busy and couldn't come back in a short time, and then hung up the phone. He didn't tell me the details, how can I answer you?"

"As you are my good sister and Zhuang's cousin, if I don't ask you, who should I ask?"

Zheng Jianxin's angry and playful answer made Lili awkward. But seeing her smiling face, she finally felt a little relieved.

What Zheng Jianxin didn't notice was that when she turned around to do her own things, Lili's face was filled with guilt in her dim eyes.

After settling down, Zheng Jianxin began to worry about her future. As a girl who had just come out of the countryside, Zheng Jianxin had an instinctive vigilance and resistance to strange men, especially "bad men" from Hong Kong and Macau like Zhong Haicai. Although she was grateful for Zhong Haicai's generous help, she clearly warned herself not to get too close to Zhong Haicai. She did not go to Zhong Haicai's construction site to deliver herbal tea.

She had a plan for business: selling sugarcane. This was discovered by Lili when she took her for a walk on the beach. She thought it would not be difficult to learn.

She borrowed fifty yuan from Lili, rode Lili's old bicycle, ran to Shangchong Fruit Wholesale Market to buy a bunch of sugarcane, and rode to Gongbei Lovers Road to sell them.

On the sidewalk of Lovers Road, the coconuts and betel nut trees were tall and beautiful; the almonds, mangoes, and bodhi figs had large crowns and shade; the flowering shrubs such as crape myrtles, osmanthus, bougainvillea, and Chinese Perfume Plant were bright and eye-catching with elegant fragrance. It looked like a southern coastal city. During the day, there were mostly tourists from other places, and at night, there were mostly couples. There was a constant flow of people here day and night, which was a good place to do business.

Zheng Jianxin imitated the way others sold sugarcane and cut the sugarcane into three or four sections, each section costing one yuan. When a customer wanted to buy, she would cut the sugarcane with the machete and peeled off the skin in a few strokes, then put it in a plastic bag and handed it to the customer. Zheng Jianxin also paid attention to packing the peels in garbage bags to avoid being scolded by sanitation workers. Zheng Jianxin sold from afternoon to late night and made more than 30 yuan a day. Zheng Jianxin was secretly happy that this small business could also make a living! More than 30 yuan a day, one could make 1,000 yuan a month!

A week passed. One afternoon, urban management personnel wearing armbands drove away seaside vendors. Nervous shouts came from a distance: "The urban management is coming!" "The urban management is coming!" With the shouts, the urban management trucks quietly arrived. Several experienced vendors quickly gathered the plastic sheet on the ground with their hands, picked it up and disappeared. Drink bottles and fruits that slipped off the plastic sheet rolled all over the ground.

Zheng Jianxin panicked. She quickly picked up the basket and put it on the back seat of the bicycle. She held the handlebars with one hand and protected the basket with the other hand to leave. Several urban management officers had already blocked her way.

The urban management officers did not speak, and their faces were gloomy. One of the urban management officers grabbed the basket and threw it directly onto the truck. A security guard who was helping the event had amazing strength. He grabbed the bicycle with both hands and smashed it into the truck like a basketball player shooting. It clashed with the shelves and pallets confiscated from other vendors in the truck, producing the loud sound of "bang, bang".

This scene shocked Zheng Jianxin. She felt the fear of being caught as a thief, or the humiliation of being slapped in the face as a beggar. She was trembling all over, and a feeling of collapse came over her. Her face turned red and she couldn't speak.

The machete was picked up from the ground by an urban management officer, who walked forward slowly.

Zheng Jianxin followed the urban management officer and kept begging him to return the machete to her: "I borrowed the machete from the landlord......"

The urban management officer finally stopped, turned around and looked at Zheng Jianxin coldly, shaking the machete in front of Zheng Jianxin. Zheng Jianxin thought he was going to return it to her, but the urban management officer didn't move his head or blink, and threw the machete into the sea with a flick of his arm......

Zheng Jianxin was so angry that she burst into tears! The urban management officer got into the truck and drove away. The truck ran over the scattered fruits on the ground, causing the juice to splash.

She kept chasing the truck and ran into the urban management office. Her mouth was dry, so she picked up a paper cup and gulped down half a bucket of water, shouting and asking for her bicycle and compensation for the machete, but no one paid any attention to her. She just sat there and refused to leave until the Urban Management Office was ready for dinner.

She was so hungry that she didn't know where she got the courage from, so she picked up the chopsticks on the table and started eating. An old urban management officer who had been silent all the time suddenly asked her a question: "Do you have a temporary residence permit?" This question made Zheng Jianxin's heart "thump" and her legs weak.

When she was in the factory, the police also checked temporary residence permits several times. The factory passed checking with excuses and a "good" attitude. On Gongbei Street, the police drove a sealed truck to check temporary residence permits from time to time. It was said that they checked temporary residence permits of rental houses in the middle of the night, especially for young women. If they didn't have a permit, they would be stuffed into the sealed truck one by one without saying a word, and immediately locked up in a shelter and sent to Foshan outside the second line (border inspection for entering the special zone). Thinking of this, Zheng Jianxin jumped up like a spring and ran out of the Urban Management Office quickly.

Zheng Jianxin ran towards the beach without looking back. She was worried that the old Urban Management Officer would call the police to arrest her. On the way, she picked up two bottles of juice and a bag of bread that had just been crushed by a car, and ran along the Lovers' Road until she stopped at the "Zhuhai Fisher Girl" statue.

After she stopped panting and calmed down, Zheng Jianxin leaned against the coastal guardrail to eat and drink. But she still felt uneasy, as if everyone around her was looking at her, and someone would identify her as a person without a temporary residence permit at any time and call the police to take her away. She felt like a thief who came to this city specifically to do shameful things.

The night gradually came and there were fewer tourists. She looked at the statue of the Fisher Girl and thought, "The Fisher Girl" was also a migrant worker, right? Otherwise, how could she stay here alone like me, homeless?

After much deliberation, Zheng Jianxin had to find Zhong Haicai and said that she was willing to deliver herbal tea to the construction site. It would be good to have a job for the time being, and then asked him to apply for a temporary residence permit for her.

Zhong Haicai's rental house is as messy as a doghouse

Zhong Haicai was overjoyed at Zheng Jianxin's arrival. Gaolu Real Estate Company issued a temporary residence permit for "employee" Zheng Jianxin.

Zheng Jianxin delivered herbal tea to the construction site with a four-wheeled small truck during the day. In her spare time, she rode Lili's old bicycle to buy some fruits for the sisters (former female colleagues) in the factory at night.

The foreign-funded factory where Zheng Jianxin originally worked had no living facilities around it. The food provided by the factory cafeteria was of poor quality. Many workers had blisters at the corners of their mouths and oral ulcers due to insufficient nutrition. If they ate some fruits regularly, they would heal quickly.

When Zheng Jianxin was in the factory before, they pooled money and took turns to buy in the city. Now that she had time, she did not forget these sisters and deliver fruits every two or three days. As the number of deliveries increased, more and more workers asked her for help, and they would give Zheng Jianxin some errand fees each time.

Zheng Jianxin was concerned about Xu Zhuang, her former coworkers, and she had not forgotten how good Zhong Haicai was to her. One day after dinner, she went to Zhong Haicai's rental house, which was downstairs from Lili, to help him with some housework, otherwise she would feel uneasy. As soon as she entered Zhong Haicai's room, Zheng Jianxin was shocked by the scene in front of her: the bed was piled with clothes and socks that had not been sorted out, the wooden sofa was a pile of used beverage cans, and there was not a single cup on the coffee table, but it was piled up with empty biscuit boxes and opened cans...... There was nothing neat in the whole room, and the air was filled with a strange smell.

Zhong Haicai and Achang turned a blind eye to this, and were leisurely drinking beer and watching TV in an extremely limited space.

"Did I scare you?" Zhong Haicai saw her eyes and was surprised and embarrassed by her arrival. Zhong Haicai, like many Guangdong men, still wears long trousers even when the weather was hot. At most, he would roll up the corners of his trousers and had a pair of sandals on his bare feet. They were used to bending one leg and sitting down with the heel on the edge of the chair wherever they went.

Zhong Haicai obviously had just picked his toes. He put his legs down and stood up.

"You should make an appointment." Achang shook his legs and laughed slyly, "It's also good for Brother Zhong to clean it up a little. Haha...... This is a typical residence of a bachelor. Pretty girls must have never seen it......"

Zheng Jianxin looked at Zhong Haicai and asked, "Aren't you a big boss?" Zheng Jianxin had indeed never seen a room so messy, even in her hometown. "Tomorrow will be. -- When 'Blue Dream' is built!" Achang rushed to answer, with a smile on his face, "Today...... It's still Zhu Bajie (a character in the classic novel *Journey to the West*) carrying straw -- no people is there to help, and no money is there to help!"

Zhong Haicai poked him, glared at him, then turned to Zheng Jianxin, shrugged and smiled a little embarrassedly, which was considered to be tacitly agreeing with Achang's words.

The main Cantonese dialects are Cantonese (Guangzhou dialect), Chaozhou dialect, Shantou dialect, Hakka dialect and Leizhou dialect. People in Hong Kong and Macao speak Hong Kong Cantonese. Most of them communicate with each other in Hong Kong Cantonese. After the reform and opening up, everyone learned Mandarin without any prior agreement, and the language of communication between each other was sometimes Mandarin (National Language). Zhong Haicai spoke Hong Kong Cantonese, and Achang spoke Chaozhou dialect. Sometimes they communicate with each other in Mandarin.

"Uncle, let me clean up for you." Zheng Jianxin shook her head. She, who always loved cleanliness, really couldn't stand such a scene.

"Okay, okay......" Zhong Haicai nodded quickly, and the awkward situation was resolved. Otherwise, the "happy" guests would not even have a place to sit. He was happy, and his cheeks showed unshaven black and white stubble.

"Today is not the Qixi Festival, how come there is a goddess descending to the earth?" Achang screamed with envy and jealousy, "Isn't it God's arrangement?! Brother Zhong, you are so lucky!"

Goddess? God? Zheng Jianxin smiled. Zheng Jianxin was working, and the two Macau construction workers who were used to looking at pretty girls were so close to Zheng Jianxin, who was only wearing a V-neck T-shirt and a pair of three-quarter pants that exposed her calves. Their eyes were straight.

The two men felt a little sorry and wanted to help, but she said something to make them sit back down: "Forget it, if you can do it, would this room be like this?"

The two of them couldn't watch TV, so they had to stare at her movements with four eyes, and move their butts when she asked them to, and lift their feet when she asked them to, watching the things in the room being stacked, flattened, and placed in order one by one, and the bulging garbage bags were thrown out of the door. After everything was put back in place, Zheng Jianxin started to scrub the furniture and utensils, and then mopped the cement floor. It took more than two hours to clean up.

Looking at the completely new and different room, Zhong Haicai just smiled, his eyes never leaving Zheng Jianxin. And Achang was jealous, and kept yelling that Zheng Jianxin would help him clean up sometime.

"200 yuan an hour!" Zheng Jianxin held the water that Zhong Haicai poured for her, rubbed her fingers, and looked playful.

"Robbed, blood drawn......" Achang cried so sadly.

Zheng Jianxin ignored his words and looked around the room with satisfaction. Suddenly, she noticed the crucifix on the wall at the head of the bed -- it was the only thing in the room that remained clean before she cleaned it up. She asked curiously: "Uncle, are you religious?"

Zhong Haicai looked at the image of Jesus and was very proud. The meaning was that he belonged to an organization and was well-educated. He nodded vigorously: "Yes. I am...... I am ...... Yes, a Catholic. The 'God' made me a good person, and I am a good person!"

Macau is known as the "City of Catholic Holy Land". In terms of area, it is a place with the most churches in the world. The lower-class laborers will also go to church to worship in order to have a spiritual sustenance or to see something new.

"Ha, Brother Zhong is a good person." Achang laughed happily. Zheng Jianxin wanted to laugh, but found that she couldn't. Since then, Zheng Jianxin would come to clean up Zhong Haicai's house every few days, wash the clothes that had been in the washing machine for several days, and buy some fish and meat at the market to make him a sumptuous dinner. At such times, Zhong Haicai would appear particularly happy, and he would like everything he saw. Even if a mouse slipped across his feet, he would not shout and beat it.

"Ajian, see what I bring back?!"

"What?" Zheng Jianxin, who was cooking soup, looked at Zhong Haicai who was excited and yelling as soon as he entered the door. "Macau salted fish, a world-class specialty!"

Zhong Haicai waved the shopping bag in his hand like he was offering a treasure, and his tone became gentle: "Ajian, you take a rest today, let me do it!"

"You? You can cook?" Zheng Jianxin looked skeptical, looked at the bag and said: "Pickled salted fish can also be famous all over the world? Do you think I'm a country girl who's easy to please?"

"I'm telling the truth." Zhong Haicai saw that Zheng Jianxin didn't believe it, and he got a little anxious, "I went to the island specifically to buy it in Coloane. There are dozens of shops specializing in selling salted fish there. The flagpoles under the eaves are all hanging strings of salted fish. Entering it is like entering a Bagua formation (maze), making people lose their sense of direction."

Zheng Jianxin understood a little: Macau is small and highly internationalized, but there are not many things that people can talk about with relish. It's easy to remember if it's a little bit special. The world-famous salted fish on Coloane Island should also benefit from this, just like egg tarts.

"Just sit and wait for the food. The salted fish is fishy and salty before it's done. It's easy to hurt your hands. If so, my heart will feel pain!"

Zhong Haicai rolled up his sleeves and took the salted fish while laughing and singing. His skillfulness surprised Zheng Jianxin a little. She chatted with the old man who was happily talking about how to make the salted fish more delicious.

Zhong Haicai really didn't lie. The unique fragrance of the salted fish filled the room while it was still in the pot, making Zheng Jianxin sniff. When Zhong Haicai brought it to the table, she had already set the dishes and waited.

Her performance made Zhong Haicai even happier. As soon as he sat down, he picked up a piece and put it in Zheng Jianxin's bowl: "Try it and see if I'm bragging!"

Zheng Jianxin responded and put the salted fish into her mouth, chewed it gently for a while, and slowly swallowed it into her stomach. Then she said to Zhong Haicai, who was full of hope and followed her movements: "Not bad. Fragrant but not greasy, salty but not choking."

Zhong Haicai didn't quite understand what she meant by "choking", but he knew she was praising him.

He raised his thumb and shook it and said: "This is really a good thing. In the past, in the countryside, I could eat a big bowl of rice with such a small piece. I lived like this for several years."

Looking at the beautiful girl in front of him and eating the salted fish in his mouth, Zhong Haicai had a satisfied expression on his face. Halfway through the meal, Zhong Haicai suddenly stood up as if he remembered something. He excitedly but a little embarrassedly picked up a woven bag that he had placed beside the bed when he just entered the room, handed it to Zheng Jianxin and said mysteriously: "Open it and take a look."

"What is it?" Zheng Jianxin put down her chopsticks and opened the woven bag to look inside. It turned out to be a bag of women's tops, short skirts and shorts, and various colors of cloth.

"Why did you buy so many women's clothes?" Zheng Jianxin took out one and looked at it. "The style is really good!"

"I bought it for you." Zhong Haicai laughed and scratched his bald head with an embarrassed face. "I don't know your......your size, so I asked Lili what she wears and bought it accordingly. Anyway, you have similar figures, it should be suitable......"

"This......you......" Zheng Jianxin blushed and didn't know what to say when she held the clothes. The scene and feeling of her father buying clothes for her when she was a child came to her mind.

"Don't talk about you, me, and ......, just take it!" Zhong Haicai waved his hand in relief when he saw Zheng Jianxin didn't decline. "You always help me, I should show some appreciation!"

"Thank you!" Zheng Jianxin put down the clothes and motioned Zhong Haicai to continue eating. "Uncle, you are so nice."

"What did you call me?" Zhong Haicai stopped holding the chopsticks and asked curiously. Zheng Jianxin smiled coquettishly and said like a child to her father: "Uncle, do you like me to call you Mr. Zhong?"

"I don't like it at all." Zhong Haicai picked up the chopsticks again, but he didn't dare to look Zheng Jianxin in the eye. He only looked at the dishes on the table and said hesitantly: "Call me Brother Zhong, it's more intimate......"

"No." Zheng Jianxin's answer shocked Zhong Haicai all over, and then she shouted like a naughty boy, "I want to call you...... Lao Dou (Dad), haha......"

Zhong Haicai realized that she was joking, and he breathed a sigh of relief and was amused by her imperfect Cantonese. He drank a mouthful of soup, sighed contentedly, looked at Zheng Jianxin and said: "Ajian, I will take you to Macau in the future. There is a women's street in Macau, there are many things, you can pick whatever you want."

"To Macau?" Zheng Jianxin's face was immediately full of longing. She had heard a lot about Macau, and after arriving in Gongbei, she felt its charm more closely. Every time she looked at Macau on the other side of the sea, she would wonder when she could go there to take a look.

Now, Zhong Haicai, a Macau native, said that he would take her there, which made her look forward to it even more. Picking up the cup of Jiujiang double-distilled white wine on the table and taking a sip, Zhong Haicai's dark face turned a little red, and under the light, it looked like a mixture of Guan Gong (or Lord Guan, which refers to Guan Yu, a historical figure and deity in Chinese culture) and Bao Gong (or Lord Bao, a Chinese politician). He took advantage of the alcohol to continue Zheng Jianxin's words and said: "Well, I will tell people that you are Mrs. Zhong and the boss lady in the future!"

"Brother Zhong, you are really good at joking." Zheng Jianxin took his drunken words as a joke, but her face still turned red, she smiled slightly with her hands covering her mouth, and her chopsticks could not be held steadily.

"Are you kidding?" Zhong Haicai also laughed, "I'm not kidding. If there is anything in the future, if someone bullies you, just tell Brother Zhong. I have friends who have stabbed people with knives and played with guns with both hands......"

"Doesn't that make me a gangster?" Zheng Jianxin didn't take his words to heart, and still looked innocent and cute.

"Isn't the underworld good?" Zhong Haicai straightened his back and said with great spirit, "Brother Zhong is Zhong Kui (a legendary figure) standing at the intersection, specializing in catching evil spirits and protecting you, a beautiful girl!"

Zheng Jianxin laughed, "I want your protection? Ha, then I'm a big sister?"

"You want to be my (big sister)?" Zhong Haicai's face flashed with excitement, he raised his thumb and took a big sip of wine, "Great, great! Ambitious! Let me tell you, I have dated several women, but compared to you, you are a fairy in the sky, and they are......the......what is it on the ground? Ignore it, I will never touch them again. Brother Zhong only wants you, love you for a thousand years! Ten thousand years!"

"Brother Zhong, you are drunk. Can you live that long? Then you will become a ten thousand year old demon?" Zheng Jianxin continued to laugh, and did not take his nagging words too seriously.

When Zheng Jianxin first arrived in Zhuhai, she saw people here making jokes about relationships between men and women without any scruples, with frivolous words and casual behavior. She felt uncomfortable and even disgusted, thinking that they were shameless. Lili once scolded all the men in Macau as perverts. However, after a period of exposure, she knew that they were frank, straightforward, humorous and open-minded, so she was no longer surprised and got used to it. Anyway, even if these people were not like this, many mainland TV, books, magazines and even billboards on the street were like this, and she couldn't avoid it even if she wanted to.

However, Zhong Haicai's face turned the color of liver, and the fire in his eyes made Zheng Jianxin numb. She was flustered and said a few words to Zhong Haicai and hurriedly found an excuse to leave the room. She was relieved when she ran to the street.

Zheng Jianxin ran to the statue of "Zhuhai Fisher Girl" again. She wanted to accompany the "Fisher Girl" and talk to her. The sculpture of "Zhuhai Fisher Girl" was sculpted by Guangzhou artists when the city was established and the special zone was established, in order to have a symbol for the city. The "Fisher Girl" stood in the sea of Xianglu Bay, holding pearls in her hands. Looking at the "Fisher Girl", Zheng Jianxin suddenly thought: "The Fisher Girl" has a graceful image, and it should also have a story, a story of breathing out rainbows. She wanted to try to write a story for the "Fisher Girl", a migrant girl.

9

Lili, dealing with three men
from Hong Kong, Taiwan and Macau

There is a saying among migrant workers: Guangdong is hot, and corn does not need to be roasted by fire, it will be cooked in the sun.

In early summer, Zheng Jianxin experienced the heat of Guangdong. To be precise, it was hot and humid. At night, the small rental house was as hot as a steamer.

A small electric fan given by Lili was hung in the mosquito net: three small plastic blades were turning, and its wind force was like a cattail leaf fan. One could only feel the existence of the wind when her face was half a foot away from it.

Zheng Jianxin took out an unfinished book from the small square handbag that Xu Zhuang bought for her not long ago. It was "*Pioneers*" bought in the county town a few years before, which was about the development of the American West.

The light was too dim, and she couldn't read after a few pages. She put the book aside. She lay on the bed and closed her eyes for a while, but couldn't fall asleep; she counted sheep and tossed and turned several times but still couldn't fall asleep. Instead, she sweated all over, and mosquitoes buzzed in her ears from time to time, which made Zheng Jianxin upset.

There was no way, Zheng Jianxin had to get up and find a pen to write down her thoughts on visiting "Zhuhai Fisher Girl" that she had always wanted to write but had never written. As soon as she put her feet on the ground, a mouse quickly jumped past her feet, and she couldn't help but scream and jumped back to bed.

Patting her chest, Zheng Jianxin's eyes involuntarily focused on the photo of her with Xu Zhuang, Lili and others on the table. What followed was self-pity: If Xu Zhuang was here, why would she be like this?

"Brother Zhuang, where are you?" After being in a daze for a while, Zheng Jianxin became more and more upset, and Zhong Haicai's eyes burning with fire flashed in front of her from time to time, which made her almost unable to help but scream.

"Shower!"

Guangdong people call taking a bath "shower", which is really the most accurate. Who takes a bath several times a night? But it's not strange to say that you take a shower several times a night. Zheng Jianxin had taken shower for the third time tonight.

The tap water was warm. But after washing from head to toe, the whole body was finally refreshed, but the mind was also clearer, and she didn't want to sleep. Walking out of the room, Zheng Jianxin planned to enjoy the wind -- walking on the beach was her favorite thing to do. Not long after she arrived in Zhuhai, Lili took her to the beach to feel the sea. After that, Zheng Jianxin would go to the beach alone whenever she had time, watching the tide and listening to the sea breeze, thinking about her lover who was cruising in the sea and working hard for their future. At that time, even if Xu Zhuang was not around, she felt that his heart was very close to her.

The lights in Lili's rental house were still on. Zheng Jianxin called her out, and seeing that she was free, she waved her down to walk with her.

From Gongbei Bay at the port to the city, Lovers' Road is a bay road that winds along the coast and the mountains for more than ten kilometers. The name is so romantic. There is a wide green belt between Lovers' Road and the seawall, and at night, it is soft and romantic.

Lili and Zheng Jianxin leaned on the stone railing. Lili wore a light brown vest and a pair of floral suit shorts, and her two beautiful legs were bright white in the night. Lili lit a "520" brand cigarette, and the fragrance spread.

The lights of Zhuhai and Macau are connected, and they look like one city. Adding brilliance to the night sky, in the distance are the colorful lights and changing neon lights of Macau's high-rise buildings, and the bow-shaped bridge across the sea is decorated with lights like pearls, making people feel like floating in the air.

The sea was quietly receding. The waning moon was covered by thick dark clouds, occasionally floating out, showing its face and then going back. Looking at the motionless flowers, plants and leaves around her, Zheng Jianxin exhaled heavily: "The room is as stuffy as a steamer, and I can't sleep at all."

Lili hummed again and said: "A typhoon is coming. If I were in my hometown, this would be the coolest and most comfortable time, with the smell of soil and mountain flowers everywhere."

"I miss home too." Zheng Jianxin glanced at her and asked: "Is there any news about Xu Zhuang?"

Lili shook her head. She shook off "Xu Zhuang" as if she didn't hear Zheng Jianxin's question. After a while, she pointed to the coastal highway on the Macau side and said: "Look, that sports car is so beautiful, is it a Ferrari?" Lili didn't know much about cars, but she remembered it because she heard people say that Ferrari was a good car. "I really want to learn how to drive. When I can drive a little red car on the street like those girls on the street, how cool it would be!"

Zheng Jianxin stood up and walked to the coconut tree next to her. Looking at Lili's self-indulgent look, she stroked the straight trunk and said in a daze, "This is indeed a city that makes people nostalgic, but I don't even have a stable place to live. I still remember writing an essay called 'My Ideal' in junior high school. Ha, ideal......"

When people were young, they thought life was beautiful and simple, but now "ideal" is mocking them.

"Your essay is about the Red Army passing through Wumeng Mountain and watering the red camellia with blood. It was really well written and published in the regional newspaper. What do you want to write when you are here?"

Lili said the last sentence casually, but Zheng Jianxin answered seriously: "I want to write about the story of the Zhuhai Fisher Girl. When I saw the statue on the first day in Zhuhai, I felt that she must be a migrant girl!"

Lili laughed at her wonderful association. Finally, there was a little wind, shaking the palm leaves next to them gently, and the flower bed farther away was filled with the faint fragrance of Chinese Perfume Plant.

Zheng Jianxin looked at the night sky over the sea. The lights of Macau cut out a golden outline for her, and the side profile was even more soft and beautiful. Lili felt that Zheng Jianxin was like a goddess at this moment, pure, dignified, and admirable. Despite this, she still didn't take her good sister's words seriously: "Don't be silly. Nowadays, people care about money and power. It's useless for a working girl to have ideals!"

After a while, Lili changed her tone and said with a smile: "My good sister, this place is only one step away from Macau and Hong Kong. Why don't I find you a good husband and let you rise to the top and become a phoenix?" She said it so easily, as if she didn't know the relationship between Xu Zhuang and Ajian.

Zheng Jianxin didn't care about Lili's jokes, and it was better not to mention her lover. She turned her head and pouted and said: "How can I be as beautiful as the four beauties in Gongbei? They are good at seducing men's souls!"

Zheng Jianxin only learned from Mingming's coffee shop a few days before that there were four beauties in Gongbei, and Lili was one of them. Lili was speechless, just raised her face and looked at her, and the two laughed at the same time.

Lili looked at the bright lights of Macau and Gongbei, and after a long while she said with some sadness: "It would be great if the world was either full of men or women, then there wouldn't be so many troubles. Alas...... the relationship between men and women is just like Zhuhai and Macau. They are both twin cities and the same city while they are both the same city and twin cities......"

She stood up and leaned against another coconut tree: "Among the three of us, I was the first to come out. I worked hard for three years and finally got a Taiwanese boyfriend. In less than half a year, I had a house, a car, and opened a coffee shop, and brought my brothers and sisters out."

Zheng Jianxin shook her head and said: "Why should we...... rely on others? We also have our own hands and feet......"

Lili shook her head: "I have only seen clearly here that having money means being the boss, having money means having face and dignity, and no one will ask you where your money comes from." Then she casually cited an example: "Being prostitutes, rich ones are envied and called romantic and capable, and brought to the tables with wine; the working ones are disgustingly called a hooligan! The office staff who are prostitutes are despised and said to have problems with the relationship between men and women......"

Zheng Jianxin looked at her quietly, and after a while hesitantly asked: "Sister Lili, that Zeng Sheng...... and Bai Lang...... how did you......"

Lili avoided her gaze and said a little unnaturally: "What? I know you have been scolding me in your heart, right?" Lili knew that sooner or later, Ajian would ask her. Although Ajian had been in Zhuhai for more than half a year, everyone was in a hurry when they meet, not to mention that she was always sticking with Xu Zhuang.

Zheng Jianxin shook her head: "I didn't...... you know...... no matter what, we are the best sisters!"

Lili was silent for a while, then sighed and said: "You know, when I first came here, I worked in a shoe factory run by a Hong Kong man in Jida Industrial Zone. I pasted leather and lining on the toe and heel of the shoe. The piecework wage was 1.2 cents per piece. At that time, all the large shoe factories in Zhuhai used glue without ammonia and benzene. In order to save money, our boss used glue containing ammonia and benzene, which cost 100 yuan per barrel. But this ammonia smelled pungent, and benzene was a carcinogen. Of course, after evaporation, the leather was pasted on the shoes, and the shoes had no smell. But we worked twelve hours a day, and often worked until two o'clock in the early morning. Except for a few hours of sleep, we lived in this air all day long. "One cent for one piece of work, how many toes and heels did I have to paste so that I could get 500 yuan a month! My current lumbar muscle strain is the cause of the disease at that time. After work, I was so sleepy that I wanted to sleep, and I had to wait for one or two hours in line to take a shower. In winter, there was no hot water at the end of the shower...... I'd had enough. "

Zheng Jianxin nodded. Looking at the prosperous city in front of her, Lili continued: "Just coming out of my hometown, I felt more real than on TV. We country girls were like Grandma Liu entering the Grand View Garden. We found everything was new. Bars, discos, nightclubs, we wanted to experience everything. "

Zheng Jianxin looked at her face full of memories, but still didn't quite understand. Among her group of good sisters, Lili was the hardest-working and most efficient in farm work, and she could do everything; she was the most daring in doing things, and she would do whatever she thought of without considering the consequences; she spoke quickly and had a sense of music, which made people love to listen to.

"Jida is an urban area, and it was already lively at that time. There were several dance halls and nightclubs around the factory."Once I passed by a nightclub, and thinking of the extravagance of such places in movies and TV, the charming and seductive dancers, and the rich and powerful who spend money like water, I couldn't help but stop and took a look."

Lili's face became more complicated, and her voice was slow: "The gap between reality and expectations is always too big. This gap forced me to take this step today."

"What do you mean?"

"Let's not talk about those men, but those women who come in and out, or the girls......" Lili shook her head unconsciously, with a mixture of self-mockery and pride on her face, "Except for the occasional one or two who can be regarded as having regular and bright features, most of them are far more ugly than we. They only rely on cosmetics to decorate the facade and clothes to wrap their bodies to be presentable."

"So, you felt unfair?" Zheng Jianxin finally came back to her senses and let out a long breath.

"Yes, I felt it was unfair." Lili smiled strangely, "they could go to high-end places and earn hundreds of yuan an hour, while we worked like slaves for only that much a month...... I felt very unfair at the time."

Zheng Jianxin looked at the indescribable melon-seed face in the dim light opposite her, and was silent for a long time before saying, "Then what?"

"Then......" Lili sighed lightly and said, "A fat man, 'bright head', wearing a neat white suit on a hot day, appeared in front of me with a big belly, shaking a cigar and smiling, and said to me in barely understandable Mandarin, 'Pretty girl, come in and have some fun'!"

"You went in?" Zheng Jianxin asked unnecessarily.

"I went in." Lili sighed again, "Although his invitation made me hesitate and shrink, and even tremble a little in my heart and body, I still followed him in. Looking back later, I don't even understand whether that trembling was fear or excitement."

Lili added, looking at Zheng Jianxin, her eyes no longer dodging, finally getting rid of the last layer of demons in her heart.

"That man was Zeng Sheng, right?" Zheng Jianxin finally understood how Lili became what she is today.

Lili nodded: "Yes. When I went inside, I saw the scenes I had seen on TV, the sound system that shook the ground, the soft and comfortable sofas, the polite waiters...... Everything made me, who had never seen anything before, at a loss. I just followed Zeng Sheng like a puppet. He asked me to drink, so I drank. He asked me to play rock-paper-scissors, so I played......"

Zheng Jianxin was a little sad. She didn't want to blame Lili's choice at that time, nor did she want to judge Lili's current life. It was just that her good sister's moral concepts were contrary to her own, which made her not know how to deal with herself.

"I was a little dizzy after drinking, and the lights in the hall dimmed.

Zeng Sheng asked me to dance, but I said I didn't know how to dance. He said it was very simple, and I would learn it after following him for a while. Then he held me and took me to step forward and turn in circles. The air in the dance hall was very fragrant and comfortable, the lights were very soft, and the music was very charming, which made people a little drowsy. It was the first time I experienced this feeling."

After removing her makeup, Lili's face was dreamy, her eyes were calm, and she was as beautiful as a fairy. Compared with the enchantment in the daytime, she seemed to have changed into a different person.

This feeling made Zheng Jianxin very distracted.

Then Lili's tone changed drastically, and she pulled the corner of her mouth with contempt: "Mr. Zeng is an old pervert. I don't know what Mr. Zeng's name is now. People in Guangdong, Hong Kong and Macau call Mr. Wang and Mr. Li as Wang Sheng and Li Sheng, so I called him Mr. Zeng at the beginning, and call him Zeng Sheng after a long time. He didn't turn around twice before his hand that was holding my waist touched my buttocks, and he pressed his face against mine, and he kept trying to press his chest against mine. At the beginning, I saw that the men and women next to me were almost the same, so I endured it. Later, his hand reached into my shoulder and sleeves and tried to touch my breast. I pushed him away and tried to leave. He quickly grabbed me and kept apologizing in poor Mandarin. I was angry and amused, and I was too embarrassed to refuse."

"Then he behaved a lot better, talking to me while dancing. I knew he was from Hong Kong, and he also knew that I was a migrant worker who had just come out and it was my first time to come to such a place. Ha, I was really honest and simple at that time, and I told the truth about everything. I think he also saw this point in me, and then he used the example of the man and woman next to him, constantly tempting me, and slowly held me again."

"But when I touched his body, I couldn't help but think of the big white pig in my hometown. Being close to a pig, I got goose bumps all over my body; and letting him take advantage of me was really unbearable, so I shook him off and ran away. I didn't breathe a sigh of relief until I ran out of the door of the karaoke hall. "

"Then how did you two......"

"He chased me out. "Lili interrupted Zheng Jianxin, "He chased me and yelled at me. I thought he was not going to give up, but I was not someone to be trifled with, so I yelled at him in front of the security guards, the receptionist and the guests at the door, 'What else do you want?' Guess what? Ha, he looked at the crowd at the door innocently, stuffed three 100-dollar Hong Kong dollars into my pocket with a flattering look, and whispered that it was a tip for me, and asked me to take it. "

Zheng Jianxin knew there was more to come, so she said "hmm" and didn't say anything.

"Looking at the Hong Kong dollars in my hand, should I take it or not? I was a little torn. This was the first time I held a Hong Kong dollar, and it would be a lie to say that I was not moved, but......"

Zheng Jianxin nodded in understanding. For mainlanders, Hong Kong dollars had a noble meaning, and were a capital for showing that they were superior and different.

"Zeng Sheng said to me, take it, you made me very happy tonight, and you deserve it." Lili shook her head with a smile, as if she still thought his words were strange, "I saw sweat on his forehead at that time. I was sweating in an air-conditioned place. I thought that with his figure, he must have been very tired to chase me and asked someone to pay the bill. Therefore, I think he was not a bad person. It would be a waste not to take the money.

"When I wanted to leave again, Zeng Sheng grabbed me again and said that he would treat me with a seafood supper. He also smiled and told me not to worry, there were lights everywhere, and he would not have the courage to rape me. I was indeed a little hungry at that time, and the temptation of seafood made me follow him without thinking much. That's how I met him."

At this point, Lili sighed and looked at Zheng Jianxin: "Ajian, tell me, if I was not so curious at that time, if I ignored Zeng Sheng's invitation and left, what would my life be like now? I would still be a worker on the assembly line in the factory, right? Even if I work hard, I have education, and the best I can do is to be a workshop team leader."

Zheng Jianxin couldn't figure out what she wanted to say, so she had to say "um" again and didn't say anything. Lili pulled her to sit on the bench. Lili reached into her bag and took out a cigarette, sniffing it greedily.

"Back in the factory, lying on the bed, I looked at the three Hong Kong dollar bills over and over again, feeling that half a month's salary was so easy to get. Looking at the workers on the beds in the dormitory, thinking that they had to work hard for more than ten days to earn three hundred yuan, at that moment, I actually felt like a rich person......"

Zheng Jianxin was stunned. She didn't know how this good sister became so vain. How long had she been out from the countryside at that time?

It is said that society is a big dye vat, but one doesn't expect that the pollution capacity is so strong.

"It's ridiculous, isn't it?" Lili smiled, walked to Zheng Jianxin indifferently, put her arm around her shoulders and said slowly, "I just like this feeling. With money, I can walk with my head held high, look at brand-name fashions, and eat the expensive seafood I like. When I was in my hometown, I longed for such a life. This is how people in the special zone live, not like a working ant who is busy all day long."

Zheng Jianxin didn't agree with her words, but it was difficult to refute, so she could only remain silent.

"Later, every time I saw the three hundred Hong Kong dollars, I would think of the fragrant nightclub, think of Zeng Sheng, and wonder if he would ask me out again. After a few times, if I was bored and Zeng Sheng was not free, I would encourage a few good-looking sisters to go to those places before dinner, and men would come to chat with us. Once we entered the KTV room, we would order the fastest-produced fried spaghetti or something else to fill our stomachs, and then sing with them, drink red wine, eat fruits, order drinks...... Ha, we felt so enjoyable at the time, and at the end, we would get a few hundred dollars for tips. Is there anything better than this kind of life? Even gods are no more than this, right?"

"Then, those men......" Zheng Jianxin held Lili's hand on her shoulder and asked carefully.

"Hey, it was just holding hands, hugging and making sexual advances. Later, I thought it was nothing. It's the same if my husband holds me in bed at home. I won't lose a piece of meat. How can I have so many delicious foods and drinks with my husband, not to mention money!"

Zheng Jianxin lowered her head and was speechless. In her opinion, this good sister had gone crazy. But what could she do? This was the lifestyle that Lili chose herself, and she was willing to do it, which did not harm anyone, and the income she earned could make her family live a better life. Was there anything wrong with this? Morality? Zheng Jianxin smiled bitterly in her heart -- the weight of morality in this era was not as heavy as a piece of paper money. Looking at the sea water coming and going, Zheng Jianxin was at a loss. When did the world become like this? When did people become like this? When did her good sister become like this?

"Once, Zeng Sheng brought a friend to ask me to go singing together," Lili continued, her tone was with proud and a little sharpness. "That day I wore a tight dress -- remember, when dating a strange man, you can't wear a short skirt or shorts, so as not to be taken advantage of and bullied. -- His friend saw that I had big breasts, and reached out to grab them lustfully and said, 'Pretty girl, let me check whether it is real flesh or silicone?' I slapped his hand away, untied the elastic band of his casual pants, and threw the half-smoked cigarette in. Hahaha, it was really satisfying to see him jumping and screaming in anxiety. Ajian, do you think it's funny?" Lili held Zheng Jianxin and laughed.

"You are so hot. Didn't you turn him into a eunuch?!" Zheng Jianxin smiled when she thought about that scene.

"No, Zeng Sheng gave him a glass of water." Lili laughed for a long time before she stopped, sneering, "From then on, none of Zeng Sheng's friends dared to touch me. He also liked my style, and from time to time he gave me some not very expensive but very beautiful bracelets and necklaces. Later, he said he would give me 5,000 yuan a month for 'household expenses', and when he came to Zhuhai, I would accompany him to 'live' together."

At this point, Lili glanced at Zheng Jianxin with a bit of strangeness, and then said: "The money promised by Zeng Sheng is deposited into my bank account on time every month. Sometimes he is in Zhuhai for two or three days a month, and more often he is not seen for two or three months. I often go out for a walk when I am bored in the rental house. That's how I met Zhong Haicai downstairs."

Speaking of Zhong Haicai, Lili curled her lips imperceptibly: "There is no man who doesn't want to cheat...... Oh, one time Zhong Haicai invited me to dinner, and that's how I met Bai Lang, Achang and others."

Bai Lang was handsome and enthusiastic as his name revealed, and had extensive knowledge. He spoke fluent English from time to time, was talkative and humorous, and could easily capture Lili's restless heart and empty body. Zheng Jianxin could imagine all this, but she couldn't imagine that Zhong Haicai, who seemed to be honest and simple, also had ambitious desire for Lili. Lili didn't like him for either his money or appearance.

What Zheng Jianxin could not have imagined was that Achang, who looked like a naughty monkey, was also flirting with Lili. Achang was very good at taking advantage of loopholes. Whenever Zeng Sheng and Bailang were not in Zhuhai, he would go to Zhuhai from Macau every day and find all kinds of excuses, whether right or wrong, to run to Lili's room to chat with her. He called her "Sister Lili" all the time and flattered her very often, which made Lili feel enjoyable.

In addition, he was diligent and always rushed to do heavy work for her, such as carrying gas tanks. Although Lili despised him as a poor boy who wanted to eat seafood for free, Achang took the initiative to pay for the small money for daily life and clothes and gifts. After a long time, she got used to him. When she was in good mood, she would deliberately tease him, asking him to lick her toes and trim her nails, and enjoy the feeling of being a queen.

Achang was also happy to do such things. Since he did not have Zeng Sheng's wealth and power, nor did he have Bailang's chic demeanor, he worked hard to do the hard work. Zeng Sheng and Bai Lang were away for much more time than when they were there, and he had plenty of time and opportunities, so he finally took off Lili's clothes.

Zheng Jianxin didn't want to ask or listen. She walked towards the seawall against the sea breeze. The tide receded, revealing the reefs and the beach. The strong stench from the mud and garbage in the ditch close to the seawall made her stomach bloated and nauseous.

When Zheng Jianxin returned to the stone chair, Lili tilted her neck and smoked as if nothing had happened. In the green space behind Lili, palm trees stretched out countless long green belts. Next to the bushes under the palm trees, colorful rhododendrons, oleanders, and roses were in full bloom. The fragrance of flowers wafted from time to time in the air, that was magnolia and Chinese Perfume Plant.

Zheng Jianxin looked at Lili under the soft street light and couldn't help laughing. Lili exhaled a puff of smoke and asked inexplicably: "Why are you laughing?"

"I think you are as beautiful as a flower fairy!" She laughed out loud, then held her arm around Lili's neck and sat beside her. Zheng Jianxin had been away from her hometown for more than half a year, and she felt like she was watching a movie or dreaming about the city. As a village girl, Zheng Jianxin walked into a modern city, as if she had suddenly fallen into a strange world full of brilliance, and faced scenes of social life one after another. She was puzzled by the phenomenon of money and lust. Lili, however, was like a scalpel for dissecting a corpse, revealing the mystery from time to time, and interpreting her personal actions vividly. Lili's words and experiences opened a corner of the social curtain for Zheng Jianxin.

After finding out the truth of Lili's life, Zheng Jianxin felt much more relaxed. Then came the worry about Lili's future and her own future, which made her mood much heavier, accompanied by anxiety, fear and confusion.

As the saying goes, "At home, you are not afraid of poverty, but on the road, poverty kills you." Zheng Jianxin thought, if Lili was replaced by me, or one day I couldn't make it, would I follow her path? Thinking of this, she withdrew her familiar, strange and wary eyes from Lili, and a chill ran up her spine. A firm voice sounded in her heart: "No, never, even if I go back to my hometown to farm for the rest of my life, no, never......"

The wind was a little stronger, and the leaves on the top of the tall and straight coconut trees fluttered. The waning moon slid into the floating clouds. Zheng Jianxin couldn't help shivering in this scene, and a familiar scene appeared in her mind.

The two bottles of water that Lili brought had long been finished. Lili played with the empty bottle in her hand. Zheng Jianxin went to the sugarcane stall and bought two pieces of sugarcane, and the two of them started eating. Lili chewed in small bites, and Zheng Jianxin sucked the juice of the sugarcane hard, making a "tsk tsk" sound, and it tasted very sweet.

"Sister Lili, if I can't find a suitable job, I will go back to my hometown! I suddenly thought of the first night I came to Zhuhai, do you remember? You took me here......" Zheng Jianxin sighed softly while looking at the wide grass on the side of the road. It was a farewell party for the old batch of migrant workers returning home. As she spoke, she packed the sugarcane residue into a garbage bag. "Instead of working for five or six years and going back sadly, it's better to leave now, which is equivalent to not having been to the Special Administrative Region. Maybe that's better."

Lili said "hmm" with her beautiful eyes blurred: "It's really bad. You just arrived and you feel the separation." She paused, exhaled a long breath, and said calmly, "What can you do if you go back? What can you do?"

10

When the migrant workers returned home, they left their bitter youthhood in the Special Administrative Region

It was a day in November last year, and the stars were shining. The waves gently hit the embankment, as if singing a soothing ballad. It was winter in the hometown, but there it was as warm as spring. Even at night, people wear short sleeves and shorts. This may be the best season in the subtropics, but the party that night didn't warm the hearts of everyone present.

The protagonists of the party were five sisters from neighboring villages, all of whom were 26 or 27 years old. One of them was cousin Chahua that Zheng Jianxin first wanted to find when she arrived in Zhuhai. They came to Zhuhai when they were about the same age as Zheng Jianxin, 17 or 18 years old, and left their youthhood in this city.

And now, they were leaving, leaving this place where they had dedicated nearly ten years of youthhood to build a glorious city. They were "old", they wanted to start a family, they wanted stability, instead of leaving their hometown endlessly, with nothing to settle down. That afternoon, Chahua told Zheng Jianxin while packing her luggage that she got off the bus at the city bus station when she first came to Zhuhai. At that time, the city bus station was in a small courtyard next to No. 1 Middle School on Xiangzhou Street. At that time, Chahua was very puzzled: Why was the urban area of the special zone not as big as the county town in their hometown? A main road turned out to be a small gravel road. There were no tunnels at that time, and Ningxi was a farmland. When they arrived at Jida, they saw construction sites everywhere for roads and houses, and they felt the atmosphere of the construction of the special zone.

What they talked about most at the party was the past. When they first arrived in Gongbei, the seaside was still empty and dark at night. People from Gaosha Village who could go to Macau went there. There were few people here and it was deserted.

At the end of Lianhua Road was the customs, a small building, and there were few people entering and leaving the country. The current port building was originally an open space connected to Macau, and a barbed wire was set up on the open space. Looking at Macau through the barbed wire had become a common sight for the place. The open space in Weiji Village in front of the barbed wire had formed a small free market, where Chaoshan people sell smuggled second-hand goods, mostly used suits and coats.

The barbed wire fence facing north on Yingbin South Road was now wide, busy, and lined with buildings. At that time, except for the newly built Yindu Hotel, the entire gravel road was dark. At the end of Beibai Road was the entrance of Beiling Village.

They recalled, talked, and smiled at each other. The smiles were bitter, helpless, and also proud. Over the years, they had carried sand, carried cement, mixed concrete, and followed the contractor to build one building after another, but they had always lived in "sauna-like" sheds and eaten the simplest meals...... When they participated in the construction of the port square, the retaining wall of the foundation pit collapsed, and they were rescued from the farmers' houses in disrepair......

Chahua came from Deyue. She worked while standing to plug in circuit boards on the assembly line. Chahua said: "At that time, except for five or six hours a day when I slept on my stomach, I stood up for the rest." As she said this, she lifted her skirt, and her legs were bulging with crooked blue veins. Zheng Jianxin knew that this was called varicose veins.

"I was paid 150 yuan a month for five or six years, and I ate old rice with sand. Now you are better off, you can earn 500 or 600 yuan as soon as you enter the factory!" She told Zheng Jianxin that no matter what factory you enter, the most important thing was to learn a technical job and get a salary of more than 1,000 yuan a month.

They built this city, and they knew every street and every building like the back of their hand, and they were very familiar with it. When they shed sweat, they also devoted their feelings. They liked to walk around on the street, and their hearts were filled with a special beautiful feeling. They had a sense of accomplishment. In this city, they could see their own traces everywhere. This city was a part of their soul. However, Chahua said that this place did not belong to them! Because they did not have a local household registration, no one had thought of moving their household registration from the countryside to here. As the city became more and more prosperous, they felt strange. To this city, they were just passersby.

They built this city and created today's glory, but in the end, all they had was a meager income and a memory full of sweet, sour, bitter, spicy and salty flavors.

One sister especially caught Zheng Jianxin's attention. Her neck and arms were covered with scars, and one would wonder if there were more scars on her body under the clothes. It was a fire in a warehouse of a garment factory in Qianshan in the summer of 1994, which left her with the mark of the special zone in Yongbian. The fire alarmed the officials from Beijing who were inspecting Zhuhai, and they visited the hospital to comfort the wounded.

During the conversation, Chahua suddenly leaned on Lili's shoulder and cried, saying that she missed her child. Later, Lili told Zheng Jianxin that not long after Chahua came, she met a local boy. The boy said that Guangdong girls' look could score 90 points out of 100 from the back, 70 points from the side, but would fail (less than 60) from the front. Northern girls were all pretty, with good figures and white skin. Guangdong people in the Pearl River Delta are accustomed to calling other provinces the north, and all migrant girls are collectively called northern girls. There is a sense of discrimination. But it has become a trend for Guangdong men to marry northern girls.

So they fell in love. After the child was born, the boy's parents who looked down on northern girls wanted their son to marry a local nurse and live a realistic life. They did not allow the boy to marry Chahua and forced them to break up. At that time, the main means of transportation in Zhuhai was a private minibus around the city, which cost one yuan to get on. At the beach of Shuiwantou, the boy's mother gave them 30 minutes to say goodbye to the child for the last time. The mother shouted several times that the time was up, but the three of them were still reluctant to leave. In the end, the mother forced them to get on the minibus, but when it was time for Chahua to get off, they were still reluctant to leave. In this way, no one knows how many yuan they paid, and they stayed on the minibus through Jida, Qianshan and back to Gongbei, round and round, until midnight. In the past, She could still find an opportunity to sneak a peek at the child from a distance, but in the future, it would be impossible.

Some migrant workers in their restless youth tasted forbidden fruit under the sweet words of various men...... While they sweated here, they also left behind all kinds of indescribable bitter love. Their parents in their hometown had already arranged their marriages and urged them to go back to get married. In the future, they would go to the fields with their husbands, serve their husbands, eat and sleep, and return to the track of rural life. One batch after another of migrant workers are all walking back like this. This is the fate of migrant workers.

Their attachment to this land and their inseparable feelings, as the spark of life inspired by the dream of the special zone is disillusioned, are covered with a layer of tragic color. That night, Xu Zhuang was also there, just listening quietly with his head buried, smoking from time to time.

Although the main theme of the "farewell party" was talking and laughing, no one could laugh, because the topic -- tomorrow -- was simple but heavy.

There were food and drinks on the lawn, and Lili and the others followed the cheering, excitedly pouring beer and making loud noises. Finally, the passionate people couldn't help but clap their cups and sing loudly. At first, one girl sang, and gradually several girls sang "Olive Tree" together: "Don't ask me where I come from...... Why I wander, wander far away......"

Drinking, shouting, singing. Lili suddenly held two sisters who were going back home, trembling all over, crying sadly, as if there was a hidden pain in her heart that she couldn't say and was unknown to others: "You can go back home, I don't even have the face to go home......"

The people present were silent for a moment, Zheng Jianxin and Xu Zhuang looked at each other, not knowing how to comfort, nor whether they should comfort, they could only listen, watch, and think quietly.

Lili's crying gradually became lower, and the hoarse crying turned into a trembling sob, and the sob turned into a nasal sound with tightly bitten lips, humming straight into people's hearts. Zheng Jianxin held Lili tightly, looked at her fellow villager, and watched the gradually dimming light in her eyes, and slowly her own tears came out.

The plastic sheet on the grass was in a mess, and the other girls cried again. After the song ended, only Xu Zhuang and Zheng Jianxin were left on the beach. Zheng Jianxin was shivering with cold, and she held Xu Zhuang's waist.

She asked: "Brother Zhuang, will we go back one day?" Xu Zhuang stroked the cowboy hat beside him with his hand, and said in a low voice after a long time: "No, no!" He hugged Zheng Jianxin tightly, looking at the waves pushing back and forth, "Others can live here, we have to live here too, live like a human being......"

Zheng Jianxin said: "When I came out, my father reminded me that everyone has a sky above their heads, it is good to go out, and not be tied to the land here, you have to learn skills and live without looking at other people's faces......"

11

Xu Zhuang is in prison, I will wait here, wait for him

The clouds in the subtropical sky are very strange, often very low. At this time, dark clouds were floating above Zheng Jianxin's head. Thinking of the scene of the five sisters returning home when the millennium came, Zheng Jianxin couldn't help but shudder all over her body, and she held her own body with her arms tightly. Walking in the modern bustling city of Gongbei, the dazzling sight made her feel like she was in a dream. Only then did she realize that she had lived in vain! One day, she would return to the countryside like her five sisters and suffer from poverty. She seemed to see her future and her ending at a glance. She resented fate, wondering why fate had thrown her to this place to be teased.

Lili touched Zheng Jianxin's arm, and sensing a layer of sticky cold sweat. "This damn place is so humid that people can't sweat. It's uncomfortable to hold it on the skin!" Lili cursed.

"By the way, Ajian, how do you feel about Chen Xiao? I see how he treats you......" Lili suddenly teased Zheng Jianxin. Men are easy to deceive. If Ajian flattered him and played a "play" with him, wouldn't she get money? More importantly, it could help Ajian to get rid of his longing for Xu Zhuang.

"Him?" Zheng Jianxin shook her head firmly, "What's the relationship between him and me? Putting aside the grudges between my family and his family, hum...... He earned some power with the blessing of his father, his wife is so fierce, and his heart is full of twists and turns, hypocritical man, what a crap!"

When the topic turned to men, in Zheng Jianxin's mind naturally appeared Xu Zhuang. Lili moved her mouth and wanted to say something, but seeing Zheng Jianxin's resolute look, she finally swallowed her words. After thinking for a while, Lili changed the subject: "Where did you go this morning? I went to look for you, but there was no trace of you!"

"I went to deliver fruit to the sisters in the factory. I told you."

Lili said to her with a tone of approval and sarcasm, "You still can't forget those poor sisters!"

"We are all poor sisters, how can I forget them?"

After Zheng Jianxin quit her job, she had more free time, so she took the initiative to buy some fruit to send to the sisters. If she didn't go for a few days, the sisters would miss her.

Zheng Jianxin finally calmed down. She took a few steps forward and looked at the dark sea in the distance. She looked at Lili with a melancholy look. After a long time, she asked tentatively: "Sister Lili, you haven't told me yet, Xu Zhuang...... Is there something wrong? Why haven't you sent me any information for so many days?"

"No, no. Don't be such a pessimist." Lili shook her head and denied, "How could something happen? Didn't I say he just went on a ship?"

"Where did he go? Europe or Antarctica?" Zheng Jianxin turned her head and looked at Lili, who looked a little flustered, "How do you know he's okay? Did he send you any information? When? Why didn't you tell me?"

"This......this......"

Faced with Zheng Jianxin's series of questions, Lili became more flustered and guilty. She avoided her gaze and looked aside, "Ajian, it's going to rain, let's go back, it's late!"

Then she stood up. These days, whenever Xu Zhuang was mentioned, Lili would talk about something else, and tonight she was even more flustered.

Zheng Jianxin's heart sank, and she became persistent: "No, tell me, tell me, what are you hiding from me? Why are you hiding it from me?" Zheng Jianxin stood up, walked back and grabbed Lili's shoulders, her voice getting louder and louder, and finally she almost yelled hysterically,

"Hurry up! Did Xu Zhuang have an accident?! Tell me......"

Lili didn't dare to look at Zheng Jianxin, she turned her head to the side, her eyebrows drooped, her rosy lips had lost much color, and she trembled slightly.

"Sister Lili, what happened to Xu Zhuang? Tell me now......" Zheng Jianxin shook Lili hard, as if this would shake the truth out of her.

"Ajian, don't ask!"

Lili finally couldn't hold on anymore, choked and slowly squatted down, tears streaming down her eyes. Zheng Jianxin's eyes went dark, her body swayed and staggered a few steps, and she was about to fall. She thought to herself that Xu Zhuang must have had an accident at sea. Did he capsize and disappear or was he injured and disabled?

Lili was frightened by Zheng Jianxin's condition. She stood up suddenly and held her, gently patted her back, and said loudly: "Ajian, don't scare me. Things are not as bad as you think. Azhuang was just detained in Hong Kong for smuggling......"

The two people's extreme actions attracted the attention of passersby, and they cast a few strange eyes at them from time to time. After hearing Lili's words, Zheng Jianxin finally slowly recovered her breath. She pushed Lili away, wiped away the tears in her eyes, and asked: "What's going on? Tell me clearly, why did you hide it from me?"

Lili lowered her head with shame. In the cool sea breeze, her face and chest were hot and sweaty, and a large area of her vest was wet. She twisted her hands and said hesitantly, "A few days ago, Xu Zhuang helped Zeng Sheng smuggle goods and was caught by the marine police in Hong Kong waters. It was late at the night when I asked you to go to the dinner party. I didn't know it at the time. Zeng Sheng called me on the third day to tell me about it, and then he disappeared."

"Zeng Sheng didn't go to excuse Xu Zhuang?" Zheng Jianxin breathed a sigh of relief, but her mood became heavy. "He is the owner of the goods, would he dare?"

Lili shook her head, "He said that Xu Zhuang's case was not serious, and even if he was sentenced, it would only be one or two years at most."

"One or two years?!" Zheng Jianxin screamed, "It's easy for him to say that, then why doesn't he go to jail?" She was so excited that she could feel her heart pounding, her messy hair and sweat stuck to her cheeks, blurred her eyes, and her feet were shaking.

"He said he would compensate Xu Zhuang in the future." Lili lowered her head and her voice became lower and lower.

"You're still speaking for him? You......" Zheng Jianxin was furious, stamped her feet fiercely, and pushed Lili: "Oh...... You've always known that Xu Zhuang did something illegal for Zeng Sheng, right? Why didn't you tell me? I'm still...... you......" Zheng Jianxin pointed at Lili's nose.

"Xu Zhuang also knew......" Lili glanced at her, said softly and lowered her head again.

"Okay...... I'm the only one who was kept in the dark. You...... you......" Zheng Jianxin's blood surged, pointing at Lili, not knowing what to say.

After a long time, Zheng Jianxin put down her hand, sat down on the grass, staring blankly at the direction of Hong Kong, the sea was dark. Her heart was also dark. The sea breeze blew, and before the typhoon came, the leaves that had been suppressed for a long time rustled, and the storm was coming. Zheng Jianxin raised her hand to tidy up her messy hair, tears in her eyes, and murmured: "Two years...... I'll wait, wait here......"

Lili felt a pain in her heart, and held her tightly in her arms. The dull thunder came from the sea, spreading all around, enveloping the two young women shaking.

12

Ajian shouted over and over again, and found that she couldn't even open her mouth

Zheng Jianxin dragged her heavy steps and slowly walked back to the rental house. Looking at her figure under the tree, she suddenly felt like a lonely ghost. Two hooligans came towards them in the alley, glanced at Zheng Jianxin, and couldn't help whistling: "Pretty girl, are you off work?"

Zheng Jianxin was already feeling very upset, and was furious when she heard this. She picked up a brick next to her and threw it at the two people: "You are blind. Are you looking for death?"

The two hooligans were startled and quickly dodged the bricks, cursing: "F..k, you are pretending to be innocent......"

Zheng Jianxin screamed as if she was stabbed, picked up another brick and chased after them, scaring the two guys away in panic, and dared not say a word again. After being disturbed by the two hooligans, Zheng Jianxin's mood was not so heavy, but her body and mind were more tired. As soon as she entered the room, she fell on the bed and didn't even want to move a finger.

When the sea breeze passed through the high-rise buildings and blew into the urban village of Gaosha Street, its power did not decrease significantly. It blew some clothes hanging outside and the unfastened window leaves and sheds, but it finally took away some of the stuffiness of the crowded place.

The sound of the wind passed through the air holes and door cracks, shaking the mosquito net, and the lights seemed to ripple. Xu Zhuang in the photo seemed to be alive, smiling gently and affectionately, looking at Zheng Jianxin. "Brother Zhuang, didn't you say you would come to see me?" Zheng Jianxin felt a pang in her heart, "I've been waiting for a long time, why haven't you come yet?"

Xu Zhuang smiled at her again, his face full of apology, and turned away without saying a word. "Brother Zhuang......Brother Zhuang......"

Zheng Jianxin rushed over to grab him, but a barbed wire suddenly appeared in front of her, blocking her way. Zheng Jianxin shook the barbed wire frantically, wishing to tear it apart, so much so that she didn't notice that her hands were bleeding. Xu Zhuang turned his head and looked at her. He shook his head gently, waved his hand, and stepped into the thick fog in front of him, disappearing without a trace.

"Brother Zhuang......" Zheng Jianxin cried heartbreakingly and fell to the ground, helplessly pinching the soil on the ground, "Come back soon, I'll wait for you! -- No matter how long it takes, I will definitely wait for you......"

A loud "bang" and the sound of broken glass startled Zheng Jianxin and she jumped out of bed, only to find that it was another dream. Looking up and around, it turned out that the second-floor window was hit by the strong wind, and the broken glass knocked down the door. The strong wind rushed into the room, and the whole room was filled with a humming sound. The pale lightning flashed silently at the head of her bed, and thunder exploded one after another outside the door. Zheng Jianxin's unsettled soul was even more uneasy.

Wiping away the tears on her face, Zheng Jianxin found a large piece of advertisement paper and double-sided tape, and stood on a small plastic stool. When she was about to seal the small hole for air (working as a window) , a lightning that tore half of the sky came towards her, scaring her. Before she could come to her senses, a gust of wind blew the paper back again, and the huge thunderclap shook her heart at the same time, making her unable to help but pat her chest to calm herself down. The wind was getting stronger and stronger, and the window paper was blown back and forth quickly, hitting the window frame and making a bang; the strong wind rushed into the room, and the small window for air became a wind tunnel, blowing her hair messy and her pretty face painful. Before she could completely calm down, the sound of dense rain had already sounded in the distance, and the sound was getting louder and louder, approaching this side quickly.

Zheng Jianxin, who had been familiar with this sound since childhood, became even more flustered. She stretched out her hands to grab the swaying window leaf, and her palm accidentally scratched the glass fragments on the window frame, and blood gushed out. Zheng Jianxin screamed and reflexively put the wound to her mouth to suck, but her feet on the stool were unstable and she fell to the ground after a few shakes. Before she could get up, the crazy rustling sound had already rushed out of the window, and then another gust of wind blew in, and raindrops as big as little thumbs poured in like bullets, soaking Zheng Jianxin's body in an instant.

Lightning, strong wind, heavy rain, hurt, loneliness...... Zheng Jianxin sat on the ground motionless, letting the raindrops hurt her skin, letting the strong wind make her tremble all over, letting the lightning make her face pale, her eyes dull. After a long time, Zheng Jianxin finally couldn't hold it back anymore, straightened her whole body, clenched her fists, and screamed with all her strength.

For her, this was the end of the world. At this time, the thin door was pounded loudly, and Zhong Haicai's screams rang out outside the door. "Ajian? Ajian? What are you doing? Open the door......"

Zheng Jianxin moved her neck but did not respond, letting the storm continue to rage on her. Zhong Haicai screamed louder and pounded on the door even louder.

Zheng Jianxin burst into tears. At her lowest point, it was not her lover Xu Zhuang or her good sister Lili who came to her side, but Zhong Haicai, a down-and-out man from Macau. Zheng Jianxin opened the door. Zhong Haicai, who was mostly soaked, rushed in anxiously with his fat body shaking. Seeing Zheng Jianxin letting the rain fall on her, he breathed a sigh of relief, but shouted even more anxiously: "Ajian, what are you doing? Get up quickly, you'll get sick like this."

He rushed to Zheng Jianxin, pulled her aside without saying

anything, rolled up the quilt on the bed with great skill, pulled out the plywood on the bed board, and nailed it to the small window, blocking out the wind, rain and lightning. After doing all this, Zhong Haicai, who was out of breath, finally calmed down. He looked at Zheng Jianxin, who had been silent and motionless from beginning to end, and picked up the towel hanging on the rope by the wall and handed it to her: "Wipe it quickly! Don't let the rain make you catch a cold!"

Zheng Jianxin took the towel, glanced at him, and then wiped the tears from her face, and then slowly wiped her neck. Her whole body had been soaked. Her white short-sleeved shirt was tightly attached to her body, outlining her exquisite curves, and her skin was barely visible, almost transparent.

Zhong Haicai was so nervous that he didn't know what to do, and his fat hands unconsciously clenched into fists. He turned around quickly, and then he realized that the whole room was full of water, and even the quilt and pillow he had just rolled up were wet.

"You can't sleep here!" Zhong Haicai pointed to the floor and the quilt and said to Zheng Jianxin, "Go to my place tonight!" Then he pulled her out.

Although Zheng Jianxin was reluctant, she looked at the situation in the room and didn't know what to say, so she had to follow him. The street lights were dim, and there were only a few pedestrians.

The wind was whistling, hitting the trees and signs on the roadside. The commercial anchor stalls that were crowded and bustling in the past were closed. Under the raging wind and rain, the iron awning tarpaulin of the rental house was intertwined with the wind and made strange noises.

As soon as Zheng Jianxin opened her umbrella when she went out, it was blown away by the strong wind. Zhong Haicai pulled up his raincoat to cover Zheng Jianxin, put his arm around Zheng Jianxin's shoulders, and said, "This is Tropical Storm Maria! I heard about it in Macau. It rained heavily just after I came back. I missed you and came to see you because I was afraid!"

Zheng Jianxin said "um" and didn't say anything. The strong sweat odor emanating from Zhong Haicai made her almost suffocate, but it was not easy to break free in this situation. She had to stretch her neck out of the raincoat and quicken her pace to let the wind dilute that feeling.

Arriving at Zhong Haicai's rental house, Zheng Jianxin immediately took a shower, and then her mood slowly calmed down. The wind and rain were still outside the window. The cold air from the air conditioner in Zhong Haicai's rental house made Zheng Jianxin's skin cool and comfortable. Zheng Jianxin stood in front of the window wearing Zhong Haicai's T-shirt and wiped her hair.

The hem of the round-necked shirt almost fell to her knees. Zheng Jianxin didn't dare to look at Zhong Haicai's face. When she just walked out of the bathroom, Zhong Haicai looked at her, his eyes lit up, and his pupils ignited the same fire when he first saw her at the "Pearl River Moon" dinner party, his eyes were straight. It was not until she pretended to glare at him angrily that Zhong Haicai avoided her awkwardly.

Zheng Jianxin's underwear was also wet, but she was not used to it and dared not wear only a sweat shirt and be in the same room with a man. Although it was uncomfortable to wear wet underwear, she could only endure it, and it would not take long for her body temperature to dry it.

Zhong Haicai's eyes wandered around Zheng Jianxin from time to time and involuntarily. Every time Zheng Jianxin shook her hair and turned around, he looked away like a thief with a guilty conscience. With Zheng Jianxin's sharp intuition, she knew what Zhong Haicai was doing without turning around. She had a good impression of Zhong Haicai, although his jokes were sometimes too much, but his glibness was a low-level manifestation of rough humor. In general, she felt that he was like her elder and was trustworthy. But he was a single man in his prime after all. If she stayed here overnight, even if no one else knew, she would feel guilty.

Zheng Jianxin was struggling in her heart. She also thought about going upstairs to Lili's place to squeeze in for a night, but she had just had a really unpleasant quarrel with her at the beach. If she went upstairs like this, she would be embarrassed.

After wiping her hair, Zheng Jianxin noticed that there was a pile of books on the coffee table, and they were all new. Zhong Haicai was not a man who read books, and she had never seen him read a book: "Why do you buy so many books?"

"I bought them for you." Zhong Haicai spoke, and he exhaled softly to explain: "You are educated, I want you to read them when you are bored, to relieve your boredom. Oh...... These books are not expensive, they are discounted at the Guanzha bookstall, and the books that are as thick as bricks are all ten yuan each, so cheap!"

Zheng Jianxin picked up the books and looked at the titles, and couldn't help laughing. They were old books like "One Hundred Thousand Whys", "Legends of Ancient and Modern Times", "Men Are From Venus, Women Are From Mars", no wonder the bookstore cleared them out for the bookstall.

"Who would read these books now?" Zheng Jianxin laughed more and more as he read.

"This......" Zhong Haicai scratched his head again and said with a silly smile, "I don't know how to read very well, but I bought them because they were thick and big. I don't know if they are suitable......"

Zheng Jianxin was halfway through laughing when she suddenly remembered a question and asked, "Hong Kong and Macau are more advanced than our mainland. How come you don't know how to read?"

Zhong Haicai became more embarrassed by her question and almost pulled his hairs off. He hesitated for a while before saying, "There are very few people who were born and raised in Macau. Most of them are immigrants from the Pearl River Delta over the years." He recalled the past, "My hometown is on an island not far from Zhuhai. My family was so poor that we couldn't eat. Most people in Huizhou and Shenzhen fled to Hong Kong, and people there fled to Macau. During the Cultural Revolution, I was a militiaman, catching fugitives, but a few militiamen threw away their guns and became deserters. I tied a gasoline barrel on my body and almost drifted to the high seas. I became a Macau citizen after Macau's amnesty a few years ago."

Zheng Jianxin finally understood. She knew something about that era from the elders at home and from books.

"You are so brave! Smuggling is risking one's life to survive", Zheng Jianxin said admiringly. She blinked her eyelids playfully and said humorously, "Now we can smuggle to Macau like you did before."

"That's right, that's right." Zhong Haicai laughed, and then pretended to be mysterious: "But it's easy for you to go."

Zheng Jianxin asked puzzledly: "Why is it easy for me?"

"Just marry a Macau man!"

Zheng Jianxin was embarrassed and angry, giggled, and threw the towel on his face, "You are so bad!"

In the past a few months, Zheng Jianxin faced the man's flirting and frivolous words. Although she still held on to the dam she built in her heart, the superficial defense of keeping people away from her had been replaced by a hippie smile and retort that could cope with it easily.

Zhong Haicai looked at Zheng Jianxin's cherry-like red lips under her blurred eyelids, and his heart felt like an ant scratching, itchy. In order to hide his discomfort, Zhong Haicai suddenly thought of drinking. He poured a glass of juice for Zheng Jianxin, who didn't drink, and drank it himself.

Zheng Jianxin flipped the book in her hand and smiled again, "Thank you, Brother Zhong, you are thoughtful. But I have to make money to support myself now, so I don't have the mood and time to read!"

"Anyway, I bought the books, don't give them to anyone, keep them!"

Zheng Jianxin nodded again, accepting his kindness. Looking up at the quartz clock on the wall, it was almost one o'clock in the middle of the night, and Lili was probably asleep. What should I do? Really spend the night here?

Seeing her like this, Zhong Haicai immediately brought out a quilt and pillow and put it on the sofa, smiling flatteringly at Zheng Jianxin: "You go to the inner room to sleep, I'll sleep on the sofa."

Zheng Jianxin struggled in her heart for a while, looking at Zhong Haicai's honest smile, she sighed helplessly and said: "I'll sleep on the sofa, that's your bed."

"That won't work." Zhong Haicai shook his head, with a sincere face, "You are a guest, and a girl. If others know that I'm 'abusing' you, they will blame me to death!"

"So you can be so flirting." Zheng Jianxin glared at him coquettishly and didn't decline.

"It's unfair!" Zhong Haicai cried out, "It's all Achang who taught me how to coax...... and I learned it from Bai Lang......" He knew that he was doing something bad, so he smiled embarrassedly and didn't say anything more.

"You're still saying no?" Zheng Jianxin was both angry and amused, and she started a jingle in Cantonese, which was as bad as Zhong Haicai's Mandarin: "To explain is to cover up, and to cover up is to be useless!"

"Okay, okay......" Zhong Haicai quickly raised his hands in surrender, but his face was full of joy and comfort, as if he had just drunk a large bowl of iced sour plum soup. Zheng Jianxin walked into the inner room, and the cool air hit her face. An old window air conditioner was running with a clattering sound. There was a Western-style table lamp at the head of the bed, which was as old as the air conditioner. The lampshade was a little damaged, which Zhong Haicai might have bought from a street stall. But the orange light still made Zheng Jianxin feel warm -- this small world that had nothing to do with the wind and rain outside made the "homeless" herself feel like a warm home.

Seeing Zhong Haicai take out the sheets that she had just washed two days ago, Zheng Jianxin smiled at him gratefully, just like her father preparing things for her when she was back home. A saying runs: It is so good to stay at home for a thousand days, but it is hard to go out. Zheng Jianxin's nose was sour. She opened the curtains and stared at the wind and rain outside for a while. There were waves of wind and rain outside, and thunder was still ringing from time to time. She felt uneasy and closed the curtains tightly.

Zheng Jianxin wanted to tidy up the quilt and pillow. When she looked up, she found that a corner of the mosquito net had fallen off. Zhong Haicai reached out to hang it up. Zheng Jianxin said "I'll do it" and jumped onto the bed. She pulled the corner of the mosquito net, stood on tiptoe, hung it on the horizontal bar, and stretched out the wrinkled mosquito net.

This time, the sweatshirt on her body was not long enough. Zhong Haicai looked at Zheng Jianxin's back, Zheng Jianxin's plump buttocks and exposed round legs. This mysterious temptation instantly released all the male hormones of men. Zhong Haicai's face turned red, his chest rose and fell rapidly, and his two nostrils whistled like bellows.

"Ajian......" Zhong Haicai could no longer suppress himself. He roared and rushed over to hold Zheng Jianxin's waist. Then he pressed his face tightly against Zheng Jianxin's neck and fell on the bed. Zheng Jianxin, who was suddenly attacked, had a black vision in front of her eyes. She was still dazed and had not yet reacted to what was going on. When she realized what was happening in front of her, she struggled with her hands and feet in panic and shouted: "Brother Zhong......Uncle, don't......don't do this, let me go......"

Zheng Jianxin struggled and twisted her upper body as hard as she could, slapping Zhong Haicai's shoulders hard, trying to get rid of his madness. Zhong Haicai was already burning with desire at this time, and ignored Zheng Jianxin's pleas. Zheng Jianxin, who had no strength left after being tormented by the wind and rain, struggled for a while and lost her strength. She just cried and shouted for the man on her to let her go.

"I want you! I want you! I want you......" Zhong Haicai roared like a monster and pressed her down. There was no gentle words to comfort her, only constant ups and downs and collisions. The great pain and boundless shame made Zheng Jianxin cry, beat, and beg. Zhong Haicai could not hear or see anything and ignored it. The wind and rain were still raging outside, and the huge noise drowned out the noise coming out of the room. Shouts, cries, cries for help, fighting, collisions, and panting echoed and mixed in the room. The shame and fear caused by the burning pain deep in the body finally made Zheng Jianxin completely collapse, and she fainted with a scream.

Seeing that the lovely girl under him had stopped moving, Zhong Haicai shook her shoulders in panic: "Ajian, what's wrong with you? Wake up, don't scare me......"

After a while, Zheng Jianxin slowly woke up, staring at Zhong Haicai's dark face without blinking, and suddenly screamed and kicked him to the ground, jumped off the bed with disheveled hair, grabbed the kitchen knife on the kitchen counter, pointed it at Zhong Haicai with both hands, and cried bitterly: "You......you......I......" The muscles on her cheeks were twisted due to extreme anger and sadness.

Zhong Haicai trembled all over. There was another gust of wind outside, which blew against the window and the curtains were lifted high by the wind that came in from the gap. Zheng Jianxin felt a chill all over her body, and when she looked down, she found that she was not wearing a single piece of clothing. She screamed and threw away the kitchen knife, grabbed her clothes and rushed into the bathroom. Zheng Jianxin slipped on the cold tiles with a thud. She covered her mouth and cried, slapping the ground, her mind was as confused as paste.

Zhong Haicai outside realized what he had done, and moved to the bathroom, slapping his face and confessing: "Ajian, it's all my fault, I'm a beast. ...... Don't do stupid things, I...... I really love you, I have loved you since I saw you for the first time! I...... I will marry you, buy a big house, take you to Macau...... I swear, I swear to God......" At the end, Zhong Haicai kept making the sign of the cross on his chest.

"Get out! Get out!" Zheng Jianxin screamed hysterically, tears streaming down her face.

"Ajian......" Zhong Haicai wanted to say something else.

"You're not going to leave, are you? I'm leaving!"

Zheng Jianxin stood up with all her strength, quickly put on her wet clothes, opened the bathroom door, looked at Zhong Haicai with hatred, kicked him aside, opened the door and rushed out. Zhong Haicai was frightened, and hurriedly put on his beach pants and rushed out. Fortunately, Zheng Jianxin was still not very clear-headed, and the wind and rain were heavy, so she couldn't run fast. Zhong Haicai finally caught up with her on the beach with all his strength, opened his arms to stop her, and begged in horror: "Ajian, don't do this. You can kill me or cut me up, don't think too much......"

"Stay away from me!" Zheng Jianxin looked at him expressionlessly, as if she was looking at an inanimate object -- or as if a lifeless object.

She stammered: "I...... I, I won't die......"

Zhong Haicai was relieved a little, and slowly moved a few steps away with trembling thick lips, his eyes still staring at Zheng Jianxin, and kept praying to God.

The sea and the sky were a chaotic whole, covered by thick black clouds. The lights on the Macau side were vaguely visible in the rain and fog. Zheng Jianxin leaned against the guardrail, her eyes piercing through the rain and fog and looking towards Hong Kong -- that is where Brother Zhuang is now detained.

The strong wind uprooted the trees as thick as bowls, some fell on the sidewalk, and some lay horizontally on the guardrail. The banyan trees protected by support frames also leaned to the left or right. The branches and shrubs in the flowerbed were in a mess. The ravaged tiny petals fell into the grass and soil.

The rain flowed down Zheng Jianxin's shoulder-length black hair, strand by strand, intermittent but continuous. Her clothes were soaked again and clung to her body. Zhong Haicai, who had been staring at her, no longer had lust in his eyes, and his face was pale. The rain flowed down from his short hair, slid down to his cheeks, neck, and shoulders, washing his naked, fat upper body. Zhong Haicai hadn't stayed in the rain for such a long time. The numbness, itchiness and coldness made him shiver a few times, and his eyes looked at Zheng Jianxin with a little more timidness.

Zheng Jianxin still didn't move, and her eyes became unfocused. She couldn't hear the sound of wind, rain and sea water at all. She suddenly thought terribly: She was dead, and it was her body that lived here. Zhong Haicai bent down and stood timidly not far away, shivering. Rain flowed from his head. He shouted loudly: "I'll give you money! Send it back to the countryside!"

Zheng Jianxin's mind was blank. Zhong Haicai's shouting seemed to come from a far away place, and it was faint and inaudible. She desperately slapped her head to wake herself up. She finally heard her heartbeat, followed by the sound of breathing, and she tried to calm herself down. She lifted her hair with both hands, and stared at the distance with confused eyes.

Another gust of wind blew, and Zheng Jianxin only felt numbness from head to toe, and felt a little dizzy.

"Brother Zhuang, where are you? Do you still love me? Are my parents and grandpa okay? Lili...... why should I quarrel with you?" She regretted not going to Lili's house to spend the night, but fell into a trap and fell into the tiger's mouth.

As if unable to bear the long-term wind and rain, Zheng Jianxin's body suddenly trembled again and again, and then her whole body shook uncontrollably. Finally, her feet could no longer support the weight of her whole body. She slowly squatted down and sat on the cement road under the guardrail.

Her body was still shaking.

Zhong Haicai was terrified. He opened his arms and wanted to hold her but didn't dare. He could only look at her anxiously, constantly hitting his cheeks, and shouted: "Ajian, what's wrong with you? Let's...... let's go back first, and talk it out......"

Zheng Jianxin only felt that her body was not under her control at all, as if her soul had been pulled out of her body. "Am I dead...... Am I dead......" Zheng Jianxin shouted over and over again, but found that she couldn't even open her mouth.

Seeing Zheng Jianxin sitting on the ground holding the railing and unable to move, Zhong Haicai's fat body was also shaking, and he suddenly roared: "Ajian, get up! I'll give you money, I'll give you money!

Send it back to your hometown for you to treat your father's injuries and your grandfather's illness......"

Zhong Haicai's roar seemed to come from the horizon, faintly reaching Zheng Jianxin's ears. "Dad, Grandpa......"

Zheng Jianxin finally regained consciousness. Yes, Grandpa. The grandfather who didn't have the old rural idea of favoring boys over girls, who cared for her like a baby, and who made her feel more caring than from her parents -- he was now seriously ill and bedridden.

Money...... Money...... Grandpa needed money to treat his illness, money to treat his father's injuries, money to buy fertilizers, and money to live at home...... Zheng Jianxin's body slowly calmed down, and she turned her head slightly to look at the man beside her.

She looked dull. He just raped her, and now he said he would give her money. What did he thought I was? A prostitute? A mistress?

Zheng Jianxin felt her body trembling uncontrollably again.

"No......" Zheng Jianxin screamed, raised her hands and slapped her head frantically, shouting with all her strength, "Dad......Brother Zhuang......"

The constant pain finally made Zheng Jianxin feel alive. She could feel her heartbeat, hear her breathing, and feel the pain...... It hurt so much that she felt her whole face swell up.

Zheng Jianxin stood up suddenly. Seeing her self-harming behavior, Zhong Haicai, who was at a loss, was shocked again. Macau was just around the corner, with spots of light shining in the darkness, like a large piece of heavy rusty iron; the sea continued to hit the rocks on the embankment, again and again, with a sound like thunder; the palm leaves swayed back and forth, and the large long leaves were fluttering, constantly dropping drops of water, hitting the looming telephone booth......

Looking at the telephone booth beside her, Zheng Jianxin's eyes finally focused, and Xu Zhuang's thick body and angular face appeared in front of her again, with a smile on his lips and a gentle look......

Zheng Jianxin's heart twitched suddenly, she choked, her lips trembled, and she murmured word by word; "Brother Zhuang......Brother Zhuang, where are you? Where are you? "

What responded to her was the sporadic dull thunder in the distance. This thunder was different from the thunder she heard in her hometown when she was a child. It was not only mysterious, but also ruthless, so ruthless that it made people feel chilled......

Zhong Haicai trembled all over, looked around in panic, slapped his cheeks from time to time, and kept making the sign of the cross on his chest: "Lord...... forgive me, forgive me......"

Walking into the phone booth, Zheng Jianxin gently stroked the microphone box, just like stroking Brother Zhuang's shoulder. The scene of talking on the phone with Xu Zhuang came to her mind again and again. She felt heartbroken and couldn't help herself...... Such a scene may never happen again. Seeing her crying silently while holding the microphone, Zhong Haicai thought she was going to report the case. The fear in his heart became heavier, but at the same time he also felt a sense of relief.

After a long time, Zheng Jianxin finally put down the microphone, sat on the ground against the phone booth, staring blankly at the sea. She regretted coming to Guangdong. She wondered what kind of invisible force had pushed her and Xu Zhuang and the others here! It was like pushing a person who couldn't swim into the sea. We struggled as hard as we could, but no one paid attention, no one pulled us up, and pointed out a way out. What kind of unfair fate was this?

The rain was getting lighter, the wind was getting lighter, the sea water beat the embankment repeatedly and rhythmically, the concrete pillars of the guardrail were cracked by the waves, and finally broke, and then fell into the sea, making a thumping sound. The rain turned into raindrops, floating in the light of passing vehicles.

Zhong Haicai was stunned for a while, and also sat on the edge of the green belt, looking at her, motionless. Shaking off Xu Zhuang's shadow, Zheng Jianxin thought of her hometown, her parents, and her grandfather again. If she were at home, she would definitely throw herself into the arms of her grandfather who loved her the most and cry about the humiliation she had just suffered -- this humiliation that she wanted to tear Zhong Haicai and herself into pieces and could not wash away.

She believed that her grandfather would give her comfort, strength, and advice from his wisdom gained from a rough life.

But what can I do now? Report to the police and sue Zhong Haicai? It has only been a few days since Macau returned to China, and everything related to people and things in Macau is very sensitive. Maybe he will use the fact that I voluntarily rented a house from him to blame me, and then even if I jump into the sea I cannot clean myself; tell Lili? How can she help me? With her current thoughts and the life she has lived, she may even persuade me to temporarily submit to Zhong Haicai; gather fellow villagers to seek justice for me? What is justice? In the end, what else can I do except asking Zhong Haicai to pay? Leaving a bunch of rumors to fellow villagers, how can I live in the future?

What should I do? Bear it silently, as if I was bitten by a dog? My lower body is still burning and painful, my body is cold, and I can't help trembling every time the wind blows.

But Zheng Jianxin still didn't want to move, not at all, staring blankly at the sea, turning a blind eye to Zhong Haicai's face of regret, shrinking and hope.

The rain stopped. Zhong Haicai looked at the sky and then at Zheng Jianxin. He didn't know what to say, and he didn't dare to approach her. Time passed by little by little, and the night gradually faded. The sea level in the east began to turn white. Sanitation vehicles brought sanitation workers and began to clean up the "battlefield" ravaged by the typhoon. There were still several cars overturned by the typhoon lying on the road. The morning light shone on Zheng Jianxin, whose hair was messy and her body was in a mess. Although it cast a layer of red on her pale face, she still looked lifeless. Her clothes were not completely dry yet, and her pants and feet were covered with half-dried dust, like a construction worker who had just come out of a day of hard work at the construction site.

Many passersby looked at them with strange eyes. The patrolman also stared at them for a long time before slowly riding his motorcycle away. Seeing this situation, Zhong Haicai immediately forced himself to cheer up, and stood up and pretended to do morning exercises, gesturing with his hands and feet to do Tai Chi. During this period, although he hesitated several times whether to carry Zheng Jianxin home by force, he didn't dare to do it in the end.

In this way, Zheng Jianxin looked at the sea, Macau and Zhuhai without saying a word for nearly ten hours. Sometimes the scenery in front of her was a film that was not fully exposed, gray and gloomy; sometimes the scenery in front of her was an overexposed film, unreal and pale. She sat until noon and was dizzy from the sun, and her lips were chapped. She slowly got up, shook off Zhong Haicai who wanted to support her, and staggered back to Gaosha Street and her own rental house.

Watching Zheng Jianxin enter the room and close the door, Zhong Haicai was stunned for a while, then touched the fat on his body, slapped himself twice, and walked back to his own rental house with his head down.

13

Zhong Haicai sneered at himself:
If you have no money and still want to pick up girls,
it would be strange if you don't run into a ghost

After taking a shower and changing clothes, Zhong Haicai sat on the sofa, staring blankly at the messy bed he had made last night, and he was filled with endless regret.

He opened the bottle of wine and poured two big gulps into his upturned mouth. His eyes rolled around and thought about it: It was very common for people from Hong Kong and Macau to pick up girls in Gongbei. It was easy for friends from Macau to pick up girls from the north. Some of them had changed partners and nothing happened. But as soon as he picked up a girl, he ran into a hot potato!

I don't understand why there are still uncivilized girls like Ajian now? A friend from Macau said that to make a northern girl obedient, you must do enough "foreplay"; another friend from Macau said, yes, "foreplay" meant "money play!" If I had given Ajian money before the battle yesterday, it would have been great to make her obedient......

Zhong Haicai regretted having sex with a beautiful girl like Zheng Jianxin, a virgin. If he had replaced her with some other ordinary-looking northern girl, it would have been much better; Zhong Haicai regretted being careless and not putting "money" first; Zhong Haicai hated himself not for failing to think about "money", but for not having money on hand.

He laughed at himself coldly: "I have no money, but I still want to have sex with women. It would be strange if I don't run into a ghost!" He made a cross on his chest, slapped his face, opened his mouth hard, and poured half a bottle of wine......

When Zheng Jianxin started to deliver herbal tea to the construction site, he was the first to run out to help. When his co-workers teased him that he was in heat, he was even more happy to do so; when Zheng Jianxin came to clean the house for him, cook for him, and wash clothes, it was his happiest time. He looked at Zheng Jianxin like he was looking at his virtuous wife, listening to her nagging and accusations of dissatisfaction with his disorganized life, but his face was satisfied and happy. He was no longer lonely, as if he had a home again, a home where he lived naturally and comfortably, rather than a cold, lonely rental house without a sense of belonging.

He still remembered the days when he first smuggled into Macau and lived in a shed. When it became dark, all he could do was to lie on a wooden bed propped up with a few bricks, thinking about his home on Yinbao Island, his wife Liang Xiangyun, who was four years older than he, and his son who was as strong and naughty as himself.

Yinbao Island is one of hundreds of islands on the vast sea of the Pearl River Estuary, facing Hong Kong and Shenzhen in the east and Macau and Zhuhai in the west. Zhong Haicai and Liang Xiangyun grew up on the island. Sugarcane and bananas were planted on the island according to the orders from the superiors. Due to the untimely purchase and the low price, the three meals of the farmers could only be sweet potato porridge with pickles, and few families could have salted fish. Wild amaranth and purslane, which were usually fed to geese or cooked to feed pigs, were also cooked and salted as food by Zhong Haicai's parents when they were hungry. The people on the island lived in more difficult conditions than those on land.

Most of the Hakkas who settled here as refugee were more accustomed to farm life, and not many people went out to sea to fish. The island is very large, and each household of villagers had a lot of land. Farmers often married early because of the need for labor. When Zhong Haicai was fifteen, his parents took in the nineteen-year-old Liang Xiangyun and held a wedding for them, which was considered a marriage.

Zhong Haicai had smuggled to Macau by sea a few years before. In 1988, the thirty-four-year-old Liang Xiangyun could not stand the poverty of her family, and she missed her man, so she also smuggled to Macau. In the middle of the night, she sat in a wooden tub and set off from the Tangjiawan beach in Zhuhai. When she arrived in Macau, she could see the lights of the buildings when she looked up. The waves pushed the wooden tub back into the sea again and again, and it could not reach the shore. The wooden tub was shaking and almost capsized. Liang Xiangyun was tossing and turning in the wooden tub. No matter how she mustered up her last bit of strength to paddle the board, it was useless. She could not swim, and faced with the helpless and desperate situation, she thought she was going to be drowned. Her heart was hanging in her throat, thinking that it was over, and she would not survive.

On the shore of Macau, two or three figures were moving, one of them was the extremely anxious Zhong Haicai. Zhong Haicai opened his eyes wide, and his head kept turning left and right, searching the dark sea, not missing any black spots. More than three hours passed, his neck was sore, and his eyes were dry. He was sure that a black spot in the waves was a person, Liang Xiangyun. He and his co-workers walked hand in hand quickly to the beach, to the water that was up to their necks. Zhong Haicai decisively grabbed the wooden basin with one hand and dragged it towards the shore.

The life of illegal immigrants in Macau was not as good as imagined. The two lived in Taishan Street near the Border Gate, and started a new family life in a shanty wooden house they built by themselves. The next year, they had a daughter. The uneducated couple gave her an auspicious and loud name - Huahua.

Zhong Haicai worked at a construction site, and Liang Xiangyun took care of their daughter while opening a breakfast porridge shop at the street corner with a fellow villager. The couple was busy inside and outside, and their life was still acceptable. Two or three years later, Zhong Haicai took out the little money he had saved with a bank loan and bought a two-bedroom house not far away.

Running a porridge shop, Liang Xiangyun had to get up at four in the morning to grind rice and cook porridge, which was more difficult than farming in her hometown. This made Liang Xiangyun complain frequently, and she wanted to change this endless life every day. One day, passing by a casino, Liang Xiangyun, who was full of ideas of getting rich overnight, was eager to try and sneak in through the side door. It is said that if you enter a casino to gamble, you can't go through the main door, otherwise you will be unlucky. She planned to try her luck with the money for rice.

When she had to leave, Liang Xiangyun, who only dared to place small bets, actually won more than a thousand yuan. This made her very excited, thinking that she was amazing and lucky, and she would be rich and prosperous in a short time. From then on, whenever she had time, she would go to casino. If she won, she would stay there to win more; if she lost, she would change to another casino to change her luck. In half a year, she lost more and won less, and even borrowed a lot of debts from relatives and friends.

Zhong Haicai had no idea, and he was still busy at the construction site from morning till night every day. Gradually, Liang Xiangyun became addicted to gambling and had less and less interest in running the porridge shop. She was always thinking about how to win back the money she lost and pay off her debts.

She lost all the money she earned from running the porridge shop, and then continued to borrow money from everywhere to gamble, and came up with all kinds of tricky excuses to make people lend her money. As the number of times increased, there were more complaints among relatives and friends, and they finally knew that she had lost in gambling. Through gossip, finally Zhong Haicai learned it.

Zhong Haicai was furious, slamming the table, slamming the stool, and throwing the plate to quarrel with Liang Xiangyun. Liang Xiangyun began to repent and blame herself, and swore to quit gambling. After a few days, she couldn't help it and walked into the casino. She would not come out until she lost all the money on her. The most hateful thing was that she "pawned" his heirloom, the "Little Golden Clock", and sold it.

"Little Golden Clock, Little Golden Clock......" Zhong Haicai cried loudly for the first time in his life, and he cried for three consecutive days. Zhong Haicai finally despaired. After thinking for a long time, he realized that dried fish could not be used as a pillow for a cat. He did not want to spend his whole life with a gambling woman, so he left his house and daughter to Liang Xiangyun. He said, "We are divorced and I will no longer care about you. Don't come to me for your affairs."

Since then, Zhong Haicai, who was left with nothing, rented a house in Gongbei, Zhuhai, and resumed his life as a single man. The cost for living here was cheaper than in Macau. From then on, like many migrant workers in Macau, he went to Macau to work during the day and returned to Zhuhai at sunset. Three years passed in a flash.

The hard and tight life made Zhong Haicai only be able to sigh at the high housing prices in Macau as more casinos were built. In addition, he was approaching old age. In a few years, he would be fifty years old. No woman was willing to be with him sincerely. He once thought that he would be single for the rest of his life and would never have a harmonious family life.

Bai Lang brought him the hope of getting rich and Zheng Jianxin made him feel at home again, Zhong Haicai's heart, which had been silent for a long time, fluctuated again: he had to have money. Only with money could he find and keep a woman.

Over the years, he watched Macau people get rich in the SAR and other places in the mainland. Macau was small, and most people knew each other, and the news was heard from time to time. Getting rich, money, was like a will-o'-the-wisp, always dangling in front of you, very close to you, but you couldn't catch it no matter how hard you tried to grab it. You followed and ran to grab it again. Still you couldn't catch it. In more than 20 years since Zhong Haicai came to Macau, he had been trying hard to find opportunities.

The year before last, he heard that a large hotel in Luoyang, Henan Province, the mainland had just been built and was about to be renovated, and there was a profit of one million yuan to be made if it was contracted, so he flew several times with a friend in Zhuhai, and spent more than

200,000 yuan on intercession and gifts -- most of which were borrowed from friends. Later, it turned out that the "boss" cheated more than a dozen construction companies and was arrested.

Zhong Haicai also raised funds for mainland companies in Hong Kong. When the agency fee was calculated to be more than 10 million, the nine agents discussed in the hotel in the middle of the night on how to divide the money. But running around in the end, it was all in vain.

Zhong Haicai was selling air conditioners and heaters to the mainland for a Taiwanese company. At that time, Zhong Haicai often went to Zhuhai Hotel for coffee, met the boss of a local trading company and sold his products to him. A batch of inferior air conditioners and heaters made a large number of people uneasy, and was sued by the customers. Right now, there were more than 20 returned air conditioners in Macau, and all the money had been lost.

In addition, Liang Xiangyun lost money in gambling and owed debts in recent years, which can be said to be a double whammy. Now that he met Bai Lang, Zhong Haicai felt that the clouds had been cleared and the sun was shining. Real estate was not empty but real. Building houses was visible and tangible. No matter how much you make, there must be people who want and live in the houses. Bai Lang spoke eloquently from foreign real estate experience to the current real estate development in China, from the room for real estate development in Guangdong to the novelty of the Lanmeng Water Village Resort project, which made him excited.

Of course, what finally moved him was the huge profit margin and the return on investment of more than ten times. Under Bai Lang's instigation, Zhong Haicai mortgaged his house in Macau and borrowed more than 300,000 Hong Kong dollars to transfer to Gaolu Company's account. He also borrowed 200,000 yuan from his fellow workers, and handed over a total of 500,000 yuan to Bai Lang. Bai Lang used his money to pay 100,000 yuan for the land deposit and 400,000 yuan as the start-up capital for the project.

Zhong Haicai finally waited for his fortune and got rich! Bai Lang not only made him a shareholder with 25% of the shares, but also shared 5 million yuan in profits once the house was sold a year later! This was the smoothest period of his life.

His peach blossom luck (love) followed his fortune in good timing. Wasn't this God's favor and arrangement for him as a "good man"? When people have money, they have courage. You need money to find a woman. It's not difficult to have any kind of woman with money. He set his sight on Zheng Jianxin, the "angel" sent to him by God. As if Zheng Jianxin was already his woman, he would always feel happy and overflowing with joy when he worked, walked, and slept.

He loved Zheng Jianxin, but he didn't know how to express his feelings. Although he had learned a lot of mushy love words from Bai Lang, and a lot of vulgar words that made women angry but happy from Achang, once he faced Zheng Jianxin, who had a face as beautiful as his daughter, he was nervous and couldn't say the words on his lips.

Last night, he thought that God sent an "angel" to his bedside, and he was so excited that he kept making the sign of the cross on his chest. But he didn't expect that God released the devil in the magic bottle of his soul, and then immediately fixed him as a sinner in purgatory. Zhong Haicai was panicked.

Zhong Haicai, who felt like a thorn in his back, asked Lili for the detailed address of Zheng Jianxin's hometown, and immediately went to the company to borrow 30,000 yuan to send it to her father in the name of Zheng Jianxin at the post office, and explained that 20,000 yuan was for building a house for the family, and 10,000 yuan was for the treatment of grandfather and father.

After remitting the money, Zhong Haicai hurriedly bought a nutritious breakfast. He came to Zheng Jianxin's door tremblingly with the remittance slip in his hand, knocked on the door, pushed it open and walked in. Looking at Zheng Jianxin who was still lying on the bed, he persuaded her to eat breakfast, gently put the remittance slip on the bedside, and whispered: "Ajian, I...... I...... I remitted 30,000 yuan to your home......"

Zheng Jianxin closed her eyes and did not look or move. Her body trembled slightly, and a stronger sense of humiliation surged in her heart, sour and painful. 30,000...... What kind of money is this? Do you think you can buy me and be done with it?

Looking at Zheng Jianxin's pale face and chapped lips, Zhong Haicai looked around blankly, said "Oh" and ran out again, bought a large bowl of sour plum soup and brought it in, persuading Zheng Jianxin to drink some to moisten her throat and relieve the heat. Zheng Jianxin turned a deaf ear to him and tried to turn her body to face him.

After sitting there for a while with the sour plum soup in his hand, Zhong Haicai looked around the room. There was still a lot of water under the window, so he quickly picked up the mop and started to clean it up.

While mopping the floor, Zhong Haicai realized that 30,000 yuan seemed not enough to settle Zheng Jianxin. He didn't know where he got the courage from, and tremblingly said: "Ajian, you......just forgive me, I really love you and like you......I will marry you, buy you a house, and take you to Macau......"

Zheng Jianxin was still speechless. Zhong Haicai didn't dare to look at her, but just said similar words over and over again, until he finished mopping the floor, and then he realized that she didn't know when she fell asleep. Looking at Zheng Jianxin's pale and tear-stained face, Zhong Haicai once again made a cross on his chest.

At noon, Lili came over with a bouquet of flowers. Seeing Zheng Jianxin's dazed look, she thought she was just not awake yet, so she didn't ask much. She said that Xu Zhuang's matter couldn't be covered up at home, and she had to go home to talk about it, and would be back in a few days, and asked her to take care of herself.

Soon Zhong Haicai came again and said that he bought her lunch and asked her to eat it anyway. But Zheng Jianxin didn't even open the door for him. There was no other way, Zhong Haicai had to put the lunch box at the door, repeatedly told Zheng Jianxin to get up and eat, and then he walked away, looking back every few steps.

There were still many things to do on the construction site, and he didn't have time to keep begging here. Zheng Jianxin didn't report the case after all, which made Zhong Haicai feel relieved. If he lost this woman who made him love so much because of the beastly behavior he made on impulse, he would really become a sinner who would never be forgiven even by the merciful Lord.

In the afternoon, taking advantage of his free time, Zhong Haicai drove a small four-wheeled truck back to Gongbei in a hurry. Looking at the lunch and fruit that had not been touched at the door, Zhong Haicai's heart sank.

He knocked on the door and begged, but Zheng Jianxin still ignored him; the same was true when he came back from the construction site at night. Zhong Haicai was worried that something would happen to Zheng Jianxin, and he wandered in front of her door. In the late night, Zhong Haicai, who never smoked, bought a pack of Sanwu brand cigarettes and sat on the curb. He smoked half of the pack one by one. He was about to collapse and fell asleep by the flower bed.

At dawn, Zhong Haicai bought breakfast and knocked on the door again, begging and confessing. He only heard Zheng Jianxin's weak but sharp and angry cry from inside: "Get out! Get out! I don't want to see you, never......"

At noon, Zhong Haicai knocked on the door again to deliver food, but there was no response after knocking for a long time. He put his ear to the door and listened carefully. It was a series of weak groans. His heart jumped: Oh no, someone was going to die. He rushed in.

The whole room was full of stench. Zheng Jianxin was lying on the ground, her pants were wet, and there was a large pool of light yellow vomit around her face. The basin of sour plum soup fell to the corner of the wall, and the red and purple soup was spilled all over the floor.

Zheng Jianxin hadn't had a drop of water for more than two days. She got up and wanted to drink something. She saw the sour plum soup next to her and drank two big mouthfuls without thinking. The weather was hot and the room was stuffy. The sour plum soup had been left for two days and one night and had gone bad. However, Zheng Jianxin, who had suffered endless pain and severe dehydration, had become insensitive to her mouth, tongue and nose and could no longer distinguish, which led to vomiting and diarrhea.

Picking up the unconscious Zheng Jianxin, Zhong Haicai only felt that her whole body was very hot and she was shivering from time to time. He shouted in his heart that it was not good. He gathered all his strength to hold her and staggered out of the room. He rushed to the street to stop a taxi and shouted to the driver: "The fastest speed, the nearest hospital! Hurry......"

Zheng Jianxin's condition even shocked the doctors and nurses in the hospital. They quickly organized diagnosis and rescue. After working for several hours, they finally pulled her back from the edge of death. At night, Zheng Jianxin finally woke up slowly. Zhong Haicai, who was waiting in front of the emergency room, felt relieved and asked about her happily. "I have completed the hospitalization procedures. The doctor said that you are weak and frail now, and you have been hungry for so long, so you can't eat hard and greasy food. You can only drink some porridge to restore your body and stomach function."

Zhong Haicai said as he opened the thermos, scooped out a small bowl of porridge made from fragrant rice, and carefully stirred it, fearing that it would be too hot for Zheng Jianxin to swallow.

Zheng Jianxin opened her eyes, still confused in her heart and cold on her face. She looked at the pale ceiling and didn't know how to deal with herself. Her appearance scared Zhong Haicai so much that he was in a panic again. He didn't stir the porridge until he was sure that she was really okay.

Her stay in the hospital lasted for a week, and Zheng Jianxin's body was basically back to normal, and the doctor allowed her to be discharged. During these seven days, Zhong Haicai handed over all the work on the construction site to Achang and others, and stayed by Zheng Jianxin's side. In addition to running to the lab and getting medicine, he also took great pains to prepare her three meals a day -- as long as she wanted to eat and the doctor allowed it. Zhong Haicai made a soup of smilax glabra and spring bone soup (Chinese herbal soup) at home to clear away heat and fire, relieve summer heat and dampness, and also went to the big hotel to buy expensive and delicious Lingzhi, Tianma and black chicken soup to nourish the body, improve intelligence and calm the mind.

In addition, Zhong Haicai also bought a lot of high-end fruits suitable for Zheng Jianxin to eat and put them in the bedside table, so that she could always have something to take and eat; every late night, he would go to a western restaurant not far from the hospital to buy milk tea, western cakes and other things for her as a midnight snack, so that she could replenish as much as possible, hoping that she could get better as soon as possible to relieve the guilt in his heart.

The middle-aged woman in the same ward was even jealous of Zheng Jianxin for the care she had. She saw when Zheng Jianxin was getting up and taking a shower, Zhong Haicai immediately went out to buy a lot of high-end brand bath towels, underwear, and skin care products, she was even more envious. She asked Zhong Haicai curiously, "Why doesn't your daughter talk? She ignores you?"

Zheng Jianxin, who had just stepped into the bathroom door, heard this and Zhong Haicai's embarrassed laugh in response.

For a whole week, Zhong Haicai, who was dedicated and conscientious, still didn't get any good looks from Zheng Jianxin. On the way back from the hospital, Zheng Jianxin walked in front with empty hands, and Zhong Haicai followed with all things, panting every three steps. After walking for a while, Zhong Haicai saw that she had no intention of calling a taxi or taking a bus, so he couldn't help asking: "Ajian, where do you want to go?"

Zheng Jianxin ignored him and kept walking forward without looking back. Her body had not fully recovered, so her pace was not fast. Although Zhong Haicai was not sick or in pain, he was a little exhausted after a week of hard work. In addition, he could not run fast with his hands full of things, and could only barely keep up with her pace.

Seeing that Zheng Jianxin had no intention of stopping, Zhong

Haicai thought that she just wanted to find a place to be quiet by herself, so he quickly freed his hands and took out money and stuffed them into her hands: "Take it, walk slowly, I won't bother you anymore."

Zheng Jianxin stopped, turned around, raised her hand, and threw the money hard in Zhong Haicai's face. Ignoring the passersby who looked at her, she walked forward without saying a word. Looking at Zheng Jianxin's back, Zhong Haicai silently picked up the money and continued to follow her silently.

In this way, Zheng Jianxin spent nearly an hour to walk back to Gaosha Street. Zhong Haicai put the things at Zheng Zhongxin's rental house first, and finally breathed a sigh of relief. Zheng Jianxin still ignored him. In order for Zheng Jianxin to rest and to avoid embarrassment, he returned to his rental house and fell asleep on the bed.

After sitting on the bed for a long time, Zheng Jianxin began to pack her things. Zhong Haicai had already cleaned the room and sprayed it with air freshener, which smelled of a faint lemon scent. Looking at the fairly tidy room, Zhong Haicai's dark and honest fat face appeared in front of her again. She remembered his panic and worry when they were at the beach, the knock on the door when meals were delivered on time every day while she was bedridden, and the dedicated service when she was hospitalized. She sighed softly.

She believed Zhong Haicai's words that he loved her, and believed that he would really buy a big house for her...... But this could not make up for the humiliation caused by his rude rape. The person she loved was not him, but Xu Zhuang. She believed that if Xu Zhuang were the one who took care of her and promised her these days, Xu Zhuang would definitely do it better and more attentively.

Because she knew Xu Zhuang, knew how deep his love for her was, and knew that Xu Zhuang would do anything for her. Because she also loved Xu Zhuang, and could make any sacrifice and effort for him. This was the love she wanted. But......but now she was a dirty woman, could she still deserve Xu Zhuang's love that was as deep as the sea and as soft as brocade? What would happen if he knew that she had been abused?

Zheng Jianxin trembled all over, and the pain came again, so much so that she couldn't help but curl up and slowly squat in the corner.

"Brother Zhuang......" Zheng Jianxin sobbed softly, hitting her head against the wall again and again, hoping to get an answer.

Although Xu Zhuang was in jail in Hong Kong now, she knew better than anyone that he was in jail because of her. When he was still in his hometown, Xu Zhuang vowed to make a lot of money in Guangdong to give her the best life and the most meticulous care. He went smuggling with Zeng Sheng without telling her, and smuggling was the first step to realize his dream. This step was too risky!

Although Zheng Jianxin was disgusted, she never insisted on stopping it. She noticed it but didn't investigate it. As the saying goes: Chickens and ducks have their own ways to urinate. People were crazy about making money, so let them work hard. As Lili said, there were not many rich people who could expose everything they had to the sun. What made her angry was why Xu Zhuang and Lili had been hiding it from her, making her bear the huge blow without any psychological preparation.

If it weren't for this, she wouldn't have quarreled with Lili, wouldn't have followed Zhong Haicai to his house and felt embarrassed to ask Lili for a place to stay, wouldn't have been raped by Zhong Haicai......

Her heart was bleeding, and she kept thinking, reciting, crying, and resenting, fighting desperately in her heart. Zheng Jianxin's consciousness became more and more blurred, and she slowly fell asleep against the wall.

The sun was setting in the west, and the light seeping in from the small window to the east was getting dimmer and dimmer. Her whole body was sore as if her muscles and bones were broken, making Zheng Jianxin, who was curled up in the corner with her legs hugged, like a trapped beast in a cage, not knowing how to deal with herself. The small fan hanging in the mosquito net was turning lonely.

Chen Xiao said mysteriously:
I feel there is another Chen Xiao like me around

"Pah, pah, pah!" Several strange knocks on the door.

Zheng Jianxin leaned over to listen carefully. At first, there were two heavy knocks, and then two very light knocks, so light that it was faint. It could be seen that the visitor was a little nervous in his tentative mood.

This was obviously not Zhong Haicai. Zheng Jianxin glanced through the crack in the door and saw that the figure was Chen Xiao. Chen Xiao was wearing a navy blue suit and holding a black briefcase. Zheng Jianxin just opened the door a little bit, and he saw that it was Zheng Jianxin, so he pushed the door open.

"Zheng Jianxin, Zheng Jianxin, I have been thinking about you. I just got off work......" Chen Xiao straightened his glasses, rubbed his hands subconsciously, looked at the dim little room, felt the stuffiness of the air, and immediately said, "I haven't eaten, and you haven't eaten either? Let's go and eat!"

Zheng Jianxin stood still. Chen Xiao couldn't see her face in the dim light. Zheng Jianxin wanted to refuse him, but she was exhausted and worried that she would die in the hut without anyone knowing. The desire to survive made her hesitate. She said "No, no", but she was reluctantly pushed out of the door by Chen Xiao.

Chen Xiao took Zheng Jianxin to Gaosha Street, a western-style restaurant called Kekexili facing the sea. Chen Xiao and Zheng Jianxin sat on a sofa at a long table in the hall. Chen Xiao's eyes scanned the hall from time to time, fearing that he would meet someone familiar. Zheng Jianxin felt nauseous and said she didn't want to eat, but just wanted to drink something. But Chen Xiao ignored her completely and ordered the most expensive steak, vegetable salad, and a glass of green mint wine in this restaurant according to the high-standard reception he had planned in advance. He himself was frugal and only ordered a spaghetti with meat sauce. He said it was like Chinese fried noodles, which he loved very much.

Chen Xiao drank the free boiled water in big gulps. When he placed the order, he stated that he was not spending public funds to show his honest character. After placing the order, Chen Xiao raised his head. Zheng Jianxin, who was usually gentle and amiable with red lips and white teeth, now had a pale face and bloodless, with dark circles under her eyes. He couldn't help but screamed: "You, why......are you sick? Is it serious?"

Zheng Jianxin shook her head lightly and gathered her hair: "It's hot."

Chen Xiao sighed sympathetically for her extremely poor living environment and didn't ask more questions. Then he spoke according to the content of the speech he had prepared in advance.

"I can't stand my mother's attitude towards your sister, and I can't stand it!" Chen Xiao seemed to come here specifically to apologize to Zheng Jianxin. He didn't dare to look at her directly and lowered his head. Zheng Jianxin didn't say anything. When it comes to her sister, Zheng Jianxin really had nothing to say. In Chen Xiao's mind, compared with the Chen family, the Zheng family is weaker, and his mother was condescending and had no sympathy for the weak. And this was exactly the gap he needed to eliminate. He rubbed his hands, mustered up the courage to raise his head to face Zheng Jianxin, like a primary school student who had done something wrong and admitted his mistake to the teacher, and said solemnly: "Ajian, don't worry, I will properly arrange for you and Aliang in the future. This is my concern, and I will definitely take care of it to the end."

Zheng Jianxin concentrated and pondered for a while, and a disdainful smile appeared at the corner of her mouth, saying: "Rich or poor, it's probably fate, right? Don't expect anyone to save anyone."

Zheng Jianxin's words were concise. Chen Xiao understood what

Zheng Jianxin meant, and his face turned red and white, which was extremely unnatural. He sighed and took a big sip of water.

Zheng Jianxin is one of two sisters. The elder sister is five years older than Zheng Jianxin. Her name is Aliang, and she looks as beautiful as Zheng Jianxin. In those years, young people in the village began to leave the mountains and come to Guangdong to work. Aliang, who was the same age as Zheng Jianxin now, also told her father that she wanted to go out. Grandpa listened and thought about it for more than half a month. This person who didn't want to bother others in his life was finally "trapped" by "poverty" and had to bow his head and said helplessly: "Okay, I'll write a letter to your Grandpa Chen and try to ask him to find you a job there!"

Grandpa Chen is Chen Xiao's father. He and Zheng Jianxin's grandfather worked in the revolution together when they were young. When the area was liberated, they were both famous bandit-suppression heroes in the local area. Grandpa Chen was the deputy battalion commander in the army, and Zheng Jianxin's grandfather was the village militia captain who "supported the front" (supporting the front to deliver supplies, escorting the wounded and sick, etc.). Later, Grandpa Chen followed the army to Wuhan, and finally transferred to Guangzhou. Grandpa stayed in the village.

After the Spring Festival, Aliang went to Guangdong with the young people in the village. She took her grandfather's letter and found the Chen family in a small courtyard at the foot of Baiyun Mountain in Guangzhou. Grandpa Chen and his wife kept changing nannies at home, and Grandma Chen was always dissatisfied. She was anxious to find someone. Seeing that Aliang was clean and agile, she kept her as a nanny.

Zheng Jianxin came to Zhuhai from her hometown and passed by Guangzhou to visit her sister. Grandpa Chen's house had six large rooms. Three of them didn't talk much. Grandpa Chen, who walked with difficulty, wore an old military uniform that was almost washed white all day long and sat at the desk to read newspapers. Her sister poured tea for him, peeled fruit for him, helped him walk, and took care of his life.

Grandma Chen, who was more than ten years younger than he, was much more energetic. She had short gray hair with small permed waves. She wore exquisite poplin clothes with lace embroidered on them. She went to a famous beauty salon twice a week. In addition to being strong and arrogant, Grandma Chen had a perceptible hostility towards Zheng Jianxin's sister. It could be seen that Grandpa Chen protected her sister.

Grandma Chen did not allow Aliang to call them "Grandpa" or "Grandma": there was no relationship between them, how could a nanny get close to her! What should she call her? She used to be called the chief, but now she has retired. If Aliang called her "chief", didn't that mean Aliang was just someone sent by the unit? Grandma Chen looked at the TV and saw the advertisements saying "Royal Garden" and "Noble Spirit". She thought of the characters in the palace TV series and felt very familiar with them. She was inspired: "From now on, call him Master! Call me Madam!"

Grandpa Chen was so angry that he pounded the floor with his cane: "You are a feudalist!"

Grandma Chen rolled her eyes and pointed at the TV: "Don't you watch the TV series of talented men and beautiful women every day?"

Grandpa Chen sighed and didn't know what to say. Zheng Jianxin felt awkward when she heard Aliang calling them "Master" and "Madam". It was like going back to ancient times. Zheng Jianxin had heard that when Grandma Chen was young, she had made contributions in suppressing bandits. She always ran to the front during the army's rapid march and fought against enemy with the male comrades. However, Zheng Jianxin "experienced" her fierceness when she met her.

As soon as Zheng Jianxin knocked on her door, she was blocked outside by Grandma Chen's bright eyes and smiling voice. She handed out a big brush and said, "Brush the dust off your clothes before entering the house!" Her sister later said that Grandma Chen loved cleanliness and treated all guests, including her son and daughter-in-law, like this. In addition, she did not allow outsiders to sit on the sofa, and handed them a small stool to sit on. After the guests left, she took the small stool to

133

the yard to dry in the sun for a while, saying that it was disinfected.

It was conceivable that her sister's life in that environment was helpless and difficult. No wonder Aliang was silent, with grievances in her eyes. Chen Xiao watched Zheng Jianxin kept her head down and ate silently, ignoring him. He sighed and said, "My mother's temper gets weirder as she gets older...... I tried to persuade her, but she quarreled with me whenever I did. I know she was mean to Aliang, but she couldn't bear to let Aliang go, saying she was used to bossing her around......"

After a long while, Chen Xiao said again, "Everyone's life is not happy! You see, I'm a married person," At this point, he stopped eating, put down his fork, looked out the window, and sighed deeply, "What's the difference between being married and not being married? My wife complains and scolds me as soon as she sees me. She used to say that I was three 'low' people: low (short) stature, low social status, and low salary. My mother asked old comrades for help several times. Now I am an official at the deputy department level and have been sent to Macau to be a representative for the company. The salary is not low, 70,000 or 80,000 yuan a month. Ajian, you have seen the world, and she compares with others again, complaining that I can't make a fortune and am a chicken scratching for food...... Hey, she is finding fault again, saying that I am three uglies, small face, ugly, big nose, ugly, bow legs, ugly...... I can't even afford a 100,000 yuan car for her......" As he spoke, he turned to money.

"You have told me all this many times, why are you telling me this?" Zheng Jianxin knew that his wife was fierce and Chen Xiao lived a cowardly life.

"Life is cold...... Alas, you don't want to go back to that electronics factory. What else do you want to do? I'll help you find it...... I care about you very much. When people here see a pretty girl, they are like flies to blood. I'm afraid you'll make the wrong friends......" Chen Xiao stuttered.

Zheng Jianxin glanced at him and looked out the window. She couldn't listen to his nonsense. Chen Xiao shook his head several times and rubbed his hands again: "Now that the country is open and reforming, nothing is standardized. Standardization needs time."

He hesitated as he took out a pile of materials from his briefcase, flipped out a newspaper and said: "The value created by American workers, the boss uses 39% to pay the workers' wages, and also has to buy insurance for the workers, etc., which adds up to 60%. Our Chinese workers create a value of 100,000 yuan a year, 40% should be more than 4,000 yuan a month! But the enterprise is independent and not required to pay so much. The current salary is obviously low, but there is no way. When the bosses can't recruit workers, they will understand!"

After a while, he had to say: "Let me help you find a suitable job as soon as possible, suitable, that is, a decent job. Don't worry about whether you work or not, every month...... I will help you with some money...... I will rent a house for you...... I will come to see you often......"

As he said, he took out an envelope from his briefcase and carefully pushed it in front of Zheng Jianxin. Needless to say, it was filled with money.

"What, you support me? To be your mistress?" Zheng Jianxin asked Chen Xiao in rapid tone. To exchange a woman's body with money, she didn't expect Chen Xiao would use this trick and treat her as a commodity. Was this a rule difficult to escape in developed areas? Yesterday's humiliation still made her heart bleed, and today she became the target of the hunter again. Zheng Jianxin's muscles were trembling with heat. The Zheng and Chen families had a feud before, and because of the unhappiness of her sister being a nanny, Ajian was very sensitive. After hearing what Chen Xiao said, her original grudge against the Chen family turned into disgust. In order to see the inner depths of the so-called upper-class hypocrites, Zheng Jianxin suppressed her anger and asked calmly while staring into the eyes of this "fly".

Zheng Jianxin's words made Chen Xiao feel like he was stabbed in the head, especially the word "mistress", which made Chen Xiao's heart tremble. He pursed his lips and waved his hands quickly: "No, no, no, that's not what I meant, don't get me wrong......"

He gently put his hand on the table, and felt that it was not easy to defend himself. Zheng Jianxin swallowed back her words before she could curse Chen Xiao. She wanted to save some face for this poor "fellow villager" who was at least an official, so she glanced at him fiercely: "I don't understand what you are saying, I'm leaving! Goodbye!"

"No, no, no!" Chen Xiao's forehead was covered with sweat, and he stretched out his arms to stop Zheng Jianxin, "You, you let me talk, listen to my explanation!" The people at the next table looked over here. Zheng Jianxin looked at Chen Xiao's begging expression, and didn't want to end up falling out with Chen Xiao, so she sat down, lowered her head, and turned her back to him.

"Misunderstanding, misunderstanding! Alas, I am often misunderstood!" He paused, "I can't do business, be a welcomed person, or speak properly at the company; at home...... I've said it before. I have no friends, no family, I just want to find someone to tell the truth to! You come from my hometown, just like the unpolluted mountain flowers and clear springs in our mountainous area, you are worthy of me telling you! ......"

Zheng Jianxin's mouth was dry, so she turned around and drank a sip of water. Chen Xiao suddenly approached Zheng Jianxin very mysteriously and whispered, "I feel that there is another Chen Xiao around me who is the same as me, but it is not me; but others put some of his despicable things, such as telling lies and looking for women, on me."

He paused again, and said seriously, "I just met an old friend, he said that I looked much better than the past two days. I said that I was on a business trip in the north and just returned to Guangzhou last night. He said that I was really good at joking, and when he saw me two days ago, he talked to me for a long time...... Don't you think it's strange? -- There are really two me in this world? "

When he spoke, his eyeballs behind the glasses kept turning, and the light shining on the glasses seemed like four strange lights were flashing. He sighed and swayed his shoulders, as if he felt much more relaxed. Zheng Jianxin was scared and her legs and feet were cold. He mistakenly thought that Zheng Jianxin was willing to listen to him because she was silent. He frowned slightly, still with a mysterious look, but a little proud. His throat jumped and he swallowed his saliva: "Hypocrisy is everywhere. We live in a world of emotional hypocrisy. It is said that 'everyone has a lover, but those who don't show it are masters'. I am going to write a novel. The content is that one day the authorities announced that all current marriage certificates would be invalid, so that those hypocritical officials, state-owned enterprise bosses, and professors would show their true colors and walk out their lovers in the sun amid cheers......"

Listening to Chen Xiao's ramblings was really a living torture. The weak Zheng Jianxin stood up resolutely and walked straight out the door. "Ajian! Ajian! " Chen Xiao wanted to explain something, but seeing Zheng Jianxin had already walked out, he could only sigh, lowered his head and supported it with his hands, and his glasses fell off one ear.

Zheng Jianxin dragged her tired body back to the rental house. The stench of rotten fruit peels and waste in the narrow alley, mixed with the stench from the sewer outlet, filled the alley. Especially after the durian peel was exposed to the sun, the paint-like smell was strongly pungent and suffocating.

Chen Xiao's ugly appearance made Zheng Jianxin annoyed and amused. The son of a veteran revolutionary, a person who had been to college, was wretched and perverted. After leaving the mountains, she realized that the special zone was a kaleidoscope. He was another kind of person who was on par with Zeng Sheng and Bai Lang. Zheng Jianxin spitted, smiled bitterly and let out a breath.

She went into the house and closed the door in a hurry to block the stench, but the stench was still pervasive. It came in from nowhere and filled the house. Living here day after day, she became dull to this faint stench and could no longer smell anything. Just like the stench, Zheng Jianxin could tolerate the damp and hot weather. When a person first enters a hot bathhouse, his breath is blocked by the steam. When he cannot escape, he will get used to it.

Zheng Jianxin turned on the light and found a small piece of rent-demanding paper from the landlord stuffed under the door. She sat on the only small plastic stool that could be sat on, holding the rent-demanding paper. She searched her handbag and clothes pockets but only found a few dollars, not even enough to buy a five-dollar lunch, let alone pay the rent. She climbed onto the bed and lay on her back out of inexplicable anger. She gritted her teeth and pounded the bed board hard. A penny can make a hero fall. Her current situation was not different. Money, money, money......

Zheng Jianxin thought about this and that. She thought of her grandfather who was waiting for money for medical treatment every day. Every time she saw his thin body lying on the bed, every time she faced his helpless and pitiful eyes, she would feel sad -- he was a militia hero who followed the People's Liberation Army to fight bandits and walked through the rain of bullets, but now he was a completely different person. Touching the remittance slip that Zhong Haicai sent to his family, which was still untouched on the bedside, Zheng Jianxin just blinked and closed her eyes, shedding two lines of hot tears. She trembled, felt sour, and hurt in her heart. It was more humiliating than being raped that night. Is this my price? ...... I sold myself out ......

But when she thought about the significance of the 30,000 yuan to her family, her heart, which had been troubled by the lack of money at home day and night, suddenly relaxed. Rubbing a few pieces of money, Zheng Jianxin struggled in her heart. What should she do? Wait for Xu Zhuang to be released from prison and return? ...... But what would it be like then? She didn't dare to think about it.

Now she needed to eat and live! Lili went back to her hometown, unable to solve her urgent problem: should she look for Mingming? In front of this sister who was dressed brightly like a proud peacock, should she beg like a beggar to borrow money? When she was in the factory, Zheng Jianxin took a few sisters to visit Gongbei, wanting to see the world, and took them to the coffee shop to see Mingming, a fellow villager who had made a fortune . However, Mingming seemed to not know those people, ignored them, and didn't even give them a sip of water. She blocked them outside the door and said lightly, "You girls are shopping, go to the opposite side to see the sea", and sent them away.

Later, Lili sent her a message: "Don't bring dirty fellow villagers to Mingming's store in the future."

She understood that Mingming had changed, had money, and looked down on her fellow villagers. Lili said, "With money, people will definitely change. "Zheng Jianxin smiled bitterly and shook her head. Who should I go to? I don't interact with other fellow villagers much, and I'm not familiar with them, so I can't ask them. What should I do? What should I do?

Ask the landlord for a few days' grace and find a job tomorrow? Should I go to the factory again to waste my youthhood? When Zheng Jianxin thought of the ten-plus hours of working, the cheap and hopeless working days, she felt a sense of fear. Go back to my hometown? This voice had appeared in her ears every time she was unhappy in the past six months. However, the louder voice was: Never go back, even if I die outside!

The barren land in the mountain village had bound the people there from generation to generation, and the people there regarded the spread of rumors as an important spiritual enjoyment, making fun of each other and scolding each other. Talented people, however, were like birds without wings, unable to fly. Standing in the fields, people could see the end of life from the day they were born. It was not the life she imagined, it was not the life she wanted. But in this bustling city, who would know her?

It is said that one must rely on oneself, but when even oneself cannot be relied upon, what should she do? "When the granary is full, one knows etiquette; when food and clothing are sufficient, one knows honor and disgrace", but what if the granary is empty and food and clothing are insufficient? What should be done? When life is down and out and there is no food to eat, there is no longer the basis to bargain and condition to live. Just like a drowning person struggling for life, even if there is only a straw in front of him, he must grab it; like a lonely boat that is about to sink, no matter how valuable the things on the boat are, they must be thrown away.

It is all for survival! Only by survival can there be hope! Only by survival can there be a future!

Looking at the rent reminder in her hand, and then looking at the remittance slip next to the pillow, she felt the hunger burning in her stomach. Zheng Jianxin knew that she needed a harbor. Zhong Haicai's timid and hopeful eyes, and the honest and kind smile appeared in her eyes. Zheng Jianxin bit her lips heavily and tore the remittance slip into pieces.

Clenching her fists, turning her palms, and the paper scraps fell. And what is the difference between her like broken stems and floating duckweed and these paper scraps? Zheng Jianxin's bitten lips were dripping with blood, and she waved away her tears with one hand. She knew that her dignity, love, and happiness were shattered from then on. When the customs clock pointed to twelve o'clock in the middle of the night, Zheng Jianxin carried all the luggage, walked through the night, and knocked on the door of Zhong Haicai's room.

Zhong Haicai opened the door and saw that it was Zheng Jianxin, his face full of astonishment. Then he trembled and shrank, and then looked at the luggage in her hand, blinking in confusion.

Zheng Jianxin stared at Zhong Haicai , calmly, word by word: "I want to marry you! I want to live with you and marry you!"

Zhong Haicai, who didn't dare to breathe for a long time, finally came to his senses. He didn't believe it was true. Suddenly, his eyes lit up. He slapped his face with his palms and said with a trembling mouth: "Yes, yes, yes......" He couldn't help stamping his feet, "Definitely! Definitely! "I must......"

Just a moment before, he was kneeling in front of the cross of Jesus, repenting, atoning, begging for forgiveness from the savior; just a moment before, he was listening to the knock on the door, waiting for the disaster to come.

Zhong Haicai felt uneasy all day long, as if there was a rabbit in his chest.

Bai Lang said that there was an urgent matter in the Blue Dream project and he should go to him, but he ignored it.

Finding a woman on a whim usually lead to the same result: those married would make their families restless by their wives. Zhong Haicai himself was single, so he didn't have to be afraid. Some would bring a few burly fellow villagers to the placed where they lived and would beat the men up, or beat the men up as soon as they found them. Some would clamp the men's ears with pliers and force them to write a note for an IOU of several hundred thousand yuan.

He didn't know what tricks Zheng Jianxin would use, or what kind of punishment she would use. When he heard that she was going to marry him, he couldn't believe it. How could such a good thing happen? He couldn't even think about it. A fair and pretty girl came to this poor man to be his wife? Zhong Haicai's blood flowed faster and he stood there dully, unable to move.

Zheng Jianxin didn't say anything else.

On the low table was the porridge left by Zhong Haicai. Zheng Jianxin filled a bowl and ate it silently.

Zheng Jianxin was in the bathroom, taking a shower. The water was running, and she took a long, long shower.

Zheng Jianxin wrapped herself in a bath towel and lay on Zhong Haicai's bed. She closed her eyes calmly, like a martyr waiting for the moment of execution.

But Zhong Haicai hid in the corner of the hall, so scared that he didn't react.

15

Taiwanese businessman Bai Lang didn't have a penny. What kind of investment did he make?

"Knowledge is power", "Experience is capital", Bai Lang, a lecturer at a university in Taiwan, believed in these two sentences. Bai Lang, who was unwilling to stand on the podium and deal with students all his life, had a premonition that reform and opening up were unstoppable when he first learned that the mainland had established a special economic zone. He persuaded several classmates to come to Guangdong to try to make a fortune. He believed that with the knowledge he had learned from studying in the UK and the experience of traveling half the world, he would definitely be able to make a big splash in this virgin land that had just been developed.

In October 1988, Zhuhai held an investment promotion conference, and people from more than 80 cities in China came to participate in foreign investment promotion. Financial groups, businessmen, and manufacturers from the United States, Singapore, Japan, Australia, and Hong Kong, Macau, and Taiwan all came to discuss investment. This was Bai Lang's first visit to Zhuhai. With an uncertain and nervous mood, he entered the mysterious land of the mainland in an adventurous manner.

At that time, Taiwan had just opened up to Taiwanese veterans to visit relatives in the mainland for only one year, and there were very few Taiwanese businessmen in the mainland. Bai Lang's appearance was quite welcomed by some city investment promotion groups.

He had an outstanding appearance, wearing a fitted linen suit, a thick slicked back hair, a pair of gentle gold-rimmed glasses, a neatly trimmed short mustache along his upper lip, and a high-end cowhide briefcase in his hand. He would bow deeply to any mainland official he met, important or non-important, shake hands with a smile, and then hand over his business card with both hands, accompanied by the words "Please give me your guidance". He said this with sincerity and without losing the identity of a business owner. Even when facing young service staff, he would bow before speaking, say "Hi, Hi" twice, nod his head to greet them, and then say "Please give me your guidance", without any other small talk.

His business card was printed with a company whose details no one knew: "Taiwan, Gaolu Investment Co., Ltd., Bai Lang, Chairman".

Guangdong not only made Bai Lang as excited as Columbus discovering the New World, but more importantly, there were so many industrial, transportation, and energy investment projects in the investment promotion groups of various cities, especially the regulations specially formulated by the central government a few months ago to encourage Taiwanese investment, and the special preferential policies such as tax and customs exemptions, which made him feel like he saw piles of gold in front of him, making him rub his hands and excited.

At night, lying on the bed of Gongbei Hotel, one of the best hotels in Zhuhai at that time, he flipped through his notebook and the investment documents distributed at the meeting, and could not fall asleep.

Bai Lang had a habit of taking out a notebook from his briefcase immediately when talking to someone, and taking out a "Parker" pen from his suit pocket (he never used convenient ballpoint pens or signature pens) to take notes from time to time. The person talking with him immediately felt respected and had a good impression of him. Whenever he spoke to others, he would immediately pull out his notebook, and the listeners would immediately feel the basis of his words and trust him.

Many investment projects regarded as advanced technologies here had been very mature and had been promoted and put into practical use in Taiwan, and some were already the second generation. Especially for labor-intensive enterprises, such as shoemaking and clothing enterprises, the monthly salary of workers in Zhuhai and Dongguan was two to three hundred yuan, and the price of labor in Taiwan was ten to twenty times more expensive than that in the mainland. There were also more specific preferential policies of the special zone for Taiwanese enterprises, which attracted Bai Lang.

Bai Lang dug up all the acquaintances and friends in Taiwan in his mind. As soon as the investment promotion conference ended, he flew back to Taiwan with half a box of information, and went from Taipei, Taichung to Kaohsiung without stopping, holding briefings one after another, calling on relatives and friends to invest in the mainland! He was a go-between, and his interests were very flexible. His Gaolu company would own a certain number of shares in the company that successfully attracted investment in the future, or receive commissions and labor fees.

Bai Lang settled in Zhuhai. The reason he told outsiders was that he liked Zhuhai's greenery and quietness -- it was very similar to European cities. In fact, he had been to Shenzhen. Most of the investments in Shenzhen were big-handed, hard-core and bloody, and there were many experts. The living there was expensive like Hong Kong, and Bai Lang's "karate" ("empty-hand dealer" in Chinese) could not hide.

In addition, Zhuhai is adjacent to Macau, and mobilizing Taiwanese friends to come to the mainland for inspection, even if there was no satisfactory project at the moment, it was worthwhile to gamble in Macau. Over the years, Bai Lang had a wide range of "connections" on both sides of the Taiwan Strait.

Bai Lang often accompanied his Taiwanese friends to hotels and nightclubs. Through his friends' introduction, he soon met Lili, one of the four most beautiful girls in Gongbei. And soon Lili became one of Bai Lang's social ties.

Half a year before, Zeng Sheng heard Lili said that a friend of her friends was a Taiwanese businessman who came to the mainland to invest in real estate. The people talking was unintentional, but the listener was interested. Zeng Sheng's heart moved and he must meet this Taiwanese.

Although Hong Kong and the mainland had different systems for decades, the economic and trade business had never been interrupted. Taiwan and the mainland had been separated for many years. The Taiwanese had just arrived and urgently needed advice from experts. Wasn't it an opportunity for him?

It was a coincidence that Bai Lang's eyes had long been on Zeng Sheng. He knew that Zeng Sheng was supporting Lili with money, while he was taking advantage of Lili with a rubber check. He didn't dare to face Zeng Sheng, because his inferiority complex made him have no dignity. But a glimmer of hope made him ignore his face, and he begged Lili to introduce him to Zeng Sheng. Lili passed a message in the middle, and Zeng Sheng and Bai Lang hit it off.

Lili introduced various bosses to Zeng Sheng with no efforts to avoid suspicion. If they made money in business, she could get some commission. Lili also kept an eye out for business opportunities suitable for her.

Zeng Sheng and Bailang agreed to meet at the Western Restaurant of Zhuhai Hotel.

Zhuhai Hotel was one of the only high-end hotels in Zhuhai at that time. It was located on Jingshan Road, Jida, and was the hotel where the municipal government received dignitaries.

The Western Restaurant was on the east side of the lobby. Looking through the large glass window, an ancient incense burner in the garden-style square made this hotel very elegant. Zeng Sheng's "foreign affairs" activities were mostly carried out here instead of Gongbei. What he wanted was to give people the first impression that he was a regular businessman. This small Western restaurant was very busy with people coming in and out from all over the world. The men were dressed noble and the women were dressed fashionable. Most of them were business dignitaries from state-owned enterprises in the mainland who went to the special zone to invest and do business. Many of the consultations and negotiations for large and small projects in Zhuhai in the early days were conducted and concluded there.

Zeng Sheng usually kept a low profile, dressed casually, with a big head which was bald, and was inconspicuous wherever he went. But once he wore a brand-name suit and changed his appearance, especially with his big belly, he looked like a big boss of Hong Kong businessmen. When Bai Lang first met him, he really looked up to him, and he was happy and hopeful in his eyes. Every time Bai Lang met an investor, he seemed to have a premonition of the occurrence of miracles and the arrival of his turn.

Zeng Sheng didn't talk much, maybe because he had difficulty speaking Mandarin, or maybe because he was not good at expressing himself verbally. He took out an album from his pocket and gave it to Bai Lang. Bai Lang opened it and saw that they were all photos of him with officials and big businessmen. Zeng Sheng pointed at the people in the photos and explained one by one: there were people from Beijing, Guangdong, and Hong Kong. Some of the local officials were known to Bai Lang, and some were celebrities he had seen at the Merchants' Fair. Bai Lang didn't know those celebrities but concluded what Zeng Sheng said was true.

After Bai Lang looked at the photo album, Zeng Sheng slowly and casually flipped through his own photo album page by page.

Zeng Sheng drank coffee with Bai Lang, and talked about his import trade business with a bit of pride. Bai Lang understood his intention. He wanted his funds, to do business together, and to expand the business. Zeng Sheng prepared his import and export trade list, import approval documents, profit calculation table and other documents very well, and handed them to Bai Lang respectfully, waiting for his attitude and his answer.

Bai Lang's eyes moved from the paper on the table to Zeng Sheng's face. Without saying a word, he took a sip of coffee and took off his glasses to wipe them with a cloth.

Bai Lang tutted his lips, as if sighing from the bottom of his heart, and said: "The profit is really considerable!"

Zeng Sheng nodded gently, and said in the soft voice of Hong Kong people when speaking Mandarin: "I originally worked with people in Beijing. The people at lower level were so bad that they abolished all the branches. This kind of business is generally not valued by people who don't know the inside story......" There was a sly light in the corner of his eyes, "My boss doesn't easily give people such high profits...... If you don't have enough money, you can introduce some Taiwanese friends to join. I know Taiwanese like to own shares in small businesses......"

Zeng Sheng imported waste and second-hand goods, such as bad motors and used plastics, from Japan and South Africa, dismantled them, sorted them, and sold them to the mainland. In Bai Lang's opinion, although there was some money to be made, it was a small profit after all. Bai Lang wanted to start a business in the mainland, a big business, and achieve a brilliant career and life, and make a fortune. He would never associate with people like Zeng Sheng who did business dealing with garbage.

He said to Zeng Sheng: "Thank you Mr. Zeng for your trust and preference for me. As the saying goes, different trades are like different mountains. Everyone will be drooling over your huge profits, but my mind is on real estate, which is my main trade, so I can't accept Mr. Zeng's kindness! In the future, I would like to drink and chat with Mr. Zeng frequently, keep in touch, and slowly learn how to make money from Mr. Zeng. When there is a good business, we can cooperate well!"

He rejected Zeng Sheng. Bai Lang came with enthusiasm. In his opinion, Zeng Sheng was a "garbage collector" who could easily be attracted to his real estate project. He could also get some Hong Kong businessmen through him, and establish relationships with the Hong Kong financial community through Hong Kong businessmen to raise funds from Hong Kong, the world's financial center. Unexpectedly, Zeng Sheng had his eyes on him. After he rejected Zeng Sheng, it was difficult for him to speak to him. Bai Lang touched the brown leather briefcase containing the project plan, and tried to open it several times, but finally retracted his hand.

The two frustrated people looked at each other, hiding their inner disappointment and unhappiness, showing an attitude of not being able to make a deal but still being friendly, and gave each other an unnatural smile.

After that, they knew each other's background and lost the charm to each other, and even belittled each other among their friends: Zeng Sheng: "Without a cent, nothing, what investment? A beggar came to the mainland, and still wanted to make a fortune?" Bai Lang: "He is full of lies, uneducated, and does garbage collection business!"

But Zeng Sheng's small photo album greatly stimulated and inspired Bai Lang.

At first, he thought that this set of behavior of raising one's status by pulling a big flag was close to the trickery of the underworld, which had existed in Taiwan for a long time, so he sneered: "Damn, child's play!" He scolded, but the small photo album could not be shaken off in front of Bai Lang. He didn't even have the heart to eat dinner, and immediately understood the importance of the small photo album, which was also an indispensable prop for him.

After that, whenever there were foreign business activities, Bai Lang would take the initiative to hand over his business card to the officials, give them compliments he had prepared in advance, and arrange for his friends to take a group photo. Soon, Bai Lang also had a photo album, which he put into his briefcase along with a pile of useful business cards and various documents he had accumulated. After that, whenever he discussed projects with people, he would not forget to take out the business card and photo album for people to browse.

He set his eyes on the real estate industry. At that time, the Pearl River Delta had just realized the value of land. Real estate, as a commercial development, had just started, and Bai Lang was a prophet.

Blue Dream Water Village Timeshare Resort
-- What a beautiful picture

In the mid-1980s, real estate became popular in the Pearl River Delta, and many bank investment companies and even some grassroots credit cooperatives flocked here to send money to support real estate development.

In order to get performance, those banks sent representatives to lend money to anyone to buy land as long as he had a project, and then mortgage the land to the bank in return. This was common in Huizhou Daya Bay and Zhuhai's West District. Some plots of land were transferred three or four times, and many people profited from it. Although it was still a wasteland after many years, each plot of land had an owner. Some people said that there was a bank president buried under each plot of land.

Bai Lang hurriedly established Gaolu Real Estate Company in a joint venture with others as a Taiwanese businessman. The registered capital was 2 million US dollars, which was invested in five installments over five years. Since "Gaolu" was a Sino-foreign joint venture, foreign investors must have their own funds. The first installment was 20%, 400,000 US dollars. Bai Lang borrowed the money for the capital verification from a Taiwanese industrial and commercial enterprise. He used it for one month and then paid it back. After that, he began to use banks for his purpose.

Bai Lang "ran to occupy wasteland" and signed contracts for three plots of land with the Land and Resources Bureau in one go. He thought that if he had a partnership, he would have money, and he could transfer the land to Taiwanese businessmen, or cooperate with Taiwanese businessmen to develop the land, and use the land as collateral to borrow more money from banks. After more than a year, he achieved nothing: his transfer to Taiwanese businessmen was unsuccessful; he asked for loans from the banks in Hong Kong and mainland, but was turned down. Not only did he spend all the more than 1 million New Taiwan dollars (equivalent to more than 300,000 RMB) he brought from Taiwan, but also the deposit of 500,000 RMB he borrowed from the contractor and deposited into the Land and Resources Bureau was confiscated.

Every day he stayed in the mainland, he felt more: the gap between the mainland's backward ideas and information and the world was narrowing, which meant that his room to make money was narrowing. He was in debt, but he was not discouraged. To get out of the predicament, he must have new projects to find money. And the new projects must be projects that did not require buying land or spending money. Would there be such a good thing? It was difficult! Bai Lang often frowned in private, combed his hair with his five fingers, and wiped his glasses.

Bai Lang, as a foreign businessman, wore a navy blue suit and continued to travel around the Pearl River Delta accompanied by a college student recruited by the company, looking for money and projects. Once a friend took him to a village rich in longan. When walking on the river bank full of longan trees, he found that the river here was crisscrossed and the scenery was beautiful. Suddenly, a more bold and advanced idea emerged: to engage in real estate development in the countryside.

He found the village committee and spent several hours explaining his ideas. He asked the village to provide the land, and he would provide the project plan, management team and fund raising, and the two sides would cooperate in development.

Bai Lang's speech was bold and loud like his father's military generation, and had the rigorous logic of a cultured person. His incitement and appeal soon convinced the villagers. At that time, a town or even a village in Shunde each had a nationally famous product. The village committee was suffering from the remoteness of the village and the inconvenient transportation, which made it difficult to attract foreign investment. If a large project settled in the village, foreign investors would build a wealth road to their doorstep, everyone was smiling. After listening to his speech, the town leaders said: "The God of Wealth has arrived, it's good, it's feasible!"

After signing the letter of intent for cooperation, Bai Lang started looking for start-up funds without stopping. As long as the project started, he could use the project as a backdoor to ask for huge funds from the bank that wanted to lend out all the money at that time, and successfully complete the project.

In his imagination, the management method of time-share resort hotels, which had long been operating in developed countries in Europe and America, was still a blank in the mainland. Once the project was completed, the wealth hidden in the market gap caused by the information gap would definitely be surprising to all.

What he lacked now was a start-up capital that was neither too big nor too small. Bai Lang was desperate for capital. Just like a man who was sick, he tried every means to make friends with bosses, big or small, and the coffee shop became his office. He had been to Japan when he was in college, and he used the salesmen who kept bowing to pedestrians on the streets of Tokyo as a role model to inspire himself. After Bai Lang and Zeng Sheng failed in their talk at Zhuhai Hotel, Bai Lang directly told Lili what he wanted. Lili couldn't think of a big boss, so she had no choice but to recommend a person who was related to real estate development. This person was Zhong Haicai, the foreman of the Macau site who lived downstairs from Lili.

When Bai Lang heard about Zhong Haicai's situation, he felt that this was the person he had longed for and was looking for. He had a premonition that things would be successful with Zhong Haicai.

When he saw Zhong Haicai, Bai Lang had no objection to Zhong Haicai's slovenliness. He was eager to invite Zhong Haicai to taste Taiwan's high mountain cloud tea with an unconcealed intimacy, as if he had met a friend he hadn't seen for many years. He took out the photo album and showed it to Zhong Haicai page by page. The mayor of a certain place was his old friend......

Before Zhong Haicai finished reading, he took out a box of business cards and pulled out more than ten business cards of large construction companies, saying that he had contacted them all, but was not satisfied with any of them: "If you join, I will be relieved about the project supervision! The quality of the projects done by mainlanders is really worrying! We just want to bring advanced foreign technology to the mainland. Engineer Zhong, our project will play a demonstration role in the mainland. You can't refuse. You are familiar with Hong Kong and Macau, so you have to help me!"

When he heard that he was going to be hired as the client's representative to manage the project, and it was a project worth hundreds of millions and for five or six years, Zhong Haicai blinked his eyes and couldn't believe it was true. He habitually patted his cheeks lightly, and he didn't hear what Bai Lang said afterwards. Bai Lang knew that Zhong Haicai was a cement worker on the construction site in Macau, but he kept calling him "Engineer Zhong". Zhong Haicai knew that he was a cement worker in Macau, but he accepted the call of "Engineer Zhong" without much correction. He had never been valued so much before, and he felt comfortable.

Bai Lang changed the subject and talked about the economic benefit analysis of the project. Zhong Haicai opened his eyes wide and shouted: "It's a huge profit!" The benefit was not Zhong Haicai's business. The speaker might seem unintentional, but the listener was. Zhong Haicai was a little restless, like a person who had not eaten and saw the rich dishes in other people's bowls, and instinctively became greedy and jealous.

"Why do others have the opportunity to make a fortune?" Zhong Haicai asked secretly.

Bai Lang noticed the change in Zhong Haicai's facial expression, and he knew that the time had come. He smacked his lips, wiped his mustache with his left thumb, and touched his glasses with his index finger. He looked a little embarrassed, but then he turned to be understanding and said, "You will contribute so much to the project in the future. I know it's unfair to just pay you wages. How about giving you some shares? Not much......" He hesitated for a moment, "three million Hong Kong dollars, let me see how much I can get......" He fiddled with the calculator on the side.

"Three million?" Zhong Haicai's upper lip twitched, and he shook his hand quickly.

Although Zhong Haicai was very excited when he heard the wonderful prospects described by Bai Lang in a very convincing tone, he stopped when it came to investment. Zhong Haicai's monthly income was only a little more than 20,000 yuan when he was working at full capacity. He had to make a living, and Liang Xiangyun would instigate her daughter Ahua to ask for money every now and then. The remaining money was used for eating, drinking and listening to music with friends, and he was a person from paycheck to paycheck. At the end of the discussion, Zhong Haicai slammed the table and firmly promised that 500,000 yuan would be no problem.

The next day, he returned to Macau and told Achang and other co-workers about the "big business": "Now everyone has food to eat!" He borrowed 200,000 Hong Kong dollars from Achang and other co-workers at high interest rates. It was really difficult to borrow more. The deed for the Macau house was in his hands. After a slight hesitation, he mortgaged it to the bank and borrowed 300,000, a total of 500,000 Hong Kong dollars, which he handed over to Bai Lang.

Bai Lang described to him that after the project was completed and launched on the market next year, his 10% share would be able to get at least more than 5 million! After the house was redeemed and renamed Liang Xiangyun, Zhong Haicai could buy a big house in Macau and live comfortably for the rest of his life.

He also made a bad assumption and made a risk assessment in his mind. However, as long as the project was there, no one could move the built house. If he couldn't catch the moon, so why should he be afraid of not being able to catch a star? Thinking of this, he felt at ease.

Zhong Haicai accompanied Bai Lang to select the construction team, and the contractors of the two affiliated construction companies provided advance funds until the roof was completed.

Bai Lang had 500,000 yuan from Zhong Haicai as start-up capital, and he set up his business. He returned to Taiwan and used the same fascinating storytelling method, invited two old classmates to join, promising not to pay wages but to share dividends. The two old classmates hired two engineers. They lived together in the Gongbei Overseas Chinese Hotel. They worked day and night for half a month and wrote a long project plan. The project was officially named "Guangdong Blue Dream Water Village Timeshare Resort".

Bai Lang held this plan like a pastor holding the Bible, and he was never tired of preaching it to people like playing a recording.

Bai Lang and the village committee signed a formal development contract:

The project covers an area of 500 mu, with eight canals forming a network. Time-share resort houses account for 60%, 667 rooms, and cover an area of 300 mu; commercial housing accounts for 20%, covering an area of 100 mu, and high-end double-story detached houses, medium-priced double-story detached houses, and cheap double-story townhouses would be built; the remaining 100 mu would be used as supporting land, such as helicopter airports, hospitals, parks, and office buildings.

The plan had a very detailed explanation, and even the location and number of garbage bins were clearly marked. The resort houses would pay the village committee 8,000 yuan per mu of rent every year from the time they move in, and the rent increases year by year.

The chapter "Sales Sample" in the business plan states:

Blue Dream Water Village concept; time-sharing resort house concept; private cars and yachts can be directly moored in the holiday house; sea, land and air concept...... *Hong Kong, Macau, Guangzhou, back garden concept......*

Beautiful environment, free check-in method, convenient transportation, and all-round high-quality services, this was Bai Lang's concept of "Blue Dream Water Village Timeshare Resort". He believed that the resort would definitely trigger a revolution in the mainland holiday hotel industry, tourism and leisure, and investment concepts.

Bai Lang recruited a group of sales staff in the city. He used inflammatory words to teach the promotion sales staff. Customers could buy a standard room to live in any seven days of the year for 20 years; if they would not live in, the management company could rent it out at a five-star hotel fee; buy now for 120 yuan per day, and rent it out after completion for a net income of 300 yuan per day, with a profit of 180 yuan......

Bai Lang said that once the sale started, 100 million cash would be received within two months. All problems such as project funds and land funds had been solved! Once the project started, there would be proof for bank loans, and the subsequent funds of 300 million would be raised through Hong Kong.

Soon, a group of people who specialized in capital business in Guangzhou brought people who did capital business in Hong Kong to the resort for inspection. Bai Lang shuttled between Guangzhou and Hong Kong. The financing procedure was complicated. First, he had to find investors in Hong Kong and sign contracts with them. The investors planned to deposit the money into a bank in Hong Kong. The Hong Kong bank also asked Bai Lang to find a receiving bank in Guangzhou. The two banks also had to sign a contract. After Guangzhou Bank applied for a credit scale from the superior bank, it could discuss the contract terms with the Hong Kong bank.

It took Bai Lang more than three months to find out the way. Bai Lang spent half of the 500,000 yuan that Zhong Haicai brought on financing. Bai Lang was generous when entertaining, and he went to high-end Western restaurants and seafood restaurants. When he was not entertaining, he was extremely frugal and hid in the room with his negotiation assistant to eat instant noodles.

The financing intermediary notified Bai Lang again and again to submit additional materials, and notified Bai Lang again and again to "go back and wait for good news." But again and again, for various reasons, Bai Lang's expectations were dashed. He often didn't even have money to treat people to a meal. Whenever his Taiwanese friends came or invited officials from related departments to dinner, he would ask the business owners he knew in Zhuhai to pay the bill, and he would often borrow money from his friends for three to five thousand yuan. The local Taiwanese businessmen or local acquaintances said behind his back that he was a liar. Gradually, he couldn't even borrow small amounts of money.

Bai Lang lived and ate in the contractor's shed, and his eyes were always red from staying up all the time. His wife suffered from severe gout in Taiwan and couldn't stand up straight for a long time. She would call him from time to time to complain: asking for money for treatment, his son always went to the Internet cafe, skipped school, and asked him when he would return to Taiwan...... Every time, he was heartbroken. He said that on the day the project was completed, he would find a corner and cry alone.

When he couldn't relieve his mental pressure and inner pain, he would take the contractor to karaoke to sing. He sang "Ghost" in English in a tactful and moving way.

However, the best way for him to vent his emotions was to find a woman. The target was of course Lili, a woman who understood him and had feelings for him, a woman who could sleep with him whether he had money or not. When Lili was not available, he would go to the front of a big hotel and pick a girl from a group of streetwalkers, bargain the price to the lowest, and take her to the hotel to have sex with her. Only then did he feel the reality of life, without hypocrisy or humiliation. Only then did he truly feel like a human being. His crazy movements in bed frightened the lady, and she shed tears of begging for mercy in pain. He also often shed tears of pain on the girl's naked chest and cried with her head in his arms.

17

Migrant girls open a fresh fruit shop together

Zhong Haicai worshipped Zheng Jianxin as a bodhisattva, and he regarded it as a repentance of the sin to God not touching her at night.

Zheng Jianxin did not let herself be idle. In addition to doing housework every day and delivering herbal tea to Zhong Haicai's construction site, she would also buy some cheap fruits every few days and deliver them to the factory for those sisters.

It was Sunday, and Zheng Jianxin rode a bicycle to the factory with a large basket of apples, lychees and other fruits. Aju and Afang, who heard the news, welcomed her to the newly built seven-story dormitory building not far from the factory, and carried the fruits into the dormitory.

"Wow, it's really a big upgrade!" Zheng Jianxin "inspected" and found that the 16-square-meter room had four bunk beds, which was much better than more than 20 people living in a large house. At the top of the building was a bathroom with ten showers. "It's much more comfortable now, and I don't have to worry about not being able to take a shower!"

Aju wiped her sweaty neck. Her skin was surprisingly white, but she was chubby and sweaty when she moved. Her left hand kept rubbing the joint of her right thumb and said, "These are all documents from above. The factory cannot be inhabited. I'm afraid there will be a lake (fire) disaster......"

"Look at your big tongue!" Before Aju could say anything, the quick-talking Afang laughed and retorted to her, "It's not a lake disaster, it's a fire! "

The three of them laughed.

Jianxin stopped laughing: "Guangdong people don't say 'tongue'.

157

'tongue' is homophonic with 'erosion', which is not good for doing business. Otherwise, why restaurants call pig tongues as 'pig profit'?"

Afang held Zheng Jianxin's shoulders: "Haha, you are talking about Guangdong superstitions after living with your Macau husband!"

"I don't believe in these! I'm just telling you. Be careful not to make the narrow-minded Guangdong people unhappy!" She looked down and saw that Aju was still rubbing her fingers, "Why does your hand hurt?"

Afang said: "It's because of work! "

Zheng Jianxin knew that Aju was at the next procedure after her "printing" on the assembly line. After the drying processing, Aju wound the wire on the magnetic core, that is, winding the enameled wire. The winding was electric, and she had to move the wire up and down by herself. A finished product had fifty coils, not less or more, and it had to be arranged evenly and not bulge.

Aju said: "Now the piece rate has increased. The original quota was to roll 350 coils per hour, 1.8 yuan. You know, it's the same price as printing, and now it has been raised to 5.5 yuan." At this point, Aju glanced at Afang and smiled: "Now there is overtime pay!"

Zheng Jianxin didn't understand what Aju meant by smiling eyes, and stared at Afang. Afang was tall and strong, with a pair of beautiful legs under her denim shorts. She shook her short braids, chuckled, and whispered: "I went to the Labor Bureau to complain against the boss lady, and the Labor Bureau came to investigate. Now the overtime pay for working at night is 1.5 times, and the overtime pay for working on Saturdays and Sundays is twice. Now everyone can get more than 1,000 yuan a month!"

"Good!" Zheng Jianxin punched Afang's shoulder twice.

Aju said: "Alas, what's good about it! The food cost has increased, and the shampoo outside has increased in price. I want to eat better and wear better, but I am still a person from paycheck to paycheck! "

"What are the bosses doing!" Afang said, "It seems that the salary has been adjusted three times, but each time it was after the government proposed the minimum wage line, there was no way not to adjust it! The salary is calculated to be a little lower than the minimum wage, and then the overtime pay and bonus that the workers can get are calculated so that the total amount just exceeds the minimum wage. The boss is always thinking about making money from our hard-earned money! Last year, the average monthly salary of employees in the province was 2,454 yuan, and we barely got half of it. Alas, what should we do?"

Aju frowned slightly and whispered to Afang: "You have to be careful, I think the boss's eyes are not right when she looks at you! "

Afang shook her pigtails twice and said the vulgar curse words just learned: "F..k her mother, I learned from Sister Jian, I will fire her before she fires me! As the saying goes: People are equal who don't ask for help!"

Aju pretended to be pitiful: "But we may not be able to find a good husband in Macau like Sister Jian!"

Aju's words were full of meaning. Recently, someone is introducing a date to Afang, who was the nephew of a villager who went to Macau a few years before and drove a taxi in Macau.

Afang's face turned red, and she laughed and started to fight with Aju, "I don't rely on anyone, I just rely on my own hands!" Zheng Jianxin looked at Aju again, her eyes asking "What about you?"

Aju made a face and said self-deprecatingly, "I have become a leftover girl!"

Zheng Jianxin said: "There will be bread, and everything you want will be there, just wait for fate, fate is coming soon, don't worry, Aju! "

Zheng Jianxin stopped smiling, and her watery eyes moved around their faces twice in approval. She was 70% sure about what she was going to say to them next.

Wipe the sweat off her face, Zheng Jianxin pointed to the baskets full of various fruits, and said to the sisters who gathered around with a smile: "Okay, these are enough for you to eat for a week. Just eat a few lychees a day, it will cause internal heat; dragon fruit can be kept, and northern apples can be kept for a week."

The female workers were very happy, and they shared the fruits. Aju poured water for Zheng Jianxin, and Afang took out a stack of money from the drawer and handed it to her: "Ajian, thank you, this is this week's labor fee."

Zheng Jianxin took the money and looked at it: "Why is it so much, it doesn't take so much. I bought these fruits in bulk from the wholesale market. Lychees are "small year" this year, and the better varieties, glutinous rice cakes are more than ten yuan per catty when they are on the market. Now in July, there are a lot of fruits. Outside, they are selling for 6 yuan per pound, but we can buy them for 10 yuan for 3 pounds. Lychees are almost off the market, and longans will be available in ten days. I want you to eat fresh ones!"

Aju pressed her hand and said, "Then you should take them. We all want to thank you very much! If you hadn't sent us fruits every week in the past few months, we would have collapsed long ago."

"That's right," Afang also chimed in, "Sisters often eat your fruit, so you should charge some labor fees! This is what we should do."

Speaking of this, she chuckled, "I know you are the wife of a boss in Macau and you are not short of money. But if you don't take this money, we will feel uneasy. Maybe one day you will forget about us and stop sending fruit; maybe one day it will be difficult to meet you after leaving for Macau!"

"Well......" Zheng Jianxin thought about it and stopped declining. She took the money, put her arm around Afang's shoulders, and said with a smile: "Don't talk about Macau!"

Looking at the way the female workers were laughing and sharing the fruit, Zheng Jianxin motioned for the two to sit down and whispered: "I have always had an idea. There are so many factories here and many people working. You say, how great it would be if I could send them fruit every day!"

"Are you Superman?" Aju screamed, "There are at least 5,000 workers in this factory, how much food do we need? Can you deliver it? Besides, where do you get so much money to buy fruit?"

"Then let's pool our money!" Zheng Jianxin smiled with her index finger hooked. Aju pouted: "Am I stupid? I finally earned some hard-earned money, why should I buy fruit for others for free?"

"What about you?" Zheng Jianxin smiled and blinked at Afang. Afang tilted her head and thought for a while, then she understood what she meant. She smiled and raised her index finger: "I agree!"

Aju looked at her index finger: "What do you agree with? Hey, what are you laughing at?"

Afang made a face and said: "You are an idiot, but you are worse than an idiot. Can Sister Jian let us buy fruit for free? She is trying to get us to do business!"

Aju looked at the smiling Zheng Jianxin and suddenly realized: "Okay, okay!" Then she whispered: "I heard that the bosses of several factories here want to move their factories to Vietnam or Myanmar, but they haven't decided yet. I've been thinking about what to do next!" She looked at Zheng Jianxin and her eyes lit up, "That's good. Let's pool some money and open a 'Fruit Girl' fresh fruit store to deliver fruit to the workers here!"

"Haha, who said she's an idiot? She is not an idiot at all!" Zheng Jianxin said teasingly. "That's right!" Aju took advantage of the situation and made a face at Afang, "I'm smart, I understand the reason -- if a grandmother doesn't let her daughter to marry, how can she have a grandson to hold!"

"I said you were fat, and you gasped immediately" Afang was not to be outdone, she raised her hand and started to play with her, and accidentally hit Zheng Jianxin.

The three girls screamed and laughed and rolled into a fight.

After the fight, sentimental Aju asked worriedly, "Sister Jian, can we do this for a long time?"

"Yes!" Zheng Jianxin said affirmatively, "The factory is far from the city, and to do business with migrant workers is not profitable, so vendors are unwilling to come. The fruit shops around the factory buy market-priced fruits from formal channels, and their prices are higher than the market price. Aren't you not eating because you can't afford it? The goods we buy are half, or two or three times cheaper than the market price. We make small profits but quick turnover. If the migrant workers don't buy ours, whose will they buy?"

"So you have planned it all?" Afang and Aju said in unison, admiring Zheng Jianxin.

"How dare I tell you without a plan?" Zheng Jianxin sighed, "In this society, if you want to make more money and change your fate, you have to rely on your own brains. As the saying goes, people with one mind are stronger than tigers!"

Afang nodded with deep feeling and said in Cantonese: "How can you get worldly wealth without hard work!"

"You speak Cantonese really well!" Zheng Jianxin praised her.

Aju revealed her secrets: "She has already prepared for a long-term plan!"

The three of them laughed happily. After the other workers had divided the fruits, Zheng Jianxin told them her plan again, "A single thread cannot make a line, and a single tree cannot make a forest", to see if anyone is willing to join and work together. She said it very clearly and thoroughly, "this business will also be very hard, and the profit may not be much at the beginning, but it is our own business, we don't have to suffer from others' anger, and we don't have to be bounded to the assembly line, asking for permission every day to go to the toilet,   "

Finally, three more sisters expressed their willingness to join.

This result made them very excited and proud. They could make money without being bullied by others. For them, what could be better than this? Moreover, they jointly invested in the business, so they were the bosses and masters!

Then several people got together to start planning, striving to consider every detail.

Zheng Jianxin said: "We want to turn the seemingly mediocre business into an outstanding enterprise; we want to turn our small capital and thin profit, and scattered and long sales outlets into opportunities for our business; we want to turn our current vision and enthusiasm for doing business into facts and make money." She looked at everyone, "And the most important point is that we should treat our co-workers well: a relaxed working environment means mutual friendship; a relaxed economic environment means that after making money, we should keep enough three funds (reserve funds, welfare funds and enterprise development funds), pay according to work, and give all to co-workers; a relaxed development environment means that co-workers should continue to learn, improve themselves, and change their destiny with knowledge! "

Zheng Jianxin's words opened Afang and Aju's minds; Zheng Jianxin's words expressed what they were thinking but didn't know how to express accurately. The two were so excited that their hearts were pounding.

They finally had their own careers and created their own lives. Girls laughed and sang when they were happy. Zheng Jianxin said: "Can I sing a song for you? 'We Promised Not to Break Up'."

Hearing the title of the song, Aju happily shouted: "You sing a love song? "

Zheng Jianxin smiled but didn't answer, she started to sing:

We agreed not to break up, I don't mind your poverty, you don't mind my ugliness;
We agreed not to break up, for a new life, for equality;
We agreed not to break up, our fingers are connected to our hearts, we hold hands;
We agreed not to break up, we will move forward together, and never break up.

The melody was beautiful, the lyrics were easy to remember, the sisters sang together......

The next day, Afang and Aju resolutely quit their jobs at the factory, and came to Zheng Jianxin's home on Gaosha Street in Gongbei. They took out more than 10,000 yuan they had collected, rented a house in

Xiawan, bought a few old bicycles for delivery, a beam scale and a large bamboo basket for fruit, and started their entrepreneurial career.

Every morning, Zheng Jianxin took the five sisters to the Guanwai Fruit Wholesale Market , buy those fruits that cost ten yuan a bunch. These fruits that were damaged, rotten, or not good-looking due to transportation or long storage were useless to wholesalers. It was troublesome to pick them up, time-consuming and labor-intensive. It was a pity to throw them away directly, so they were shoveled out with a big shovel, poured out in a big basket and piled on the ground, so that people who needed cheap products could pick them up by themselves to buy, or the fruits could be sold at a low price by piles.

What Zheng Jianxin and her friends had to do was to pick out the good or not-so-rotten fruits from the piles and send them to the factory area to sell. The price of the fruits produced in this way was naturally much lower than that on the market.

Picking and choosing among a pile of fruits that exuded a strange smell were a tiring and torturous job, especially for girls. Sometimes they have to wear masks to continue working.

"People should have ambitions, and horses should have spirits!" This was what Zheng Jianxin encouraged her sisters every day.

"Compared to working in the factory, it's not very tiring, but there are too many rotten ones......" This was what Afang sighs every day.

"This is nonsense. If they were all good fruits, wholesalers would be stupid to sell them to us in bulk. Or you can seduce them and let us benefit from it. This is what Aju and her friends would tease every day.

After picking out the good fruits, Zheng Jianxin and her friends would wash them several times until all the foreign matter and odor on them were washed away.

It was noon when they finished all this. After eating fast food lunch, they rode their bicycles carrying various fruits and set off -- Zheng Jianxin's bamboo basket were always the fullest and heaviest with fruits.

They walked and stopped along the way, and arrived at the factory area near dusk, then dispersed and rushed to the gates of various factories.

At this time, it was the time for workers to change shifts. They were very happy to see someone delivering fruits to their doorsteps. The fruits would be sold out in less than two hours.

After a few days, the business was going smoothly. Zheng Jianxin and her friends made a rough calculation and found that the average daily sales were around 2,000 yuan, and they made a net profit of nearly 350 yuan after deducting the cost.

The fruit business was going very well. Zheng Jianxin and Afang discussed it and decided to pull a few more sisters out of the factory and expand the business scope to factories in other places to benefit more workers.

Since they were going to do business, they must do it legitimately, so as not to be caught by the "urban management" and have the baskets thrown into the sea. For this reason, Zheng Jianxin, after discussing with several sisters, went to the Industrial and Commercial Bureau to register a business license and legitimately opened two branches in other factory areas in Zhuhai. Afang and Aju were responsible for each, with unified distribution and unified prices.

The expansion of the business made Zheng Jianxin even busier. In her spare time, Zheng Jianxin began to read some management books and got inspiration from them. She bought social insurance for all the people in the fruit shop so that they would have no worries and work harder and more attentively.

Zheng Jianxin's approach touched Afang and the other sisters, especially the new comers who had no shares in the fruit shop. They not only worked hard, but also spread the goodness of Zheng Jianxin and the others everywhere, and brought in a few more people for the fruit shop.

"Fruit Girl", the reputation of the fresh fruit shop for its cheap prices spread among the workers. In addition to their stability and punctuality, workers from various factories basically patronized their business, making their business increasingly prosperous.

Zheng Jianxin was more excited than anyone else. However, she was not in a hurry to share the money with her sisters. Except for the necessary daily living expenses and working capital, the rest was saved.

She made it very clear: Zhuhai and Zhongshan are adjacent, there were so many factories, and there were more than 100,000 workers in the two neighboring towns. They shouldn't just focus on one factory. They would open chain stores in the future and extend to the factories they could reach.

Afang and the others agreed with Zheng Jianxin's words. Thinking about expanding the business in the future, their eyes flickered.

After doing the fruit business, Zheng Jianxin no longer delivered herbal tea to Zhong Haicai's construction site, but worked hard from dawn to dusk until she was so tired that she couldn't even stand.

She worked so hard , first of all, to make more money and truly had a career of her own, and then she would keep herself busy until she was numb, so as to avoid Zhong Haicai. At night, she would do her accounts and read until Zhong Haicai started snoring before going to bed, to avoid Zhong Haicai's sexual desire that always made her fearful.

18

As a wife, Ajian lives like this

The "Blue Dream" project was progressing smoothly, and Zhong Haicai was intoxicated in the dream of getting rich, and he crossed his chest from time to time. He put on a formal posture: he wore a suit and tie in the hot summer, saying that he often dealt with officials and it was a work requirement. But he was really not used to such formal clothes in a suit and leather shoes, and his muscles would twitch here and there from time to time, which made him look very weird.

In the past few years, whenever he was lonely, he would always beg Lili to introduce him to a girlfriend. Although Lili said that she lived an unclear life, she would never associate with girls who made a living by sex, so as not to make people mistakenly think that she was with them. She always said without care "OK, OK, I will introduce you if there is a suitable one". Most of the northern girls Lili knew were well-educated. They were self-righteous, and some were shrew. No one liked him who was old and poor. Achang once said to Lili: For those of them who live at the bottom of society, life was just to work and make love.

With Zheng Jianxin, the home in Gongbei was like a magnet. Zhong Haicai rushed back as fast as he could after work, and no longer hung around with Achang and other workers. As long as he was with Zheng Jianxin, he would change his work clothes, shave off his stubble, and clean himself up. After getting off work, he rarely went out and never touched other women. Achang said: "Ajian has purified Zhong Haicai's soul! "

In the first few nights after Zheng Jianxin moved in, Zhong Haicai was afraid of irritating her, so he slept on the sofa obediently and didn't even dare to approach the bed.

For Zheng Jianxin, she stepped into Zhong Haicai's house, and fate made her Zhong Haicai's woman! She looked at Zhong Haicai's naked body on the sofa, restless in the long night, and felt uneasy about her own stalemate. On the night when Zheng Jianxin decided to start a fruit business, she took the initiative to pull Zhong Haicai's hand to the bed, told him her thoughts and decisions in a friendly manner, and asked him for some capital to make up for the share.

Zhong Haicai, who had been living in fear for the past month, saw his beloved woman finally turning from coldness to warmth, how could he not be happy and open his heart and flatter her.

Then, Zhong Haicai tentatively put one hand around Zheng Jianxin and stroked her slender waist with the other hand. Zheng Jianxin immediately got goose bumps all over her body, but she did not resist on the surface. Zheng Jianxin was nervous and frightened, and her body was trembling, like a patriot who was ready to die on the execution ground, lying on the bed with her eyes closed, motionless.

Zhong Haicai saw that the time had come, and he was overjoyed. He couldn't wait to take off Zheng Jianxin's shirt and her shorts. Zheng Jianxin closed her eyes tightly and didn't dare to even look at him. She was worried that as soon as she saw his lower abdomen she would not be able to help but jump off the bed and run away. She tried hard to treat him as her husband, just bear with it.

Zhong Haicai felt that he was dreaming, the most wonderful dream of his life. Zhong Haicai could no longer bear it, and he turned over and covered her, pressing her white and tender body deeply into the mattress......

Tears seeped out from the corners of Zheng Jianxin's eyes. She was motionless, clenched her fists and tensed her whole body to let Zhong Haicai ravage her, thinking about how to start the fruit business tomorrow and in the future......

After a long roar, Zhong Haicai finally stopped and let out a long breath.

Zheng Jianxin also let out a long breath, used all her strength to push away the fat on her body, picked up her clothes and walked into the bathroom expressionlessly.

After closing the door, Zheng Jianxin turned on the shower to the maximum, rubbing her body over and over again, trying to wipe off every trace of Zhong Haicai and every trace of his smell from her body......

At this time, Zhong Haicai was intoxicated with happiness. He was very proud that God had given him a beautiful fairy who was hard to find in Macau and Zhuhai!

After that, Zhong Haicai danced happily all day long and showed off to everyone he met, constantly boasting about his charm in front of Achang and other workers. He was only willing to reveal a little bit of privacy: "Ajian's white arms feel as smooth as silk", which made Achang and his group of people envious. They all said that he didn't know how many lifetimes he had cultivated for his blessings, which made people jealous.

Zhong Haicai also said: "Even if there are women prettier than Zheng Jianxin, are they as virtuous as her? Even if there are women more virtuous than her, are they as pretty as her? "Zhong Haicai's tongue was rarely so eloquent, his words made the workers furious.

Every morning when she combed her hair and looked in the mirror, Zheng Jianxin would secretly admire her own beauty when she saw her jade-like face. At this time, she thought of Zhong Haicai's face with wrinkles on his forehead, and she sighed in her heart, "If only he could be 20 years old, how nice it would be!"

Whenever she and Zhong Haicai went out on the street and met with strange eyes from pedestrians, she sighed in her heart, thinking how nice it would be if she was 40 years old all of a sudden, and older!

In the dark night, when she smelled the stinky smoke coming out of Zhong Haicai's mouth, she would immediately turn over and face him in anger. She thought, if it was Xu Zhuang instead of Zhong Haicai, she would tenderly offer herself to him and snuggle up to him like a little bird, how ecstatic that would be.

Whenever Zhong Haicai wanted to kiss her secretly at home, she would vigilantly shake her head left and right to avoid his mouth. She thought, if it were Xu Zhuang instead of Zhong Haicai, she would definitely greet him warmly, how intoxicated that would be.

Whenever they went out on the street, Zhong Haicai would walk behind her with inferiority and keep a distance. She thought, if it were Xu Zhuang instead of Zhong Haicai, she would definitely hold his hand, how comfortable that would be.

However, all this was just her thinking, thinking, and in the end, she was dreaming and soul-destroying.

She regretted that she had lost too much, and that what was irreplaceable was lost forever. People in her hometown said that she and Xu Zhuang were a perfect match, but due to some strange circumstances, they were not destined to be together. She could no longer hear Xu Zhuang reciting Whitman and Tagore's poems to her. In the face of the harsh living environment: noble emotions and "petty bourgeois" sentiments were all torn to pieces and were worthless!

Sometimes she looked at Zhong Haicai with sympathy. If Zhong had not found her, but a woman of similar age, without education and without many aspirations, Zhong would have received the woman's true love and careful care in life even in the hardest days. It was his misfortune that Zhong possessed her.

Zheng Jianxin was diligent, and cooking and washing clothes were not a problem. But her deep rebellious consciousness made her wait for Zhong Haicai to finish work, let him drag his tired body to do it, and she watched from the side. When Zhong Haicai went to take a shower, she thought that if it were Xu Zhuang, she would wash his feet for him; but in reality, she angrily called Zhong to come over and wash her feet over and over again. She got some pleasure of revenge from it intentionally or unintentionally, and looked at the most unfortunate man in the world with a bit of gloating eyes!

Zheng Jianxin came through with a complicated heart like this. The saying goes "love grows over time", and slowly Ajian got used to it. Since she was his woman, whether she loved him or not, whether she loved him deeply or not, she should give him everything a woman could give to her husband! When she couldn't do it, she forced herself to do it hard......

Zhong Haicai served Zheng Jianxin meticulously. Every day, he finished work early and cooked delicious soup for her to come back. After dinner, he washed her feet to promote blood circulation, and then followed her to the beach for a walk; when he went out in the morning, he repeatedly reminded her to be careful at work, to wear a mask when picking fruits, not to ride fast, and to let people who buy fruits line up......

Although Zhong Haicai rarely went out after work, he was always uneasy at home. He didn't know which unpleasant words or rough actions would make Ajian frown. He would peek at Ajian's face from time to time. He often worried about how to hide, but didn't know what to hide. He often sighed subconsciously, and his life was really tiring.

A few months later, Zheng Jianxin felt that Zhong Haicai was not so bad after all -- at least he was impeccable in housework during this period, so she slowly regained her calm and stopped torturing him. However, Zheng Jianxin's anguish could not be eliminated. Every time she went out with Zhong Haicai, the strange expressions of passersby made her feel like a thorn in her back, and she wanted to stay three meters away from him. She was not afraid of others laughing at the mismatch between the two. What she could not stand was the contemptuous eyes of those who regarded her as a "mistress" who was greedy for money: "Mistress!"

For this reason, Zheng Jianxin sometimes urged Zhong Haicai to go back to her hometown with her several times a day to get a marriage certificate. Only when she truly became his wife, she felt that she could stand in the sun with him and accept everyone's scrutiny.

Zhong Haicai also felt that he was in the wrong. But he simply could not spare the time to go back to Guizhou in the mainland with Zheng Jianxin to handle the marriage procedures. Bai Lang said that shareholders would not be paid wages, so Zhong Haicai had to go back to Macau to work. Bai Lang also found various excuses to ask Zhong

Haicai to go to the "Blue Dream" construction site to discuss work every now and then, but there was nothing important to discuss when he went there. When Bai Lang did not look for him, he himself went to the "Blue Dream" construction site with concerns. In order to make Zheng Jianxin happy and at the same time make up for his guilt, though he did not know computers, he bought a laptop from Macau for Zheng Jianxin to play with.

19

Chen Xiao shouted "What a tragedy!"

Chen Xiao went to Russia and Eastern Europe, and met Achang when he came back through the customs gate. Achang told him that Zheng Jianxin and Zhong Haicai lived together and moved to Zhong Haicai's house.

This unexpected thing for Chen Xiao was like a bolt from the blue, which shocked him so much that he couldn't speak for a long time. After a long time, he rubbed his hands slowly, regardless of the public occasion, and actually shouted: "What a tragedy, what a tragedy! ......" Then he cried with his mouth twisted.

Achang held Chen Xiao and walked out of the customs building, persuading him as they walked: "Mr. Chen, why are you doing this? What's strange about a woman being with someone?"

"You don't understand! You don't understand!...... The jade is broken and the fragrance is gone!" Chen Xiao's mouth was drooling, "What is tragedy? It's the destruction of beautiful things for people to see. The Special Administrative Region is a shitty place, it pollutes a person faster and more severely than the Chernobyl nuclear pollution...... Ajian is for money, for becoming a Hong Kong and Macao citizen......"

Achang understood that what Chen Xiao meant was that a beautiful flower was stuck in cow dung, and a heavenly dog ate the sun. "As long as she is willing, it is none of our business whether them match or not!"

"Talented woman, talented woman!" Chen Xiao couldn't stop sighing. Aliang once showed him the clippings of Ajian's essays "Praise Life" and other articles. He was furious, "But Zhong Haicai is illiterate! An illiterate who can only write his name!"

Achang didn't care whether Chen Xiao was fair or felt guilty for not

173

caring enough, and whispered, "Is it because you can't eat grapes, you are jealous, and you say others are jealous, and you are sad and hopeless!"

Chen Xiao waved his hand and punched Achang in the ribs: "What do you know!"

Chen Xiao's heart was in pain and self-blame that outsiders could not understand.

Achang saw that he was worried, so he pulled him to a cafe to sit down.

Chen Xiao pulled the tie around his neck and slammed the briefcase heavily on the table.

Chen Xiao's feeling for Zheng Jianxin was complicated, and this complicated feeling was mixed with the unclear grievances between the two families. During the "Cultural Revolution", Chen Xiao accompanied his father Chen Bo to the countryside to seek refuge and met Zheng Jianxin's grandfather and father.

In 1950, the hometown of Guizhou was carrying out land reform and suppressing bandits at the same time. Zheng Jianxin's grandfather Zheng He was the village party secretary. He cooperated with the land reform team to divide the floating wealth of the landlord Chen Bo's father's family. After Chen Bo knew about it, he rode back to the village overnight, pointed his whip at Zheng He and said angrily: "I risked my life to fight against bandits in the mountains, but you raided my house. Whoever took anything from our house must return it in the same state!" The land reform team reported Chen Bo's problem to the Party organization. Chen Bo made a self-criticism and was punished. From then on, Chen Bo and Zheng He, a pair of young good friends in the village who vowed to liberate the world's toiling people, had a feud.

Zheng He was promoted to the section chief of the county agricultural bureau because of his solid and outstanding work performance. In the difficult economic period of 1960, in order to reduce the pressure of administrative expenses, the state proposed to streamline the government and called on cadres to be transferred to the countryside. Zheng He took the lead and led his family to move back to the countryside to be farmers.

Although Zheng He served as the deputy secretary of the village, the villagers spread rumors behind his back that he had made mistakes in the county town: "If he hadn't made mistakes, could he come back? He must have been fired!" What mistakes did he make? No one could tell. In that era, the country was poor and officials had nothing to embezzle, so it must be a problem of love affairs! Word spread from one person to ten, and from ten to a hundred, and Zheng He's affairs were fabricated in great details.

In Chen Xiao's opinion, the root cause of Zheng He's misfortune in the countryside was that he did not follow the town leaders and the village secretary closely. When the class struggle was being carried out in the countryside, Chen Bo's father, who was a "landlord", died, and Chen Bo's ex-wife was promoted to "landlord's wife" and was constantly criticized. Zheng He thought of his comradeship with Chen Bo and his sympathy for the widowed woman, and sent firewood to her on her sickbed in winter. When the "Four Cleanups Campaign" was launched to investigate "four unclean" cadres, Zheng He was labeled as "four unclean" and resigned. From then on, he became a person with historical problems that several generations of people in the village looked at differently. And his wife and children kept complaining and scolding him every day: "If you hadn't been sent down to the countryside, we would all be city dwellers now, and we wouldn't be peasants who have to endure endless hardships......"

When Chen Bo returned to his hometown to seek refuge, the two old comrades went to the fields to work and chat. When returning to the city, Chen Bo grabbed Zheng He's hand and said with emotion: "Brother, you are a good person, and you will be rewarded......"

Chen Bo and Zheng He sang the song they often sang when they were young, "We Promised Not to Break Up":

We promised not to break up, eat meat together, drink together;

We promised not to break up, you don't mind my poverty, I don't mind your ugliness;

175

We promised not to break up, for a new life, for equality;

We promised not to break up, ten fingers connected to the heart, forever hand in hand.

After Chen Xiao's father returned to the city and resumed his post, he gradually forgot about Zheng He. He remembered what Zheng Bo said: "When we were fighting for the poor, we were all together. After the revolution was successful, everyone was busy with their own things." Chen Xiao described himself as a man with conscience, and he often felt guilty when he thought of this.

Zheng Jianxin's tragedy made this guilt Chen Xiao's lifelong repentance. He regretted it. Why didn't he come forward and arrange a good job for her? Besides, it was not difficult to arrange a clerk in a company or his branch here, but he just stuffed her into a circle full of cheap labor and dealt with it hastily.

While lamenting Zheng Jianxin's question, he couldn't help but lament himself. It was that vain wife Jiaojiao who pushed him, who didn't expect wealth and didn't know how to do business, to the road of business. He lost two business deals in a row, which made him very anxious. His superiors and colleagues looked at him sideways for being a person who got promoted by nepotism. Some even avoided him as if he were an infectious disease. He was like a spiritual beggar wandering on the street, not knowing where to go.

He didn't want to go home. Whenever he approached the stairs, his heart would tighten. When he entered the door, he would see Jiaojiao's cold and ferocious eyes: "Money, where is the money you earned?!"

He also hated Mrs. Tong and her husband. In order to repay and please their former boss Chen Bo, they easily transferred Chen Xiao to the foreign trade company with a few words. Mrs. Tong often instigated Jiaojiao: "If you can't make money, don't blame me for not helping. The foreign trade company goes in and out of Hong Kong and Macau every day. You can do public and private business. Some business can be promoted to do kickbacks and commissions...... Look at Luoluo's husband taking money home every day!"

Under the instigation of others, Jiaojiao looked at Chen Xiao like looking at a hornet's nest, with holes full of problems. When she heard that others had made some money, she would get angry and put the blame on him for not being able to manage money: "Look, the house that others bought for more than 3,000 yuan per square meter has increased to more than 6,000 yuan...... Look, Mrs. Tong's Hetian jade bracelet that cost 20,000 yuan has increased to 50,000 yuan, and it is said that it will increase...... You have eaten your food in vain, and your father gave birth to you so mentally retarded......"

Without money, there is no dignity; if you can't make money, you can't be respected. Chen Xiao became the object of people's ridicule. When his wife was scolding him in front of others, they showed more contempt. When he was in Guangzhou, he had his own philosophical research topic. With books as company, Chen Xiao was not afraid of loneliness. There were countless good friends in the books. Entering the books was like entering a warm world. When he arrived at the company, except for talking about business and money, it was like falling into an ice cave, without a smile, without a warm word. People who were very familiar to him seemed to be strangers. They stood back to back and quietly and busily looked for various ways to make money.

Jiaojiao said bluntly: "What does it mean to be able to make money? It's to put your face in your pants!" After not seeing each other for a few years, old friends who made money and got promoted felt that they had status. In addition to continuing to smile at people with higher status, they mostly looked down on those who were not as good as them. There were also a large number of old friends who had not made a name for themselves, and they all lived in seclusion very tactfully. The people Chen Xiao saw were like the negatives of undeveloped black and white photos, just white figures, flat, silent, and bloodless.

Only when he thought of the pure Zheng Jianxin did he feel a little warm in his heart. Zheng Jianxin was a ray of light in his dark kingdom and an oasis in his dirty world. Now this beautiful idol was also smashed to pieces by the cruel life, and was polluted and changed by the temptation of money......

And Achang couldn't understand all this. Why do people live and how to live, this century-old topic has never been as confusing as it is today. Chen Xiao's heart was like a dry well. He loosened his tie, took off his glasses, and let out a heavy breath. Who could understand him? He opened his mouth, picked up the glass, and poured the bloody Madri Sa into his stomach.

Chen Xiao drank and cried: "I killed Ajian, I killed Ajian......" He was crying and shaking his head, sighing, and rubbing his hands.

Achang looked at his lost and insane appearance and found that his eye sockets were turning red, and then his eyes gradually became moist and shiny as if they were coated with oil, and his eyeballs were blurred. The guests around kept peeking at this place. Achang hurriedly pulled him up, "Let's go, let me take you to a place to change your mood, I guarantee you will broaden your horizons!"

Chen Xiao was not good at drinking, but he indulged himself in drinking. "What are you afraid of? It's water. I hope it's dichlorvos!" He used wine to mourn his broken heart.

Achang helped him to a nearby sauna and massage parlor.

His face turned red all the way to his chest. Achang smiled and handed him to the female technician and walked away. The female technician was about 20 years old, and her clothes were thin and revealing.

The female technician helped him to the big bed in the massage room.

The female technician asked in a low and considerate voice: "Sir, what do you want to drink......"

Chen Xiao's nose pulled the bellows (snoring), making a humming sound.

The female technician asked him loudly several times, and he said: "Tea, tea......"

The fragrant Tieguanyin tea arrived.

The female technician took a large laminated card, pushed Chen Xiao intimately, and said in a delicate voice, "Sir, sir, what service do you want?"

Chen Xiao still had a snorting sound. "We offer health massage here, with more than 20 services. Tell me where you feel uncomfortable or tired!"

The female technician looked at Chen Xiao who didn't respond. In order not to delay her work, she put a hairpin in her mouth, put her long brown hair on top of her head into a bun, and then took off Chen Xiao's suit.

Chen Xiao heard the girl's crisp voice in a daze. The scenery in front of him was picturesque. It was the mountainous area of Guizhou or some other fairyland. Otherwise, how could there be a strong fragrance, and a group of fairy-like girls swimming in the white mist with smiles......

The female technician said in a coquettish voice: "People who work in office buildings always have more cervical vertebrae strain. The first item is 'whispering'."

The female technician gently leaned on Chen Xiao. Her face was close to Chen Xiao's face, and she gently twisted his neck and his ears.

In the dream, the fairy's velvety fingers stroked Chen Xiao's face. Subtle changes were also taking place deep inside Chen Xiao's body. This gradual boiling shocked Chen Xiao so much that he woke up all of a sudden. He sat up suddenly and looked at the girl in front of him with very little clothes. He was shocked and terrified. He felt like he was in hell, and then he felt guilty!

He cried "Ah" and covered his face and cried.

He and Jiaojiao had been sleeping in separate beds for more than a year. Under Jiaojiao's scolding and the contemptuous eyes of everyone, his instinctive desire for warmth was not only extinguished psychologically, but also physically unresponsive. For a person who was incapable of making money, this was logical. Any more desire would be a luxury that should not be begged for.

What was incredible was that he was in the same room with a strange woman! Besides Jiaojiao, this was the first time he saw another woman's body with his own eyes. Of course, like many men, he had also fantasized about other women taking off their clothes. But that was a fleeting thing that was immediately driven away by the consciousness of "shame". In his heart, he had an unextinguished yearning for passionate love. Today, he not only desecrated the nobleness of "love" in his heart, but also fell into such a state.

"Wake up, you filthy person!" He buried his head deeply under the pillow, shaking his body and crying, "This is a crime! This is a crime!......"

20

Grandpa, your granddaughter apologizes to you from the bottom of her heart

More than a month later, Lili came back from her hometown.

When she learned that Zheng Jianxin and Zhong Haicai lived together, Lili first absolutely did not believe it, then was struck by thunder, and finally sighed deeply.

After asking Zheng Jianxin why she did this, Lili grabbed a kitchen knife and went downstairs to kill Zhong Haicai.

Seeing Zheng Jianxin's resigned look, she had no choice but to give up, but she felt deeply guilty.

"It's all my fault" Lili held Zheng Jianxin's shoulders with tears. If she had taken good care of Ajian, she would not have made such a big mistake. In such a short time, the world had turned upside down. The good sisters and cousin Xu Zhuang were no longer a pair of beautiful couple, and Ajian had become someone else's wife!

It was almost the first time in her life that she realized the "impermanence of life" and the ruthlessness of life! What also puzzled her was that Zheng Jianxin not only did not seek revenge and punish to the bad guy after being raped, but took the initiative to be his wife. It was not Ajian's character to give up on herself! What's more, Zhong Haicai had no charm, no money, and no manner. She couldn't know what Zheng Jianxin wanted from him?

However, Zheng Jianxin kept silent and didn't want to talk more. As soon as the topic changed, she happily talked to Lili about her fruit business, which changed Lili from cry to joy and she congratulated her repeatedly.

Zheng Jianxin deliberately didn't look at Lili's eyes, where into depth there was a trace of worry and self-blame. Lili also brought bad news to Zheng Jianxin.

Grandpa Zheng was dead!

When Lili handed Zheng Jianxin the letter from her father, she was mentally prepared, but she still couldn't help shaking all over, kneeling on the ground, crying.

When Lili spoke, in Zheng Jianxin's mind appeared the sad face of her grandfather who had never had a comfortable meal in his life, and her heart was like a lake filled with bitter sour water.

She felt guilty about her grandfather and could never forgive herself. She had seen her parents complain about her grandfather endlessly since she was a child. Sometimes her mother even gnashed her teeth and hated her grandfather, as if her grandfather was the source of all sufferings. She always blamed Grandpa for everything: "If it weren't for your Grandpa, I would be using tap water and washing machines in the city, and I would not have to use a washboard!" She would also complain when she went to the toilet: "People in the city poop at home and turn on the lights, but I have to run outside in the dark and cold. Who here has ever seen what electric lights look like? It's really a dark world!" Once at dinner, Grandpa was sick and didn't want to eat. Mother poured Grandpa's bowl of rice on the ground and yelled: "You think it's not delicious, right? You can't even eat this peasant meal. Think about what you have lived for? How many generations have you harmed?"

Grandpa was silent. In the 1980s, Grandpa, who was in his 50s, went to Chongqing and worked as a "bangbang man" (bale-hauler) at Chaotianmen Wharf. He was the first migrant worker in the village.

One day, he was carrying a load for a young female cadre. When he arrived at her home, her father-in-law, a director of a district, recognized Grandpa. He was a cadre under Grandpa when he was a section chief in the county. He hurriedly called out, "Old boss, why is it you!" He was kind-hearted. He took care of Grandpa's food and drink for a few days, sent someone to take Grandpa to the hospital to treat the sequelae of cerebral infarction, gave him money and clothes, sent a car to take Grandpa back to the village, and told him that "health is important and he can't work anymore." He also wrote a letter to the town government, introducing Grandpa's exemplary deeds in those years and saying many words praising the "old revolutionary."

Since then, the villagers and parents had changed their views on Grandpa. But the fate of "second-class citizens" he brought to his descendants was still "unforgivable."

Zheng Jianxin was invisibly influenced by her parents' words and deeds. When she was a child, she didn't like Grandpa to touch her. She also learned a few words from her mother and scolded Grandpa as "harmful spirit" and "not letting me go to kindergarten......" Later, when she grew up and became sensible, she felt pity for Grandpa, but she never said a word of repentance to him. This became her biggest regret in her life.

For three consecutive nights, Zheng Jianxin went to the beach to burn paper money for her grandfather. She knelt on the ground and cried to her grandfather with tears in her eyes: "Grandpa, facing the sky and the earth, your granddaughter apologizes to you from the bottom of her heart and repents to you! Please accept it!......"

Scenes of her grandfather's past passed by her eyes one after another. She remembered what her grandfather said: When we were fighting for the poor, we were all together during the revolution. When the revolution succeeded, everyone was busy with their own things. Child, you should work hard on your own and be a good person. You can't do things that harm others and benefit yourself! This was the grandfather's last words.

Knowing that Lili was back, Bai Lang and Achang of course came out one after another to get close to her, and a few days later, Zeng Sheng, who had been hiding for a long time, also appeared.

Zeng Sheng pushed Xu Zhuang into the fire pit and he was imprisoned. Zheng Jianxin regarded him as an enemy, but she didn't make a fuss like a shrew, shouting and killing. She knew that it would be useless. Zeng Sheng, who knew he was in the wrong, tried to avoid her as much as possible. When he couldn't avoid her, he smiled flatteringly and said he would treat her to tea, dinner and gifts.

In response, Zheng Jianxin just snorted coldly and didn't respond.

A few days later, Lili found out that she was pregnant. She panicked and hurried to Zheng Jianxin to discuss what to do.

"Whose child is it?" Zheng Jianxin frowned. This was really a confusing account.

Lili counted on her fingers for a long time before saying uncertainly: "It should be my husband's."

Zheng Jianxin looked at her suspiciously and said, "What are you going to do?"

"If I know what to do, why do I come to you to discuss it?!" Lili felt very aggrieved.

"You have to make sure whether you want to give birth first." Zheng Jianxin looked at her and asked calmly.

After two months of doing fruit business with a few sisters, her tone and demeanor became a little bit bossy.

After thinking for a while, Lili nodded affirmatively: "Yes! I like children."

Zheng Jianxin said "Oh", pondered for a while, and then said: "Then go back to your hometown to give birth! I think there may be a Three Kingdoms war for this child!"

Lili sighed and nodded, and then her eyes lit up again, rolling around. "What are you thinking?" Zheng Jianxin knew her very well and knew that she must be thinking some bad thoughts again.

"Nothing." Lili smiled, shook her head, stood up, and said while touching her belly without any fat.

She unbuttoned her dress, shook off her dress, and showed Zheng Jianxin her naked body. She touched her belly with her hands and showed it to Zheng Jianxin: "It's still flat and smooth. I'll go back in a few months. My baby...... Let's go back to our hometown to enjoy the beautiful mountains and rivers and the pollution-free air, not to mess around in this smoky and itchy place......"

Lili was going back to her hometown to give birth. After getting on the train, she sent a text message to Zeng Sheng, Bai Lang and Achang, saying that the climate and environment here were too bad, and she wanted to go home to take care of the baby and come back after giving birth. There was no need to see her off as they were busy.

Achang, who knew the inside story of Lili's life, was half-believing and half-doubting whether it was his child, but Zeng Sheng and Bai Lang were overjoyed. They said they would send money to Lili, send things and nutritional supplements, so that she could rest assured to take care of the baby and give birth smoothly. Of course, Lili would accept any offer.

As for Zeng Sheng's suggestion to find a snakehead to take her to Hong Kong to give birth on the due date, Lili turned it down on the ground that she was afraid that his wife would find out and kill her. In fact, for Zeng Sheng, it was just a lip service, just to make Lili happy and give her a rubble check, so he would not get himself into trouble.

21

Are you Ahua? You are so pretty

When Zheng Jianxin came back every day with a tired body, Zhong Haicai was often already home.

Looking at the big-bellied man who happily welcomed her into the house, and looking at his fat face who fawned on her like a pug, Zheng Jianxin calmly accepted his serving of meals, washing dishes, mopping the floor and doing housework.

A sense of revenge rose from time to time in Zheng Jianxin's heart.

She felt that Zhong Haicai was as unfortunate as herself.

Even so, three months later, Zheng Jianxin was horrified to find that she was pregnant!

This made her blame herself for being careless and regretful.

And Zhong Haicai was overjoyed, the three great joys in life: marrying a wife, having a child, and getting rich. Zhong Haicai felt that God really favored him too much.

When the Chinese New Year was approaching, Zheng Jianxin's belly was already slightly bulging. To be on the safe side, Zhong Haicai would not let her deliver fruit by bike. He only let her take the bus to the store to help during the day, and read books, calculate accounts, or plan the next step of the business at night.

That night, Zheng Jianxin was looking at the account book. Zhong Haicai came back from work in Macau. He looked angry and a little embarrassed. He stood at the door and looked at Zheng Jianxin, scratching his scalp, wanting to do something but not knowing how to do it.

"What's wrong with you?" Zheng Jianxin asked, putting down the things at hand.

Zhong Haicai was about to speak when a cute little face suddenly appeared behind him. She looked at Zheng Jianxin with twinkling eyes and stuck out her tongue and said, "Hello, Auntie......"

Zheng Jianxin was stunned for a moment and immediately reacted. She stood up and walked to the door. She bent down and looked at the little girl who had come in, then gently hugged her and said, "You are Ahua, right? You are eleven years old, right? You are so beautiful! Your 'dad' often talks to me about you. Have you eaten?"

Ahua shook her head, tears welled up in her eyes, and said aggrievedly, "No, my mommy hasn't come back yet, and I don't know how to cook......"

"What's going on?" Zheng Jianxin looked at Zhong Haicai in surprise.

"She has forgotten everything because of gambling!" Zhong Haicai was angry, "She didn't even remember that the school was closed today. If the teacher hadn't called me, no one would know if she starved to death!"

"Well," Zheng Jianxin thought for a while, and then said to Ahua, "Ahua, why don't you live here? Auntie will make delicious meals for you every day. During the day, you go to the fruit store with Auntie. You can play or do homework. Auntie will teach you if you don't know."

"Okay." Ahua threw down her schoolbag and jumped up, "Thank you, Auntie. My mother never taught me to do homework. She just shook her dice and listened to the sound all day, saying that she wanted to learn from the gambling saint."

Zheng Jianxin looked at Zhong Haicai, who spread his hands and looked helpless.

Without saying anything more, Zheng Jianxin asked the father and daughter to wash their hands, put away the account books, and took out the hot food to eat.

Looking at Ahua who was praising the deliciousness while eating voraciously, Zheng Jianxin couldn't help but touch her belly, with infinite pity in her heart.

The days that followed passed quickly, and the Blue Dream Water Village Resort project was progressing smoothly, which made Zhong Haicai more and more confident in making a fortune. He boasted to Zheng Jianxin from time to time, describing an extremely bright future.

Zheng Jianxin just listened and smiled without saying anything. She now had her own business, as long as she managed it well, she no longer had to rely on anyone.

She selected the appropriate management methods and concepts she saw in the book and applied them to practice, and taught Afang and other sisters to run the fruit chain store better and better. She bought a second-hand small truck specifically for delivery, because the daily delivery of more and more fruits must be improved in efficiency; secondly, it also allowed those sisters to not have to ride back and forth dozens of kilometers every day so hard, freeing up more manpower to pick fruits.

After opening another branch, Zheng Jianxin bought most of the cheap fruits in the fruit wholesale market. More than a dozen girls were busy and happy every day.

In August 2002, Zheng Jianxin and Zhong Haicai's child was born smoothly. It was a chubby boy. Zheng Jianxin thought for a long time and named him "Huihui".

Having a son in his old age made Zhong Haicai happier than winning a jackpot of ten million. He called his friends to eat at the food stalls and it was very lively.

Liang Xiangyun had known the affair between Zhong Haicai and the Northern girl for a long time. She felt sour in her heart, but she knew she had no reason to blame Zhong Haicai.

As she lost more and more gambling, she became so anxious that she didn't care about anything. She used this as an excuse to ask Zhong Haicai for money. Zhong Haicai, who was pestered again and again, would give her some money to keep his ears clean, and warned Achang and other workers not to tell Liang Xiangyun about his rental house in Zhuhai.

Lili successfully gave birth to a baby boy in her hometown. In October, the child stayed in her hometown after 100 days, and Lili returned to Zhuhai.

Zheng Jianxin looked at her face and figure, which were plump and more feminine like hers, and teased her for a long time before asking in a low voice: "The child......"

Lili knew what she wanted to ask, and showed her the 100-day photo of the child, made a face and said: "It's a boy. It must be my husband's, and he looks exactly like him."

Zheng Jianxin looked at the photo and found that it was indeed as she said, so she was relieved and said: "What are you going to do in the future? Continue to mix with them?"

"Since you are doing well, how about selling fruits with you?" Lili patted the dashboard of the small truck and said with a smile.

"It's more than I can wish for, having a big beauty as a signboard." Zheng Jianxin was happy to have her.

"I can't do what you are doing. I can't stand that kind of hardship." Lili sighed and said with a sigh. "During the time at home, I used the child as an excuse to ask Zeng Sheng for some money. This time, when 'Blue Dream' is built, I will ask Bai Lang for more commissions, and I will work for another year or so. Then I will go back to my hometown to open a clothing store and live a stable life."

Zheng Jianxin said nothing.

Time passed as usual. Zheng Jianxin ran the fruit shop with diligence, took his son out for a walk when she had time, and tutored Ahua. Zhong Haicai crossed the border to work on the construction site in Macau every morning, and returned to Gaosha Street at night. After having a son, Zheng Jianxin basically corrected her role as Zhong Haicai's unregistered wife, buried her feelings for Xu Zhuang deeply, and concentrated on building a small nest for four people including Ahua. Lili continued to wander among Zeng Sheng, Bai Lang and Achang, using all means to accumulate capital for the future.

Lili pinched Zeng Sheng's chest muscles hard:
What the hell

One night, Zheng Jianxin's cell phone rang. Picking it up, Lili's low voice came: "Ajian, Zeng Sheng is here, he will definitely not leave; Bai Lang said he would look for me tonight, so I have to turn off my cell phone. If they ask you, just say that I played mahjong with you all night in Xiangzhou and slept at girlfriend's house. OK!"

Zheng Jianxin replied in a very bored voice: "Got it!"

Putting down the phone, Zheng Jianxin felt unhappy. What kind of life was Lili living? In the past, it could be said that it was because she left her hometown, her heart was empty, and she was greedy for pleasure and vanity for money, but now she was already a mother, does she still need a little dignity? A life of vanity and debauchery was a sin in the local dialect! If she were not her good friend and sister since childhood, she would have parted with her long before.

In the nearly two years since she left the factory, she was very frustrated to find that many women here were living in this helpless and embarrassing way. When she was puzzled, she remembered a sentence Hegel said when she was studying philosophy in high school: "What exists is reasonable."

She couldn't change this reality, so she could only accept it. But she couldn't completely look at and deal with Lili, her good sister.

"How could the world become like this?" Zheng Jianxin held her head and buried her head deeply in her knees.

Upstairs, Lili put down the phone in the bathroom, answered Zeng Sheng who had been calling her outside, turned off the faucet, walked out naked, wiped her hair with a towel while walking, and said to Zeng Sheng lying on the bed in a charming way: "I'm here! I'm here! Why are you in such a hurry? I won't fly away!"

Lili picked up a stack of money that Zeng Sheng had placed on the bedside table and weighed it in her hand. She pouted and muttered, "That's all?" Pushing the money aside, she sat heavily on the edge of the bed with her buttocks that became more round after giving birth to a child, and Lili continued to wipe her hair.

Zeng Sheng put a cigarette in his mouth and put another in Lili's.

He blew out a smoke ring and said, "Five thousand yuan, you still think it's too little? Oh...... You also know that my business has not been very good recently. I can't find a good helper like Xu Zhuang. It just doesn't work...... Ah, don't be angry, it's all my fault, okay? It's okay if you don't let me see my son, but every time I look for you, you can hardly see me once......"

"Who said you can't see your son?" Lili interrupted his drooling, "Look, look, this is the photo, here you go! Do you dare to bring him back to Hong Kong? If you do, your wife will eat him alive!"

"Am I afraid of her? Really!" Zeng Sheng raised his voice a little fiercely, "In a few years, when it's time for my son to go to school, I will help him immigrate to Hong Kong to study!"

"Bullshit! Do you mean what you said?" Lili glanced at him coldly and curled her lips, her voice higher than his, "You said you would buy me a house before, where is the house, are you still going to buy it? After sleeping with me, you haven't seen me for a month or two. You think I don't know, you are tired of me, and you go to find pretty girls again! You Hong Kong pervert!" As she said that, she pinched his chest.

Lili's shrewishness and sharp words made Zeng Sheng unable to retort, and he was embarrassed to let the neighbors upstairs and downstairs hear their talk, so he hurriedly shushed her to keep her voice down.

The weather was hot, and every house had its windows open, and any loud noise could be heard clearly upstairs and downstairs. Finally, Lili was calmed down. Zeng Sheng held her waist with one hand and kneaded her, and held the photo of the child with the other hand.

From time to time, he grinned proudly and laughed "Oh wow".

Lili's cell phone rang, and she was so scared that she quickly covered it. Why did she forget to turn it off? She quickly pressed the power off button.

"Who would call you so late?" Zeng Sheng asked.

"It's just that group of girlfriends who have nothing to do and want to play mahjong...... midnight snack......" Lili hesitated and secretly breathed a sigh of relief.

Zeng Sheng said "hmm" comfortably after hearing this. Lili raised her eyebrows and pressed her palms against his chest to prevent him from pressing down, "If you don't take a shower, you sleep on the floor!"

"Do you think I'm dirty? Go, go, go, I'll go right away!" Zeng Sheng didn't dare to argue anymore, and hurried into the bathroom and closed the door with a snap, followed by the sound of running water.

Lili raised her body and stared at the bathroom door. She picked up the phone and dialed back the number she had just received the call: "......From Taiwan to Macau? That's good, don't gamble! I thought you were back in Zhuhai!......It may not be possible tomorrow. I'll call you when I get back from Guangzhou. It'll only be two or three days! Kiss you! Bye!"

After Lili finished speaking, she quickly turned off the phone, went back to lie on the bed, covered with a towel blanket, and took a long puff of cigarette as if nothing had happened.

After a while, Zeng Sheng came out, and then the phone rang. He cursed in Cantonese "F..k your mother" in a very disappointed way, picked up the phone, and immediately frowned to signal Lili not to make a sound, pressed the answer button and put it to her ear: "Wife, you haven't slept yet...... I'm in Guangzhou, and I can't go back for a few days. My friend who owes me money hasn't come yet. It's really hard! Wife, don't worry about it, I will take care of everything. Don't talk too much, my phone battery will be dead, go to bed early, good night!"

After saying that, Zeng Sheng collected the phone line, and his face showed a smug look again.

Lili pinched his chest muscles fiercely: "Eating from the bowl and looking at the pot, what a joke!" Zeng Sheng didn't agree, and replied with a smile: "I'm tired of leaning on my back with my yellow-faced wife in bed! I'm happy to see you!" As he said that, he chuckled.

In Zeng Sheng's drunken eyes, Lili saw that she was just his "doll". Humiliation rose from the bottom of her heart. She punched him hard in the chest and cursed: "What the hell!"

"Wife," Zeng Sheng called Lili flatteringly, his face became serious, "Wife, I'm actually very sad, who can I tell? The business can't go on, it's too dangerous." He was referring to Xu Zhuang's incident and said, "I still can't breathe because of the two million I lost. I've been doing boats for half my life, it's so hard and painful to give it up!"

"So do you want money or life?" Lili asked sternly with cold eyes.

"Of course life! I'm also thinking about changing my way in the future. My father sent a message from the United States: he wants to invest in high-tech holographic imaging engineering in the Science Park, and wants me to work in the company, starting from the lowest level as a worker. My father wants to transform me into a new person. Haha! My father is testing me. If I work hard, maybe the pearl factory will be handed over to me! Hey, do you want to learn some skills too?"

Lili's eyes turned, thinking of Zeng Sheng's only boat, and said: "That's high-tech, I don't understand. Now Zheng Jianxin is running a fruit company, you take 50,000 yuan, not much, count it as your investment!"

Unexpectedly, Zeng Sheng thought about it for a while and was quite happy: "Okay! Bring me the shareholding contract, and I will pay you next week. You have to have a serious job, right?"

The next morning, Zeng Sheng left for something, and Lili felt relieved. In the afternoon, she went to the beauty salon to get her hair done, and then went to Mingming's coffee shop to relax.

Next, Bai Lang was coming again, and she had to be energetic to deal with it.

Beauty salon, Luo Luo and Mrs. Tong

When Lili went to the beauty salon, she specifically asked Zheng Jianxin to go with her. "Women need to maintain their appearance since they are 20 years old. Don't women rely on their faces? With a good face, it can be very useful for both official and unofficial work!" Lili said that this beauty salon was a new product, with a trial price, and she would treat her, and she forced Zheng Jianxin to follow her.

It was indeed a new product. A retired military doctor named Auntie Tian from Chongqing used a natural wild plant, wild thorn, produced in Daba Mountain, for beauty treatment, which was immediately welcomed by the females in the Special Administrative Region who pursue new things and have a spirit of innovation. This plant grows on the wind outlet of Daba Mountain, is resistant to drought, and retains moisture. The nuts have a milky white thick liquid, which is analyzed to be a rare natural element for skin care and freshness preservation.

The store rented by Doctor Tian was not far from the border inspection station with the five-star red flag hanging, giving people the illusion that it was opened by the Army. No one from the taxation and industrial and commercial departments would think of coming here to check. Not to mention that any enjoyment starts with the rich and powerful, and the cars parked at the door were all high-end cars for the wives.

Since it was run by the "troops", the simple conditions of the shop were understandable, and it also increased the credibility and friendliness of the product.

Zheng Jianxin followed Lili into the shop and saw that there were three or five massage beds in the two rooms, one large and one small, on the two diagonal corners. The room was dark, the air conditioner had just been turned on, and there was a stuffy atmosphere. Because it was afternoon, the people who took a nap had not come yet, and the work had not started yet. There was a woman in her early fifties lying on a bed in the big room, wearing a dark blue long skirt, probably made of soft high-grade silk. The skirt was pulled down, revealing her white and thick thighs. The big wavy hair covered half of her face, with delicate skin and a cute slightly upturned nose. Her name was Luo Luo.

She was smoking, her hand holding the cigarette hanging under the bed. She glanced at Lili, then looked away, looked at the ceiling, and smiled, "You're here? And you brought a pretty girl with you!" She said this politely, half-turned her body, and nodded to Zheng Jianxin as a greeting.

Zheng Jianxin saw the friendly look in Luo Luo's eyes.

On the way here, Lili mentioned that several regular customers here were wives of officials and rich women, and told their strange stories vividly. Zheng Jianxin often heard about how rich people lived, but had never saw the real rich people. She was very curious about "them" and wanted to see them. This was also one of the reasons why Zheng Jianxin wanted to come here today.

Among these women with backgrounds, Luo Luo's father was the most powerful official. When the special economic zone was just established, Luo Luo's husband came to Zhuhai and served as the deputy chief engineer of a technology company run by a central enterprise. Luo Luo followed, and the unit provided her with housing and cars. She often entertained guests in restaurants, and she rarely cooked. She had plenty of time to enthusiastically read the fashion magazines her husband brought back from Hong Kong on business trips, and she knew all kinds of brand-name clothing and accessories. If Luo Luo wanted to open a fashion store, she would definitely be an excellent boss. Unfortunately, she only planned to brag about it at parties with her friends. Whether she judged other women or herself, whether she dressed up or not, she had a yardstick, that is, world famous brands and popular clothing styles.

Unfortunately, before her Chow Sang Sang necklace, which had been altered many times, was brought back from Hong Kong by her husband, he had secretly fallen in love with a young rich woman in Hong Kong. With an excuse of long-term sick leave, he ran to Shenzhen to set up an electronics company for a city in the mainland and served as general manager. Without waiting for Luo Luo to shout and make a fuss, her husband handed over the house, car and several shops in Zhuhai that he earned from doing business with others to Luo Luo, and used money to shut her up.

The husband's "desertion" was soon successful. Before he flew to Shenzhen, he left her a signed divorce agreement and asked her to decide.

People often say that a dead camel is bigger than a horse. In front of others, Luo Luo still supported her spirit as a member of the second red generation (sibling of revolutionary officials). She never felt sorry for herself in front of people, and always showed her noble origin and acted as if she was unshakable.

She gently ordered Lili to move aside, and Lili obediently pulled Zheng Jianxin to the small dark room.

Zheng Jianxin didn't want to, she said she just liked the bright and airy room there. Doctor Tian couldn't stop her, so she lay on a bed by the window. Luo Luo sat up suddenly and asked curiously: "How can you do this?" Luo Luo half smiled when she spoke, which was her temperament of being a lady of a noble family and being polite.

Zheng Jianxin said: "We spend the same money, why can't we be equal? You can use this bed, but I can't?"

"Then, what if Mrs. Tong comes?" Luo Luo still had a negotiating tone.

"Isn't there a bed over there?"

"But that's a small room, and she's the wife of an official, how can it work?" Luo Luo turned to Doctor Tian for help.

Without waiting for Doctor Tian to speak, Zheng Jianxin pointed to the two empty beds next to her, "Aren't these empty beds? How many people are there?" Luo Luo was a little embarrassed. She wanted to say it tactfully but couldn't find the tactful words: "How can she lie with you, a migrant worker girl?"

When Zheng Jianxin first came in, she was quite fond of Luo Luo's elegance and friendliness, and had some respect for her. But Luo Luo's words seemed gentle, in fact they were bullying, which made Ajian a little unhappy. Now such direct discrimination against the poor made her extremely disgusted with Luo Luo's sour Shanghai accent. She slapped the bed angrily, "What's wrong with a migrant worker girl? Here are two beds, and I won't interfere with her!" She had more to say, but was stopped by Luo Luo:

"Okay, okay, I won't say anything. Let's see what that woman will do in a while. She has a bad temper!"

While talking, Doctor Tian and her assistant began to clean the skin of the three of them with facial cleanser, and soon applied a white ointment on their faces, leaving only their eyes exposed.

Zheng Jianxin was thinking about Mrs. Tong who might come at any time. She wanted to see what kind of remarkable person she was.

Sure enough, the sound of high heels clacking was heard after a while. The sound stopped and someone entered the house.

"Oh, Luo Luo, I'm a little late!" The voice was crisp and sweet, as if she was apologizing to Luo Luo, and also as if she was tired of doing things.

Zheng Jianxin turned her head and looked at Mrs. Tong who came in with fragrance of perfume. Mrs. Tong was wearing a lavender cicada wing satin Chinese-style top with medium sleeves and pure silk black flared pants. Maybe because of the high heels, her waist was stiff. Her face was like an actor who had just come off the stage and had not yet removed her makeup, with pink chin and rosy cheeks. Two small braids were folded into two strands and tied behind her ears with thin ribbons, just like the fat dolls in the New Year pictures, which was a bit cute. But she had a shriveled chin that people could remember at a glance, which made people look uncomfortable.

Luo Luo pointed at Zheng Jianxin and introduced her as Lili's friend.

Mrs. Tong immediately greeted her with a warm compliment: "Hey, what a great figure! There are so many pretty girls in Gongbei!" While talking about others, she was posing, leaning her upper body to the right, and shaking her right hand in the air. This was the action of well-educated and humorous Western people in movies and TV.

The one who came in after Mrs. Tong was actually Chen Xiao's wife Jiaojiao. Jiaojiao's waist was as thick as her hips, like a gasoline barrel, and she was recognizable at a glance. Zheng Jianxin had just arrived in Zhuhai, and Chen Xiao took her to his home in Fushen Garden to get acquainted. For some reason, Jiaojiao was carrying a travel bag.

Jiaojiao knew that Lili often had beauty treatments. Mrs. Tong and the others knew that she was one of the four most beautiful girls in Gongbei, and were shocked by her sexy appearance. In addition to being jealous of beautiful women, women also appreciate their beauty, and evaluating beautiful women was their main topic. Jiaojiao didn't expect Zheng Jianxin to come for beauty treatment. She immediately realized that Zheng Jianxin was on Lili's path. She glanced at Zheng Jianxin with disdain and snorted at her arrogantly, with a gloating laugh.

Zheng Jianxin closed her eyes and ignored her.

Jiaojiao pushed away the mineral water that Doctor Tian handed to Mrs. Tong, searched out a small bag from her bag, and took out Mrs. Tong's special thermos cup. She glanced at Doctor Tian and said, "Mrs. Tong, drink this. It's the ginseng health tea that Beijing has just developed."

She handed the cup to Mrs. Tong with both hands, turned around, and told Doctor Tian with a serious face: "The governmental organization has arranged for Mrs. Tong to go abroad to Europe for inspection. You have to do it several times seriously."

Doctor Tian nodded slightly: "Yes, yes, yes."

Now everyone's face was covered with a thick layer of white skin care lotion, lying quietly, waiting for the nutrient solution to penetrate the cells of the facial skin, to activate cells, and make them radiant. Zheng Jianxin closed her eyes, a little sleepy.

Mrs. Tong seemed like a person who could not sit still. Her lips were surrounded by skin cream, and her lips opened and closed unnaturally. She still said to Luo Luo hesitantly: "The doctor from South Korea has arrived, and we just arranged for him to stay."

"What did the doctor say?" Luo Luo asked.

"He said that we need to do another operation, and the left mandible needs to be cut thinner, so that the cheeks will be symmetrical!"

Luo Luo didn't seem to care, and smiled sympathetically: "Oh, it's really painful, is it worth it......?

Since Luo Luo's father was a high-ranking official in a big city, much higher than Mrs. Tong's husband, who was at the department level, she didn't think her status was lower than Mrs. Tong, and she didn't flatter Mrs. Tong, and sometimes she spoke bluntly. Luo Luo calculated in her mind that this was Mrs. Tong's third cosmetic surgery. She went to Guangzhou several times before, and also went to South Korea once, to raise the bridge of her nose to make it slender and straight; she shaved her lower lip to make the upper and lower lips thicker.

"The doctor is here, how can I not do it? ...... Unlike you, who was born with thin eyebrows and eyes......" Mrs. Tong felt Luo Luo's contempt for her beauty treatment and her jealousy that someone helped her pay for 80,000 or 90,000 yuan.

Luo Luo's husband ran away, the big tree fell, and there was no place to report the money she spent. Despite this, in Mrs. Tong's heart, Luo Luo was still a friend she could interact with. Although Luo Luo was no longer as glorious as before, often opening her wallet to pay the bill after eating and shopping, the noble temperament that seemed to be born with the children of high-ranking officials was still there, which made her, who grew up in the mountains, often feel inferior. Luo Luo was knowledgeable and was her enlightenment teacher in etiquette and consultant in fashion consumption. Since Luo Luo lost power and became lonely, she sometimes dared to ridicule and tease Luo Luo. Although Luo Luo's father had been famous, he had retired and died more than ten years before, and no one knew him. Apart from her own pity for her, who in Zhuhai knew who she was? Luo Luo's pressure on Mrs. Tong's heart gradually disappeared.

Luo Luo was really moved, her chest heaving, and her voice was a little choked, because they were lying down and no one could see her eyes.

After a while, Luo Luo seemed to say to Mrs. Tong, or as if talking to herself: "I came to the Special Administrative Region by mistake. I still have a job and relatives in Shanghai. Now I am alone, without organization (Party), family, friends, enemies, family affection, or love."

She sighed and turned to Jiaojiao and said: "Now I am afraid of the night, facing the long night of loneliness. At that time, I was looking forward to a phone call. I couldn't sleep in bed, and I was trembling with fear even if there was a slight noise. Hey, how is your 'dwarf' recently?"

Luo Luo thought of Jiaojiao's husband from her own singleness, so she asked about Chen Xiao.

"Don't mention him, he is really a chicken, he scratches for food all day long, and he doesn't make much money!"

Mrs. Tong said, with contempt in her words: "Don't underestimate the dwarf, maybe he has many ideas and many tricks! "

People are very strange. Men always think that other men's wives are better, but women always think that other women's husbands are not good. They don't compare with others, but only with those around them.

Zheng Jianxin hated to hear these words, and was a little impatient. She moved her body and the bed squeaked twice. Mrs. Tong and Luo Luo both felt Zheng Jianxin's reaction.

"The short guy is from Wuhan." No one knew what Mrs. Tong wanted to say. "Where is Wuhan, on the Yellow River?" Mrs. Tong asked.

Jiaojiao didn't know what the relationship between Wuhan and the Yellow River was, so she couldn't answer for a while. Although Luo Luo had been a phoenix fallen from the heaven and was not as good as a chicken, she had always looked down on this arrogant bumpkin Mrs. Tong from the bottom of her heart, and just smiled without answering.

Mrs. Tong asked again: "Which is bigger, Wuhan or Zhuhai!"

"Is it a question?" Jiaojiao told the truth, "There are three towns in Wuhan, one district under a town is larger than Zhuhai! "

Mrs. Tong tilted her head towards Zheng Jianxin, as if speaking to Zheng Jianxin: "The north must be very poor, otherwise, why do people come to Zhuhai to make a living?"

This also irritated Luo Luo. She retorted: "Who is as lucky as you? You can help outsiders with a piece of paper to mark out a piece of land and set up a project. You don't have to spend a penny to transfer it to the developer to get cash, and you can also get a row of shops and collect rent every month; you don't spend a penny and you are still a shareholder of a foreign-funded enterprise......"

"Stop talking nonsense, the foreign investors of the Deyue factory asked me to put my name on it." Mrs. Tong defended, "Last month we handed over all our shares to a company to buy out, and we are quitting."

"Quitting? Good, you made a fortune again! " Luo Luo knew that using backdoor to raise the stock value and using connections to get state-owned enterprises to buy at high prices was a way for the powerful to make money.

When Zheng Jianxin heard about "Deyue", she shuddered. She was fired from that factory. Unexpectedly, she accidentally met the Chinese boss here. She swallowed her saliva and felt hot in her heart, as if she was nauseous.

When the time came, the skin care lotion was spread into a layer of mask. Doctor Tian and her assistant peeled off the mask, washed everyone's face with clean water, and then used their hands to apply a moisturizer similar to floral water on everyone's face. Suddenly, the whole room was filled with fragrance.

After Mrs. Tong sat up , Doctor Tian gave her a few back pats. As soon as she stopped, Jiaojiao immediately handed Mrs. Tong's thermos cup to her with both hands. Mrs. Tong blew slowly and carefully at the hot air twice, and then took a sip gently. Mrs. Tong was very insightful. She paid attention to learning everywhere and strove to act as a well-educated woman. The fixed posture of drinking water was learned from palace dramas. The imperial concubines would blow twice before drinking covered tea. But Mrs. Tong didn't know that it was to blow away the tea leaves floating on the water. No matter what she drank, including beverages, she used the fixed posture, blowing twice left and right, and her movements were so gentle.

In the afternoon, Mrs. Tong was going to a blind date for her son. The girl's family was a family in Guangzhou with a hundred million of assets, a real estate businessman. Mrs. Tong knew that they were attracted by her son's grandfather's position in the government. Mrs. Tong wanted to find a rich in-law for her son, and now money was indispensable for everything.

Jiaojiao carefully took out a shirt from her travel bag for Mrs. Tong to change into, and stuffed the wrinkled shirt from sleeping on the bed into the bag. Mrs. Tong changed into a dark green short-sleeved shantung silk shirt, with small white lace on the cuffs and Chinese-style front, and a dark red gem on the collar. When Mrs. Tong stood up, Jiaojiao took the opportunity to gently straighten Mrs. Tong's cuffs and the hem of her top. Then she took out a comb from Mrs. Tong's special makeup bag and stood behind Mrs. Tong to comb her messy hair.

The phone in Mrs. Tong's LV handbag worth more than 20,000 yuan rang. Jiaojiao hurriedly took it out and handed it to Mrs. Tong. Mrs. Tong said "hmm" and "um" for a while. After hanging up, she pondered for a while and whispered to Luo Luo: "An old comrade in the province has been double-regulated (under investigation)! " There was regret in her voice.

After a while, a tender light appeared in her eyes, and she smiled with a sour tone, "He has a few mistresses, all of them are young...... I didn't expect that the official is over 70 years old and still in such good health, it's rare!" After saying that, she stood up.

After listening, Luo Luo said calmly: "Ancient officials were all literati and scholars. In the Tang Dynasty, there were official prostitutes belonging to the government, who were both beautiful and talented; besides, the TV is all about the palace and the harem all day long, and the emperor had women in groups. Now some officials have power and money, it would be strange if they don't have women!"

Mrs. Tong wanted to go out, but suddenly heard this. She thought that she couldn't talk about the officials behind back, especially in front of the masses. She turned around and said very seriously and analytically: "Some men go to prostitutes to satisfy low-level physiological needs, which is morally corrupt; our officials look for lovers because they love life and have high-level spiritual needs. There is a difference between the two! "

After saying that, she smacked her lips and glanced at Lili. Everyone present could hear what she said, intentionally or unintentionally putting Lili and the others in the low-level ranks.

Lili's Achilles' heel was being grasped. Facing the insult, her face was burning and she was short of breath and speechless.

Zheng Jianxin was combing her hair in front of the mirror, and with a "snap" she pressed the comb onto the table and said coldly: "Is there a difference between having sex in bed? Then show us a noble love!"

When Mrs. Tong and Zheng Jianxin looked at each other, Mrs. Tong didn't mind the collision of the common woman with her at all, and just said "Oh", "What a beautiful girl!"

When she learned that Zheng Jianxin was "looking for a job", she frowned and said, "Don't complain about the factory being tiring, who hasn't been tired? Working in a factory doesn't have any technical content, and you can't blame the society for your own inability. It's much better to find a job than in the countryside! " At the end, she said earnestly and with a hidden meaning: "Gongbei is a very chaotic place, and men are very bad now. Women should respect themselves and don't make mistakes in their lifestyle!" The last sentence was the standard phrase that many officials often used to admonish their subordinates at cadre meetings.

Zheng Jianxin didn't like the officials' wives in the first place, and felt disgusted by Mrs. Tong's nonsense. Mrs. Tong was a stranger to her, but she scolded her. Thinking that Mrs. Tong was her former boss, she had a grudge against Deyue Factory. The complicated mood made her open her eyes wide. She suppressed the anger in her heart and said calmly: "Do you want to be a slave laborer? People can't even support their own survival with low wages. Do they deserve it?"

As she said, she pushed open the window: "How much technical content is there in building these buildings and paving these roads? How much technical content do those who took away a lot of money have? If the miracle of the special zone economy is not because of us workers, is it because of the people who made trade in land, because of you? "

Mrs. Tong didn't expect that her kindness would be in vain. The deep grooves in the flesh of the skin that had just been taken care of and smoothed by skin care products were exposed again, and she was so angry that she couldn't speak.

When Jiaojiao saw someone contradicting Mrs. Tong, she rushed over and stood between Mrs. Tong and Zheng Jianxin, shouting, "Who dares to talk to Mrs. Tong like this in Zhuhai?" She pointed her finger in the air and almost poked Zheng Jianxin's forehead.

Lili was also a little panicked. She pulled Zheng Jianxin into the hut: "Mrs. Tong also meant well......"

Jiaojiao didn't give up, "Dare to offend Mrs. Tong, Mrs. Tong can arrest anyone in a minute with just one word! What's more, 'outside girls' and 'streetwalkers'?"

When Jiaojiao said "outside girls" and "streetwalkers", everyone present heard the hidden meaning, and was blaming someone.

Zheng Jianxin was so angry that her lips trembled. She took a step forward and cursed, "Who are you talking about?" She moved her arms to hit her.

Mrs. Tong had the generosity and broad-mindedness who didn't care about the little man's mistakes. She reached out and grabbed Jiaojiao: "Forget it, forget it. Has Wang the accountant arrived? Ask him to come in and pay the bill." A young man who was waiting in the car outside came in and paid the bill.

Doctor Tian said that the trial price had expired, and now it was time to open a membership card. Ten times got two free, a total of twelve times, the material cost per person was 300 yuan, and the labor cost was only 30 yuan, 330 yuan, ten times 3,300 yuan, three people, 9,900 yuan. Long and long (in Chinese the pronunciations of nine and long are the same), how auspicious! There was no invoice but a receipt.

Doctor Tian looked at Mrs. Tong as if to confirm, Mrs. Tong nodded, and Accountant Wang accepted the receipt written by Doctor Tian.

Before Mrs. Tong left, Zheng Jianxin heard her say to Doctor Tian, "I'm going to treat a beautician from South Korea to dinner tonight. You can come along. Oh, it is just add a pair of chopsticks to have you as a guest! Please help me with some advice. He said I need at least two more operations. After sawing the jawbone flat, I need to cut and lengthen the corners of my mouth. Big-mouthed beauties are popular now! I also need to make a chin to make it fuller. You can imagine how much I'm suffering. Fortunately, I'm a veteran with more than 20 years of Party membership. If it were anyone else, they wouldn't be able to stand it!"

"Make a chin?" Luo Luo asked puzzled. Zheng Jianxin and Lili were even more curious and stretched her ears.

"Oh," Mrs. Tong smacked her lips, looked at Luo Luo and then at Doctor Tian, "Do you think I'm doing this for good looks? No......" Then she said mysteriously, "Two months ago, I rushed to Xijiao Mountain in Nanhai and met a fortune teller who was selling things on the street. He said that if my chin was rounder, my life would be better in my later years!

"Do you know what a chin is? People often say that when looking at people, they should look for a 'full forehead and round chin'. The forehead is the sky, representing Yang, referring to men; the chin is the earth, belonging to Yin, referring to women. The fortune teller said that a full chin, solid and rich can bring good fortune in old age! Besides, I am not doing this for my husband's prosperity. If I get better, Old Tong will be safe and sound! "

After listening, everyone breathed a sigh of relief. She talked in a mysterious way, although it was pretentious, but it seemed to have a basis.

Luo Luo nodded gently, thinking about the knowledge in the chin. Zheng Jianxin and Lili often saw fortune-telling stalls on the street. Zheng Jianxin told Lili not to believe these deceptive words. "You and I are not bad-looking, why are we so unlucky! Today, I heard here that there is such a saying about human organs."

Because it came from the mouth of an official's wife, Zheng Jianxin was extremely disgusted. She muttered to Lili: "Alas, she has eaten too much (so that she has wasted her energy)!"

Doctor Tian knew how to talk, and immediately agreed with Mrs. Tong, saying, "No matter what, you do better and better each time. Your temperament is radiant wherever you go. One can feel your unique nobility and elegance at a glance!" Mrs. Tong suddenly became like a shy girl, glanced at the doctor, and asked in a naive way, "Really?"

Lili and Mrs. Tong were already very familiar with each other. While patting her face with her palms to let the water penetrate into her skin, she blurted out a sentence, "The most important thing is to have another operation. Please have a fortune teller to pick up a good date!"

Mrs. Tong heard it, "Pooh", glared at her, and stomped her feet. "Unlucky!" She turned sideways and thought again, "This is a good reminder. Thank you, beautiful Lili!"

Jiaojiao quickly took out a small notebook and wrote it down.

The fragrant wind wrapped the three noble women out of the door, and Mrs. Tong could still be heard saying as she walked: "I am too kind-hearted, and I am willing to talk to anyone! The fortune teller has quietly advised me several times not to contact people who are lower than I or poor people, because it is unlucky and will hinder my husband's career! I always forget it, hi!"

After the three left, Doctor Tian breathed a sigh of relief. Usually, Mrs. Tong and her friends would talk to Doctor Tian for a long time about women's beauty, health care, body shaping, weight loss and other topics, delaying business.

Zheng Jianxin was still angry and cursed: "What kind of world is this? People love the rich, and dogs bite the poor!"

Lili took out her wallet to pay the bill. Doctor Tian smiled and said, "The trial price is 20% off, 120 yuan, 240 yuan for two people." At the end, she reminded, "Don't tell others! I am doing this at a loss for you! I hope you can bring more girls to help my business!"

After leaving the beauty salon, Zheng Jianxin shook her head and said, "With a little money and a little power, she is so arrogant, funny!"

"Mrs. Tong also came from the mountain valley!"

"What about coming from the mountain valley? Look at the rural people in the newspaper who have master's and doctoral degrees. Once they have power, they are more greedy and become faster! A learned person once said that when a slave becomes a master, he will never give up the title of master!"

"Alas," Lili sighed with empathy, "How can people not mess around in this world?"

Zheng Jianxin said, "This place can be written into a TV series!"

"It's lively enough. These people don't worry about food and clothing, have endless money, and are happy wherever they go all day! And they look down on everyone!" Lili said.

Yingbin Avenue was crowded with people and traffic. Zheng Jianxin looked at the crowd passing by her and suddenly said to Lili: "What's the name of the TV series? Give it a name!"

"Farce, 'People Who Have Nothing to Do'!"

"Okay! Okay!"

Ajian hung the "marriage certificate" on the wall like a certificate of honor

What should be passed is passed, what should continue is continued, and what should be entangled is still entangled. Days pass by like this, and the city was constantly changing at a rapid pace.

More than half a year had passed.

Zhong Haicai was waiting for the big hen "Blue Dream Water Village Resort" to lay golden eggs.

At night, Zhong Haicai liked to take a few sips of wine. He grabbed the wine glass with his rough fingers and looked at the sleeping baby on the bed with a proud and comfortable look, and the blue veins on the back of his hand were throbbing.

After taking a sip of wine, Zhong Haicai squinted his eyes and said to Zheng Jianxin who was picking longan: "Wife, just wait for another two or three months, I promise to buy you a house by the sea. In addition to household expenses, I will give you 10,000 yuan a month, and you can save it yourself...... Hey, it's just a few thousand yuan, it's nothing!"

Zheng Jianxin pouted impatiently: "Come on, you just know how to talk nonsense. As the saying goes, if you say good things three times, even a deaf person will be annoyed!" She muttered, "It's only a few days before the end of the month, are you worried about how to pay the rent next month?"

Zhong Haicai was about to argue when his cell phone rang. After looking at the caller number, Zhong Haicai picked up the phone and answered: "Oh, oh, okay! You want me to treat you to night tea and music? Okay, okay...... That's it! See you later!"

The call made him look a little excited, and his dark face and sagging cheeks glowed a little red. After changing his clothes, Zhong Haicai touched his pocket and said to Zheng Jianxin hesitantly, "Boss Bai's cousin is coming from Taiwan, I have to go and see him......"

"Then go quickly!" Zheng Jianxin was already a little annoyed by picking longans. Zhong Haicai hadn't become a boss yet, but he acted like one. He often neglected his family and always came back sweaty. He asked Zheng Jianxin to pour tea and serve him, and kept talking about his "Blue Dream Water Village".

"This......" Zhong Haicai rubbed his hands and looked embarrassed, "You know, I haven't received the project payment yet, and I paid the workers' wages with my own money. I don't have much money on me now...... Can you give me some money first......"

"Except for living expenses, my money is all public funds of the fruit shop, how can I use it?" Zheng Jianxin didn't give in.

"You don't even give me face! I'm a man, how can I go out without a little money?" Zhong Haicai raised his eyebrows in anger, and when he turned around, he bumped into Zheng Jianxin, knocking her off the stool and onto the ground.

"You know you're a man, don't you? Don't forget that you still have more than 500,000 yuan in debt, and you just dream all day long......" Zheng Jianxin sat on the ground and accused, her face full of grievance.

Zhong Haicai hurriedly helped her up and apologized repeatedly: "I'm sorry, I didn't mean it...... Wife, wife......"

"What wife?" Zheng Jianxin was even more annoyed, and said to Zhong Haicai with a stern face, "No matter how busy you are, you must go back to Guizhou with me to get a marriage certificate! The child is two years old, and I don't want people to call me a bitch!"

"Well......" Zhong Haicai knew he was in the wrong, so he lowered his head and stood there without saying a word.

Seeing him like that, Zheng Jianxin sighed, went to the bedside and got 2,000 yuan for the fruit payment and handed it to him: "Go! Don't get drunk again!"

"Of course, of course, my wife's words are the imperial decree......" Zhong Haicai responded, imitating Achang's playful manner and making a weird salute, which made Zheng Jianxin laugh, and then he opened the door and went out.

Zheng Jianxin kept yelling about getting a marriage certificate, making Zhong Haicai's ears calloused. This matter had to be done sooner or later. Fortunately, the construction site was free these few days, so Zhong Haicai returned to Macau to find a law firm to prepare documents for the marriage certificate. The lawyer asked him if he had been married. Zhong Haicai said he had, but they had broken up for many years. The lawyer asked him if he had gone through the divorce procedure. Zhong Haicai said he had never obtained a marriage certificate in mainland China and Macau, nor had he obtained a divorce certificate. The clerk asked him to sign a statement that he had no spouse to show that he was legally responsible, and the lawyer signed as a witness. Zhong Haicai borrowed money to buy a plane ticket and immediately went back to her hometown, the provincial capital, with Zheng Jianxin to get the marriage certificate at the Foreign Marriage Registration Office. It took five days.

During these five days, Zheng Jianxin didn't even go back to her hometown. Zhong Haicai said that he would wait until he became rich before returning home with her, it wouldn't take half a year or a year. Zheng Jianxin thought about it and listened to him.

"Fruit Girl" Fresh Fruit Store has spread all over remote factory areas and places with dense migrant workers, making Zheng Jianxin and her friends earn a lot of money. In addition to saving a part as development funds, the five sisters who founded it could get a lot of dividends every month, and the employees also had a lot of bonuses according to various systems.

The marriage certificate that she had been worried about for more than two years was finally obtained, which made Zheng Jianxin's heart completely settled, and she felt that she could finally hold her head high and live a life with a clear conscience. So, as soon as she returned to Zhuhai, she framed the "marriage certificate" and hung it on the wall like a certificate of honor.

After learning that Zheng Jianxin had returned, Ahua, who was already in the first year of junior high school, also rushed over from Macau on the weekend, teasing and congratulating Zheng Jianxin with a playful smile.

After more than two years of getting along, Ahua was even closer to Zheng Jianxin than to Zhong Haicai and Liang Xiangyun. Sometimes, when she heard Liang Xiangyun say bad things about Zheng Jianxin, she would refute her mother, saying that her mother knew how to stab people in the back besides gambling.

The "Blue Dream" was shattered, and Bai Lang ran away

After returning from Guizhou, the first thing Zhong Haicai did was to "report" to Bai Lang at the "Blue Dream Water Village". However, Bai Lang's phone was turned off, and when he went to the Gongbei Fushen Garden where he rented, the house was "iron general" (the lock) guarding the door. Zhong Haicai felt something was wrong, and he hurried back to the construction site of the Blue Dream Water Village Resort early the next morning to check the situation. What he never expected was that the construction site had stopped, and Bai Lang ran away! The office was crowded with people demanding project funds and material fees, as well as villagers who were owed wages.

As soon as Zhong Haicai arrived, someone recognized him: "He is from Macau, a foreign businessman, we asked him for money!"

Zhong Haicai argued that he was not the boss, and he did not specifically manage the project, but was just a technical consultant. But no one listened to him, and the besiegers pushed and beat him. Then someone wanted to beat him, and some calmer ones tried to dissuade them. Finally, a group of people dragged him to the police station.

The police station immediately reported to the superiors and the town government. The mayor and the town investment promotion office staff immediately came to the police station for a short meeting. At the meeting, a cadre from the town government took out a foreign investment registration form and asked Zhong Haicai: "Mr. Zhong, you are a shareholder, why is your name not on it?" But then he changed the subject and said, "Since everyone knows that you are a shareholder, the shareholder is the boss! You have to bear legal responsibility!"

Zhong Haicai complained repeatedly, recounted the matter of his loan to Bai Lang, and said that he was just a small foreman on the site in Macau, not a boss. Before going to Macau, he was a farmer in Yinbao Island, a neighboring town.

After studying the case, the police station and town cadres were in a dilemma: they could say he was a fraudster, but there was insufficient evidence. However, the Taiwanese businessman Bai Lang had already run away, and he could not be allowed to run away again. He could not be imprisoned, released, beaten, or scolded. He was a compatriot from Hong Kong and Macao, so they had to pay attention to the policy. They asked their superiors for instructions on how to deal with the case. The superiors replied: There were currently no documents or regulations on this issue, and they were asked to make reasonable arrangements based on the specific circumstances.

Several cadres brainstormed and came up with a solution: 1. Temporarily withhold his Hong Kong and Macao compatriot return permit so that he could not leave the country; 2. Let him stay in a hotel and send someone to watch over him; 3. Let his family send money.

They had no hope for the last one, but they still wanted to have a try.

Late at night, Zheng Jianxin got the news and was going to see Zhong Haicai, and Lili couldn't stop her.

The small truck happened to be in the repair shop for maintenance, and Zheng Jianxin rode her bicycle without saying a word. Most of the more than 20 kilometers of the journey were rural dirt roads. There were no main roads, no street lights, only the pond reflecting the moonlight. The bicycle was bumpy and rattling on the uneven road, and every time she passed a house, the dogs kept barking. She passed through several villages, rushed to the police station, and found the hotel. It was already dawn.

After a day of torture and shock, Zhong Haicai, a grown man, hugged Zheng Jianxin like a lost child who finally saw his mother and burst into tears: "I was deceived by Bai Lang so badly! So bad!" He couldn't sleep all night, and was restless, thinking about the loan in Macau,

and now there was the house where Liang Xiangyun lived in Macau......
What would happen if she poked a hole in the sky?

In just one day, Zhong Haicai's stubble grew, his clothes were torn,
and there were several bloodstains on his face and chest.

"Why are you crying!" Zheng Jianxin pushed him away and said
sternly, "You can't steer a boat but complain the bend of a river. Are you
a man?"

As soon as they heard that someone had come from Boss Zhong's
home, who looked like his daughter, people immediately rushed to Zheng
Jianxin to ask for money.

Zheng Jianxin yelled at these people: "I also came from the
countryside. Let's be honest. I have money to support one person, but I
don't have money to give you. Forget it! If you want to lock up my
husband, I won't leave!"

The town cadres learned from the village cadres and farmers that
Zhong Haicai was indeed not the boss and had no money. If they
detained her again, she would become a burden, and it would be
meaningless to provide her with food and accommodation. So after
discussion, they decided: "Continue to detain the certificate, Zhong
Haicai must be available at any time." After the announcement, the town
government sent a jeep, put Zheng Jianxin's bicycle at the back of the
jeep, and sent the two of them back to their home in Gongbei.

To be fair, timeshare resort was a feasible hotel management model
with considerable development potential. There were precedents abroad.
But Bai Lang started it a little too early in the mainland. There were not
many people with spare money, and people were not so rich that they
could not find places to invest. Although Bai Lang's sales team was
targeting large cities such as Hong Kong, Macau, and Guangzhou, there
was no money for publicity. It only conducted pyramid selling among
relatives and friends. The feedback was that the market response was cold,
and almost no funds have been recovered in more than a year.

Seeing that the sales situation was not good, the bank would not
continue to lend him money, and it also tried to force Bai Lang to repay

the previous loan. With the capital chain broken, the only outcome of the project was to be suspended and stranded.

Zhong Haicai, who was not specifically involved in the project management, did not get any clue about it in advance. Bai Lang "pawned his clothes to buy wine, cared about his mouth but not his body", and always said "the situation is good and will get better and better".

The night before Bai Lang escaped, a good construction site was messed up by debt collectors. Bai Lang's suit was torn by the workers, his glasses were broken, his neck was pinched, and he was thrown into the foundation pit. Bai Lang thought he would be buried alive. He was so scared that he cried out "I am a Taiwanese businessman, I am a Taiwanese businessman" while crying loudly, kneeling on the ground to beg for life: "I have parents and children to take care of, please leave me a way out!"

Bai Lang's plan failed. He could no longer support it. He left more than 20 business plans and said he would return to Taiwan to find investors, but he never returned.

The real cause of Bai Lang's failure was that he had no capital of his own. He overestimated his consciousness and energy. He wanted to rely on his interpersonal relationships to cheat others of their funds to cover his losses, and finally hurt others and himself......

For this result, Achang and his friends were even more panicked and didn't know what to do -- the money they raised for Zhong Haicai to lend to Bai Lang was hard-earned money.

Zhong Haicai's dream of getting rich was shattered! He didn't know what to do in the face of a debt of 500,000 yuan -- it was simply a drop in the bucket to repay the huge loan with the wages that had not yet been received for the Macau project.

Zhong Haicai was stunned and completely collapsed. He was like a wooden chicken (motionless) for three consecutive days, sighing and gasping at home. He didn't eat, drink or move in the hot weather. Zheng Jianxin kept shouting and shaking him, fearing that he would become persistent vegetative state (PVS) due to excessive shock.

Men are fragile at critical moments. Although it is said that women are stronger than men, Zheng Jianxin only showed calmness. She and Zhong Haicai were husband and wife. This debt of 500,000 was a common disaster for the family. How to repay it and how to settle it, Zheng Jianxin felt a heavy stone in her heart. She had no appetite to eat, just sat with Zhong Haicai, and kept drinking water...... Women look for men to find a harbor, Zhong Haicai -- what kind of harbor was this!

26

Liang Xiangyun said at home in Macau:
"The sky is falling"

The bankruptcy of Blue Dream Water Village Resort was like an earthquake. More than a month later, it affected Liang Xiangyun in Macau who had nothing to do with it. After having a simple lunch alone, Liang Xiangyun looked at the empty bowls and plates on the table, lit a cigarette and smoked silently. Some past events could not help but come to her mind.

Ever since Zhong Haicai said he broke up with her and moved out, it was only Ahua who came back from boarding school to accompany her on weekends. Perhaps because of her own mistakes and negligence, Ahua spent most of her free time in Zhuhai with Zheng Jianxin and others, and only came to see her occasionally.

The emptiness and loneliness made Liang Xiangyun very depressed. But she didn't know what to do because she had a gambling habit. Gambling made her husband leave, and half of her daughter belong to someone else.

Every time like this, she thought of Zhong, and she hated Zhong Haicai with gritted teeth.

She clearly remembered what Zhong Haicai said when he left home: "There is nothing valuable in the house, only debts; I will leave this house to you. Now we are divorced, I will have nothing to do with you in the future!"

But Liang Xiangyun did not let Zhong Haicai go: He didn't give her money in the divorce! Liang Xiangyun had always been upset. Especially after learning that he and a northern girl rented a house in Gongbei and lived together and even gave birth to a son, she was furious. She always tried to use this as an excuse to make Zhong Haicai "bleed", otherwise she would mess with them and make life difficult for them.

One day, Liang Xiangyun, who had just passed the border from Zhuhai, was stopped by the experienced and sharp-eyed Macau marine police.

"Pull it up and have a look." The inspecting marine police pointed to her abnormally bulging trouser legs and said.

Liang Xiangyun timidly pulled up her trouser legs to her knees, revealing two pieces of raw pork tied to her calves with transparent tape.

"You are smuggling again!" The marine police were familiar with Liang Xiangyun and other professional "water ghosts" who went back and forth several times a day, but no matter how familiar they were, the law must be enforced.

There were legal regulations for the entry of animals and plants in Macau. Vegetables could be imported within a reasonable amount per person each time. Animals and meat were not allowed to enter without quarantine and customs declaration. Carrying them was illegal, and hiding was smuggling.

In order to take the pork, the marine police pulled too hard, causing Liang Xiangyun's body to shake. She fell to the ground and cried to passersby in a pretentious manner: "Sir (police) hit people, hit people!"

At this time, Zhong Haicai happened to pass by. Seeing that it was Liang Xiangyun, he walked over with a dark face and helped her up: "Get up! Stop making noise!"

Liang Xiangyun saw that it was Zhong Haicai, but she stopped crying immediately and said angrily: "It's you? Go to your northern girl. Don't bother me!"

Zhong Haicai apologized to the marine police and pulled her away in a bad mood: "Let's go. Don't show off here!"

Liang Xiangyun immediately followed Zhong Haicai into the groups of people entering across the border.

"You are fine, my daughter also wants you. I am left behind alone;

the son born by the mistress has grown up, right?" Liang Xiangyun followed Zhong Haicai, jealous.

"What mistress? Don't talk nonsense!" Zhong Haicai didn't look good to her.

"You want to get rid of me before you have paid me for the breakup? Don't even think about it!" Liang Xiangyun grabbed his arm, "You'd better be sensible, otherwise I will make your good life impossible!"

"What do you want? Are you done? " Zhong Haicai turned his head and glared at her.

"If you don't give me money, it won't end! "Liang Xiangyun looked like a dead pig that was not afraid of boiling water, "I will fight against you as long as I am alive!" After saying that, she twisted Zhong Haicai fiercely and walked out.

Zhong Haicai rubbed his twisted muscles, looked at Liang Xiangyun's back as she quickly passed the customs, shook his head angrily, but looked helpless.

Thinking of this, Liang Xiangyun finished smoking a cigarette and was still too lazy to move. While she was thinking, she heard the sound of shaking iron bars and the voice of strangers at the door: "Is anyone at home?" Liang Xiangyun opened the door and looked at the two strangers in suits, a man and a woman, outside the iron gate and asked: "Who are you? What's the matter?"

The man holding the document looked at the doorplate and said: "We are from the law firm. This is Mr. Zhong Haicai's home, right?"

"Yes!" Liang Xiangyun nodded, "But he...... moved away several years ago!"

"Excuse me, who are you to him?" The woman looked inside through the iron bars on the door.

"What do you want?" Liang Xiangyun didn't know how to answer for a moment, so she had to ask back.

The man raised the folder in his hand: "He borrowed money from the bank, and the bank did not agree to extend the loan. We are here to see the house."

He wanted to open the iron door and come in.

"See the house?" This was too much. Liang Xiangyun held the door tightly to prevent them from coming in, "No! I don't know about his borrowing money. I am his wife, and I also have a share in this house. You can't move it!"

"Do you have the marriage registration documents?" The woman looked at her and asked.

Liang Xiangyun was speechless, stunned for a moment and then reacted immediately, and said quickly: "Yes, yes, in the countryside of the mainland!"

The man and woman looked at her, "Oh", and said: "Then we will come back in a few days."

After that, they turned around and left.

Liang Xiangyun was relieved, but she thought that Zhong Haicai must have borrowed money from the bank to mortgage the house. She was kept in the dark , and she felt as if she was hit by a club. As soon as she came to her senses, she realized that this was a disaster from heaven, so she closed the door and hurriedly called Zhong Haicai to curse him: "You bastard, you don't even give me a place to live! Do you want to go to jail?"

Zhong Haicai on the other end made a few groans and hung up the phone without saying anything. When she called again, the phone was turned off.

Liang Xiangyun, who was still furious, took out her cigarette to vent her anger. She walked around the room a few times before she calmed down a little and sat down to think of a solution.

Zhong Haicai worked in Macau, and she knew when he would get paid. Every time he got the money, she would go and make a scene, and Zhong Haicai would give her some living expenses. In the past three years, she only knew that Zhong Haicai was doing real estate in the mainland, and rarely "caught" him in Macau. Four years before, she agreed to "break up", So she was too embarrassed to go to him every day to "beg for alms". But today, someone from the law firm came. It must be that Zhong Haicai had used the house as collateral to borrow money without her knowledge. Now the bank was going to auction the house, Liang Xiangyun had become a fish in the pond that was about to be in trouble!

Liang Xiangyun had always believed that Zhong Haicai gave her the house, so she didn't think about transferring the ownership. "Zhong Haicai, you are so scheming and cruel. You dare to borrow money with my house!"

Liang Xiangyun was so angry that her lungs were about to explode. In any case, the house could not be sealed, otherwise she would have to sleep on the street. Even though she was chased by loan sharks every day before, she never thought of mortgaging the house, but now she was cheated by Zhong Haicai.

No, she must keep the house. Didn't I divorce Zhong Haicai a long time ago, and the house belongs to me? She was unsure in her heart, and hurriedly picked up the phone to consult a fellow villager who ran a company. The fellow villager said that she couldn't do it without a divorce certificate. The house was the common property of the couple, and it would be difficult for Zhong Haicai to sell it unilaterally! But she and Zhong Haicai had never obtained a marriage certificate, so what should she do? ...... There was no way, but she should find a way.!

After thinking about it, she jumped up, found a travel bag, packed a few things, and then called Ahua and said: "Your mother will return to the mainland and the countryside early tomorrow morning, the sky is falling......"

When she left the next day, she specially burned incense for the "door god" placed on the ground outside the door. The god tablet was inserted in a square iron box that had been used to hold moon cakes, and the incense burner was a lotus-shaped plastic box. After burning incense, she put a small apple in the box and replaced the small glass with a new glass of water. In front of the iron box was a round iron box of the same size with a hollow lid. She burned some paper money respectfully.

27

Xu Zhuang was released from prison and looked for Zeng Sheng and Ajian

The seaside of the city was always the place where most people lingered, especially at night. There were many people enjoying the cool air in the Lovers' Road Green Space, some playing with their children, and bursts of laughter from men, women and children.

Although the temperature difference between day and night in the subtropical climate is not large, the sea breeze brings some coolness to people after all. The lights of the Macau Bridge lightly cast a layer of halo here.

Zeng Sheng also had a rare leisure time this night. He held Lili and sat on the grass to watch the sea and feel the cool breeze.

Zeng Sheng took the "Temporary Receipt for the Shareholding of Fruit Girl Fresh Fruit Company" given by Lili, looked up, and was stunned: "Why, I paid the money and wrote your name?"

"Look at you, you are like a rabbit afraid of being caught all day, always worried, you are not like a human being, you are like a ghost, do you dare to show your face? Besides, will Zheng Jianxin take your money if she knows it's you?."

Zeng Sheng understood that he was fooled by the cunning Lili. Then he thought that he hadn't given Lili any money in the past few years, and always promised to "buy a house", it was a small revenge by Lili now. It was time for him to "fall" and finally made a "contribution" to reduce Lili's complaints. He handed the "Temporary Receipt for Shareholding" back to Lili.

Zeng Sheng covered his face and said, "What the hell? I just do a small business like transporting food. My big boss, smuggling cars and engines, made a fortune a long time ago and built a building in Beijing. Now he is doing a formal business. As for me, I have quit from illegal business. In the future, I will invest the little money I earn in the formal projects......"

"Your father's investment in high-tech, is there any news?" Lili asked while putting the temporary receipt into her handbag.

"It's almost there, I'm waiting for him, he said he will arrive next month."

He sighed: "The boat, I won't run it!...... I have been working on the boat for half my life, and my father scolded me for not doing my job properly......"

Lili accused him again: "You are doing a business that harms others and yourself. You could cover the fire but could not hide the smoke!"

Zeng Sheng waved his hand and suddenly burst into laughter: "It's so interesting. Every time my father called, he always asked me at the end, 'Have you found the whereabouts of Miss Zhenzhu (Pearl)?'......"

Lili clapped her hands and laughed.

Zeng Sheng had told Lili the story of Zhenzhu many times. She was very moved by the old man's persistence in his first love. Zeng Sheng's hometown is Xianglu Bay, Zhuhai. Xianglu Bay was a large fishing village in history. Zeng Sheng's family had been fishermen for generations. Grandpa went to Hong Kong before liberation, became a fishing boat owner. After the liberation, in response to the call to build a new China, in 1955, he returned to his hometown with Zeng Sheng's father, Zeng Tianpeng, who was 15 years old that year, and two large sea boats, and became the vice president of the fishery cooperative. When Zhuhai County was established in 1956, his grandfather was invited to join the CPPCC. In 1961, class struggle began, and it was necessary to separate from Hong Kong capitalism. The boat could not go to Hong Kong. His grandfather was labeled as a capitalist and was constantly criticized. The 21-year-old Zeng Tianpeng said goodbye to his 17-year-old fiancée Zhenzhu and sneaked to Hong Kong, and then to the United States, working in a distant relative's restaurant while studying. In 1980, Zhuhai established a special economic zone, and his father came back to invest in a factory and sell national brand pearls in Europe and the United States. Historically, Zhuhai was rich in pearls, and they were tributes to the imperial families.

"You have to tell your father about the whereabouts of Miss Zhenzhu, and give an explanation!"

"They are all dead, what can I say?" Zeng Sheng said, "Zhenzhu was also criticized in the village and ordered to clean toilets for poor farmers every day. Later, she went to Hengqin Island with her father to raise pearls. According to people, she was swept away by the sea water while driving piles...... No, my father knew it at the time, so he got married and gave birth to me. But he won't give up hope, always asking...... "

The sea water came and went, and the sound of "swishing" was sometimes heavy and sometimes light.

The sea is eternal and unchanging. But the people and things on the seashore are like movies, changing very quickly. This is what people often say "a hundred years pass in the blink of an eye". Zeng Sheng's story made Lili feel like she was in another world.

The two were talking affectionately, when a knife suddenly fell in front of them and stabbed into the lawn with force.

The two looked up in shock, only to see Xu Zhuang standing two meters away with bare arms, wearing a yellow vest and green beach pants, with a stern and angry face.

Xu Zhuang didn't wait for the two to speak, he took two steps forward and grabbed Zeng Sheng's neck, his voice as cold as ice: "Zeng Sheng! I'm back!"

Zeng Sheng was a little breathless, and he turned his head to see that it was Xu Zhuang. He twisted Xu Zhuang's hand and said: "Hey, brother, let's talk it out, let's talk it out!"

Lili was also surprised: "Cousin?! You came out? Don't......"

"Cousin, don't worry about it!" Xu Zhuang didn't even look at Lili, staring at Zeng Sheng, his fingers didn't relax at all, "I smuggled for you, took the blame for you and went to jail in Hong Kong...... Humph, but you visited the prison twice and it's fine; I came out, you didn't answer my calls, didn't reply to my messages, and you were free and easy!"

"Xu Zhuang......" Zeng Sheng said with a flattering smile, "No, no, I'll give you some money! I...... I'm helping you to take care of your cousin......"

"Stop farting!" Xu Zhuang pushed him down on the grass and said in a hateful voice, "If you know what's good for you, pay me the hard-earned money within three days, otherwise...... the barefoot are not afraid of the ones wearing shoes!"

"I'll give it to you, I'll give it to you!" Zeng Sheng trembled and took out the money and gave it to Xu Zhuang, "Take this first, brother......"

Seeing Xu Zhuang take the money, Zeng Sheng said, "I've read the information, I'll deposit the money into your account tomorrow", and then ran away.

He knew Xu Zhuang's temper very well. If he stayed there, he might really be beaten up.

Looking at Zeng Sheng's back and sneering a few times, Xu Zhuang put away the knife, sat down on the grass with a grim face, and sighed softly. Lili handed him a cigarette, and after lighting it, she lowered her eyelids and kept silent. He just nodded and shook his head in response to Lili's question.

After a while, he finally asked: "Cousin...... Where is Ajian?......"

Lili hesitated for a long time before saying : "Don't look for her...... She has been very depressed for a while...... Now her husband is in debt, and life has never been peaceful......"

"Husband?" Xu Zhuang's thick eyebrows were raised, and his eyes were wide. Ajian got married? His face changed color in an instant.

"A Macau man named Zhong Haicai......" Lili didn't dare to look him in the eye.

Xu Zhuang stopped talking. His arms were shaking, and his ten fingers were digging into the grass tightly, making a thumping sound; the faster beating heart made a drumming sound. Lili heard it and felt scared. Xu Zhuang smoked heavily, and the sparks on the cigarette shot back violently.

The sea water was rolling in the dim starlight. The broad leaves of the palm trees collided with each other in the night wind, making bursts of noise.

Xu Zhuang in prison missed Zheng Jianxin madly, but because of guilt and fear of being blamed by her, he did not dare to write to her, but asked about Ajian in the letter to Lili. In order to vent his emotions, he wrote a diary and poems every day. He wrote and then revised, revised and then tore it up, putting all his thoughts and deep feelings into it.

Among the prisoners, the reason why he deliberately became the vanguard of the Big Circle Gang and was the first to rush up and beat people in gang conflicts was mostly to vent his anger at being framed by Zeng Sheng and his thoughts for Zheng Jianxin. Only in this way could he divert his attention and not go crazy because of excessive pain.

In addition, he also tried every means to please the prison guards, so that they would not be in a bad mood and make things difficult for him because of a small matter, or even make things difficult for him in reducing his sentence. He wanted to get out of prison as soon as possible, regain freedom as soon as possible, and meet Ajian as soon as possible. Ajian was everything to him.

No wonder the cousin mentioned Ajian less and less in her letters to him, and when he mentioned Ajian, she only said "selling fruits" and "everything is fine".

Xu Zhuang had imagined several possible living conditions for Ajian. Although the various conditions were different, the results were the same: Ajian waited for his return infatuatedly in the hardship. He never thought that Ajian would get married! The daughter of the prime minister waited for Xue Rengui in the cold kiln for eighteen years (a Chinese ancient love story), and he had been away for only three years. Was this something that "Ajian" who had made a vow to him and had a spiritual connection with him could do? Just because of this failure, did his "Ajian" completely deny him? This was not something his "Ajian" could do!

Why was this happening? Why was this happening? Xu Zhuang's heart was broken. His two hands subconsciously kept grabbing and pinching the soil on the ground, and two holes were dug on both sides of his body. He missed Ajian every day in the past three years. He planned how to make a living after being released from prison, such as making money, being with Ajian, and letting Ajian live a life of ease and comfort.

Ajian was his whole world, and the world in front of him suddenly became unrecognizable. Ajian was the whole meaning of his life, and all this seemed to have no meaning. Ajian was the "home" in his heart, the "home" that the "wanderer" in prison always wanted to return to, but the "home" was gone......

This man who was as strong as a mountain, as if his spine had been pulled out, became limp like a puddle of mud, his eyes staring straight and dully at the neon lights of Shuangcheng in the distance, the flashing lights were like a group of demons dancing......

No, I want to see Ajian, see Ajian, I want to ask her, ask her! He ran to Lili's building at a brisk pace. Lili said that the window below her window was Ajian's window. He looked at it carefully. The light was on in the window. Ajian was in the house! — His heart couldn't help but beat wildly again.

Am I going to rush to her house like this? What should I say to her? Make her feel overwhelmed and sad? If her husband is at home, the two men will inevitably quarrel and make her tremble in fear? No! No! She is the saint and goddess in my mind. I can't hurt her, even the slightest harm......

Xu Zhuang didn't know what to do. The woman he loved was so close but he couldn't see her. He was so close but he couldn't tell her that he existed!

Xu Zhuang leaned against a telephone pole. There was a drooping wire above his head. He didn't care about his safety. His eyes were always looking at Ajian's window. The light in the curtain went out, replaced by the faint light of the table lamp. Xu Zhuang kept looking at the faint light until it went out......

Xu Zhuang kept smoking, sometimes taking big puffs, sometimes holding the cigarette between his fingers and forgetting to smoke, until the cigarette burned his hand.

Cigarette butts were thrown all over the ground.

Men don't shed tears easily. In the hard days, tiring days, days of being bullied, including in prison, Xu Zhuang never shed a tear. At this moment, the tears lingered in his heart and silently flowed out, bewitching his eyes and washing his entire face......

28

A couple's road of mixed joy and sorrow

Zheng Jianxin's old window air conditioner hummed all night and didn't cool much, so the house was still stuffy. At dawn, the vendors who were surrounding tenants made breakfast food, and the whole building was filled with the smell of oil smoke. Zheng Jianxin got up and pushed the stroller with the child to the beach to get some fresh air. A well-used small checkered handbag was hung on the stroller to hold books.

The wind in the early morning was cool. Zheng Jianxin sat on a stone bench by the lawn, combed her hair, stood up, and teased her son who was already naughty and running around: "Huihui, just play here, don't run around!" Then she took out a book from the bag hanging on the cart and slowly started reading.

The tide rose before dawn. The sea water looked deep and solemn, beating the stone embankment with full force. A layer of mist floated on the blue sea, exuding a very refreshing fragrance.

Zheng Jianxin looked at the sea, thinking that the tide would slowly recede in a while, and there would be another tide in the afternoon, ups and downs like life. If the sea is also emotional, then the tide sand is the language it confides with.

Zheng Jianxin sighed for no reason and silently asked in her heart: "Oh sea, do you also have happiness and sorrow?"

With a cry, two seagulls quickly passed by in front of her eyes, and did not stop because of Zheng Jianxin's sigh.

The blue sea tide kept beating the embankment, and the sound continued. As Zheng Jianxin was thinking, her eyes suddenly darkened. She turned around in surprise and saw a person standing in front of her: hollow leather sandals, white trousers, and a light yellow round-neck short-sleeved T-shirt.

Looking up, she saw a face with sharp edges and full of tenderness. "Xu Zhuang?! ......"

Zheng Jianxin screamed, and her eardrums roared. This face had appeared in her dreams countless times in the past three years, making her surprised, crying, and guilty......"

"Ajian......"

Xu Zhuang walked to her and wanted to hold her hand.

Zheng Jianxin's fingertips trembled as if she was electrocuted, and a chill ran through her body.

They looked at each other, but were speechless. For a moment, they didn't know what to say, let alone where to start.

Looking at the child who was playing happily with a small stone next to him, Xu Zhuang pulled her to sit on the stone bench.

Xu Zhuang was full of regret. The experience of more than two years of prison life enabled him to endure the pain that ordinary people could not endure, including the humiliation. Even though his heart was turbulent, he could show indifference. He couldn't find the first sentence to say to Ajian, what to say.

Xu Zhuang finally spoke and said to her softly: "I know everything about you." After a long time, he continued, "I hurt you......"

Zheng Jianxin felt the pain of being torn apart in her heart, and her face turned red and white due to the strong mixture of sadness and joy. She bit her lips and looked at the man she had been thinking about day and night again and again. His body was originally long and thin, but now his shoulders had become wider, with chest muscles, full of masculinity; his originally fair face was now brown-red; his original thick eyebrows had not changed, but the smile under his eyebrows had changed, replaced by a deep gaze, and a thin beard on his lips.

Looking at his expectant eyes, Zheng Jianxin's tearing pain in her heart became stronger.

She knew that there would be such a day sooner or later. But when this day came without warning, she didn't know how to deal with it, nor did she know how to explain to him in regard to her current situation.

She couldn't find any words, she just hoped that Xu Zhuang would beat her hard and scold her viciously, so that she could stay away from him from now on and cut off the past. This thought made Zheng Jianxin tremble all over.

Trying to control the abnormal movement of her body, Zheng Jianxin lowered her head and held back her tears, trying to pretend to be calm and change the subject: "Brother Zhuang......it must be very hard in prison?"

Xu Zhuang sat down slowly, and after a long time he said: "Not bad."

"That's good. "Zheng Jianxin replied, but she opened her mouth but didn't know what to say.

Xu Zhuang stared at Zheng Jianxin: Although she was a mother, her plump and dignified figure, which was unique to mountain girls, remained unchanged, but her face which was less rosy and immature, had been replaced by a radiant and mature look; the original pair of passionate eyes now occasionally passed through a few strands of melancholy.

The two were silent for a while.

They used to be close lovers, people who talked about everything under the flowers and the moon, but after a slight turn, everything changed suddenly.

Luofu already has a husband, and the governor has no wife yet...... (a Chinese idiom)

Xu Zhuang's heart twitched.

Looking around, the small checkered handbag on the stroller made Xu Zhuang's eyes light up and his heart warmed up, that was what he bought for Ajian. Several years had passed, it's old, and Ajian was still using it......

He picked up the book Zheng Jianxin was reading and laughed dryly: "Why, are you still reading college textbooks? "

Zheng Jianxin noticed the change in his eyes and quickly turned to look at the child, so as not to lose her composure: "I signed up for a correspondence course at the business school last year to learn e-commerce. I think only knowledge can change destiny!"

Xu Zhuang nodded.

There was another silence.

After a while, Zheng Jianxin finally couldn't stand this atmosphere anymore and said, "I opened a fruit chain store with a few sisters, specifically for migrant workers. The business is pretty good, and life is quite fulfilling; I go to Gongbei Night School twice a week to attend classes."

Xu Zhuang nodded, pointed to the several motorboats shuttling back and forth on the sea, and also avoided the topic: "A motorboat is just a toy, I like to drive a big one. Standing on the big one, the waves splashed and flew under my feet, drawing a beautiful arc, and then returned to calm, with a slightly salty sea breeze blowing all the exposed skin, taking away the heat while also making people sober. "

After a pause, he looked at Zheng Jianxin quietly, wanting to say something but stopping himself, still couldn't help explaining what had happened. He smiled and said, "I knew what I was doing at the time. I don't really have any hatred towards Zeng Sheng, and I'm a little grateful that he let me see the real world outside." After a pause, he said, "I know what I need."

Zheng Jianxin didn't know what to say about the past. She avoided his gaze, her face blank. After a while, she stood up suddenly and said, "I'm going to the fruit store to get busy!"

"Wait......" Xu Zhuang also stood up and held her, "I came here to tell you that a shipping company in Shenzhen wants me......"

Xu Zhuang followed her.

Zheng Jianxin glanced at him, and her heart softened.

Pushing the stroller slowly, Zheng Jianxin looked at the child who was chattering and moving non-stop, her nose was sour, unable to suppress her emotions, and her eyes looked into the distance dejectedly: "Do you know why I named the child Huihui? Huihui means discouraged......"

Xu Zhuang trembled all over, and after a while, he murmured and blamed himself: "It's all my fault. I couldn't protect you......"

He stopped and grabbed Zheng Jianxin's arm: "Ajian, take the child and leave him, let's live together! I love you, never change!"

Zheng Jianxin had expected him to say this, and was not surprised. She said bitterly: "Brother Zhuang, everything is too late."

"That old man Zhong is not only mediocre, but also illiterate. He is not worthy of you at all. You and he are worlds apart. What's the point of getting together?" Xu Zhuang roared excitedly.

Then his eyes turned red, his voice was a little choked, and he said sadly: "When I first came to Zhuhai, I told you that we are poor but not cheap! ...." Unexpectedly, his Ajian also followed the old path of many girls...... He knew that he had to take a big responsibility for Ajian's current situation, but how unfair was fate to her? Xu Zhuang hated the culprit Zhong Haicai to the core!

"No, no, old Zhong treats me well usually." Zheng Jianxin looked flustered and embarrassed, as if a virgin whose clothes were suddenly torn off.

Xu Zhuang frowned and was a little unconvinced: "He has a wife in Macau, you......"

"I know, but they broke up four years ago......" Zheng Jianxin's face was burning, and she couldn't help but raise her hand to cover her face.

The bright sun began to heat the air, and the sea breeze wrapped in humid heat filled the air, making Xu Zhuang sweat a little and his mouth dry. He licked his lips: "But can you be happy? Come with me, take the child, and settle down in Shenzhen or Zhuhai as you like......"

"Don't say it! "

Zheng Jianxin glanced at him, stood with her back to him and said sternly. She felt like a stone was pressing on her heart, and she was suffocated.

"You are willing to be a mistress?" Xu Zhuang's Adam's apple moved twice, and he couldn't help but raise his voice sharply.

Zheng Jianxin was particularly sensitive when she heard the word "mistress". Today, this word came from the mouth of her lover in her heart, and she was so angry that her face turned pale.

You also regard me as a mistress? "Mistress" The word was like sharp needles, piercing Zheng Jianxin's bones. As soon as Xu Zhuang arrived, she immediately smelled the familiar scent on him. She had ignited the fire of girlish love for him, and she associated everything about her beautiful future only with him. This was the man she thought about day and night, her cheeks were flushed, her eyes were watery...... But now she had to forget all this, she was a married woman! And he, Xu Zhuang, was just a passer-by! ...... However, this person whom she wanted to entrust her life to, took risks for money and pushed both of them into the abyss.

Others can call me a mistress, I can bear it; but why do you, Xu Zhuang, call me a mistress? Even you, Xu Zhuang, wronged me! Even if I am a mistress, who forced me to be a mistress? I could have married the person I love and lived my own romantic life, but the ordinary dream that ordinary people can have was shattered by the a hand invisible to Xu Zhuang! It can never be recovered......

Zheng Jianxin was mixed with love and hate. She held back her tears, turned around, and curse words that she couldn't believe she would say came out of her mouth: "Son of a bitch!" At the same time, she raised her hand and slapped Xu Zhuang's face!

She didn't let herself cry, only her chest rose and fell sharply.

The child was frightened and cried, but she didn't care.

The sudden slap shocked Xu Zhuang.

He covered his face, but calmed down immediately. He insisted on finishing what he was going to say: "I will go to work next month, and I will have a monthly salary of more than 20,000 yuan......"

Zheng Jianxin avoided his burning gaze again and turned to leave. Xu Zhuang stopped her: "Ajian, have you really forgotten the red camellia in your hometown?" Yes, the hillside was layered with red plum camellia flowers. At night, they sat on the hillside and smelled the fragrance of flowers......

"Ajian, have you really forgotten when we first came to Zhuhai? "Yes, when going out, Ajian wanted to hold his hand, afraid of losing herself. Xu Zhuang held her hand, and both of them had sweat on their hands......

These memories disturbed Zheng Jianxin's feelings. The bitter water from her heart hung on her long eyelashes, but she would never let Xu Zhuang see it. She turned around firmly and shook off Xu Zhuang's hand.

Xu Zhuang's words poured out like a river with the gate opened. He was out of breath and heartbroken: "Do you know how much I missed you in prison? Do you know that I wanted to tear down the whole prison to find you? Do you know how many letters I wrote to you but didn't dare to send them out in the end? I looked forward to coming out day and night, looking forward to being by your side, but what about you? You...... you...... why don't you call the police to arrest him? You still follow him and continue to let him insult you, why is this! Just for that little money? Do you still remember the vows we made? Do you remember that you said that no matter what happens, we will be together for life? What about now? What about now?!"

Every word of Xu Zhuang hit Zheng Jianxin's heart hard, impacted her nerves, washed every cell, and made her stiff and unable to move.

After a few deep breaths, Xu Zhuang hit his chest, pointed at Ajian who had her back to him, and shouted hysterically with all his strength: "I don't care about anything, I only want you! But you......"

Zheng Jianxin's head seemed suddenly slammed, her face instantly turned pale, her whole body trembled violently, and even the baby carriage shook. Huihui was so scared that he stopped crying and turned his head to look at her blankly.

After yelling, Xu Zhuang was exhausted, his feet could no longer support his body, and he slowly squatted down. His whole head was almost buried in his knees, and his hands supporting the ground were trembling slightly.

Seeing Huihui who was a little panicked and puzzled, Zheng Jianxin calmed down in an instant, but she held the baby carriage tightly with both hands, so that her joints made a sound.

Passersby and tourists did not show much surprise at their strange behavior, but they were silent when they approached, and then hurried past.

"I know you are a little vain......" Xu Zhuang's choked voice came out vaguely from between his knees, full of frustration and despair, "It was because I knew it that I took the risk......"

When Xu Zhuang first came to Zhuhai, he was most afraid to go shopping with Ajian. But Ajian, like all girls, could not resist the charm of the goods in the mall. The bags, clothes and shoes that Ajian liked were all very expensive when she asked about the prices, not to mention the necklaces and earrings in the jewelry store. Ajian picked up these things curiously and flipped through them, but had to put them down reluctantly. When Ajian saw the fashionable clothes of the passing girls on the street, she stared at them and exclaimed in admiration. At these times, Xu Zhuang's head was sweating. What kind of man was he if he couldn't satisfy the needs of his beloved girl a little bit! And Ajian's words like "When can I have......", although they were just casual words, became Xu Zhuang's pain, became Xu Zhuang's motivation to make money at all costs, and also made him resolutely leave the beverage factory......

When he came to Guangdong, he saw that everyone was thinking about money and working day and night for money. Those who mad money didn't show their joy, those who worked for nothing didn't curse, everything was going on silently, Xu Zhuang shuddered: it was like a world with white moonlight, a cluster of ghost lights dancing in front. Countless people were like marathon runners, running after it. These people were like ghosts, or turned into ghosts, running silently. This world had simply become a world of ghosts.

When he got involved with Zeng Sheng, Zeng Sheng was like a window, which made him see at once: some people were making hundreds of thousands, millions, and ten millions of dollars. These propaganda about the rich and the numbers fermented in his blood, just like someone took a piece of candy and kept shaking it in front of a child, so that the child could see it, but could never eat it. He couldn't calm down, he found a huge gap and a huge goal: "I am also a six-foot man, they can do it, I can do it too, I want to fight!" The result was "dying before achieving success", stepping on a row of landmines.

One day not long after arriving in Zhuhai, Zheng Jianxin stared at a girl's handbag on the street with envy. The handbag was small checkered, simple and unique. She told Xu Zhuang that their factory manager had such a handbag.

Xu Zhuang knew that she liked this handbag. He asked: "How much is it? Where can I buy it?"

"It's so expensive, more than a thousand yuan...... It's said to be on Lianhua Road......" Zheng Jianxin said hesitantly.

"I'll buy it for you!" Xu Zhuang promised generously.

"I don't want it, I don't want it! I'm just talking!" Zheng Jianxin refused firmly.

The next day, Xu Zhuang withdrew two thousand yuan from the bank and ran along the beach to Lianhua Road. There was indeed such a handbag in that store. Xu Zhuang was about to buy it happily, and two female tourists in fashionable clothes were also looking at the handbag, whispering that it was a replica and a fake. Xu Zhuang hurriedly asked the boss: "Is this a genuine brand?" The boss teased him for not knowing the business: "If it is real, authentic, this world famous brand, it will cost 10,000 or 20,000 yuan in duty-free shops!"

Xu Zhuang slowly put the handbag back to its original place, muttering in his heart: "Counterfeit products are illegal, don't buy; can't help these people do fake business...... "He stopped again after walking a few steps out of the store: "If I don't buy it, Ajian likes it, isn't it a waste of time?" He thought for a long time, and in order to make Ajian happy, he made up his mind: "Buy it! "

He found Zeng Sheng and borrowed 20,000 yuan from him for the first time. He ran to a leather goods counter on the second floor of Jida Duty Free Shop and bought the handbag. After that, he ate instant noodles for a month. He was so happy when he saw Ajian carrying her beloved brand-name handbag!

He slowly raised his head from the small checkered handbag, his face was covered with tears and snot, and he shook his head and continued hoarsely: "You won't understand how I felt in prison, you won't know what kind of hell it was, and you won't understand how much effort and trouble I had put in to stand here before original release time. You......are no longer you, not the you who followed me out of the village......"

Zheng Jianxin pushed the cart away without stopping, letting the bitter tears flow from the corners of her mouth and fall to the ground. For a long time, she couldn't understand why she followed Zhong Haicai and why she was so cowardly.

Now she is a married woman. Married women must stick to the code of conduct for woman. Although extramarital affairs, one-night stands, and mistresses are popular in this society, she will never follow the crowd. She must be an upright woman, a clean woman, and no exception for anyone, including Xu Zhuang.

Looking at Zheng Jianxin's back as she walked away without looking back, Xu Zhuang strode to catch up and put an envelope on the baby carriage: "Small changes, for household use!"

Ajian opened it and saw that it was a lot of money. She quickly returned the envelope to Xu Zhuang and shouted: "I am a woman with a husband and a family. I am a decent woman. Don't come to me again! I don't want to see you again! "

Such a heartless and ruthless look, such cold words, Xu Zhuang couldn't believe that they came from Ajian's mouth, and a piercing sadness surged into his heart. It was like a knife plucking his gallbladder and piercing his heart. Zheng Jianxin walked away, and he called out:

"Ajian...... Ajian......"

He took a breath and uttered a steely voice: "Ajian, I love you, forever!" After shouting, he held the envelope in his hand, his legs softened, and he fell to the grass.

A few Hong Kong dollar notes were falling......

Xu Zhuang closed his eyes. He could feel the sweat oozing from the soles of his feet. He could not hear all the noise around him, and his heart was as calm as "death" as he had never felt before. He sneered and said to himself: "For money, but what's the use of money? " He looked up to the sky and sighed: "No matter how long it takes, this resentment will never go away......"

He buried his head in the grass and cried bitterly. On the other side, Zheng Jianxin didn't walk far. Her light body swayed, and her feet could no longer support the weight of her body. She fell heavily. She felt her body was smashed to pieces. She climbed up with difficulty, knelt on the grass, and rested her arms on the baby carriage frame. "I...... I am not a mistress......" She rested her head on her arm, murmured, and tears welled up again.

The sea was quiet.

No one except the sea listened to the conversation and words of lovers.

Women drinking afternoon tea in the coffee shop

The coffee shop was open, and the sea could be seen through the large glass windows.

The words "Kaohsiung specialty simple meals, charcoal-roasted coffee, Taiwan high mountain tea" were written in dark blue and brown on the glass. The store was not large, only 30-plus square meters. Taiwanese shaved ice and snacks were placed on the counter at the door of the store, and various glassware shone under the orange light. The small square table in the store was covered with a checkered tablecloth, and the store looked clean and warm.

About every afternoon, there was a group of women who gathered here to drink afternoon tea. Some of them married men from overseas or Hong Kong, Macau and Taiwan and settled here; some went through immigration procedures and were waiting for approval; some were girlfriends or lovers of overseas men; some had given birth to children for overseas men, and overseas men had set up another "home" here. They had beautiful makeup and permed hair styles. Their hairs were dyed yellow, brown, and red, and their clothes were revealing and sexy. They had not left the country yet, but their appearances were already exotic. They drank coffee, drinks, tea, ate snacks, crack melon seeds, played around, and laughed from time to time.

They didn't have to go to work and had money to spend. Overseas men used "Love" to pull the mainland young girls with dreams out of love and embraced them in Gongbei. These women who relied on men for their fate seemed calm, but they were actually helpless. They were looking for opportunities to dispel loneliness. They exchange information, hoping that their fate would suddenly change one day. An important topic among them was immigration. Who had obtained a one-way permit (i.e., an immigration visa) and would leave in the next two days; how was someone's life after immigration, and how much money she got after finding a job. After talking about these things that could be directly or indirectly learned from, they chatted about everything under the sun.

The slim Girl A, who dyed her hair brown and tied it into a knot behind her head, shouted: "I want money too much. I lost all the money I have playing mahjong. I want to ask someone to buy an Apple phone from Macau for 8,500 yuan, and I want to learn to drive, which costs 4,500 yuan......"

The plump Girl B, who wore beggar shorts, said: "I want money too, I want money like crazy! One of my girlfriends helped her boss in the mainland to gamble in Macau. The boss won hundreds of thousands and gave her 100,000! Why can't I meet such a big fish? If I have money, a few people will pool 200,000 to pay the down payment for a cement mixer truck, and deliver bulk cement to the construction site. It is a sure profit; a mixer truck costs 2.5 million, and it can be paid off in three years. From now on, it is my own profit! "

"Buying a truck can make a sure profit? Don't be fooled, be careful!" someone said.

"No," said Girl B, "I will go to the construction site to cook, watch the truck, and contact the business myself. No one can fool me!"

Several people over there chattered and giggled.

Someone made fun of Lili, making her embarrassed, Lili laughed at herself: "I don't want to be like this! Men, not a single one is good. If I think this way, I feel that I am not wrong!"

The first girl smiled and "exposed the truth": "Among the three, Lili is very special to the Taiwanese guy. The bed creaked at night until dawn!"

Everyone laughed.

Lili blew out a puff of smoke with an angry look on her face: "Nonsense! Taiwanese guys are perverts! I wish I could drive them all away. They always cheat me by buying a house!"

Girl A: "I saw it. When the Taiwanese guy came, he brought a big bag of children's clothes!"

Girl B: "Only Brother Chang from Macau doubted it. He said to me, 'How did I become a father without knowing it! '"

Girl A teased Lili: "Who is as good as you? You brought a seed from the countryside and changed it into three, Hong Kong, Macau, and Taiwan!"

Lili laughed, raised her eyebrows and relaxed her eyes, scratched her ears and cheeks: "Don't make fun of me, who doesn't have black spot at the bottom!"

Everyone laughed again.

Nineteen-year-old Sister Lian blinked her eyes and asked: "Why can't I understand anything!"

Girl B: "There is a lot of knowledge here!"

"Bullshit knowledge! The most easily deceived and hurt are our mainland girls! "

The speaker was a girl who had just returned from Taiwan to visit her family. "I only realized when I got there that most of the men we married were bad boys or had criminal records! Then I saw that they all married mainland beauties! They came to the mainland, dressed up like decent people, well-mannered, and chose their wives like they were choosing concubines! Mainland girls are all bullied by their in-laws in Taiwan, as if we all married to Taiwanese for money! We are discriminated against! In the end, we are beaten and scolded by our husbands!"

"It's so pitiful!" A woman with big wavy hair kept fiddling with her phone, "Listen, there's a paragraph: You are the wind and I am the sand, you are the leather shoes and I am the brush, if you ignore me, I will commit suicide!"

The smoke from the cigarette was curling up.

Girl A also found a joke on her phone: "Listen to this. The person I love is already taken, and the person who loves me is unbearable to look at, either becoming bad in debauchery, or becoming perverted in silence!"

Everyone laughed: "That's right, perverted!"

In such a loose gathering, people came and went. Zheng Jianxin came in and pulled a chair to sit down, which attracted everyone's attention.

"Ajian is back! "

People can't live without groups. The closest thing life could provide to Zheng Jianxin was such a circle. Just as she didn't agree with Lili's lifestyle, she didn't agree with the bored lifestyle of this group of people either. Just as she understood Lili's helplessness, she also understood the current situation of this group of people. In the past, Zheng Jianxin accompanied Lili here several times when she couldn't refuse. Curiosity drove her to sit and listen here, broaden her visions, and dispel her unhappiness in the bustle. Now it was different. She had become a family member of Macau people. Her subconscious told her that she belonged to this group. She and they did have a common topic of immigrating to Macau, and she also wanted to get some knowledge and information from it.

Mingming was a quiet woman, about 23 or 24 years old, plump, and wearing long black hair. Because she didn't see the sun much, her face was as delicate as a white magnolia. She poured Ajian a cup of milk tea and asked, "Is your hometown good?"

"Nothing has changed."

Lili said with a smile: "You are the only one who has changed. You got the marriage certificate!"

Zheng Jianxin slowly took out the red "marriage certificate" from her bag, then opened the "marriage certificate" and held it in her hand to show everyone. Although she said she was showing it to everyone, she stared at it intently, her tender eyes sparkling with proud passion, and her face showed a satisfied expression.

Mingming said: "I have no hope in this life!" Then she lit a cigarette and said to herself as if to make fun of herself: "Mistress, just mess around like this for the rest of my life......"

Several women touched it curiously, like looking at a gem, turning it over and over, as if it were their own. The "marriage certificate" made these women's faces red. They bowed their heads, shook their heads, and sighed in different ways.

Getting a marriage certificate is the most basic right and the most common thing for any adult, but for some women here, they will never enjoy or get it. Some of them don't have, and won't have, marriages. They don't have upright lovers, and don't have marriages under the sun. Their "love" exists in the dark, living on its own. They are mentally disabled.

Girl A took the marriage certificate and was filled with another kind of joy: "Just wait for the Macau ID card!"

Zheng Jianxin smiled bitterly and shook her head gently. The debt was like a stone that made Zhong Haicai and Zheng Jianxin breathless. How could they have the mind to apply for immigration?

Mingming pointed at Girl B: "Look, she has only obtained the marriage certificate two or three years ago, and she can get the Macau ID card next month! Next month, she will become a Macau compatriot!"

Everyone cast envious eyes on Girl B. These girls from the mainland, relying on the boasting of foreign men, closed their eyes all day and fantasized about the paradise-like life in Hong Kong and Macau, a life where money was sprinkled from the sky to make people happy every day.

Zheng Jianxin asked Sister Lian: "Do you have any news about your Taiwanese husband?"

Sister Lian shook her head: "No, there are still a few debt collectors, so fierce, I am very scared! .... The landlord wants to drive me out!"

Girl A: "Alas...... People are like a bunch of grass, I don't know where to plant them."

Zheng Jianxin: "Sister Lian, why don't you live in my shop and help us sell fruits!"

When several people heard that Sister Lian was "saved" so easily, they quickly agreed: "Yes, good thing!"

Sister Lian's eyes lit up, nodded and thanked repeatedly.

Zheng Jianxin opened two more stores close to the factory last month.

Just when everyone changed the topic and talked to Zheng Jianxin about her fruit shop, Ahua's slender figure appeared outside the glass window and waved to Zheng Jianxin cutely.

"Zheng Jianxin, your daughter is here to see you!"

Several women said with a smirk in unison.

Zheng Jianxin responded to Ahua, stood up and poohed them, without any displeasure on her face.

"I'm leaving too." Lili said hello to everyone and walked to the door side by side with Zheng Jianxin.

On the way, Lili told Zheng Jianxin that she wanted to go back to her hometown in the next few days.

"Why, are you upset?" Zheng Jianxin was silent for a while before asking.

"I have seen through it," Lili said sadly, "Marriage is a rope. Since I am tied to it, I have to accept my fate and Inmiss my husband!" She said with deep understanding, "Family is a bed. No matter how long you wander outside, your own bed is still soft and your own quilt is comfortable."

Zheng Jianxin nodded in agreement and was delighted by Lili's change.

As soon as she returned to Gaosha Street, Achang came up from behind with a big bag and opened the bag and put it in front of Lili: "I bought you something from Macau. They are all childcare supplements. It is difficult to buy genuine products in the mainland, and they are expensive......"

"You are really good at pleasing people......" Zheng Jianxin smiled and patted him."

I really love Sister Lili. I will take her and take her to Macau." Achang said confidently.

"What a cougar love!" Zheng Jianxin glanced at him and joked, "Do you understand her? What do you love about her?"

Achang looked at the curves of Lili's sexy body and said affectionately: "Love is a feeling, it cannot be explained."

The mistake of love itself is a tragedy. Moreover, Achang had been deceived by Lili without knowing it. Zheng Jianxin was an experienced person, and her heart ached. She quickly turned her head away so that they would not see the tears in her eyes.

30

Liang Xiangyun placed the "marriage certificate" in a prominent position

At home in Macau, Liang Xiangyun got angry when she heard the word "celestial being" on TV. Outside the window, the lights were on. Ahua, who graduated from high school, found a job in a casino and had been working for a month.

Ahua lived at home, Liang Xiangyun was full of joy, and the family was lively. She cooked according to Ahua's time off work, wanting to take good care of her daughter. But Ahua couldn't stay at home. She went to Zhuhai every few days with her eyebrows and eyes painted.

Liang Xiangyun got angry at Ahua who was packing up to go out: "Heavenly fairy? Northern girl, vixen! You are going to find her again. She hooked your father's soul. She hooked your soul again in the past two years! Humph!" Liang Xiangyun said while burning incense at the shrine.

Ahua grumbled dissatisfiedly: "Mommy, you broke up with my father several years ago, and you don't care about him anymore!" In front of the mirror on the dressing table, she gently applied a layer of makeup powder on her face.

"Do you think I care about your father? I'm talking to you, my daughter, you treat my home as a store, and you have to leave again after walking around! Go, go, I'm an old woman, even if I die here, no one will know!" The last two sentences were said lightly, with a bit of sadness.

Ahua understood her mother's loneliness, pushed her handbag aside, and smiled: "Okay, Mommy, I'll accompany you. I will go after dinner!"

She accidentally saw two documents on the chest: "Marriage certificate? New?"

Ahua saw that the date was a few months before, and her father's name was written on it, so she asked: "Does Dad know?"

Liang Xiangyun kept wiping the table with her hands, and said contemptuously: "Why let him know?"

"Mommy, what are you doing here?" Ahua remembered that Zheng Jianxin got a marriage certificate with her father two years before, and asked in confusion.

Liang Xiangyun looked a little proud in her calmness: "It's useful, I can use it!"

"Where did it come from? Didn't you buy it at a street stall in Guangzhou?"

"Nonsense!" Liang Xiangyun said seriously, "I went to the government in my hometown to get it! It's legally binding! I've sent it to the Macau government for record!"

Ahua quickly realized that it was about the house, so she didn't ask. Ahua took out bread and ham from the refrigerator, made a fruit salad, fried eggs on the induction cooker, and put them on the table.

Liang Xiangyun said: "I want to drink!"

"Okay." Ahua opened a bottle of Portuguese red wine and opened assorted fruits for Mommy to drink.

Time had turned Mommy into a dry old woman, but her movements were not clumsy or slow. It was just that her teeth had fallen out and it was difficult to chew food. Her shriveled cheeks kept squirming. As she took a sip of wine, her back trembled slightly. Ahua felt a pain in her heart and blamed herself for ignoring Mommy's existence.

Ahua kept picking up food for Mommy and talking to her. But most of the time it was Liang Xiangyun who was talking and Ahua who was listening.

Some people say that reminiscing about the past is a symbol of getting old. For Liang Xiangyun, what she was rich in was the past. For older people, the past is warm.

Liang Xiangyun looked at Ahua's pink face and said emotionally:

"When I was young, your mommy was also a flower on the island! Your dad smuggled to Macau early, he couldn't go back for many years, and I raised your brother; I almost died when I came to Macau"

"Mom" Ahua said: "You have told the story of the backwater fish (smugglers) many times!"

"Huh? Huh, what does it mean?"

"It's many, many times. You sat in a wooden tub and couldn't get close to the port of Macau......"

Liang Xiangyun lit a cigarette.

"Now think about it, what have I got in my life? Just a Macau ID!"

Liang Xiangyun took a puff of cigarette, and the smoke floated. "When you were one year old, there was an amnesty. It was March 1990......" Liang Xiangyun had been reminiscing about the past when she was free these past two years, and she wanted to tell others about it whenever she had the chance.

"I was busy in the porridge shop at the time, and outside there were a lot of people shouting 'Amnesty! Amnesty!'

"That night, the one-kilometer road from Nanwan to Xinma Road was filled with a long line of people, shouting and yelling. At dawn, the "underground people" who were tired but happy at heart rushed into the Yat Yuen Canine Racing Field to register.

"People tried to squeeze into the stadium. They had to press their fingerprints in two places! People were hustling and screaming. Some women's skirts were squeezed off. Some people from Zhongshan and Jiangmen got the news and went to Gongbei to try to break through the customs to enter Macau......"

She was thoughtful, as if she had suddenly realized something. She took out her "Macau Resident Identity Card" from her handbag, looked at it over and over again, and said with bitterness: "Alas, I have thought about it a lot. It seems that my whole life is just for a piece of paper, a small notebook ......"

Outside the window, the neon lights flickered and changed from time to time. Ahua looked at the clock on the wall from time to time. The clock pointed to ten thirty. At twelve o'clock, the traffic crossing customs office would be stopped. Ahua couldn't help it: "Mommy, go to bed early, I have to pass the customs!"

"Looking for a boyfriend? What kind of good man can that northern girl introduce to you?"

"Mom, I am going to Zhuhai to find a job......" Ahua pouted and gave Mommy a reproachful look. Her face flushed instantly. She picked up her handbag and was about to go out. She hugged Mommy affectionately, and said to Mommy's ear in a cute and naughty way: "I will support you when you are old! Let's go back to the mainland!"

"I have something else to say!" Liang Xiangyun was reluctant to let her daughter go, and always wanted to keep her for a while.

"Today I asked you Dad, the bank is okay now......"

Ahua didn't want to listen, and said casually: "It's okay as long as you pay the interest monthly!"

Ahua opened the door and was gently pulled by her mother again. Liang Xiangyun forced a smile and held out her hand, "Give Mommy some money, money is tight......"

Ahua took three hundred-dollar Portuguese patacas, "Mommy, stop gambling!"

Taking the bills, Liang Xiangyun nodded, "Quit gambling a long time ago! Giving it to your mommy is better than being cheated by the mistress, hum!"

Ahua shook her head helplessly at her words, but was too lazy to refute anything. Liang Xiangyun sat for a long time without moving, looking at her daughter's back as she left, feeling sad. The room was always dark except for a lamp in the living room that emitted a faint light. Whether watching TV or not, Liang Xiangyun would not turn on the main lights. The room was so quiet that only the sound of the fan was heard. Although her home was in a busy city, it was like a small temple in the mountains, cold and deserted.

She curled up in the wooden sofa, with a towel beside her, wiping the sweat from her neck in the dimness. She often fell asleep while lying like this. Sometimes she woke up in the middle of the night and went back to bed, and sometimes she slept until dawn. It was late at night, and she didn't want to sleep, for fear that she would die after falling asleep and no one would find her for three or five days. Every time like this, she would leave home and go to the casino.

When she first arrived in Macau, the Hong Kong-Macau Port had not yet been built, and the ships from Hong Kong were parked at the Inner Harbor. The Inner Harbor was bustling, with one pier after another. There was a casino called "Sea Palace" built next to Pier 16 -- it was gone now. Liang Xiangyun went from Taishan Street in the North District, through Kwai Kei Street and Sha Lei Tou, to the "Pirate Ship" (that's what the locals call it) to gamble. If she won some money, she would buy fish, meat and vegetables at the "Water Market" next to it and take it home. She didn't dare to go home if she lost money after gambling. She would go to the nearby Tong Sin Hall to wait for the "rice distribution". Sometimes, people would fight for this free rice. Sometimes, after gambling all her money and having nowhere to go, she would go to the church "Rose Hall" to listen to the teachings of quitting gambling.

Now, in addition to several specialized large casinos in Macau, almost every large hotel had a casino. Sometimes she didn't gamble, but went to the casino just to relax. The luxurious decoration in the casino made her feel that life was really good. The air conditioning there was sufficient and comfortable. She sat at the gambling table for a while and asked for a free drink. When she saw other betting customers winning money, her heart was warmed, and she couldn't help but take out the only two or three hundred yuan in her pocket and bet on it. The simplest thing was to bet on size. The electronic display on the gambling table shows the record, and the number of big and small numbers was opened in turn. You could judge whether to bet on big or small number next time. Bet on the glass table with number written on it. The dice cup makes a crisp sound, and the lights light up. If you bet on the right one, you win. The more you bet, the more you win. If you bet on the pair on the small glass table, your win will be multiplied.

Liang Xiangyun had done homework on "gambling".

Not long after she came to Macau, she heard about Ye Han, the founder of Macau's gambling industry. It was said that Ye Han, who was known as "the man scaring ghosts", had a pair of particularly large ears. When the dice cup was shaken, his ears immediately stood up. From the tinkling sound of the glass dice cup, he could distinguish the difference in the sound of each dice falling, the difference in the number of dice landing, and the number of points when guessing big or small. He won every time he sat at the gambling table. The bosses of American casinos were afraid of him. Liang Xiangyun thought that if she had one ten-thousandth of his ability, it would be a huge profit and a huge source of wealth. Liang Xiangyun was so happy that she was going crazy.

So Liang Xiangyun locked herself in the house and did not leave the house for two whole months. Liang Xiangyun could endure hardships. According to the experience of Ye Han taught by her friends, she practiced over and over again, and her fingers were rubbed with blisters. Now all five fingers were covered with calluses.

The sound of the dice falling on the glass seemed to be muffled, so the number on the side in the dice cup will be small, either one or two; the side facing up could only be one possibility...... four points, the sound was difficult to distinguish between yin and yang, and the most difficult to figure out......

Then you had to practice multiple dices, shake three dices at the same time, and instantly distinguish the sound of three dices falling into the cup.

Liang Xiangyun practiced single dice without any results, so she practiced multiples; when multiples failed, she practiced single. Sometimes she could hear clearly, and sometimes she couldn't hear clearly. Not to mention being tired all day, she would count by the bed at night, and even forgetfully shouted "big!" and sometimes shouted "small!" with her eyes straight. When she was excited, she stood on the bed and shook the dice cup over and over again. She only wore a sweatshirt on her upper body. As the cup shook, her two sagging breasts also shook, slapping each other and making a rhythmic "pa" and "pa" sound.

When Zhong Haicai came home and saw this scene, he was amused, angry, and disgusted: "You are really playing tricks......"

"No, I want to become a saint, a gambling saint!" Liang Xiangyun felt very good about herself, to the point of being intoxicated.

But the dice cups of the casino had already been changed, and Liang Xiangyun failed again and again.

It was not that the skills Liang Xiangyun learned hard were useless.

One night she won 50,000 yuan with 1,000 yuan. When she returned home at dawn, she tossed and turned in bed, too excited to sleep. She had her own goal, and when she made 150,000 yuan, she would retire. With this money, she would go back to her hometown and buy a small shop in the town, live upstairs and rent out the downstairs for retirement.

Every time she went back to her hometown, the whole village looked at her with strange eyes, wondering if she had become rich and if she was a rich woman. She was disgusted with those sophisticated people. They envied those who made money in Hong Kong and Macau, and they despised those who were mediocre to the point of gloating. For this reason, she rarely went back to her hometown and rarely contacted her relatives. She spent more than ten years of her life in repeated wins and losses. Even if she lost all her money, she couldn't bear to leave. She watched others gamble and watch others win and lose. She could watch for a long time. In the casino, the unknown and mysterious answers always tempted her. Sometimes she would linger in the casino for three days. Unwilling to lose, she stepped into the tiger's mouth casino again and again like a hero who would never return......

Now, her life had an answer: she had completely given up. Except for occasionally, going to the casino was just to relax and have a cup of coffee. She didn't even look at the gambling table. When she walked out of the casino and touched the money in her pocket, she would happily say: "Not gambling means winning, this is my win!"

The following life was to face the long night. The house was empty, and the heart was empty. Was it just waiting to die? The housing prices in the mainland were rising again and again on TV. Would she never have the face to return to my hometown? As an old woman who no one cared about until her death, couldn't she hold her head up in front of neighbors and relatives? The pressure in her heart was getting bigger and bigger. She had no way out. From the window of her house, she could see the glittering Jinsha Casino. Although she was resisting in her heart, she couldn't sit still. In the end, that "Liang Xiangyun" defeated this Liang Xiangyun: "I want to go again. Life is like a dream, just fool around! At worst, I can jump into the sea. Anyway, it's all death, and it's time to die. It's the same whether I live or die......"

Such people can be seen in the gates of large and small casinos: wearing ordinary suits, pretending to be waiting for someone, turning around, and aiming at the gamblers coming in and out one by one. When you stop for a while and feel depressed, he will come over and ask you if you want to borrow money like an old friend, and he doesn't need to pledge, just an ID card is enough.

Liang Xiangyun was very familiar with such people, and she took the initiative to walk towards one of them......

Everyone will taste the ups and downs of life, but the difference is that each has its own taste. In the dark room, besides the light from outside, there was only the spark of the cigarette in her hand. She thought that after nearly 20 years in Macau, she had lived like a dream, and in the end it was still a pitiful nightmare!

She often thought that if she hadn't come to Macau, she would have been busy farming, fishing, washing clothes in her hometown. Although it was hard work, it would be so nice to have the whole family together at night, and it would be endless fun! If she hadn't left her hometown, maybe she and Zhong Haicai would be playing with their grandchildren at the beach now!

Thinking of this, she seemed to smell the fragrance of the fish soup that Zhong Haicai cooked with wild fire at the beach again......

Alas! If there was enough food for the whole family at that time, they would not have gone out and run to Macau......

Liang Xiangyun didn't miss her hometown like the fallen leaves returning to their roots. She wanted to leave Macau immediately and leave Macau forever. She wanted to be an ordinary old woman in her hometown!

But she felt like a lonely goose, crying in the fading light, wanting to fly, but unable to, without the strength......

31

Zhong Haicai said his fortune had come:
an unknown person repaid his bank debt for him

The sky won't fall, and if the sky doesn't want people to die, people have to live day by day, no matter how difficult it is. After being scared for a while, Zhong Haicai's body and spirit slowly woke up.

After hard work, the Macau bank extended his debt repayment period for one year.

There was no chance to play in the mainland. Zhong Haicai didn't chase money, the ghost fire that always fluttered in front of his eyes, and he couldn't catch up. Zhong Haicai was honest and accepted his fate. From then on, he went back to Macau every day to work on a casino construction site owned by a company of the United States. He worked overtime day and night in order to make more money to pay the bank's loan interest. As for when and how to pay back the principal, he didn't dare to think about it; he could only return to his home in Zhuhai once a week or two.

Zhong Haicai was still a man: he didn't ask Zheng Jianxin to use her money to support the family, but he reduced his expenses and sent her money monthly. He and his co-workers had afternoon tea during breaks. Instead of drinking coffee and eating sausages and bread, he only paid four or five yuan for a croissant and a free cup of tea. He quit drinking and declined dinner parties. He didn't want others to pay the bill, and he didn't pay for others either. Men don't use women's money. He wanted Zheng Jianxin to use her savings to do business.

Achang and other co-workers also expressed understanding of Zhong Haicai's situation. Instead of chasing debts, they pooled money to pay the bank interest monthly.

One day, when Zhong Haicai was working on the construction site, someone from the bank called and told him that he didn't need to pay the interest anymore. The principal had been paid off two months before. He was also notified to go through the procedures for releasing the mortgage of the house and collect the overpaid interest.

"F..k (really annoying), who is playing tricks!" Zhong Haicai hung up the phone before he finished listening to the phone call, frowning angrily, "You think I'm not unlucky, and you're making fun of me!" He kept cursing.

The phone rang again, but Zhong Haicai didn't answer it. Then another call came. He had to answer it. It was indeed the bank.

Zhong Haicai thought the bank had called the wrong number, but the bank insisted that it was not wrong. This was strange. Zhong Haicai had to run to the bank. The manager took out a receipt: "Two months ago, an unknown person in Hong Kong remitted 350,000 Hong Kong dollars, saying that he would pay off your loan. The note said that he had already told you to pay him back in three years."

Zhong Haicai was stunned after hearing this. How could such a thing happen? It must be someone in Hong Kong who made a mistake. The bank asked him to look at the bill of exchange again. It clearly had his name "Zhong Haicai" written on it. That was right!

After confirming it again and again, Zhong Haishi believed it and became extremely excited. Who cares what bank, who cares what remitter, who cares whether right or wrong, as long as the bank doesn't chase him to pay back the debt! He quickly made a cross on his chest, affirming in the name of God that this was true.

Zhong Haicai jumped out of the bank. God knows what tricks God was playing! It seemed that Zhong Haicai had had good luck! The God of Wealth had come knocking on his door!

Zhong Haicai was so happy that he felt like he was in the clouds, and his whole body was light. Liang Xiangyun was worried every day, worried that someone would come to seize the house at any time. After a long time, she didn't see any move from the bank, and couldn't help but call Zhong Haicai and asked: "Have you settled your business?"

"It was okay! A friend from Hong Kong paid off my bank loan for me!"

"I don't believe you!" Liang Xiangyun scolded. Zhong Haicai, a construction worker, how could he have a Hong Kong friend who was a rich boss?

"I'm not joking, and it's just a friend I don't know. You can ask the people at the bank and you will understand!"

Liang Xiangyun, who was half-believing and half-doubting, of course went to the bank to verify it. The result was true, and she was relieved and happy like Zhong Haicai.

That day, Zhong Haicai stopped working overtime. Not owing money to the bank anymore was a good thing for him. He wanted his body to take a breath and relieve the blood circulation in his limbs. After work in the evening, he returned to Zhuhai from Macau.

When crossing the border, Zhong Haicai bought a bottle of French red wine for Ajian at a duty-free shop, and he bought a bottle of Jiujiang double-distilled liquor for himself on the street at four yuan a bottle, to celebrate his fortune with Ajian. When he arrived at the intersection of Gaosha Street, the roadside fruit stalls were filled with red imported cherries, 80 yuan a pound. Zhong Haicai knew that Zheng Jianxin liked to eat but was reluctant to buy them, and he only had 100 yuan in his pocket at this time. After hesitating for a while, he still bought a pound.

What he wanted was for Ajian to be happy!

Zheng Jianxin felt a little agitated at first about Zhong Haicai's "happy event", but soon she guessed 80% to 90% of the reasons. Instead of being happy, she felt heavy in her heart: It was Xu Zhuang, it must be him!

Before the meal was ready, Zhong Haicai couldn't help opening the bottle of wine and drinking it in small sips with fermented bean curd and peanuts.

He couldn't help laughing while drinking. He laughed strangely, like the squeak of a baby crying, and the vertical wrinkles on his cheeks were squeezed together and more obvious. Because he stayed at the construction site every day, his eyes were swollen from the sun and the sea breeze, and there was white cement in his nails that could never be brushed off.

"Laugh? Why are you laughing all the time?" Zheng Jianxin asked unhappily, "Don't laugh so much that you become an idiot!"

Zhong Haicai took a bite of the chicken: "This is really too bizarre!" He asked her, "Who do you think that mysterious person is?"

"I'm not a god. How can I know if you don't even know?" Zheng Jianxin replied unhappily while cooking. After Zhong Haicai had enough wine and food, he was too lazy to wash the bowl. He smugly hummed the Shatin lyrics: "The hut is short and low, but you don't mind the simplicity to pick up my girl. Pearls are on the bottom of the sea, and the waves are big. It's rare to meet a true girl in this world."

Shatin is the land formed by the accumulation of silt from the Pearl River at the mouth of the Pearl River. The so-called water village is the village formed on this land. Zhong Haicai's ancestors were Hakkas who immigrated here and later settled on the island, but they always maintained Hakka custom.

Zheng Jianxin was washing dishes, and Zhong Haicai sang and walked behind Zheng Jianxin, one hand around Zheng Jianxin's waist, and the other hand into Zheng Jianxin's shirt.

"Get out!" Zheng Jianxin was feeling choked up, and pushed him away with her elbow in annoyance, and ran out of the door with a shake of her hand, leaving behind Zhong Haicai who looked puzzled and her son who was still eating at the table.

Zheng Jianxin ran to the beach in one breath, held the railing with both hands, looked at the sea in the direction of Shenzhen and Hong Kong, and after a long time, she shouted to the sky like a volcanic eruption: "Xu Zhuang......"

She seemed to hear the echo from the horizon, and the hot feelings for Xu Zhuang in her heart surged up. She murmured to herself: "Brother

Zhuang, why don't you hate me? Don't hate me! I didn't wait for you, I failed you; I am a dirty person, why do you still love me? You can't do anything with your hard-earned money, but you have paid off Zhong Haicai's debt! I know in my heart that you are all for me and my family; you love me, even your rival...... Why is this! Brother Zhuang, Brother Zhuang, my heart hurts so much!......"

Tears are like beads that have broken off the string, falling from her face in large drops, wetting a patch of lawn......

32

Ahua - a female dealer in a Macau casino,
is going to get married and settle in Zhuhai

In the coastal areas of Guangdong, the weather is hot and humid from April to early November. The buildings in the urban village are almost separated, and even if there is wind, it is difficult to blow into the house.

The fan in Zheng Jianxin's small house was on all day. The blades kept swinging left and right, and the wind that blew on people was still warm.

The sound of going up and down the stairs and noisy talking outside the house were one after another.

On the table were her son's textbooks and toys. Her son fell asleep on the table.

Zheng Jianxin sat in a daze on a small chair, holding the frame of her and Zhong Haicai's marriage certificate in her hand, thinking about Xu Zhuang in her heart. Every night when it was quiet, after she finished her work for the day, she would make a cup of tea, calm down and miss Xu Zhuang for a while. This was also a warm moment that belonged to her alone in a day.

"Brother Zhuang, where are you? What are you doing now?" She and the man in her mind were talking and answering each other.

Zheng Jianxin didn't want to think about it anymore, so she leaned her head against the bed and closed her eyes.

It was late at night, and it was much quieter outside. Looking from the window, she could can see the tall shadows of coconut trees.

There was a knock on the door outside: "Auntie Jian!"

It sounded like Ahua was coming. Zheng Jianxin smiled and opened the door and said, "The female dealer! Here she comes!"

Ahua worked in a casino, and the ladies who watch the gambling tables in the casino were called female dealers.

Ahua put down the bag she brought and said to Zheng Jianxin: "I brought you pork jerky from Macau!"

Zheng Jianxin took the things.

"Why, my dad didn't come back?" Ahua sat in front of the fan, lifted her long hair, and let the wind blow the sweat off her neck.

"I haven't seen him for a few days! He is debt-free and frivolous again, hanging out with his drinking buddies!"

Ahua held Zheng Jianxin's shoulders: "Aunt Jian, don't be angry about my dad." She knew that most men in Macau were like this, with low education, no ambition, and just messing around.

Zheng Jianxin nodded. She looked at Ahua, who was dressed pretty, and guessed that she came so late because of "Glasses". Girls in love are absent-minded, with no night and day, and they are always worried.

Zheng Jianxin smiled and asked proactively: "You have seen 'Glasses' a few times, how do you feel?"

Ahua raised her face, a little shy, and then said cheerfully: "He is a good person. He invited me to his fruit farm tomorrow. I won't pass the customs tonight, and I will sleep with you!" After that, she laughed so happily that she couldn't help herself. Ahua opened her handbag and took out a stack of Macau patacas and gave it to Zheng Jianxin. "Today I get paid. Tomorrow you can help me change it into RMB and deposit it in the bank."

"Okay! In the past few years, we all needed Hong Kong dollars, but now we all need RMB!"

"RMB preserves its value! Besides, if I put it in Macau, my mom will ask me for it every few days!"

"Glasses" is the boyfriend that Zheng Jianxin introduced to Ahua.

Zheng Jianxin met "Glasses" at a suburban fruit wholesale market.

That afternoon, Zheng Jianxin went to the wholesale market to buy cheap fruits as usual, and then went outside the market to pick out a basket of good longan from the pile of rotten fruits that others had thrown away and put it on her bicycle. Ajian was sweating all over under the scorching sun. Just as she was about to leave, her tire burst and the bicycle fell to the ground with longan scattered all over the ground.

At this time, a young man came over, wearing a pair of frameless glasses. "Glasses" said kindly, "Big sister, don't worry, I'll help you!" Then he took the plastic basket off the bicycle and said, "Big sister, I'll pick the fruits, you go to the side to fix the tire and get some fresh air in the shade!"

"Glasses" was very patient, put his briefcase on the ground, bent over, and almost lay on the ground to pick up the longans one by one into the basket. After the tire was fixed, he helped Zheng Jianxin tie the basket to the back seat of the bicycle. At that time, the back of "Glasses"'s white short-sleeved shirt was all wet, and the glasses were watery. He took them off and wiped them several times.

When they parted, he handed Zheng Jianxin a business card and said, "I am Lin Weihua, from Taiwan Zhengshun Agricultural Science Company, please give me your advice!"

"Tourist farm?"

"I'm doing fruit improvement here! Welcome to visit and guide me, big sister!"

Soon, Lin Weihua brought Zheng Jianxin a box of fruits, which was cheaper than the price she paid at the fruit market. Zheng Jianxin tried to arrange for him to meet Ahua at the checkpoint. The two of them were really destined to meet, and soon they started chatting.

Ahua took a shower, rubbed her hair, and applied night cream to her face in front of the mirror.

"Tomorrow, you should go with me, Aunt Jian!"

Zheng Jianxin said jokingly: "I am a client of his company, and I still want to be a 'light bulb' (standing in between)?"

Ahua pretended to be angry.

Lin Weihua called, and Ahua went outside to listen.

Zheng Jianxin heard their conversation intermittently in the room. The other party probably said something like "I miss you",

Ahua replied: "We will meet tomorrow, why are you in such a hurry! Don't come to pick me up tomorrow, I want to 'go incognito' and conduct a field investigation!"

Ahua came in again, her face flushed.

Zheng Jianxin said, "See how you thank me as a matchmaker?"

Ahua hugged Zheng Jianxin and kissed her on the face, "You will always be my reliable friend, respected stepmother!"

The next morning, Zheng Jianxin sent Ahua to Gongbei long-distance bus station.

Ahua wore a short-sleeved top with ruffles, a brightly printed pomegranate skirt, and brown flat shoes, exuding a girl's romantic atmosphere. She also wore a pink rattan hat on the side, which made her look sweet and elegant.

The farm where Lin Weihua worked was rented from a remote rural mountain in Zhongshan City. In the center of the farm was an artificially dug lake, and mountain springs flowed into the lake continuously. Guangdong is humid and plants grow easily. Looking up, the mountains are lush and green, connected with the crops on the ground. People here are like entering a green world.

Ahua's arrival, like a fairy descending from the heaven, caused a sensation in the whole farm. The workers working on the hillside put down their work and cast their eyes of admiration at the same time. Lin Weihua was very proud and excited!

Lin Weihua picked fruits from the fields and placed them on the table of the lakeside pavilion to entertain Ahua. Ahua ate the dragon fruit in big mouthfuls, and the juice flowed from the corners of her mouth. Lin Weihua looked at her expression in fascination and fanned her with a straw hat.

Ahua smiled at him: "Dragon fruit, so fragrant!"

Lin Weihua: "We also improved pineapples and bananas from the mainland, look......"

Rows of green pineapples on the hillside.

Ahua: "So beautiful......"

Lin Weihua couldn't hide his happy mood: "No matter how beautiful it is, it can't be more beautiful than Miss Macau Ahua!" He was usually calm and mature, but he became talkative at this time, but he didn't know what to say, and suddenly thought of his matchmaker.

"Hey, your aunt is so pretty! Not only pretty, but also very charming!" Lin Weihua chewed the fruit and said, "To be honest, your dad is like a crazy toad eating swan meat!"

Ahua covered his mouth with a piece of fruit pulp: "Don't talk nonsense!"

When it comes to family matters, the conversation is long. Ahua recounted the past: "My mother was in the casino all day, I had no food to eat, and I was not good at studying. My parents were separated at that time. My father lived here with Aunt Jian. My father brought me here and handed me over to Aunt Jian. Aunt Jian was 19 years yonger than he, not much older than I. She tutored me and was very kind to me!"

Lin Weihua sighed and said: "Good people, but bad luck. Your father, your mother......" Ahua grabbed a dragon fruit and hit Lin Weihua on the head: "What nonsense are you talking about again!" Her eyes flashed a light: "Otherwise, why would I change my fate? As soon as Aunt Jian introduced you, I agreed!" Then she laughed, "We......get married, and I will settle down here! Become a boss's wife!"

Lin Weihua was afraid that others would hear and cause misunderstandings, thinking that he used the names of "boss" and "rich man" to deceive mainland girls, so he quickly whispered: "Boss, I am an engineer! No......."

Ahua pretended to be angry: "Don't you want to be the boss?" Lin Weihua was afraid of making a mistake, so he nodded with a smile on his face: "Yes, I do, I do, boss!"

Ahua smiled, and Lin Weihua smiled too. Ahua quickly kissed him on the face, and the two were immersed in mutual admiration.

A row of weeping willows by the lake, with long green strips gently brushing the lake water. Colorful flowers bloomed on the path beside the willows. The sun was shining, the mountain breeze blew, and the fruity and floral fragrance made Ahua intoxicated.

Ahua was in the limelight and had a great time here for a whole day. Macau has narrow streets and air conditioning exhaust everywhere. This place was a paradise for her, where there was no conflict with the world and money. Thinking of this, she suddenly said to Lin Weihua: "We are getting married. I want to bring my mom to live here!" Ahua thought about the future so specifically that Lin Weihua was really shocked and confused.

Ahua had to work the night shift and return to Macau tonight.

When Lin Weihua sent her to the Gongbei Port, the lights of the big clock in the customs building were on.

The lights of the customs square at the port were flashing. The crowds of people entering and leaving the gate in different directions were like the sea, one wave after another.

Ahua was reluctant to leave Lin Weihua: "I have to pass the port, the annoying night shift!"

"You should be more energetic at work," Lin Weihua joked, "Female dealers are also officials! Standing by the gambling table, you look so proud! Wow, a lot of money flows in front of you!"

Ahua responded: "Some are happy and some are sad! All I hear are sighs!" Ahua looked at Lin Weihua's face and asked, "Do you think gambling is good?"

Lin Weihua said with certainty: "Boss, I will never gamble!"

Ahua said: "If you dare to gamble, I will chop off your hand!"

After saying that, Ahua seemed to feel that she had said it a little harshly, so she moved closer to Lin Weihua and whispered: "Kiss me!"

Lin Weihua looked around at the people passing by and felt a little embarrassed.

Ahua insisted: "Yes......"

Lin Weihua's eyes lit up, knowing that Ahua wanted a light kiss.

But he quickly kissed her hard. Ahua screamed in pain: "Bad!" But her heart was as satisfied as honey. She waved to him happily, walked quickly towards the departure hall, blew a kiss affectionately and shouted: "Bye!"

33

Huihui asked Mommy: Why do they close the gate?

For people who are busy, the days seem to pass by in a flash. Huihui was five years old. Next year, he would be of school age.

Three years before, Zheng Jianxin brought all kinds of information about Zhong Haicai and applied to the visa department of her country of origin for herself and Huihui to settle in Macau, but it had not been approved. It was said that it was a problem on the Macau side. Zheng Jianxin requested many times, and Zhong Haicai also went to the Macau Immigration Bureau several times. Zheng Jianxin asked him what the Immigration Bureau said, and Zhong Haicai hesitated and gave an unclear answer. Zheng Jianxin knew that Zhong had not even attended elementary school and could only write his own name. It was difficult for him to understand the rules without education.

That day, Zhong Haicai returned home as usual, anxiously looking at Zheng Jianxin's face to see if she would lose her temper when she saw him. He received such blows usually when they met. He lowered his waist and glanced at Zheng Jianxin who was cooking. Zheng Jianxin's face was indeed not good that day, and his heart began to beat nervously. Before Zheng Jianxin could get angry, he whispered, "The construction site has been shut down for two months. I haven't paid you for two months, and I'm eating your money...... This is all caused by the financial crisis......"

"Now the most important thing is that Huihui has to go to school!" Zheng Jianxin raised her voice, and she really wanted to hit Zhong Haicai on the head with a spatula. Zhong Haicai always answered "yes, yes" to her words. What it meant was that he didn't care, no action, no results.

"The school matter has been settled!" Zhong Haicai responded quickly. As soon as he learned that it was Huihui's school matter, he felt relieved and at ease.

Zheng Jianxin was pleasantly surprised at first, then half-doubtedly asked: "Can Huihui really go to school in Macau?"

Zhong Haicai nodded affirmatively. When he saw Zheng Jianxin smiling, a mischievous and complacent look flashed across his lips: "Huihui is my son, a Macau native! Of course he can go to Macau to study!"

Macau law stipulates that blood-related children from the mainland can immigrate to Macau. Zhong Haicai and Huihui did a paternity test and sent it back to the mainland public security department, which quickly approved Huihui's immigration application.

"Your Macau identity will definitely be approved if you wait a little longer!" Seeing Zheng Jianxin's good face, Zhong Haicai said excitedly, and then joked to himself, "You are Mrs. Zhong, who dares not to do it?" His uneven yellow teeth were revealed in his open lips.

"You just talk big!" Zheng Jianxin replied.

In this way, Zheng Jianxin's family life entered the preparation stage before Huihui went to elementary school, buying new clothes, school bags, stationery, water cups, etc.

The day before Huihui went to school, Zheng Jianxin took his son to play for a whole day, and then came to the beach to rest. Zheng Jianxin pointed from near to far: "That's the customs. After the customs, it's Macau; beyond that, there's a big construction site, where Dad works!"

Huihui asked puzzledly: "Mom, why do we need customs? Dad calls it the gate?"

"Customs is like a gate, checking the documents of passersby." Zheng Jianxin answered. "People can only go in and out if they have documents; Macau people can come and go at will, but people here have to have approval of when to go and how many times to go......"

Huihui didn't understand: "Can't the gate not be closed?"

Zheng Jianxin shook his head. This question couldn't be explained to a child in one or two sentences.

Huihui said, "I understand. Checking documents at the border gate is to prevent bad people from passing."

Zheng Jianxin answered casually, "Sometimes good people are not allowed to pass either."

"Then why?"

Zheng Jianxin felt that she had said something wrong, and thought of a random wording: "The procedures are incomplete!"

"What do you mean by procedures?"

Zheng Jianxin said nothing, interrupting the topic. This was also the question she wanted to ask, but she didn't understand herself.

"You are going to Macau to study tomorrow, so you must bring your documents. Don't lose them!"

"Why do I have to go so far?"

"Your father is from Macau. It doesn't cost money to study in Macau. The textbooks are all issued by the school!"

"Mommy, are you going?"

Zheng Jianxin hesitated for a moment and said softly, "Yes, but it will take some time to get the documents before I can pass!"

When Zheng Jianxin and the child returned home, Zhong Haicai had already returned, and Achang also came.

Zheng Jianxin asked: "Why did you get off work so early today?"

Zhong Haicai and Achang took turns washing their faces and feet in the bathroom. Zhong Haicai took a shower and changed into shorts. Both of them were very happy.

Achang put an apron around his neck and said, "I came to your house for dinner!"

He took out a bag of dried tofu from his bag and put it on the chopping board. Zheng Jianxin looked at the dried tofu and didn't understand what it meant. Achang smiled mysteriously and said, "I'll make this dish."

Achang turned on the gas and the vent fan. After the oil in the pot was hot, he skillfully fried the dried tofu in the pot, added sugar and green onions, and the dried tofu was fried bright yellow.

Achang put it on the small table and said like announcing the answer to the riddle: "Huihui will go to school tomorrow. In our hometown of Chaozhou, we will make this for the child! Hey, Mrs. Zhong, look, does the dried bean curd look like a golden seal? It means that our Huihui will have an official position in the future, and the green onion means that he is smart and capable!" He cut it into small pieces with a knife and gave each person a portion, "It won't be served for dinner, eat it now!"

"Brother, you are thoughtful!" Zheng Jianxin hurriedly asked Huihui to thank his uncle.

Zhong Haicai said to Huihui: "Tomorrow morning, Dad will boil two eggs for you. They are called smart eggs!" The dinner was very lively. Zhong Haicai squinted his smiling eyes, looked at his son from time to time, and laughed. He slapped his cheeks and joked with his son with a Hakka nursery rhyme in a rhythmic manner: "Toads are clacking, no studying no wife!"

Achang said: "Mommy, beautiful girl, handsome boy, handsome boy, afraid of not having a beautiful wife?" The room was full of laughter and chatter, so lively.

The following day, when the morning glow from the sea filled the Gongbei Port Square, Zheng Jianxin held his son's hand and walked towards the border with Zhong Haicai.

The more than 20 channels in the departure hall of Gongbei Port were filled with passengers waiting for their documents to be verified. There were more than a dozen students who went to Macau to study. All of them were sent off by their families.

Zheng Jianxin watched Huihui go to the "China, Hong Kong and Macau Residents" exit verification counter. While waiting in line, Zhong Haicai taught his son how to hand his ID to the police. After Huihui's ID was verified, he waved to Zheng Jianxin: "Bye, Mommy!" and followed Zhong Haicai.

The school Huihui attended was not far from the border gate. It was a Chinese school. After crossing the border every day, he was picked up by the teachers of the Supervision Center. The Center was to supervise tutoring, provide nutritious lunch, snacks, and pick-up services.

Huihui liked this school very much. The school had white walls, light green walls, dark blue shutters, and gray window sills. It was clean and warm. It was a building Huihui had never seen in Zhuhai.

The little classmates from Macau were polite and friendly. Once Huihui threw the tissue he used to wipe his sweat next to the trash can, and a little girl picked it up silently and threw it into the recycle bucket. Huihui blushed and said, "I'm sorry!" The little girl said, "It doesn't matter, you'll get used to it! Macau is my home, everyone takes care of it!"

The problem came from the students from Zhuhai.

The school children had known each other for less than two weeks, and the classmates from Zhuhai pointed at Huihui and talked nonsense behind his back. Some classmates said to him in person, "My mother said that you are the child of a mistress and she doesn't let us play with you!"

One day at noon, Zhong Haicai came to see Huihui. The classmate said, "Zhong Huihui, your grandfather wants you to come!" Huihui's face turned red with embarrassment, and he clenched his fists, really wanting to beat him up.

Zhong Haicai and Huihui sat together on the steps on the hillside, with empty lunch boxes beside them.

Zhong Haicai smoked a cigarette with a satisfied look on his face.

Huihui suddenly asked, "Dad, when can I live in Macau with Mommy?"

"Soon!" Zhong Haicai said, touching his head.

Huihui lowered his eyelids and said softly, "If I live in Macau with Mommy, I will no longer be the mistress's child! Dad, what is a mistress?"

"Mistress?" How come the children know about mistresses? Zhong Haicai was shocked, but fortunately Huihui didn't know what a mistress was. Even if he understood, he was not the mistress's child, and even if he was, what did it have to do with his classmates! He looked at Huihui and shook his head, "Don't talk nonsense. It's okay, Dad will get it done soon! We will live in Macau together!"

"Mommy said you only know how to brag!" Huihui couldn't get an accurate answer, so he shouted at Zhong Haicai. Zhong Haicai looked embarrassed, hesitating and didn't know what to do.

34

You must treat Ajian well,
otherwise I will chop off your "mud chicken" claws

In the afternoon, Zhong Haicai received a call from the bank at the construction site, which was another great thing!

He went to the supervision center to pick up Huihui before he got off work, and hurried through the border with his son. He wanted to tell Ajian this good news as soon as possible!

The narrow streets and alleys of Macau are noisy with cars and people. Once you pass the border, the port square is open, and the eight-lane welcoming avenue is in front of the passengers. Zhong Haicai always opened his arms and took two deep breaths of fresh air at this time. His legs and feet were immediately relieved and his mood was good.

Zheng Jianxin just bought ice cream and kept it in a cold drink box and waited for his son at the border.

On the stone bench in the square, Huihui ate ice cream and whispered to his mother that he was very tired, and then asked Zheng Jianxin when Mommy could immigrate to Macau.

Zhong Haicai looked at his young and beautiful wife and smart and handsome son, and with his good mood today, he couldn't help laughing.

Zheng Jianxin looked up and asked, "Why are you grinning?"

Zhong Haicai deliberately held back his words, he wanted to give her a surprise. He couldn't wait to hug Zheng Jianxin: "Wife, let's go to the western restaurant. Good news! Bai Lang's story!"

A few days before, Lili said that there was news about Bai Lang: in recent years, he has been working in Shanghai with Taiwanese businessmen to engage in real estate. Bai Lang acted as an intermediary as a "mainland expert", and went to government departments such as land and planning to handle procedures, and also used his expertise to participate in planning and design. He called Zhong Haicai and other friends to express his deep apologies, saying that he had just made a fortune and sent Zhong Haicai 500,000 yuan first, and said that he would send money to Zhong Haicai as interest in the next few years, and that he was organizing funds and would make a comeback to grab the Blue Dream Water Village time-share resort project.

"Ajian, the money Bai Lang sent from Shanghai has arrived! "Zhong Haicai shouted as he walked, and then laughed heartily. In the past few years, this debt forced him to almost jump into the sea. Although an unknown Hong Kong friend paid off his bank debt for him, he still owed money to Hong Kong people. He felt uneasy when he thought of this anonymous person. He couldn't tell whether it was a blessing or a curse. One day, a man with a knife would come out and ask for debts. Every wrong has its perpetrator and every debt has its creditor. With Bai Lang's money, he could pay back the Hong Kong people and settle the debt completely. It would be a relief to be debt-free!

"But how can I return it to Hong Kong? I don't know the name of that person......" Zhong Haicai frowned. It was difficult to pay back the money, like looking for a needle in a haystack.

Zheng Jianxin stopped and glanced at Zhong Haicai, and wiped the sweat from her forehead with a tissue: "Who do you think that person is?"

"Who is it?" Zheng Jianxin lifted the hair stuck to the corners of his eyes with his fingers, stared into his eyes and said: "It's Xu Zhuang!"

"Xu Zhuang? " Zhong Haicai stopped and held his breath in astonishment. He was a little unconvinced, but Ajian's words would not be false. He was a little confused and felt depressed. He scanned Zheng Jianxin's body with a half-believing and half-doubting look.

Suddenly, he seemed to understand something, and his whole body was tense, as if on fire. The salt stains left by sweat on his body made his pores itchy, and he was even more itchy because of his impatience. The blue veins on his neck jumped, and he shouted hoarsely with a dry throat: "Okay, you have never broken up with Xu Zhuang, you are having an affair behind my back!"

Zheng Jianxin raised her eyebrows and turned her head away with disdain. Every time she thought of or mentioned Xu Zhuang, her heart ached. She had no intention of paying attention to Zhong Haicai, but just said: "What nonsense are you talking about! I haven't seen Xu Zhuang for many years!"

Zhong Haicai became even more angry: "You are still quibbling! Do you think I don't know? You women like tall and mighty men...... they are compatible when walking, right? " He was so jealous that he lowered his head and cursed in Mandarin, "son of a bitch!" and raised his arm to hit her.

Huihui was anxious and pulled him hard: "Don't! Don't! Dad!"

At this time, a big hand grabbed Zhong Haicai's wrist like a vice. Zhong Haicai, Zheng Jianxin and Huihui were all shocked and felt the ground shaking under their feet. After this person landed, it turned out to be Xu Zhuang! It really fit the saying: Speak of the devil, the devil comes. This was strange! Xu Zhuang was wearing a black cotton sportswear and a small bag on his shoulder. His cold face was like an axe. He grabbed Zhong Haicai's hand and lifted it into the air. His black eyebrows twisted, and the cold light in his eyes stared at Zhong Haicai's face. With the other hand, he raised a bowl-sized fist and said to him fiercely: "You must treat Ajian well. If you do anything wrong, I will chop off your mud chicken claws! "

People in Hong Kong and Macau call cement workers at construction sites "mud chickens".

Zhong Haicai was so frightened that his wrist was clenched so hard that he kept saying "yes, yes, yes". He was worried that his rival would break his arm.

After Xu Zhuang finished speaking, his mustache jumped twice, shook off Zhong Haicai, and walked away without looking back.

Zhong Haicai fell to the ground in response. He straightened up and looked at Xu Zhuang's back, still in shock, with his chest heaving.

He wanted to get angry at Zheng Jianxin to save some face, but he swallowed his anger. He lifted the corner of his sweatshirt, wiped the sweat off his face heavily, and plucked up the courage to curse softly from his throat: "Jailed guy!"

Zheng Jianxin didn't say a word, she pulled Huihui and left.

Xu Zhuang's sudden appearance shocked Zheng Jianxin again. Where did Xu Zhuang come from?

The evening breeze messed up her hair on her forehead, and the hair on her temples stuck to her sweaty face. She knew her back was sweating.

She remembered what Lili had asked her: "Xu Zhuang often comes back to Zhuhai to see you, do you know?" Zheng Jianxin said she had never seen him, it was not true.

In Zheng Jianxin's view, the relationship between her and Xu Zhuang was like the clothes and meals of the previous year, and Xu Zhuang had long been disappointed.

Now she suddenly understood, remembering that she had seen a person who looked like Zhuang in the crowd at the border several times.

But then she thought again, was it because she often missed Xu Zhuang in her heart, and it was an illusion? She thought she was dazzled. Now she thought, that person was Xu Zhuang! He didn't go to Macau, why was he always at the border? Could it be that he just wanted to see her? Her body trembled, waves of indescribable pain surged to her chest and heart......

35

Ajian in version one and Ajian in version two

Every weekend and holiday, Xu Zhuang would rush back to Zhuhai, as if Zhuhai was his home. When he found a hotel in Gongbei to stay, he felt empty again: Who was he going to see? Was it Lili? Having a meal with his cousin was not the purpose.

Lili saw how miserable Xu Zhuang was, so she said to him, "Should I ask Ajian out for you so you can meet?"

Xu Zhuang crossed his arms and shook his head.

"Ajian has always missed you...... What's the matter? You can be lovers if you can't be husband and wife......"

Xu Zhuang stared at Lili and put off his cigarette with his fingers: "What do you think of me, my cousin? I, Xu Zhuang, am an upright man who doesn't do those sneaky things!"

The latter sentence made Lili shudder. "Hey," she retorted with a red face and bulging eyes, "The world is so chaotic, why bother pretending to be pure, who are you looking at!" She seemed to be defending herself.

He ignored Lili's feelings, just exhaled a long breath and sighed: "My greatest love for Ajian now is not to cause her trouble and let her live a peaceful life"

Sometimes in the afternoon, he took a boat from Shenzhen Shekou to Zhuhai Jiuzhou Port. If there was enough time, he would go straight to the port. He knew that Zheng Jianxin was picking up her child at the border at this time, and he looked at Zheng Jianxin from distance. If he came back late, he would run to the port early the next morning and take a look at Zheng Jianxin from distance while she was sending the child through the border. He held his breath and concentrated just to take a look at Zheng Jianxin: to see her familiar figure, her movements and appearance, to see her familiar eyes, her big eyes like a mirror, thorough and soft......

Over the years, his heart had never left Zheng Jianxin for a day. It did not fade because Zheng Jianxin was married, but became stronger. Zheng Jianxin was like a flame burning in his body. When he was free from work, when he was walking, when he went to bed, he would think of Zheng Jianxin. Zheng Jianxin was always frozen in the moment when she just walked out of the mountains, pure as the white clouds in the blue sky, blushing when touched, and limp when hugged. At this time, he would talk to Zheng Jianxin, talking about the things in his memory that were not clearly explained, and talking about the feelings in his heart at the moment. And every time they talked, there were new topics and endless words. At this moment, love flowed from the bottom of his heart......

When he returned to Zhuhai, the center of his thoughts was Zheng Jianxin. At night, he would go to the alley where Zheng Jianxin lived, looking at the lights of Zheng Jianxin's house, knowing that she was at home, he felt at ease as if he saw her, and he watched until the lights went out. Of course, at this moment, a fire would float in his heart. Just like what he thought when he first stood downstairs of her house: he could imagine Zheng Jianxin's petite body lying in the arms of the old man who always exuded the smell of sweat. And that fragrant and warm body should have belonged to him.

Ajian! You were looking for a harbor for life, but in the end, you became someone else's harbor! The old man did not bring you money and wealth, but poverty and suffering. He felt sorry for Zheng Jianxin from the bottom of his heart, and sighed to the sky for losing Zheng Jianxin! Every time at this moment, his heart was bleeding......

He thought about it, and then turned around and hated Ajian. It was she who dedicated herself to a penniless, walking dead man!

Since things have come to this, why should he miss her? No! He missed the Ajian of version one, and the current Ajian was version two.

He missed the Ajian of version one, and hated the Ajian of version two......

He thought about it, and then turned around and complained to himself: Why was I doing this? I ran back and forth from Shenzhen in two days just to see Ajian for a few minutes. We were only a stone's throw away, but we couldn't talk, just like the Yin and Yang worlds. What was this? Why bother? Especially when he saw Zheng Jianxin, Zhong Haicai and Huihui together, he immediately felt pathetic and pitiful for himself as a love thief who had asked for trouble. He made up his mind several times not to see Zheng Jianxin again! But he couldn't control himself, he couldn't do it. He scolded himself for being useless! However, just with such a glance, he was greatly satisfied emotionally, and felt extremely fulfilled and warm in his heart.

Sometimes he also advised himself that Zheng Jianxin was already someone else's woman, so what was the point of missing her? He couldn't go on like this. Find a good girl and talk about marriage, which was the best way to forget the old lover. But every time he met other girls in the coffee shop as scheduled, he immediately thought of Ajian, and a sense of guilt for betraying Ajian arose spontaneously, and he suddenly became bored with other girls and even disgusted with them on the spot. After several failed attempts to make friends, Xu Zhuang secretly vowed never to contact women again.

This Ajian was the Ajian in his mind. He blended his various beautiful imaginations with Zheng Jianxin in real life to create a new Zheng Jianxin. He often couldn't tell the difference between this Zheng Jianxin and the Zheng Jianxin in real life. Whenever he thought of Zheng Jianxin, he felt a warm current in his heart. In his heart, he lived with Zheng Jianxin, and it was Zheng Jianxin who could make him feel the warmth of this world.

Apart from going to work, Xu Zhuang spent the rest of his time missing Ajian in loneliness. When the longing and loneliness were unbearable, he tried to indulge himself. In the evening, he entered a nearby nightclub and asked for a small private room and a bottle of wine. The Mama-san arranged two girls for him. The escort girls came in with a smile and sat down close to him. When the two girls called him "husband" in a coquettish voice and pressed against Xu Zhuang's shoulder, Xu Zhuang shouted: "Get away!" The two girls were startled and whispered: "Aren't you here just for fun?"

Xu Zhuang drank half a catty of Wuliangye liquor alone, took out the golden bank card in his hand, and fiddled with it over and over again.

He remembered a joke he had heard from others before: "I'm so poor that I only have money left." He said to himself painfully: "I really have nothing except this!"

That day he was not on duty. He rushed back to Zhuhai in the afternoon and came to the port square early. He never exposed himself and didn't want to interfere with Ajian's life. People should know how to give up love. If you can't get it, you have to accept your fate and give up! Since it was her choice, you should silently bless her!

But when Zhong Haicai was about to use force on Ajian, he jumped out without thinking. He really wanted to beat Zhong Haicai up, but for Ajian's sake, he held back. He didn't want to cause trouble for Ajian. Since Ajian had chosen such a life, let her live in peace and happiness, without any misfortune.

He lived for Ajian. This was why Xu Zhuang remitted money to Macau through Zeng Sheng to pay off Zhong Haicai's debt. He knew that saving Zhong Haicai was saving Ajian! For Ajian, let alone money, he was willing to sacrifice his life...... When he remitted money through Zeng Sheng, Zeng Sheng called him a fool! He also said, "With hundred thousands of yuan, what kind of pure girl can't be found? Zheng Jianxin is already a fallen flower, is it worth it?"

Xu Zhuang punched him hard.

Zeng Sheng said again, "since you like Zheng Jianxin so much, Zhong Haicai is struggling for life now, it's an opportunity, why don't you just snatch Zheng Jianxin and the child away, why don't you do it, and help Zhong Haicai?"

Xu Zhuang replied to Zeng Sheng: "You know shit! Taking advantage of others' misfortune, wouldn't I, Xu Zhuang, become a 'villain'?" He knew Ajian's character and always despised "villains". Xu Zhuang, a man who is not afraid of going to jail, was in a dilemma when he talked about this he was in tears......

Xu Zhuang always felt this sense of loss and took a boat from Zhuhai Jiuzhou Port to Shenzhen Shekou Port alone. He looked at the vast sea for a long time, thinking about Ajian, and was confused. Am I really a passerby of Ajian?

He wrote his poem "Passerby" in a small notebook:

You are a ray of light in my emotional world,
I am a passerby beside you.
The whole meaning of my life is to make you happy,
When I escape from you,
I am also happy in my heart.
Meeting is destined,
That is the corner where the two lines meet.
We will soon go to a place where we don't know each other,
Am I a passerby in your life?

36

Is Liang Xiangyun's marriage certificate real?

After Zheng Jianxin was beaten by Liang Xiangyun at the checkpoint, she was kept in the hospital for observation and no major problems were found, so she returned home at night.

Zhong Haicai was busy, cooking for his son, eating, and helping him take shower.

Zheng Jianxin could only take a few sips of water. Zhong Haicai followed the doctor's instructions, looked at the clock, and fed Zheng Jianxin medicine.

Zhong Haicai took a shower and washed the family's clothes. It was already past twelve o'clock. Zheng Jianxin was somewhat sober. Zheng Jianxin felt a splitting headache. Half-conscious, she took a sip of the mineral water Zhong Haicai fed her. She struggled and asked Zhong Haicai: "Tell me, have you and Liang Xiangyun ever been married?"

The big eyes that were usually bright now had a few dark clouds. "Old Zhong, Liang Xiangyun said there was a marriage certificate, and she was so sure. Tell me the truth. Only when you tell me the truth, I will have a way to deal with it!"

Zhong Haicai rarely smoked cigarettes before. Since "Blue Dream" Bai Lang ran away, he was troubled by the bank loan issue and couldn't sleep every night. He bought a pack of cigarettes to relieve his boredom. One thing had just been solved, and another matter about Liang Xiangyun's marriage certificate made him restless, and he started smoking again after just quitting.

He had just lit a cigarette on the balcony to relieve his fatigue when he was called in by Zheng Jianxin. He didn't say anything when he heard Zheng Jianxin's question. The air conditioner was making a low sound of "glglglglgl", and he became nervous.

He thought of the words that the children scolded his son, and felt that the problem was serious, and he couldn't hide the matter of the Immigration Bureau any longer.

"Speak up!" Zheng Jianxin was a little anxious. Zhong Haicai held the smothered cigarette in his hand and said with a sad face: "Ajian, to tell you the truth, I don't understand either...... I went to the Macau Immigration Bureau and they said I have a wife in Macau, Liang Xiangyun......"

Zheng Jianxin asked: "Why do they say that? What evidence do they have?"

"There is a marriage certificate between me and her......"

Zheng Jianxin was furious when she heard it: "Zhong Haicai! You have a wife and you haven't divorced her, but you still dare to marry me. You lied to me! You ruined me......" She tried to get out of bed and stand up. She looked around and grabbed the kitchen knife on the chopping board.

"Don't! Don't!" Zhong Haicai grabbed the kitchen knife and held Zheng Jianxin, who was trembling all over. "Listen to me, I have never obtained a marriage certificate with her!"

"You are lying! None of you Hong Kong and Macau men are good people. You treat us mainland girls as if they are not human beings. Don't you just have a few dirty money? You play with them at will!...... Others are with rich men...... What do I want from you?"

Zheng Jianxin started crying.

Zhong Haicai rubbed his hands and stamped his feet, made the sign of the cross on his chest, and whispered: "Believe it or not......" As he said that, he also got angry, puffed out his chest, and said in a muffled voice, "You can check it!"

Zheng Jianxin frowned and felt lost. She realized the seriousness of the problem: she had become a mistress, a "mistress" with a marriage certificate! The marriage certificate on the wall instantly became a piece of waste paper! She was angry and resentful, and the corners of her mouth trembled. The person who deceived herself was the person she always thought was incompetent but honest!

"Zhong Haicai, I tell you, Macau, I don't care! It doesn't matter if I can't get through, it's not a paradise! I just want to be a woman with dignity! You made me not even know who I am!" Zheng Jianxin sobbed.

Zhong Haicai held his breath and hid on the balcony again. He had just lit up his cigarette butt, but before he could take a puff, he heard Zheng Jianxin yelling, "Get out! You smoke to death!" Zhong Haicai quickly put the cigarette butt out in the ashtray.

In the double torture of pain and spirit, Zheng Jianxin stayed up all night, staring with her eyes wide open until dawn.

Zhong Haicai soon fell asleep as if nothing had happened, snoring, with the smell of cigarettes whitish in his throat. After he had gone to Macau, he had no interest in anything except for learning to flirt with women. He didn't understand anything, and he couldn't even understand what people said. He couldn't express his meaning with words, and he was really like Xu Zhuang said, a walking corpse! Zheng Jianxin slapped him hard on the back a few times, and he only yelled twice, turned over and snored again.

Zheng Jianxin understood that she couldn't ask others for help regarding the immigration affairs.

Zheng Jianxin decided to go to the Macau Immigration Bureau to find out the truth in person. She had to get to the bottom of it! To go to Macau, she had to return to the provincial capital and apply to the Public Security Exit and Entry Management Department as the spouse of a Macau citizen to get a Hong Kong and Macau Pass. The next day, Zheng Jianxin stuffed Huihui's schoolbag into Zhong Haicai's arms: "You take care of your child! I can't stand it, I want to go back to my hometown!"

37

Ajian goes to Macau:
Go to the government department to find out the truth

Zheng Jianxin took a double-decker bus, running day and night, and returned to her hometown in the provincial capital in two days.

She went to apply for a Hong Kong and Macau Pass that day. For the mainland Public Security Department, Zheng Jianxin had a marriage certificate and her husband's Macau information, so there was no problem in processing a visitor visa.

After returning to Zhuhai, 20 days later, Zheng Jianxin received a Hong Kong and Macau Pass with a visitor visa endorsed by express mail.

On the third day, Zheng Jianxin went to Macau. In the morning, she went through customs with Huihui.

Recently, whenever Zheng Jianxin sent her son through the border, there would be strange-looking people pointing and shouting behind Zheng Jianxin, saying, "She is the mistress, the one who fought that day, look, mistress!"

In the square, two women wearing glasses stopped Zheng Jianxin. The younger one said they were reporters, and the middle-aged one said they were from the Women's Federation, doing a social survey and wanted to interview her. Zheng Jianxin was already upset and angry, and after hearing this, she got angry and cursed, "You are bats looking at the sun, you are blind, get out of here!"

In the exit hall of Gongbei Port, fingerprints had been registered with the Border Inspection Department. When passing through the border, visitors just put the ID card on the machine and pressed the fingerprint. In the channels for mainland residents, border inspection personnel checked the documents one by one and stamped the exit stamp with the year, month and date.

Huihui lined up in the "Chinese Hong Kong and Macao Residents" group, and Zheng Jianxin lined up in the "Chinese Mainland Residents" group, and waved to each other.

They passed the border inspection counter separately, and Zheng Jianxin held the child's hand again.

When she first married Zhong Haicai, Zheng Jianxin applied for a family visitor visa and stayed in Macau for three days.

Those yellow walls or red walls, coffee-colored windows with balconies, Portuguese buildings with triangular window barrels, churches with pointed roofs, and sidewalks paved with black and white granite stones made her feel like she was in a foreign country. When she went to the Mazu Temple, she saw the Chinese-style streets paved with stone slabs, the tablets of the God of Wealth worshipped in the corners of every house, and the smoking incense burners, which made her feel that she was in the old China decades before that she had seen in the movies. Casinos and hotels were busy and noisy, but the houses and streets built on the hillside were quiet and tidy. Macau, a place that she couldn't explain, made her feel novel everywhere. There were many foreigners on the street, and the pedestrians were dressed strangely, but they were all dressed neatly and spoke softly. She liked this place, and she tried to find more advantages for herself. This was the place where she would settle down for the rest of her life and live with her husband and child.

When she came here this time, she suddenly felt that this was a strange place.

In Mingming Coffee Shop, Zheng Jianxin asked the sisters who were familiar with Macau. They said that there is a department in Macau responsible for such matters, called the Identification Bureau, which issues reliable identification certificates to qualified persons and also provides accurate and clear information. She followed the route indicated by the sisters and took a minibus to Avenida da Nam Van after passing the border.

Zhong Haicai was already waiting for her in the shade of the building. He wore a white round-necked shirt tucked into his long jeans, with a waist bag hanging on his belt, and the hem of his trousers covering the top of his sandals, looking very neat. When he saw her coming, he pulled her to the office counter.

An official listened to Zhong Haicai's questions very politely and patiently, and found out the relationship between the two. The official quickly found the file, spread it out and said to Zheng Jianxin: "Miss, we have returned your immigration consultation to "the top" (Macau people call the mainland "the top" based on the geographical location) several times for a reason: Mr. Zhong has a wife, whose household registration is in Macau. This is the marriage certificate between Mr. Zhong and Ms. Liang Xiangyun."

Zheng Jianxin held her breath and listened to the official's talk. Although she was prepared, she was still skeptical about Liang Xiangyun's "marriage certificate". But when the official said it was "real", she was shocked as if being electrocuted, her face was bloodless, she was stunned, unable to control herself, staring at Zhong Haicai with angry eyes, tightly pursed her lips, locked her teeth, and couldn't speak. Zhong Haicai was anxious and stuttered to argue: "Fake! Fake! I have never held a marriage certificate with her!"

The official ignored his arguments and continued to explain to Zheng Jianxin: "Macau law treats legitimate and illegitimate children the same, and both can immigrate. We have already handled your son's immigration procedures two years ago, right?"

"Humph! Illegitimate?" Zheng Jianxin stared at Zhong Hai with a sharp look, full of anger.

Zhong Haicai was at a loss, just grinning and shaking his head. He took out a cigarette from his pocket, and immediately realized that smoking was prohibited here, so he held it in his hand without moving.

Zheng Jianxin knew that this "marriage certificate" was a bomb that destroyed her life. What secrets were hidden behind it, and the truth could not be revealed for a while. Zheng Jianxin tried to calm herself and face this reality.

"Can I make a copy?" Zheng Jianxin asked the official. Official: "No. You can check at the place of issuance." The official still helped them as much as possible and said to Zheng Jianxin, "You can write down this place of issuance. If you have any questions, you can check there. I can't help you with other things, sorry!"

After leaving the building, Zhong Haicai wanted to return to the construction site.

"Why is there nothing for you?" Zheng Jianxin refused to let Zhong Haicai go. Zhong Haicai was originally a person without ideas, and Zheng Jianxin couldn't think of any ideas for a while. Finally, Zheng Jianxin opened the parasol and followed Zhong Haicai to the construction site.

This was a supporting building for an American casino. The construction had been stopped, leaving a small number of workers to do sporadic work. When Achang and several workers saw Zheng Jianxin coming, their faces were so ugly, and they mistakenly thought it was about money. Achang stopped her and explained: "We have waited for two months and haven't received our wages. This is true. The financial tsunami is killing people!"

Zhong Haicai bowed his head and kept silent. He sat on a pile of bricks and turned his head to smoke. Zheng Jianxin shouted to Achang: "You asked him, is it just about money?" She pointed at Zhong Haicai with disdain, "What are you pretending to be? You the cheater of Macau!"

Achang asked the whole story and pulled her aside: "I can testify that Brother Zhong did not lie to you. The singer does not hide the truth from the gong player! When he met you, he had broken up with Liang Xiangyun three years before and rented a house in Gongbei; Liang Xiangyun went to gamble and owed a loan shark more than 100,000 yuan in debt. Brother Zhong borrowed money to pay it back. After the two broke up, they had no contact again!"

Zheng Jianxin licked her lips: "Then why didn't they get divorced and have a marriage certificate?" Achang shook his head and answered very affirmatively: "They had a wedding in their hometown, but they didn't get any marriage certificate. Brother Zhong sneaked to Macau."

Zhong Haicai scratched his head angrily and took two big puffs of cigarette: "I , I don't understand what's going on! Oh my God! "

Zheng Jianxin walked alone in the streets of Macau in a daze, not knowing where to go.

As she walked, she thought, Zhong Haicai and Liang Xiangyun were married, so what was she? Was she really a mistress as others called her? Was she so despicable?

After eight years of waiting and enduring, this was the result in the end.

Zheng Jianxin felt a terrible feeling in her heart, that she had been abandoned by life! Facing this strange city in front of her, facing the many strange faces coming towards her, she was like a beggar, like a lonely ghost!

In front of the Lisboa Casino, there were several girls who were obviously from the mainland. They were heavily made up and spoke Mandarin. They stopped the guests entering the casino with a charming smile on their faces: "Sir, please go to my room to rest first!"

Zheng Jianxin would feel disgusted in Zhuhai, but today she felt a little pity for them. Am I not also a fallen person? Thinking of this, she quickened her pace and walked forward. After walking through the bustling downtown area, she sat on a stone bench in the fountain square of the City Hall. The pattern of white and black stones on the ground made her head a little dizzy, and she had to close her eyes. Only then did she realize that she had not eaten lunch, she had no mood to eat, so she had to buy a bottle of water and gulp it down. Damn, water was more expensive than in Zhuhai, 2.5 yuan in Zhuhai, 11 yuan here!

After drinking the water, she felt a little restless again, and walked aimlessly through Banzhangtang Street. There were several large cosmetics stores there. When she passed by such cosmetics stores in Zhuhai, she liked the colorful large and small bottles of cosmetics displayed inside, and often couldn't help but take a few peeks outside the store. But this time, the light reflected from the glass cabinet annoyed her, so she walked away quickly.

When she walked around the Ruins of St. Paul's and came to a Christian church not far from the casino, there was a large poster at the entrance, which read: "Problem gambling suicide", "Gamblers have a 5-10 times higher suicide rate than non-gamblers". She sneered and said in her heart, "Gambling City is against gambling, what is Macau!"

Macau is densely populated, with tall buildings and narrow streets. The hot air from the air conditioners in every household blows directly into the street. It was already hot weather, and walking through one hot air outlet after another was like getting into an oven. When you want to take a breath, you open your mouth and a wave of heat falls straight into your throat, making it difficult to breathe.

In Zhuhai, there were few people and vast land. Walking in the sun for more than ten minutes would make one's body wet and difficult to breathe. What's more, Zheng Jianxin walked in Macau for a whole morning, and her sweat flowed from her calves to the soles of her shoes. There was water in her sandals, and Zheng Jianxin slipped every step she took.

As she walked, she suddenly thought of what Zhong had just said casually: "Ask Liang Xiangyun, everything will be clear!" But who would ask Liang Xiangyun? If Zhong asked, he couldn't even speak clearly so he was not fit.

Zheng Jianxin, who was eager to uncover the truth, thought to herself, since I came to Macau, I would go find her. Yes, I go to find her and ask her the question. People in my hometown often say that people with good consciences are not afraid of entering the temple gate. I don't believe she can eat me!

The sound of church bells came from not far away. The bells were not loud, but they were crisp and pleasant. Macau is small, but there are many churches. You can see one every three or five steps.

Zhong Haicai said that when the Portuguese and Europeans came to Macau, the church would mediate and judge any disputes in business. The church preached charity and gratitude, so that people from all over the world came to Macau and everyone lived in peace.

Zhong Haicai could not answer more questions about doctrines: "We are just playing, we don't have food to eat, how can we have time to listen to sermons? There are more than 30 church festivals in Macau every year. If you want to go, you don't have time to work to make money!"

Zheng Jianxin thought, yes, everyone wants to do good and be a good person; everyone says that they are good people, but fate often teases good people. Many of the sins, misfortunes and sufferings of mankind come from the relationship between men and women. Just as Lili said, if there were only men or only women in the world, life would be much easier!

Walking past Banzhang Hall, she looked back at the Ruins of St. Paul's. The fire that year burned the majestic St. Lo Church to a page-like archway. Zheng Jianxin felt that she had her own church in her heart. She didn't know when it would burn and what it would look like......

38

Liang Xiangyun exclaimed:
The mistress came to the door

Recalling the address of Areia Preta that Ahua had told her, Zheng Jianxin walked through one building after another. She checked the house number downstairs of Liang Xiangyun's house, hesitated for a moment, and walked in more forcefully step by step.

Except for her daughter Ahua, Liang Xiangyun's house usually had no guests. Liang Xiangyun was lonely all day, and sometimes she looked forward to the phone ringing or someone visiting, so when she heard the doorbell ring, she opened the door quickly.

Liang Xiangyun opened the door and saw that it was Zheng Jianxin. She was shocked and rubbed her eyes. When she looked again, it was indeed Zheng Jianxin.

"Is it really you, Zheng Jianxin?" She was panicked and at a loss as if she had seen a ghost in broad daylight. But she thought that this was in Macau, her home; and then she looked at Zheng Jianxin alone, so there was nothing to be afraid of except doubt. Liang Xiangyun, with one foot inside and one foot outside, leaned against the door to block it:

"What, the mistress came to my house, what do you want to do, I want to call the police!...... What do you want to do, take my house?"

Zheng Jianxin said calmly: "Sister Xiangyun, please forgive me for coming to your house, I want to know the truth, did Zhong Haicai and you get a marriage certificate?"

Liang Xiangyun knew the purpose of Zheng Jianxin's visit, and her worry was gone. She put on an elegant look, but she was trying to put on a little airs to suppress Zheng Jianxin, and stepped aside and said: "It is reasonable not to hit a guest who comes to my house, I can let you in!"

Zheng Jianxin nodded and thanked her and went into the house. The window of the living room was blocked by the building opposite. The room was dark, Liang Xiangyun turned on a dim light.

Zheng Jianxin saw that the living room was only seven or eight square meters. As soon as he entered the door, she saw miscellaneous items scattered in the corners. On the small dining table on the right, there were unwashed dishes and chopsticks. In the other corner was a standing fan, shaking its head constantly. The square table in front was dedicated to the shrine, and on both sides were two high-backed chairs. Liang Xiangyun sat cross-legged on the chair, lit a cigarette, and played with the dice cup on the coffee table next to her.

Zheng Jianxin sat on the chair near the fan and wiped the sweat on her face and shoulders with a tissue.

Is this the old woman who was a little crazy at the port? Zheng Jianxin looked closely today: her dark yellow cheeks were thin and sunken, and her yellow eyes, which were used to focusing on dices, glowed like cat's eyes, and peeked around from time to time. The water in her body may have been burned out in the casino, and her skin was dry and loose.

As the host, Liang Xiangyun spoke first: "I have suffered all my life because of men...... I met this heartless Zhong Haicai! He didn't learn how to be good in Macau, but learned how to seduce women...... Women will grow old one day, Macau men are like infectious diseases, looking for women, looking for women in the mainland......"

Zheng Jianxin waved her hand and interrupted her: "I just asked about the marriage certificate, and I'll leave after I finish talking!"

Speaking of this, Liang Xiangyun was a little proud: "We got it, got it!" She glanced at Zheng Jianxin, "Do you want to see it?"

"I want to see it!" Liang Xiangyun took a deep puff of cigarette, tilted her neck slightly, and exhaled a big smoke ring comfortably, just like a magician who kept people in suspense and was reluctant to reveal the answer.

Since Zhong Haicai paid off the bank loan, the "marriage certificate" that she used to resist the "building closure" was useless, and she put it away in the drawer. After a while, she slowly leaned over, opened the drawer with one hand, took out a red booklet, and handed it to Zheng Jianxin very proudly.

Zheng Jianxin opened it and saw:

Marriage certificate,

Zhong Haicai, Liang Xiangyun.

Special seal for marriage registration in XXX town in XXX city.

Liang Xiangyun really had a marriage certificate! Zheng Jianxin's chest heaved with anger. This marriage certificate was exactly the one filed with the Immigration Bureau, and it was the same place as the place of issuance informed by the Immigration Bureau! This was the ghost that had been shrouding her for several years, and this was the tight hoop curse that had been giving her headaches for several years. She finally found the source.

Zheng Jianxin didn't know what to say for a while, and didn't want to give up, so she asked in confusion: "Didn't you break up more than eight years before?" Could it be that during this period, Zhong Haicai would go to get a marriage certificate without telling her?

Liang Xiangyun suddenly realized that this marriage certificate had the biggest use, which was to subdue Zheng Jianxin, to make her laugh, and to make her cry. She began to act pretentiously.

She did not respond to Zheng Jianxin's words, but countered slowly: "Without you northern girls, would he not go home? Three bodhisattvas and two incense sticks, how could you have a share?" She tapped the marriage certificate with her fingers twice, "With this, even if he doesn't go home for ten or twenty years, I can still control him!" After that, she put away the marriage certificate and threw it on the square table with a bang.

This bang sound was like a hammer hitting Zheng Jianxin's heart, and like a cannonball exploding in her heart. Zheng Jianxin looked at the marriage certificate without saying a word. For a moment, she didn't even dare to look up at Liang Xiangyun. She could imagine that Liang Xiangyun's face was a smug smile of a winner and a look of mock towards her.

Liang Xiangyun's eyes suddenly flashed, and she wondered if another battle to defend the house had begun again? She flicked the ash off her cigarette: "Tell you the truth. You are looking at this house, right? No way!"

Zheng Jianxin covered her chest with one hand and said angrily with a frown: "Enough! Enough!"

She stood up shakily, glanced at the table, picked up the marriage certificate with force, threw it on Liang Xiangyun, and rushed out of the door angrily.

A patient with an incurable disease, hoping that the disease is not real, and then undergoing laboratory tests, another or several similar test reports with the same indicators, one will gradually believe that the time of death has come. Zheng Jianxin was in this mood at the moment. She was indeed married to a married man!

Zheng Jianxin couldn't remember where she had lost her parasol, and she didn't want to think about it. The sun was like a venomous snake above her head, and her thick hair was scattered and stuck to her sweaty cheeks and neck. Her mind was blank, and she walked quickly towards the gate. She just wanted to return to her home in Zhuhai as soon as possible, to her own home. Inexplicably, she felt an attachment to her home in her heart, as if it would be lost in an instant.

When the self-combed woman was dying, she asked someone to send little golden clock to Macau

In the evening, Zhong Haicai passed the gate from Macau in his sweaty work clothes. When he returned to his home in Gaosha Street, Zhuhai, he began to unbutton his clothes and prepare to take a shower. After entering the house, Zheng Jianxin pulled him to sit down without waiting for him to untie his belt. Her burning eyes swept across his tired eyes and his neck covered with fine beads of sweat, and then stared at him without blinking: "I went to Macau to find Liang Xiangyun!" Then she told him about her meeting with Liang.

When Zhong Haicai heard that Liang Xiangyun had a marriage certificate with him, he was shocked and his eyes became wide: "Impossible! Impossible! Yi (this) bitch!" He was so angry that his face turned purple, "Fake, fake! It must be fake! I have never returned to my hometown with her since I came to Macau, let alone got a marriage certificate! Ahua can prove it!"

Zhong Haicai did not ask how the fake certificate came from, as if he could get away with just saying "fake". He grabbed the bath towel and walked into the bathroom angrily.

Zheng Jianxin had her back to Zhong Haicai and leaned against the wall. She had just finished taking a shower and her hair was not completely dry yet. It fell on her white and smooth shoulders. Her pale face was revealed in her long hair, and her pair of black eyes now showed confused astigmatism. What happened at Liang Xiangyun's house today was a blow to her, and it was like a knife cutting a bloody mark of humiliation in her heart. She ran around in Macau all day, and what she came back with was a problem, a very serious problem. Several doubts and assumptions filled her mind.

When Zhong Haicai came out of the bathroom, she seemed to say to Zhong Haicai or to herself: "I am most afraid of people saying that I am a mistress. I didn't expect that I really became a mistress! Do you know what I care about most, Zhong Haicai? Who am I to you? A tree is afraid of damaging its roots, and a person is afraid of being hurt in heart!"

Zhong Haicai didn't say anything. He didn't know what to say.

Zheng Jianxin said, "Wow!" and stood up straight, pointing at his nose, "Since you haven't been with her, do you dare to confront her?"

Zhong Haicai had an idea and answered loudly, "Sure! I dare to confront her!"

The child fell asleep. Zheng Jianxin lay on the bed exhausted. Zhong Haicai sat on a small stool as usual, with his two bare legs exposed, constantly swatting mosquitoes; the blue veins on his calves were bent like earthworms. His old problem was knee pain, and he rubbed it with Wanhua Oil from time to time.

"Liang Xiangyun also broke my heart, so we broke up!" Zhong Haicai sighed and whispered. The loose muscles on his face trembled slightly with anger.

Zhong Haicai usually didn't talk much, and rarely had a heart-to-heart talk with Zheng Jianxin. In fact, it was not that he didn't want to talk, but he couldn't talk more than three sentences, and he was too dumb to continue, and gradually didn't want to talk anymore. Now he had to speak, and many questions rushed to his throat.

He poured a cup of strong Gongfu tea.

"When I went to Macau, there was a distant uncle in Macau named Zhong Wang. He worked as a watchman in the casino and had some connections with the underworld. He was very imposing, with thick eyebrows and a wide mouth. His hair was black and thick, smeared with oil and combed back. He always wore Chinese black yam gauze clothes and pants, and a pair of black cloth shoes with leather soles and futoni fabric. The two canine teeth on the left and right of his thick lips were inlaid with gold teeth, which made people intimidated. But he had no home in Macau -- and he never had a family in his life."

"When I first came to Macau, he took me to dinner and warned me three things: 1. I had to work to make a living in Macau; 2. I couldn't gamble; 3. I couldn't borrow money from him. After saying these three things, he said, 'I belong to the underworld you mainlanders talk about. If you respect me, call me every month and go out for dinner. If anyone bullies you, just tell me; if you look down on me or are afraid of me, after this dinner, no one will recognize each other when you leave! '"

"I told him that I didn't understand and I wouldn't ask what he was doing, but he was my uncle forever."

"Without the protection of my uncle in those years, I would have been unable to stand in Macau and was repatriated to the mainland."

"When I first arrived in Macau, I worked on a construction site, but I was not paid every month. The foreman lied to us that the boss would pay us only after the project was completed. The project was completed and it was time to pay. The black-hearted foreman, who was a mainlander who came to Macau in the 1950s, reported to the Portuguese that there were illegal workers here in order to get their wages. The Portuguese arrested illegal workers in carloads and repatriated them to the mainland every year. The night I was about to be arrested, my uncle got the news and rushed over quickly. My uncle was a martial artist, and he punched the foreman like a hammer, and then knocked down several thugs, and rescued us so that we were able to escape."

"Liang Xiangyun had just arrived in Macau, and I took her to the casino to see something new. At that time, the Lisboa Casino had just been built. I pointed out to her the tiger mouth decoration on the top of the gate of the Lisboa, which is for eating people; and the two knives decorated next to it are deadly. Cantonese people call Macau soda port, soda means alkali, which means a place to wash your pockets clean! Local people in Macau rarely go to casinos. I told her what my uncle said, Don't gamble. I said, Liang Xiangyun, I can forgive you for anything you do wrong, but if you break my uncle's teachings, I will break your legs and drive you out!"

"But over time, Liang Xiangyun unknowingly became addicted to gambling. At that time, there was an old casino called 'Water Palace' in the inner harbor. It was a gambling boat, where fishermen and lower-class people gambled. It was quite far from Guanzha Taishan Street where we lived, about 40 minutes' walk, and several streets. Liang Xiangyun often disappeared in the blink of an eye, going to gamble. She didn't dare to go home after losing the bet. She wanted to make up for it, so she even knocked on the door of her fellow villagers in the middle of the night and knelt on the ground to borrow money pitifully. I beat her, and beat her so hard that she couldn't get out of bed. But once she could move, she disappeared again and went to the casino. She knew how to play baccarat, one-point, roulette, fandui, and big bet small. Later, she went to big casinos like Lisboa. There was a Kanggong Temple between Water Palace and Lisboa. She gambled, burned incense and prayed for blessings. After losing, she drew lots, calculated her fortune, and went to the foreign church to pray for blessings. She was tossing around all day long...... I had no choice but to beat her , I was so weak that I couldn't hit her anymore......"

"My uncle died a few years ago. When he was dying, he handed me a gold-plated Western self-ringing clock the size of his palm, and held my hand tightly with both hands and said, 'Keep it as a souvenir, keep it well, and don't lose it!' I knew that the little golden clock was my uncle's lifeblood, and I swore to him that I would keep it well as a family heirloom to let him rest assured! This Western self-ringing clock looks like a heart, and the little golden clock is very beautiful with a bright yellow color, and the gems inside are shining...... But more importantly, this little golden clock is the most important concern of my uncle's life, it is my uncle's lifeblood!"

Speaking of this, Zhong Haicai trembled a little and couldn't continue. Suddenly, he cried like a flash flood, "Ah", sobbing; "This little golden clock actually was pawned and it's gone! I can't find it again! I'm sorry to my uncle, I'm unfilial! "

The Little Golden Clock was a clock made in Europe a hundred years ago. It's rare and precious, but more importantly, behind it was the sad love story of his uncle Zhong Wang.

When he was young, Zhong Wang had a childhood sweetheart, Ali, in his hometown village. There was a bad young man in the village who was doing business in Guangzhou. He asked a matchmaker to pay a large sum of money for the "big engagement" and vowed to marry her.

After being politely rejected by Ali's father, the young man's family spread the word: money could make the devil push the mill. They didn't believe that Ali would not obey, and they instigated the guards to force her. At that time, there was a custom of fighting in the countryside of the Pearl River Delta. Ali's father didn't want to make things worse but didn't know what to do.

Ali was so angry that she volunteered to be a "self-combed girl" on the ground of waiting to serve her old father.

In ancient times, girls braided their hair into braids, and after getting married, they changed the braids into buns. Girls who comb their hair into a bun by themselves to show that they will never marry were called "self-combing" or "combing up". At that time, this custom existed in Shunde, Panyu, Xiaolan, Sanjiao, and Minzhong in the Pearl River Delta, and this custom was brought to Southeast Asia.

Ali's father chose a wedding day and invited neighbors to the banquet. Ali swore to the heaven and ancestors that she would never marry. The custom there was that "self-combing girls" should not be asked to marry from the day they publicly announce that they had "combed up".

Just as everyone was in the party, Zhong Wang rushed to the sea, waving his arms and striking the water like crazy, swimming non-stop. That night, Zhong Wang left his hometown angrily and ran to Macau to settle down. At that time, the customs was mainly responsible for collecting taxes, and there was no restriction on people moving.

Zhong Wang vowed never to return home. But when he missed Ali so much that it was unbearable, he ran back to his hometown. He and Ali could only look at each other, but it was not appropriate to speak, so as not to ruin Ali's reputation, and this went on year after year. Since Ali never married, Zhong Wang did not want to marry and irritate Ali, so he never married.

Self-combed women were respectfully called "aunties", but in fact they were "lonely women". A self-combed woman who had returned from Southeast Asia lived in the aunties' public house outside the village. When she died, she gave the little golden clock to Ali as a souvenir.

According to custom, self-combed women shouldn't die in the village. There was a family in the village looking for a wife for their deceased son. Ali's nephew tried to persuade Ali to marry the dead man, so that she would have a pure body, a place to live in when she was in her old age, and people to take care of her. Ali refused because she was always thinking about Zhong Wang.

Before she died of illness in the aunties' public house in her early fifties, she took out the little golden clock and asked her nephew to send it to Macau: "You must find Zhong Wang and give it to him!"

At the end of her life, Ali opened her heart to the person she loved in this secret way: "I love you", "I have always loved you", "I love you forever......"

When Zhong Wang received the little golden clock, Ali had been dead for three months. Zhong Wang opened the packaging box of the little golden clock, and it slowly uttered clear music. It was the greetings from the pure girl Ali to Zhong Wang, and the love that Ali had never confessed to Zhong Wang.

When the music sounded at night, facing the little golden clock Zhong Wang burst into tears.

The little golden clock ticked, ticked. It accompanied Ali through her lonely life in the cold eyes of the villagers.

The little golden clock ticked, ticked. It accompanied Zhong Wang through his life of longing in the bright lights and feasting of the city.

This is the love of the older generation of Macau people.

Zhong Haicai's eyes were red, his brows were deeply furrowed, his left hand clenched into a fist, his right hand slapped his head, and he said with great regret: "Over the years, I have lost everything with Liang Xiangyun, I can't remember it, and I don't feel bad. The only thing is that little golden clock of my uncle, I protected it like my life, and told Liang Xiangyun not to touch it. I wanted to pass it down as a family heirloom. Seeing this little golden clock, I will remember the ups and downs of my uncle's decades of living in Macau, and I will remember my uncle's admonition against gambling!"

"But I failed to keep the little golden clock. Liang Xiangyun pawned it to the pawnshop at the entrance of the Lisboa Hotel. When I found out, it was already forfeited and could not be redeemed! The pawnshop staff said that it was soon bought by a foreigner!"

"Liang Xiangyun hurt my heart. I didn't hit her or scold her. I cried for the first time in my life. I cried for three days. I felt sorry for my uncle! After that, I moved out and moved to Gongbei. The food and accommodation here are cheaper. I told all my friends in Macau that Liang Xiangyun will have nothing to do with me in the future. Children and people in my hometown know......"

Zhong Haicai was silent after he finished speaking.

His eyes were red and white foam was overflowing from the corners of his mouth. After a while, he half-closed his eyes and said, "How could I get a marriage certificate with her?......"

The room was quiet, and the fan kept running, making a low humming sound.

Zheng Jianxin listened attentively. Zhong Haicai was telling from his heart and she shed tears while listening. It seemed that she could hear the "tick-tick" and "tick-tick" sound of the little golden clock. She was immersed in this sad love story for a long time.

She rubbed her forehead and temples. She believed that Zhong Haicai was telling the truth. He had never gotten a marriage certificate with Liang Xiangyun. But Liang Xiangyun's marriage certificate made her feel annoyed: she could imagine that Liang Xiangyun could stir up trouble at any time with that marriage certificate and confuse people to the extreme. Thinking of this, she blinked her eyes, thinking that two people should go to get the marriage certificate, and she remembered a common saying: "Fake is fake, and the disguise must be stripped off!" Yes, check her! Check her! For such a person and such a thing, it is useless to feel afraid, and you must have the courage to face it!

She had confidence in her heart, and got out of bed and went to the bathroom. When she came out, she took Zhong Haicai's hand: "Go to bed!"

Ahua brought the news:
Liang Xiangyun agreed to negotiate a breakup

The closest person to Liang Xiangyun was her daughter Ahua. When children grow up, they go from being weak to being strong. They are knowledgeable and have the information of the times, and parents sometimes have to listen to them.

For Ahua, on one side was her mother who she resents, loves and pities, and on the other side was her father who had a family and child. The endless entanglement must come to an end. Just like a balance, Ahua was the lever in the middle. She told Lin Weihua about her troubles.

"You are my think tank. Please come up with a solution as soon as possible on how to resolve the conflicts at home!"

Lin Weihua, who had no experience in marriage, downloaded a lot of divorce information and articles on psychological counseling from the Internet, and wrote a document "Implementation Plan to Promote Parents' Breakup (Divorce)" based on the situation of Ahua's parents. When Lin Weihua was about to hand the "Plan" to Ahua, he played a trick: saying that his scientific research results were to be paid, just like the reports issued by the RAND Corporation in the United States.

Ahua guessed that he was keeping it a secret, blushed and gave him a white look, deliberately asking: "Do you want money to sell it? Name a price!"

Lin Weihua said: "No Hong Kong dollars or RMB," and then leaned close to Ahua's ear, "I want a kiss!"

"You are so bad!" The two of them played and hugged each other.

According to the "Plan", Ahua talked with her mother for two nights. On the first night, she let her mother talk. Ahua just listened. Liang Xiangyun repeated it over and over again: from being a girl on Yinbao Island until her father betrayed her. The conclusion was that she had suffered losses and been deceived all her life. She cried and vented out her anger that the root of her misfortune was marrying the wrong man. Zhong Haicai was the root of her misfortune, and she no longer had the beauty of her youth......

Ahua kept wiping her mother's tears and sweat. When her mother said she was tired, she made Gongfu tea for her mother and handed her fruit. When her mother was moved, she hugged her mother and cried together. Liang Xiangyun patted Ahua's back in tears and said, "Daughter, you and your mother are united as one!"

The second night was Ahua's turn to speak. Ahua persuaded, "What do you want that marriage certificate for? It's just a piece of waste paper. Dad will never live with you again. You might as well go to the Civil Registry with my father to get a divorce and ask Aunt Jian to immigrate to Macau. Everyone will be harmonious. Isn't it good to have more people to take care of you?"

In fact, Liang Xiangyun did not disagree with divorcing Zhong Haicai, but wanted to negotiate on the terms with him and Zheng Jianxin.

"As long as we can talk, it's fine!" Ahua finally persuaded her mother. The plan had achieved its expected results. Ahua was secretly happy and called Zheng Jianxin early the next morning to arrange the time and place for the negotiation.

In the evening, Zheng Jianxin went to the customs checkpoint to pick up the child and met Lin Weihua, only then did she know that Ahua was coming too.

As soon as Ahua and Huihui passed the checkpoint, Zheng Jianxin found that there was mud on Huihui's white school uniform, and then there was a blood mark on his forehead. So he asked: "Huihui, what's wrong?"

Ahua hurriedly explained: "There was a fight, and my dad called me and asked me to pick him up and accompany him back. It's okay!"

Huihui twisted his body and pouted: "Mommy, I don't want to go to school!"

Zheng Jianxin looked at Huihui in confusion. "They all called me son of mistress, wild child......, several times......"

"Then you......" Zheng Jianxin knew the reason why Huihui fought, and was about to criticize Huihui, but Huihui continued: "I hit them with a brick......".

"You shouldn't have hit them, you can complain to the teacher!"

"The teacher said that I would be sent back to Zhuhai......"

Zheng Jianxin hugged his son, feeling heavy-hearted, and said nothing more. Adults' affairs cast a shadow on children's psychology. This was the adults' fault, what else could be said?

Ahua pulled Zheng Jianxin aside: "I have made an appointment with my father, you guys negotiate at Gaosha Food Street tonight! We will take Huihui!" Turning around and pulling Huihui up, "What shall we eat, KFC or Italian pizza, we will be happy, and then, let this learned person help you with your homework......"

Ahua, Lin Weihua and Huihui left.

The customs clock rang with the time signal.

The crescent moon hung high in the sky above the downtown area of Gongbei. Zheng Jianxin, Zhong Haicai, and Liang Xiangyun sat at a table in the food stalls of Gaosha Food Street. The food street was very lively every night. There were many people from Macau who came here to eat. The food street seemed to be open for Macau people. Zhong Haicai and Liang Xiangyun saw many familiar people and greeted them. Liang Xiangyun wore a clean shirt today, with a white background and a dark blue flower. Her hair was combed neatly, and the plastic silver hairpin was still inserted in the bun behind her head. She put some powder on her face and exuded fragrance.

Zheng Jianxin poured tea for Liang Xiangyun, and Liang Xiangyun tapped the table twice with her index finger to express her gratitude. Liang Xiangyun lit a cigarette and looked very relaxed. She greeted Zheng

Jianxin: "Business is very good here, most of the diners are from Macau. A plate of vegetables costs seven dollars here, but it costs more than ten dollars in Macau."

Zhong Haicai didn't even look at Liang Xiangyun, and didn't say anything. He called the waiter over and took the order: "Soup, pig lungs and tea tree mushrooms; boiled chicken, fried snails, pig feet with ginger and vinegar, lettuce with oyster sauce, a bottle of double-distilled wine, two bottles of Wanglaoji......"

Liang Xiangyun was in no hurry to eat, nor was she in a hurry to negotiate. She had been lonely for a long time, and it was a rare opportunity for her to have a dinner party. She seemed very excited, and there seemed to be no distance between her and Zheng Jianxin.

She talked more: "Guangdong people love the word 'eating'! Eating is called offering sacrifices to the five internal organs. In the past, the stomach (the belly) was called the five internal organs temple. Here, not only Chaoshan cuisine and Hakka cuisine can be eaten, but also some local snacks have emerged. Hey, northerners eat flour, and Guangdong also has it! Chaoshan pancakes, salty and sweet fillings; Dapu pancakes are cylindrical, with bean sprouts and tofu shreds; there are also Tian Ai Bao pancakes and red date pancakes......"

Liang Xiangyun had a cat face and a dog face (change of expression), and Zheng Jianxin didn't know what to do. She had to listen to her nagging patiently. Inadvertently, from the side of Liang Xiangyun's forehead, she felt a trace of kindness in her eyes.

"Are you done? "Zhong Haicai interrupted her with a stern face, "I'm talking to you about serious matters, I don't have time to listen to your nonsense, eat!"

Liang Xiangyun looked at Zhong Haicai and sighed in dissatisfaction: "Your bad temper hasn't changed at all......" Then she picked up the chopsticks. Zhong Haicai took a sip of wine, pressed down the chopsticks, and angrily questioned Liang Xiangyun: "I haven't held a marriage certificate with you, where did you get the marriage certificate?"

Liang Xiangyun didn't care, and was a little proud: "Didn't you marry me? Didn't you have a wedding banquet? Where did the boy and girl come from?" At this point, her eyes turned back to Zheng Jianxin, pretending to be reasonable: "If you want to go to Macau, I can break up with Zhong. He ruined my youthhood and can't ruin yours anymore! "She tried hard to learn to speak Mandarin, so that Zheng Jianxin would feel warmth.

She took a big sip of the drink, stared at Zheng Jianxin, and held her hand: "Break up! I have already told you my conditions, the house in Macau will be transferred to my name......"

"No problem!" Zhong Haicai was very straightforward.

"And cash in Hong Kong dollars, no, RMB, 300,000, all at once!" Liang Xiangyun put down her chopsticks after speaking, and took out another cigarette from the handbag on her chest. People from Hong Kong and Macau often do not take off their handbags when eating out, and pull their handbags to the front of their chests. This way they will not be lost or stolen.

Zhong Haicai was so angry that his upper and lower teeth chattered and he shouted: "300,000? Where can I get it?"

As soon as she sat down, Liang Xiangyun looked at Zheng Jianxin up and down. Only now did she have the opportunity to look at this northern girl so closely under the bright lights. Her eyes swept back and forth from Zheng Jianxin, making Zheng Jianxin embarrassed.

Liang Xiangyun admired her from the bottom of her heart for her adorable looks! Her black and shiny eyes and delicate and straight nose were better than hers when she was young. At this time, the hidden jealousy, mixed with the feeling of inferiority, suddenly revealed her long-standing hostility towards Zheng Jianxin. She pointed at Zheng Jianxin with her finger and deliberately said with ridicule: "Fruit stall owner!" Then she pointed at Zhong Haicai, "Didn't you give all your money to your mistress?"

Zhong Haicai and Zheng Jianxin shouted almost at the same time: "Nonsense!"

Zhong Haicai became annoyed and really wanted to slap her!

He drank two sips of wine, suppressed his anger, and turned to beg Liang Xiangyun in a low voice: "Let us go, Xiangyun, I beg you! If you don't divorce, Jianxin won't be able to go to Macau, and no one will take care of the little kid when he goes to school!"

Liang Xiangyun sneered. Zhong Haicai knew that she was bored and he would continue to be fooled by her. Since she didn't take the soft approach, he would use the hard approach and completely turn against her: "Don't be so domineering!" He panted, "I have to divorce! Eat less salted fish and have less dry mouth, otherwise, I will sue you in court for falsely obtaining a marriage certificate!"

Liang Xiangyun curled her lips in disdain and smiled coldly: "Okay! Sue me?" She widened her eyes and stared at Zhong Haicai, "Zhong, I think you are jumping into the oil pan like a toad -- looking for death! Do you know that you are committing bigamy? I will make you go to jail!"

"What, bigamy, jail? " Zheng Jianxin was stunned and spat out half a mouthful of rice.

Liang Xiangyun talked a lot of nonsense, but Zhong Haicai didn't care.

He said to her coldly: "You can eat too much, but you can't say too much!" After that, he drank and smoked in silence. Liang Xiangyun started eating as if nothing had happened. She looked at them without even moving their chopsticks, frowning.

Zhong Haicai looked like a dried eggplant, and Zheng Jianxin looked like a rotten tomato, and she felt satisfied. Well, this is God's retribution for you two. While chewing the rice in big mouthfuls, she gave instructions like a winner: "I will give you one week! Ah, remember?"

Ajian said: Wherever the marriage certificate was issued to Liang Xiangyun, we will check it there

"Three hundred thousand yuan. Nonsense! "After taking a shower at night, Zhong Haicai went to bed and slapped a handful of mosquitoes on his head, cursing Liang Xiangyun: "I gave her 30,000 yuan last year, and I wanted to settle the matter. In the end, after receiving the money, she still wanted to make trouble!"

Zhong Haicai fell on the pillow angrily and closed his eyes sleepily. Zheng Jianxin didn't let Zhong Haicai sleep, and rubbed his chest with her hands: "What do you think we should do about this?"

Zhong Haicai said "hmm" and turned over: "What can I do......"

"Will it be bigamy and will I go to jail?"

"How do I know?" Zhong Haicai turned over again.

"Will Liang Xiangyun's certificate be fake?" Zheng Jianxin pushed Zhong Haicai awake, "Do you dare to go back to your hometown and check her certificate? ......Ask the government why they issued a "certificate" to her alone?"

If a woman doesn't let a man sleep, there is nothing a man can do. Zhong Haicai simply sat up: "Sure, I will do whatever you say!"

The next day, Zheng Jianxin and Zhong Haicai took a boat to Zhong Haicai's hometown, the town that governs Yinbao Island, early in the morning.

As soon as the boat left the dock, it entered the deep sea area in a few minutes. Zhuhai is where the river and the sea meet. The sea water on the shore is often turbid, while the water in the deep sea is blue. The clean blue sky seems extremely high and far, and sometimes it seems to be above people's heads and can be easily touched. Zheng Jianxin stood by the boat, and the sea breeze lifted her short hair and the corners of her clothes. She was depressed for many days, but now she felt much better. The world was so vast!

In Zhuhai, they saw the bridge of Macau from a distance, but now they saw it from close up. One of the two bridges is like a rainbow bow, and the other is like a wave, stretching out from the peninsula to connect Macau's own two islands. The lines of the bridge are very simple: white steel cables and railings, two streamlined bridges quietly floating on the blue sea, very much like a flying girl in white.

Zheng Jianxin said in her heart: Macau, you are a dream to me, and an unsolvable mystery. After landing in the afternoon, the two took a two-yuan passenger motorcycle and rushed to the town government office building. It is close to Guangzhou, there are many foreign-funded factories, and the economy is developed. The town has a small population, clean roads, good greening, and no old houses can be seen. Zheng Jianxin sighed that it was more luxurious than her hometown county in Guizhou. In the Marriage Registration Office, Zhong Haicai was speechless and couldn't explain clearly, but Zheng Jianxin explained the purpose of the visit. A female staff member took out a thick and old file, opened a page of the Marriage Registration Application Form, and pointed it to Zhong Haicai:

"Zhong Haicai'? "It has your signature!" Zhong Haicai took it and looked at it carefully. He was so angry that his lips trembled and he stamped his feet and said, "This is not my handwriting! Who signed my name!" Zhong Haicai held the form subconsciously and refused to let go. He almost cried to the female staff, "Someone is framing me!" Then he said, "I will sue this person. I will go to jail in Macau!"

Zheng Jianxin pushed Zhong Haicai to sit on the chair and asked him to control his emotions. Then Zheng Jianxin handed Zhong Haicai a pen and asked him to write his own name on a white paper for people to see. Zhong Haicai wrote several "Zhong Haicai" crookedly.

The female staff compared the two signatures: "Not similar, not similar! Hey, the handwriting of Zhong Haicai's signature on the application form is similar to that of the female!"

Zhong Haicai hurriedly took it and looked at it again. It was indeed Liang Xiangyun's handwriting. He had lived with her for many years and was familiar with her handwriting. She had participated in "literacy campaign" in her hometown and knew more words than himself. She could understand advertisements in newspapers and write short messages. So he said to the female staff in a rough voice, "Yes, it's Liang Xiangyun's handwriting!"

Zhong Haicai was about to speak again, but the female staff raised her hand to stop him, thinking about something. "Liang Xiangyun? From Yinbao Island? Oh, yes, it's been several years. I remember that she came alone to get the marriage certificate and said her husband was busy. I said that both parties must be present in person. I remember that she brought the boy with her, took the application form stamped by the village committee, and got the marriage certificate. I'm not surprised. Old wife and young husband is our custom!" Zheng Jianxin said: "Sister, the signature Zhong Haicai were obviously signed by Liang Xiangyun. This is a fraud. Can this marriage certificate be declared invalid?"

The female staff asked Zheng Jianxin: "Who are you to him? "

"Wife."

"Wife?" The female staff member felt strange and asked, "Do you have a marriage certificate?"

"Yes!" Zheng Jianxin straightened her chest, "We both got it at the Foreign Marriage Registration Office in Guizhou Province."

The female staff member patted her forehead, thought for a while, raised her head, and scanned their faces with doubtful eyes, saying to herself, "Isn't this a true and false Bao Gong (an ancient Chinese judge) case?" Then she said to them, "This, this, I have to report to my boss, wait a moment!" After that, she took the file and walked out of the office.

Zheng Jianxin was upset and didn't even bother to look at the scenery outside the window. She sat on the wooden chair, lowered her head, and wrapped her arms tightly around her chest. Zhong Haicai stood at the window and smoked.

The female staff member came back and announced to the two: "This situation must go through legal procedures and conduct handwriting identification. Zhong Haicai, please write an application and pay 3,000 yuan in advance."

Zheng Jianxin wrote a handwriting identification application on behalf of Zhong Haicai, he signed it, and she paid the money.

"Leave your mobile phone number and go back to wait for the processing notice!" The staff said to them.

On the return boat, Zheng Jianxin and Zhong Haicai sat side by side. As the boat moved, Zheng Jianxin fell into deep thought. After many twists and turns, the mystery of Liang Xiangyun's marriage certificate was finally revealed, and she breathed a sigh of relief. However, Zheng Jianxin was still confused about how to solve the problem. Everything in the past flashed through Zheng Jianxin's mind one by one.

In this place life is extravagant and decadent, human desires are rampant. The affairs of men and women around her are all marked with money, and are carried out semi-publicly like commodity transactions. But Zheng Jianxin was not like that. Since she had made up her mind, she just followed that man, whether there was love or not, whether the love was deep or not, was not the most important thing, the most important thing was that it must be legal and legitimate.

She thought that after getting the marriage certificate and accepting her fate, she would be at ease and she would be worthy of herself. Unexpectedly, Liang Xiangyun's marriage certificate pierced her heart like a sword, subverting her beliefs and declaring that she was not a decent wife, but also a mistress, and a poor mistress. She felt that there was no one who lived a more miserable life than she!

But who could she talk to? Would Zhong Haicai listen? However, at this time, she could only tell him. The boat was moving in the boundless sea. Zheng Jianxin pulled Zhong Haicai's arm towards her. She said slowly and solemnly: "When I first came to work, I envied you Macau people who came and went freely. The wages here are a few hundred yuan, but 4,000 yuan to 10,000 yuan in Macau, ... Bringing a Hong Kong and Macau husband back to my hometown, the whole village will be glorious. Mingming's family is the first in the village to convert the thatched house into a two-story building. The villagers all said that Mingming had made a fortune in Guangdong......"

A few seagulls circled freely and flew towards the white clouds. Zheng Jianshi raised her head, tidied her messy hair, and said word by word with a sad heart: "In the past two years, I have understood more and more that I have to rely on my hands everywhere! Do you think I am going to Macau? Wrong! I want a legitimate marriage. No matter who I marry, I will accept it, but good clothes don't hold rotten meat......"

The grievance of not being recognized by others made her cover her face with her hands and sob sadly. Her body was shaking. She said loudly: "I am not a mistress! I am not! I am not! I am not!" She cried and bit her lips with her teeth, sobbing, "I don't want to be a mistress!"

The sky was quiet and empty; the sea was quiet and open. The sea and the sky seemed to be a microphone, echoing Zheng Jianxin's angry declaration.

Zhong Haicai didn't know what to say, so he had to remain silent and slap his cheek from time to time. The boat moved forward. The blue sea water hit the side of the boat. The waves occasionally hit the board and splashed on Zheng Jianxin's clothes and shoes.

Zheng Jianxin controlled her emotions, rubbed her eyes, and after calming down, she said to Zhong Haicai: "If it doesn't work, I think we should get divorced!"

Zhong Haicai had no expression on his face. A week passed. Zheng Jianxin waited for news from Yinbao Island. Because before leaving, an official in charge at the town government said: They would deal with this matter very seriously. Zheng Jianxin seemed to see a little hope.

The next morning, Zheng Jianxin rode a bicycle to send her son through the customs. Just as she returned to the fruit shop, Liang Xiangyun followed her. Liang Xiangyun's face was gloomy, her hair was messy, and there were many wrinkles on the hems of her clothes and pants. She grabbed Zheng Jianxin and said the same old thing, trembling, "Sister, if 300,000 yuan won't work, 50,000 yuan will do! I want a divorce, I want a divorce! Give me the money, and you can immigrate to Macau right away!"

Liang Xiangyun put her hands together and begged, "Give it to me now, please?"

Zheng Jianxin looked and saw two men in black round-necked sweatshirts behind her. Liang Xiangyun explained, "I lost the bet the day before yesterday and borrowed high-interest loans! Last night, I made it and won ten thousand yuan, but lost it all again at dawn...... Three days of interest-free, tomorrow it will double!"

Seeing Zheng Jianxin's disapproving expression, she turned around and was about to leave, and said to the two men in black in a low voice, "I will have money to pay you back, she owes me money!"

Zheng Jianxin tried hard to shake her off: "What nonsense are you talking about again!"

Liang Xiangyun rushed over, raised her hand and grabbed Zheng Jianxin's arm, and the foul breath in her mouth sprayed on her face: "You stole my husband and cheated my daughter's money......"

"Nonsense! Nonsense!" Zheng Jianxin was so angry that her eyes were full of sparks, and she pushed her hard, "If you keep making trouble, I will call the police!"

Immediately, a group of people gathered around, and just like last time, some were indignant, and some shouted for fighting and killing. Liang Xiangyun clung to Zheng Jianxin, a blue vein jumped on her dry temple, and white foam kept coming out of the corners of her mouth: "If you don't give me money tomorrow, I will ask someone to take over your fruit stall and sell it off! It's a fight to the death, and no one will have a good ending! Someone in my hometown is a policeman, and I want you to go to jail! Jail! This time it's real! Real!" At the end, she spat on the ground and kicked the fruit basket with her foot.

In order to protect the counter, Zheng Jianxin was pushed onto the counter, blood all over her face. However, Liang Xiangyun's words "go to jail" and "this is real" and the loud sound of her spitting on the ground made her hear clearly. That was right. This time the wolf was really here! Liang Xiangyun was at her wit's end, and her threats were fruitless. She had to change her "thinking" to achieve her goal of asking for money. She was going to take action, and Zheng Jianxin was facing an unpredictable abyss......

Lili and Ajian talked for the last time

The night sky by the sea was as close to people as the scenery of a stage. The clouds moved very fast on the dark blue background. Thick clouds covered the moon, and then thin clouds brushed the moon, trying to cover and conceal, trying to make it bright and dark. The leaves of a row of tall coconut trees swayed in the wind. Their shadows were sometimes bright and sometimes dim as the moonlight changed.

The tide in the sea was quietly and ruthlessly torn into countless waves, surging layer by layer, touching the embankment, making a rhythmic sound in the silence, dull and monotonous. That day was a neap tide. When the sea water receded, the mud around the reefs and the garbage on the beach were exposed, making the air on the coast full of stench.

"This damn place of Guangdong, it's November, the sun is so toxic during the day, and it's still so hot at night." Lili kept fanning the wet sweat on her face with her right hand. She wore a beige sleeveless, unbuttoned shirt with two corners tied in a knot, revealing a pink bra on her chest, and a pair of coffee-colored suit shorts. Her newly permed thick black hair was tied into a bun with a ribbon at the back of her head. The moonlight at night set off her long eyes and attractive figure.

Zheng Jianxin beside her said softly, "It will cool down in less than ten days or half a month," and the two continued to walk. Although she lived in the same building with Lili, it was rare for her to have a good chat. The marriage certificate incident recently made Zheng Jianxin feel uncomfortable as if a big stone was pressing on her heart. Tonight, while Zhong Haicai was at home helping the child to bed, Zheng Jianxin asked Lili to go to the beach for a walk.

Zheng Jianxin wore a sleeveless, round-neck floral shirt, pink cropped pants, and a pair of light blue soft-soled shallow round-toed ballet slippers on her feet, which made her look graceful and refreshing. She tied her hair into a braid, exposing her round shoulders like snow lotus roots and her thin waist, like a girl of fifteen or sixteen, very charming.

"Have you brought the story I wrote? How is it?" Zheng Jianxin asked Lili. A few days before, she showed Lili the "Story of Zhuhai Fisher Girl".

"I have brought it," Lili replied, "It really excavated the upward spirit of Zhuhai Fisher Girl, and it is well written and beautiful! You are really good. You are so busy every day, and you are studying at night school, and you still have to write something!"

"For me, I correct my child's homework every night, then calculate the fruit account, and then write my homework. After that, I make a cup of tea, calm down and think about my own thoughts, and pick up a pen to write."

"That means busy until midnight, so hard!"

"When I calm down, my heart is free and comfortable!"

Lili took out a small notebook. The story written by Zheng Jianxin was like this:

In ancient times, a migrant worker named Zhenzhu (Pearl) spread the technology of pearl farming to the fishing village here. From then on, Zhuhai was rich in pearls. Because Miss Zhenzhu was hardworking, she was loved by the fishermen in Xianglu Bay. Zhenzhu and the young man Apeng fell in love and wanted to settle down in Zhuhai. One spring, it rained and was windy for several months. The fishermen did not go out to sea, and every household was out of food. In order to hand over the tribute of South China Sea pearls to the imperial court, the local officials forced Apeng's father and other fishermen to go out to sea. People complained in private: the migrant girl was a witch, and it was all her fault. At night, the wind and rain were strong, the sea was boiling and the mountains were shaking. People were anxiously waiting for the return boat on the shore. The navigation torches in their hands were extinguished again and again and could not be lit......

Lili said: "I really admire your imagination, Zhenzhu ignored the rumors and led everyone to climb to the top of Yandun Mountain. The most amazing and surprising thing is--"

Lili recited as if she was performing on the stage, "On the top of the mountain, Zhenzhu's left chest suddenly flashed and fluttered. She tore open her chest, and a pearl jumped out of her chest...... The pearl sparkled...... The pearl gradually grew bigger...... She raised the pearl above her head and called to the sea, 'Aba (father) --'. The pearl illuminated the sea; ....lit up the mountains and rivers......Aba and others' boats were coming hard......

Lili stopped, she slowly retracted her hand hanging in the air, and narrated in a calm voice: "In an instant, it became calm, the sun, breeze, sea. People turned trying to find the girl. She turned into a stone, standing on the top of the mountain......"

Lili finished reciting, and the two were moved by themselves and couldn't speak. When Lili read the story written by Zheng Jianxin, she felt that Zheng Jianxin fell in love with Zhuhai. After reading it, she asked Zheng Jianxin: "Why, do you think this place is your home?"

Zheng Jianxin smiled and said: "I don't love Zhuhai, I love our special zone dream, the gold rush dream! If you have a dream, go forward bravely."

Lili, who was annoyed in Zhuhai, didn't expect Zheng Jianxin to integrate into this society. She looked at herself and couldn't speak for a long time.

Zheng Jianxin praised her performance: "Ah, goddess, you must be great to be an actor! " Lili nodded secretly and smiled faintly for some unknown reason. After walking for a while, the two sat down on a stone chair next to the stone guardrail. "It's going to rain." Zheng Jianxin looked at the sky, feeling the annoying moisture in the air and said, "Sister Lili, I don't know why, I miss you so much today!" Zheng Jianxin was full of grievances and didn't know where to start, nor did she know how to get out of the mess, so she just wiped her sweat with a tissue.

She stared at Lili intently as she spoke. Lili was stunned for a moment: "Me too. I know what's bothering you recently!" After that, she held Zheng Jianxin's shoulders with concern. "Damn Bai Lang, he came to bother me as soon as he showed up in Zhuhai these two days!" Lili sighed, seeming to be happy and angry.

Bai Lang finally returned the money he cheated from Zhong Haicai. Lili was calm when facing Zheng Jianxin. "Bai Lang is still humane. He returned the money to Zhong Haicai, and Zhong Haicai returned it to Xu Zhuang. Thank you so much, Xu Zhuang!"

"Yes, my cousin is really thoughtful," Lili glanced at Zheng Jianxin and smiled, "He has always had you in his heart......" She swallowed her saliva and didn't know what to say.

Whenever she thought of Xu Zhuang, or someone mentioned him, Zheng Jianxin's heart would beat wildly.

Looking at the scenery in front of her, Lili sighed and said, "People are like plants, it's hard to be perfect. Look at this kapok tree, the tree is tall and strong, when it blooms, the whole lovers' road is red, it feels very romantic, but once the leaves fall, the branches are full of dead branches, and they are easy to break, and they will be scattered in the wind. Magnolia, it's fragrant and pleasant, but it's hypocritical, not wind-resistant and not salt-tolerant, it's hard to grow it......"

"The moon waxes and wanes, this matter has been difficult to be perfect since ancient times." Zheng Jianxin responded.

"Ajian, are you and Zhong Haicai in love?" Lili suddenly brought up this topic. How did Ajian, this "young grass", get eaten by Zhong Haicai, the "old cow"? Lili felt guilty, had regrets that could never be redeemed, and was resentful. With such complicated feelings, Lili sometimes dared not face Zheng Jianxin.

It was difficult to explain this problem in a few words that even Zheng Jianxin herself had been confused about for a long time. She smiled as if to relieve her sarcasm, shook her head slightly and nodded: "He has been treating me better and better recently. He is afraid that I will be tired, so he does housework for me after work; he is afraid that the smoke will hurt my skin and my fingers will become rough. He said that Macau women pay special attention to hand care and don't ask me to cook......"

Zheng Jianxin sighed, "But he still wants to make a fortune all day long. He sighs when he can't make money...... He is worried that he will be old. If I leave him, he will definitely be alone for the rest of his life."

"Do you miss Xu Zhuang? "Lili hesitated for a moment and said. She had been imagining what life would be like for Ajian after Zhong Haicai was replaced by Xu Zhuang.

Zheng Jianxin looked up and didn't speak for a long time. Her beautiful big eyes looked blank in an instant. She moved her eyes and glanced at the sea of floating lanterns, lowered her voice, nodded and spoke the truth: "I think of him every day. I think of him when I'm free. But I can't love. Love is to make the other person relaxed and happy, I don't deserve it...... Love, for me, is too luxurious! Sugarcane is not sweet at both ends...... As long as I can live a life worthy of myself and be considered a person, I'm satisfied!"

Lili was so sad that she couldn't speak. Only she who understood Zheng Jianxin's experience could understand the passion of love in Zheng Jianxin's heart from these words. After calming down a little, Zheng Jianxin asked back: "Sister Lili, do you have love? Who do you love?"

"Oh...... love? I still think the countryside husband is good! Other men are animals in my eyes! "Lili stammered in response. In her mind, love is a synonym for sacredness. She avoided it because she didn't want to blaspheme it, and thought she was not qualified to talk about it.

It was late at night, and the lights in Zhuhai city and Macau across the street were much less. The night sky finally revealed its original depth, and a few stars were sparsely squeezed out, dyeing the petals and strands of flowers in the flowerbed hazy, which seemed more textured. Lili bent down, embraced the flowerbed with her hands, put her nose against the flowers, and said, "So smooth!"

"I know you love flowers."

"Yes, I also love the sea."

"What about the sun?"

"The sun is too bright; I love the night, and the moon is very gentle." The fading lights in the city seemed to have taken away a lot of the noise, and the sound of the sea hitting the shore became louder and louder, hitting the hearts of the two again and again. The two were silent for a while, quietly feeling the sound of the waves.

The sea breeze blew in waves, with coolness and freshness penetrating into their skin. No one wanted to leave, and the two wanted to hold each other like this. There were only the two of them in the world, and no one was willing to leave each other, and no one could leave. When they were in their hometown, they always had endless things to say. When they arrived in Zhuhai, they met every day, passing by in a hurry, but they had no chance to say what was in their hearts. It was not that they didn't want to say what were in their hearts. For Lili, the shameful life made her difficult to speak, and for Zheng Jianxin, the inability to express the true feelings in her heart made her avoid her. They seemed to have become strangers to each other.

"Ajian......" Lili closed her eyes and whispered softly, "Whenever I close my eyes and take a nap at the beach, I hear the sound of the waves hitting the shore, just like I hear the sound of the Uncrossable River flowing in our hometown. It feels like I'm back home...... Jian, I'm tired and want to go home, I really want to go home......"

"The sound of the river is louder than the sound of the waves, like it's roaring something!" Zheng Jianxin said as if asking Lili or herself: "Don't you think it's strange? I don't know who named the river 'Uncrossable River', it's so difficult to pronounce! "Talking about their hometown, they talked a lot.

Their hometown is in the Wumeng Mountains, where there is a small river. According to legend, a young man and woman fell in love and waded across the river every night to meet each other. The eunuch beside the Jade Emperor also wanted love, but he couldn't get it, so he was jealous and did something bad. He falsely passed on the imperial decree and waved his hand. The water suddenly became turbulent and could not be waded across, so people named it "Uncrossable River". From then on, the two lovers could only look at each other but could not hold hands, so they had to cry every night. Their love moved many people, and they all asked the Queen Mother for mercy. The Queen Mother knew about it, waved her hand on the river, and drew a bridge along the mountain, but at this time the two lovers were already gray-haired and their youthhood had passed.

Later, people called this bridge the Natural Bridge. Lili and Zheng Jianxin had to cross this bridge every day when they went to school. Recalling this, Lili's expression became lively, with a smile in her eyes. She was a charming but shy girl in her hometown. In Zhuhai, her personality changed in the past few years. She always smiled and didn't care. She often lit a cigarette with her left hand and shook her key chain in the air with her right hand like a Buddhist bead. She even used this cynical attitude to deal with Zheng Jianxin on weekdays.

But this night, as if she had changed into a different person, she fell into deep thought for a long time, and then said with some sadness: "We ran away from Uncrossable River and ran into to another invisible Uncrossable River!"

She looked at the dim sea and the dim sky, sighed, and her chest rose and fell like the sea, "Who can draw a natural bridge for me!" In the distance, the sea reflected a few colorful lights of neon lights, which turned lonely with the waves, brilliant and dazzling.

Listening to her trembling and even choking voice, Zheng Jianxin felt the pain hidden under her often smiling eyes, knowing that she was emotional, but for a moment she didn't know how to comfort her.

"Ajian, I often miss the red camellia flowers blooming all over the mountains and fields in our hometown. In fact, the scenery of our hometown is not worse than here, and the people are also hardworking and simple."

"We came out just for a change!" Zheng Jianxin smiled calmly. She called out "Sister Lili", glanced at her, and said what she had wanted to say for a long time, "Is it okay for you to be like this now? When will it end?" She looked at Lili's face and said seriously, "We can't do as the saying goes, the snake doesn't say it's crooked, but says the road is not straight, right?"

Lili turned her head and plucked handfuls of green grass. Zheng Jianxin's words hurt her deep in her heart. She knew she was degenerating. She knew she was walking in the grass of the swamp, the mud under her feet was soft and trembling, and she could slide down, sink, and be drowned at any time. But she didn't dare to think about it, didn't want to think about it, and didn't want to say it out loud. So, she smiled lightly as if she was talking about someone else: "It's just sleeping with men, what's the big deal?"

After saying it, even she found it funny that she could actually say this! She couldn't help feeling a little ashamed to say something that she used to think was sacred so simply and easily. She laughed with a bit of mockery. The muscles on Zheng Jianxin's face twitched a few times, and she also laughed. The palm trees beside them trembled in the night wind. After laughing, neither of them spoke again. After an awkward silence, Lili felt that she had to give an explanation to Zheng Jianxin and herself, and sighed, "The Chinese New Year is only two or three months away. I will go back before the New Year and sell the stocks that are hurting me...... and say goodbye to this place completely!"

"Go home?" Zheng Jianxin blinked her eyelids. This was an important topic for migrant workers. She and Lili both knew the situation of those who had returned from Guangdong. Zheng Jianxin's sister Aliang left the Chen family in Guangzhou and returned to her hometown two years before. After not being exposed to the sun and wind for several years, her eyebrows and eyes were more beautiful, and her slender figure influenced by the city had become more feminine. When her mother asked people to propose marriage in the surrounding villages, people declined politely as if avoiding the plague or the devil: "Girls who come back from the city are well-informed and beautiful, and they are too beautiful to marry." They secretly spread dirty words: "How can a girl who comes back from the city be undefiled? Nowadays, men in the city have become bad, how can such a beautiful girl be let go...... I don't know how many men's hands she has pulled...... Who wants such a daughter-in-law? She will be drowned by spit......" Aliang became a flower in the mirror and a moon in the water that no one cares about. Zheng Jianxin was worried and anxious that her sister would be tied to that barren land like her grandfather and father, living an unclear life, half-human and half ghost.

And Xiuxiu, who came back from Zhuhai, gave her husband the 30,000 yuan she earned from working in Zhuhai. Her in-laws were grateful to her and regarded her as a successful person. When the new house was built, her in-laws gradually disliked her: what kind of skin care products did she put on her face in the morning and evening, and scalded the bowls and chopsticks with boiling water before meals, which was a waste! The husband was not used to her: just when they were passionate at night, she pushed him off the bed, and asked him to take a shower before he could touch her, and after "that" asked him to wash again. The mother-in-law finally spoke: After working outside for a few years, she could not control herself, and something would happen sooner or later. So the family drove her to the fields to work before dawn, and she was beaten by her husband for any retort.

As for Chahua, she married a poor bachelor with crooked eyes and a crooked mouth, who was born with a mental disorder. Only a fool would not ask her about what happened in Zhuhai. Her husband would look for her every night, and he was so rude that he even didn't let her go during her menstrual period. Chahua didn't want to give birth to a retarded child, and every time she refused, her husband would beat her. Two years later, the mother-in-law saw that her daughter-in-law was not pregnant, and found out the reason. One night, she and her elder sister-in-law held down Chahua's arms and legs, and let her husband rape her and ejaculate into her body. Finally, they tied Chahua's hands and feet with ropes and didn't allow her to move until dawn. Chahua tried to run away many times, but was caught and beaten. Zheng Jianxin's father went to her husband's house to reason with him, and also went to the village head and the police station, but they all said it was a "family affair, difficult to manage."

Lili said: "I'm not afraid, I can control my husband!" After that, her bright eyes turned twice, and she laughed indifferently. Everything she had here, no matter how big the rumors in her hometown were, as long as her husband didn't mind, she would not have uneasy days if she kept him stable.

"But isn't life 'frozen'?" Zheng Jianxin said, "I'm afraid, I don't dare to think that I can see the end of the day at a glance!"

Seeing the end of life was to work day after day on that barren land, and to do housework day after day at home on that barren land, until she should die of illness and old age. "One day I can't make it here, I will jump into the sea and won't go back. There is no way out!"

Zheng Jianxin, like other girls who went out, often missed home. When she encountered something unpleasant, she wanted to go home. Whenever she had the thought of going home, she would think of the tragic scene when the old migrant workers returned home. Going back means walking the old path for the rest of their lives...... But walking the old path is also difficult. They integrate the urban civilization into the backward and poor farming life. This is a tragedy of life.

"Life is like a play! It's not right to go back, and it's not right not to go back." Lili lowered her eyelids, "We ran to Guangdong without any preparation, just like an actor who appeared on the stage without preparing for his role. Will there be a good result?"

"Who would be prepared!" Zheng Jianxin said disapprovingly.

"Yes!" Lili stretched out her voice, "Some people arranged their children and relatives to the business department early. When we earned a penny with a drop of sweat in the factory, some people had already earned hundreds of thousands or millions of dollars!"

In order to make a fortune, Lili kept an eye on the stock market and threw the little money she had into the stock market, but she didn't make much money. Zheng Jianxin smiled sadly and responded: "The Special Zone is like a boiling pot. Everyone lives here and runs to get a piece of meat and a mouthful of soup. Layers of people surround the pot, and we migrant workers also come, but we are a little far away from the pot......"

Lili sighed and shook her head gently. "Why do you say that? Look at us, we are like junk stocks in the stock market! Sometimes when I think of my parents, I really want to make a crack in the road and let me crawl in!"

"Don't talk nonsense!" Zheng Jianxin stopped her.

Lili wanted to say more, with a doubtful light flashing in her eyes: "People like me should not die well, right?" Zheng Jianxin hurriedly spitted on the ground and covered her mouth.

After a while, Lili said slowly: "What capital do we have? It's just a body -- isn't it just a piece of grass? Working is what you call cheap labor? As for me," she changed the subject, "I am much cleaner than those hypocritical people! None of them can touch me. Once, a well-dressed man came from Guangzhou. I saw him on TV. He said that he had admired the four famous prostitutes in Gongbei for a long time. Today, I saw her beauty and was lucky to see her. What? You said I was a prostitute? I was so angry. I controlled my temper and said, how can you admire a prostitute? I said, if you want me, aren't you afraid that it will bring bad luck to your career and wealth? I shook a handful of his money to the ground, and then took out a lighter to light the banknotes. When they saw it, they were so panicked that they called the police, but I ran away!"

"There are also people with good intentions." Zheng Jianxin laughed before she finished speaking, thinking it was funny.

"Who?" Zheng Jianxin said, "Chen Xiao! He used to be in a state of constant anxiety. He returned to Guangzhou and sometimes sent me QQ emails. He said he was auditing a university psychology course and now he feels more at ease. He also spoke very clearly, like a different person, not so crazy anymore. I asked him, 'Don't you miss money?' He replied, 'Wealth and honor are like autumn wind passing my ears!' He said he was studying the alienation of a society during the primitive accumulation period. He said money alienated the rich into being fierce and cruel, and private factory owners alienated workers into labor tools. How can we liberate people from alienation? Everyone should live like a human being!

He sympathized with us migrant workers and said that we were chewing the bitterness of the reform era......"

Lili swallowed hard with a dry throat and sighed heavily; "Yes, it would be wonderful if people could live like human beings and live decently!" She stared at the sky with a dazed look in her eyes, "But who treats us as human beings?" Somehow, Lili's mood suddenly became gloomy, "But I, I know, 'I am just a tender branch and tender leaf, don't compare me to a wallflower or road grass'. I have no way out, this world...... won't tolerate me!" The cigarette butt in her hand flickered in the wind.

When she said "won't tolerate me", Zheng Jianxin's heart skipped a beat, and she felt the branches beside her trembling. Why did she say this? Was she afraid that she would be arrested during a "severe crackdown", or was she afraid that her "multi-acting drama" would be exposed, or was she too ashamed to face her conscience? Or something else......

A drizzle came, and the leaves on the top of the coconut tree made a rustling sound. "I know you're feeling miserable." Then Lili retracted her gaze from afar and focused on Zheng Jianxin's face, complaining to her, "I never said anything to you. You used Zhong Haicai's money and just dated for a while, that's all. Why did you take it seriously, get married, and get a marriage certificate? You've ruined your life!"

Zheng Jianxin felt guilty about only one thing in her life, and that was her guilt towards Xu Zhuang. She sighed, "My heart is broken into pieces, falling like rain...... I can't even explain it myself, it's really 'cut and tangled'. But I must have a marriage certificate. I want to be a legitimate person. My life is tied up in marriage, and I'm in a 'grave'!"

Lili smiled bitterly and advised her, "Don't be so pessimistic! I really admire you. You are about to finish your college studies. At first you asked me to sign up, but unfortunately I just couldn't stick to it; you have a career, oh...... How is the company going?"

The development of the Fruit Girl fresh fruit store had been going smoothly. Zheng Jianxin had discussed with several sisters recently and rented an office building in the suburbs to set up a Fruit Girl supermarket chain store enterprise. At the same time, they also wanted to set up e-commerce and sell online, and in the future sell to customers all over the country.

Zheng Jianxin said: "Tomorrow afternoon, we will formally register for the shares, and we need to set up the office. You can help me! Don't forget, you are the major shareholder!"

"Okay. But don't call me a shareholder. I just helped you to borrow money." Lili agreed, but asked, "What can I do?"

An idea flashed through Zheng Jianxin's mind like a spark. She smiled and said: "You will be appointed as the office director. One tree cannot make a forest, and one flower cannot make a spring. How about we call more people to work together?"

Lili answered happily: "Yes, madam. From now on, I will turn over a new leaf and take up my post tomorrow. I will fulfill my mission. Please rest assured, Boss Zheng!"

"Okay!" Zheng Jianxin hugged her and laughed with tears in her eyes.

Lili suddenly remembered something and said, "I had my fortune told on the street yesterday. The fortune teller said that my 'center' is auspicious, which means that my eyebrows to the tip of my nose are good, and I will have good fortune in middle age. He also said that my 'life palace' is good, which means that my eyebrows are long and beautiful, and I will live a long life. He said that I am destined to be a boss!"

After a pause, she said seriously, "Maybe the fortune teller is right. I went to the Internet cafe to search online. I can open a jewelry chain store with several ten thousands of yuan. I want to try it in the future!"

Zheng Jianxin smiled and said, "Okay! Just be self-reliant! Get rid of those stinky men! We are not here to make a lot of money, but to pursue this process of self-reliance!"

Lili agreed and added, "Someone said that beauty is the objectification of essential power. They call us beauties, so we become real beauties, beauties who never age!"

The two laughed happily again, and this time they laughed sincerely, feeling very comfortable. The coconut trees stood tall in the drizzle and dim lights, and the sea water was dyed with bizarre colors by the colorful lights on the shore, flowing and dancing like colorful ghosts......

As long as you don't kneel,
you will never feel shorter than others

The next day, Lili was on her way to work. She didn't know why she felt uneasy and was a little confused about the life that was about to change. She habitually walked to Mingming's coffee shop again. Lili wore a red sleeveless tight-waisted dress today. She wore a silver necklace and a heart-shaped pendant on her round neck, revealing her white and smooth neck, which looked bright and beautiful.

Last night, Zheng Jianxin told her that the "office director" should dress elegantly. She had a gray suit, which she put on and took off for some reason and changed into this dress. Her bright eyes revealed an arrogant and mocking smile again.

It was still the same table and the same group of women drinking afternoon tea. When they saw Lili, they competed to welcome her with applause and shouts.

After sitting down, Lili asked Mingming: "I haven't heard you mention your husband for a while." While talking, Lili kept holding Mingming's hand, which made Mingming feel strange. They were so familiar with each other, why were they still shaking hands? She had to go to greet customers.

The woman with dyed brown hair heard what they said and smiled indifferently: "It doesn't matter if he wants to come or not, as long as he pays. You can play mahjong when you have time. It's nice to have sex with a handsome guy, isn't it? I lost more than 7,000 yuan playing mahjong yesterday! I feel sad when I think about it. This is the harvest of my parents in my hometown for a year and a half...... We are committing sins! Mingming, don't you think so?"

These women were dressed beautifully and had empty pockets. Once they had money, they spent it all, as if the money was really not theirs. So they shouted about money every day.

Mingming smiled without comment, and then observed Lili carefully. Lili finally noticed that a customer had come, so she let go of Mingming's hand embarrassedly and stood up to pace around the store. Her eyes followed the pattern on the wall and slowly saw the juicer on the workbench. She even touched the coffee distiller with her hand and turned the frother a few times. It was as if she was visiting the place for the first time. Everything was new to her and she couldn't bear to leave, revealing a nostalgic look.

It was obvious that she was worried, but it was difficult for Mingming to ask. After greeting the guests, Mingming quietly followed her. The girl who had just had a big wave hair buried her head and fiddled with her cell phone: "Hey, hey, I'll read a paragraph. 'I am firewood and you are fire. Thank you for lighting me. My love for you is as deep as a cesspool.' Damn it!"

Another woman said, "What's that!" She flipped through her phone and found a paragraph, "'I am a monkey, you are a peach, sweet peach, monkeys are happy, eat too much peach, and have diarrhea!' Bah, these stinky men!"

The women sitting around talked nonsense for a while, and there was nothing else to talk about. They waved to Lili to sit down and drink tea, and asked about Zheng Jianxin, who they hadn't seen for many days, what she was busy with. Zheng Jianxin had always been admired by them. Sometimes they also wanted to imitate her and do some serious business, but these people were used to comfortable things. They were afraid of hard work and trouble, and finally gave up halfway.

"She is persistent and motivated. She has been studying at night school for three years and is about to graduate. The fruit business has evolved from direct sales to stalls, and now it has upgraded to an office!" Lili looked at them and responded, her tone full of admiration and a bit of pride.

After listening to that, the women were full of admiration and envy. One of them said, "I really admire Zheng Jianxin. I'm afraid my life is over!"

Lili joked, "The old man in Macau pays you and sleeps with you a few times a month. Sometimes he doesn't dare to come over for a month or two for fear that his wife will find out. You don't have to worry about food and clothing, and you have money to send home. Isn't it good!" Lili had long been accustomed to acting according to circumstances. Here, she often said things that were insincere, inaccurate, and forgotten after saying them. It was both self-mockery and mockery of others.

"Yes, playing mahjong, doing beauty treatments, others call her a mistress, what's wrong with a mistress?" Several women shouted together: "A gentle heroine who robs the rich and helps the poor!" Everyone laughed. Among the laughing girls, Lili laughed the loudest and the longest.

Lili was in high spirits. Only among this group of women who shared the same suffering could she laugh heartily; without inferiority, without sarcasm, she could feel her true self. She often came here to seek the warmth of feelings.

Looking around the coffee shop, Lili suddenly said: "Why do I feel that this place is like a birdcage, and the women inside all want to fly out, but they don't know where to fly to, and they don't know how to fly out......"

As she spoke, her ruddy face twitched involuntarily, her eyes flashed with strange flames, and her face was mixed with sad and lost expressions. Then, she cried, and cried loudly.

Mingming and the other women looked at each other, all puzzled. Lili's crying suddenly stopped. She sat up straight, wiped the tears from her eyes, clenched her fist and raised her right hand, announcing excitedly: "A chicken has two claws, and a person has two hands. From today on, I will turn over a new leaf, be self-reliant, and make money on my own! From today on, I am the office director of Fruit Girl Company!"

They were all stunned by this sudden change, and then someone started to applaud first, and the others also came to their senses and applauded.

Lili blushed. She said something ambitious without confidence: "Ajian said it well, as long as you don't kneel, you will never feel shorter than others!"

Several people had tears in their eyes......

Lili ended her beautiful dream in panic

Lili was a person who had ideas and was quick in doing things. After arriving at the company during the day, she designed a series of forms such as the equity confirmation letter. While Aju was printing and waiting for verification, she quickly wrote the titles of the rules and regulations to be formulated. These copywriting tasks took less than two hours.

She spent the rest of the time directing Afang and Aju to rearrange the desks and computers in the office, and the crowded room immediately became tidy. Afang said admiringly: "Sister Lili is a prime minister!" Zheng Jianxin was happy from the bottom of her heart. With Lili in charge of internal management, she could rest assured.

Zheng Jianxin didn't know why, but she felt blocked all day. She felt so sad that she wanted to cry. She wondered if she hadn't rested well because of the marriage certificate issue in the past few days, and calculated whether her period was coming. In the end, she didn't come to a conclusion, so she didn't think about it anymore. In the evening, she went to Gongbei Night School to take the final review before the graduation exam. When she listened to the teacher's lecture, her mind was always distracted, and her right eyelid kept twitching from time to time. She rubbed it with her hand, but it kept twitching after a while.

After finally getting through the end out of class, she was about to let out a sigh of relief when she saw Ahua waiting for her at the school gate, flustered, and it seemed that she had something urgent to do.

"Auntie Jian, this is terrible!" Hua said as they walked, "I can't persuade Mommy, Mommy will write to the police and the court to report you for bigamy!"

Zheng Jianxin's heart skipped a beat, and she sighed solemnly, as if asking herself: "Is it really illegal?"

"I have to rush back to work the night shift, you think about what to do!" Ahua said and left.

Zheng Jianxin sat on a bench by the road, feeling irritated and uneasy. It's almost ten o'clock now. In her hometown in the mountains, people would have fallen asleep and the village would be silent. But here, nightlife was bustling. The heat wave of the day had dissipated a little, and people were coming out to meet friends, talk business, eat, drink, and shop. The lanterns on Yingbin Avenue were blooming, the shops were brightly lit, and the gold was overflowing. She looked at the port square, and the crowds entering and leaving the customs were at another peak of the day. Zheng Jianxin sighed in her heart, the city, the city was the concentrated expression of human desire; human desire shaped the city, and the city evoked complex human desires. Zheng Jianxin should hate Liang Xiangyun, but she often couldn't. She felt sick when she thought of Liang Xiangyun, and hated Liang Xiangyun as a person. She didn't know when she could get rid of her completely.

Zheng Jianxin thought of Lili and wanted to tell her what was happening and discuss with her what to do. She called Lili's cell phone, and Lili said she was having dinner with Achang in a tea restaurant not far from her, and asked her to come over to eat. Zheng Jianxin said she didn't want to eat anything, and Lili promised to call her after dinner. After hanging up the phone, Zheng Jianxin untied the rubber band on her ponytail, loosened her hair, took a deep breath, and walked slowly to the beach.

Looking at the gray coast, white foam was mixed with the swirling waves and was swept into the seabed, and then more foam and bigger waves came to the shore again...... Zheng Jianxin suddenly remembered a weird dream she had a few nights before.

In the dream, she was in the middle of the sea, chasing the shining pearls in the sea with countless girls. They paddled hard, but they could not get close to the pearls no matter what. Once someone stopped, they would be swept into the sea by the tide. Those who stood on the shore would applaud and laugh.

They had to paddle continuously and continue their hopeless efforts. On the crest of the surging waves, she saw a man standing on the shore. He had a face that seemed to be pieced together. It was unclear whether he was old or young. He looked strange but a little familiar. He held a big gun and shouted loudly: "Whoever is disobedient, I will shoot her if I don't like her!" After that, he raised his gun and fired at the sea, and the people on the shore cheered.

The girls around her were shot one after another, and Lili was among them. The blood dyed the turbid sea red. Only she and two or three girls were left, and they were finally about to reach the shore. At this time, a huge wave surged behind her and covered the sky. She paddled desperately, trying to escape from it all. She forgot to breathe, forgot everything, and just swam desperately.

The waves hit with a "snap", and nothing was left. The morning light sprinkled on the calm sea, and was kneaded into tiny scales by the waves, shining like gold...... Why was it such a dream? Zheng Jianxin had been wondering, what did it imply? Did it indicate success or failure for herself or the company? Lili was shot and fell down, would there be another one? Liang Xiangyun could win the lawsuit, would she go to jail? Thinking of this, Zheng Jianxin took a breath.

In the restaurant on the beach of Lovers Road, Achang was very happy. He was doing business now. Recently, he bought some Cordyceps sinensis from a businessman from Qinghai, took it back to Macau and sold it to the big boss, which added a way to make a little money. Today he specially treated Lili to a sumptuous Western meal.

He was helping Lili cut the pork chop: "Don't use too much force to cut it. If the texture of the meat is not right, it will be hard to cut......" Lili was dressed in beauty tonight, with a black vest on her sleeveless red dress, which made her look particularly dignified and eye-catching.

Lili used too much force, and the black pepper juice splashed on her face. She couldn't help but yelled that she was unlucky, and the two laughed together. The trees outside the window swayed in the breeze, and the colorful lights on the street cast their shadows on the large glass windows. Looking from the inside, different patterns were floating on the large glass windows.

At this time, Bai Lang, dressed in a suit and carrying a briefcase, happened to pass by outside. He saw Lili through the large glass and walked in. He didn't bother to greet Achang, and happily pulled her to his side and said, "Wife, you're here! Didn't you go back to your hometown to see your son?"

Lili blushed to her ears, and shook off his hand unnaturally: "Ah, Mr. Bai, I'll call you later!" Bai Lang pretended not to mind Lili and Achang's date to show his gentlemanly demeanor. In his eyes, Achang was just a small scoundrel working in Macau, and Lili was just playing with him, and he couldn't even take advantage of her. He sat down, smiling, "It's so late to eat, you sit down!" Turning around, he waved to the waiter, "I want a cup of coffee, a latte!"

Lili was afraid that Bai Lang might reveal the truth about the child if he said a few more words, so she stood up and said, "I'll take Achang away," and then she took Achang out, explaining to Achang in a low voice, "I had agreed to break up with him a long time ago, but now he's back to bother me! He's a liar, don't pay attention to him!"

Achang had met Bai Lang several times because Zhong Haicai invested in Bai Lang's project, but he was not familiar with Bai Lang. Achang was still furious about Bai Lang's tricking them. He turned around, rolled up his sleeves and said, "This guy always wants to get something for nothing. This time he's here. I must teach him a lesson!"

Lili pulled him tight and quickened her pace: "No, no, let's go!"

Bai Lang was a little puzzled by their sudden escape. He combed his bright head with his five fingers, picked up his briefcase, and chased after Lili, shouting at her back: "Wife, wife! Why are you running? I have something to say to you!"

Achang forcibly grabbed Lili, turned around, waved his fist and said angrily to Bai Lang: "What, your wife? Bai, do you have a marriage certificate? You liar, get out of here! Get it clear, Lili is my wife now!"

"No, no!" Lili tried to explain to Bai Lang. Her embarrassed face turned pale and her heart was pounding. Bai Lang pulled down Achang's arms that were waving in the air, and announced with a bit of pride and mystery: "Hey, Brother Achang, we have a child! I'm back now, so don't get involved, give Lili back to me!"

"No, the child is mine!" Achang was a little anxious, and took out a photo from his wallet, "Do you think it looks like me?" Bai Lang's face changed when he saw the photo, and he also took out his wallet and took out a photo of his son: "What's going on, this is obviously my son!"

When the two photos were compared, they were exactly the same. Achang and Bai Lang's faces changed drastically at the same time, and they exclaimed "Ah" at the same time.

Lili, who was standing aside, was ashamed and looked around in a panic. Suddenly, she was shocked. Zeng Sheng also appeared at the door of the restaurant and was walking towards her happily. Lili's blushing face instantly turned pale.

"Oh my God...... just let me go!" Lili felt like she was going to faint. She couldn't control herself, and blood immediately surged on her pale face, and blood gushed out of her eyes, and her body was steaming with heat, and her head was buzzing. She seemed to see countless pairs of black eyes like monsters, radiating light, roaring, and shaking in front of her. Her hands trembled, and her bones made rustling sounds, but she was powerless to resist. Suddenly she saw a bright light, which was an orange road. She didn't care to think too much and immediately ran along this road. The flying red skirt was like a ball of colorful clouds.

"Lili, my dear! I didn't expect to see you here!" Zeng Sheng exaggeratedly opened his arms and hugged her, "I was planning to find you later to tell you the good news, our son can immigrate to Hong Kong. My old hen can't lay eggs, so I had to pester her to agree......ah, why are you running?"

Zeng Sheng was about to hug her tightly to express his excitement, but Lili took a step back in fear and turned to run. Achang and Bailang looked at each other in bewilderment, and then they realized what was going on. They shouted at the same time: "We've been fooled!" and hurriedly chased after her......

Zeng Sheng and Bai Lang only met once in Zhuhai Hotel. After they realized what the other party was, they never met again. Moreover, Bai Lang had fled to Shanghai to avoid debt for several years; Zeng Sheng's whereabouts were secretive because of his smuggling business, and he didn't know Achang. Zeng Sheng saw this situation and heard these words. He was experienced and mature. He immediately judged that Bai Lang and Achang were jealous of each other. He squinted his eyes and calmed down, watching the fire from the other side, and cursed proudly: "Of course you have been fooled!" He took out a photo of his son from his wallet, "That son is mine, hehe! My wife in Hong Kong can't give birth to a son, so she asked me to come here to give birth to a son! Women don't care who they belong to, you guys fight! I just want a son! A son! Hahaha! Mine!"

When the three men were fighting, Lili rushed onto the road in a panic. She felt that her feet were powerless, as if she was stepping on cotton wool. She didn't care about the traffic lights on the zebra crossing that flickered and were full of strange illusions. She was walking with her head held high and walking across. When a truck that rushed to the green light didn't react in time, coupled with the huge inertia, it knocked down the woman who flashed in front, and she fell into the flowerbed beside the road with a "bang".

"Lili......"

Achang and Bai Lang exclaimed at the same time and rushed over. Zeng Sheng, who followed closely behind, twitched his mouth a few times and quietly disappeared into the crowd. The whole intersection was in chaos, with more and more people watching. The vehicles blocked in the lanes honked their horns without knowing the situation, attracting more people to watch.

When Achang and Bai Lang rushed out to rescue, a kind-hearted person had already called the police. The driver who caused the accident looked at the motionless woman on the ground with a dead look on his face. The ambulance and police car arrived at the scene quickly. After a brief inspection of the situation, the doctor quickly lifted Lili into the ambulance. Achang and Bai Lang also got in the car and rushed away.

Watching the doctors and nurses start the rescue in the car, Achang and Bai Lang, who could not help, were slightly relieved. They looked at each other with a heavy heart and immediately looked away. Achang suddenly remembered that Zheng Jianxin was still waiting for Lili's call, so he quickly called for help and asked her to go directly to the hospital. Just as he hung up the phone, Lili's mobile phone in her handbag rang. Achang took it out and found that it was Xu Zhuang calling. He quickly explained the situation to him, but he was hesitant to answer his crazy roar and questioning, so he just told him to go to the hospital.

"It's all that Hong Kong guy......" Bai Lang cursed in a low voice as he watched Achang hang up the phone. Looking at Lili, whose red skirt was stained with blood and motionless, Achang lowered his head and said nothing, with a worried look on his face. He knew that she had an affair with Bai Lang and Zeng Sheng besides him, but he didn't care. At first, he just thought Lili was a dissolute woman, one of the "four beauties" in Gongbei, and wanted to take advantage of her. Unexpectedly, after getting to know her better, he found that she was not the kind of person he thought. She was educated, opinionated, and considerate. Achang fell in love with Lili over time.

Compared with Bai Lang and Zeng Sheng, he cared more about Lili's life and death. Although he doubted that the child was not his, he would rather choose to believe it, wishfully thinking that Lili would be willing to be with him and be a lifelong partner. "God bless, Buddha bless, Sanqing (Three Heavens) bless!......" Achang kept making gestures on his chest and prayed silently, "I will believe in whoever can make Lili better!"

When Zheng Jianxin rushed to the hospital, she saw Xu Zhuang standing alone at the gate, his face full of grief and anger.

"Brother Zhuang......" Zheng Jianxin felt something was wrong, and eagerly held Xu Zhuang's hands, and Xu Zhuang's fingertips were trembling...... Xu Zhuang's eyes were filled with tears: "Dead!" "Dead?!"

Zheng Jianxin looked at Xu Zhuang in disbelief. In an instant, she felt cold sweat oozing out of the pores of her body, and her body couldn't help shaking.

Xu Zhuang bit his lower lip tightly, lowered his eyes in pain, and tears burst out of his eyes.

"Oh my God...... Don't......" Zheng Jianxin burst into tears. Lili's smile last night flashed before her eyes. "What? She's dead?" Ajian was heartbroken as if she was stabbed from behind without any defense. She held her hands and screamed "Wow". Her body softened and fell on Xu Zhuang's shoulder. The two held each other and cried bitterly.

Xu Zhuang held her tightly, as if he was afraid that she would disappear from his sight. In the temporary morgue, Zheng Jianxin looked at Lili's body covered with a white cloth and cried bitterly. Bai Lang and Achang beside her were full of regret. One was heartbroken, and the other had tears all over his face.

Seaside funeral

According to the custom of their hometown, relatives and friends should set up a mourning hall for the deceased, but the landlord did not allow sacrifice activities in the rental house. After several considerations, Xu Zhuang and Zheng Jianxin both thought that the seaside was the most suitable place to say goodbye to Lili.

The news of Lili's death spread quickly. Fellow villagers and friends were all shocked and regretful! A color photo of Lili was placed among the flowers and offerings. It was taken at this location on the beach when she first came to Zhuhai. She smiled, so innocently, so brilliantly, so charmingly. One flower after another was gently placed in front of her......

Perhaps because of the same fate, the group of sisters drinking afternoon tea in Mingming Cafe cried particularly sadly. The girl with dyed brown hair knelt in front of the portrait and cried so sadly that she couldn't get up. Zheng Jianxin wanted to help her up but couldn't, so she had to hold her and cry together.

Mingming didn't come, and someone sent a message saying that she was not feeling well. Zheng Jianxin understood that it was a refusal. It must be that the so-called Taiwanese "husband" was afraid of bad luck and didn't even allow her to attend the final farewell. Mingming had really changed! She had become so hard-hearted that she was not a fellow villager, let alone a sister. Zheng Jianxin often felt that human feelings were thinner than paper from Mingming.

The night in early winter was cold. The grass and trees also showed sad green and sad red. The lights of Macau looming in the distance reflected the changing light patterns in the mist, which looked very scary. The sea was at low tide, and waves were retreating one after another.

Zheng Jianxin and Xu Zhuang silently spread the paper money one by one into the sea, and the sea water quickly swept them away, out of sight, and swept them into the depths of the sea.

The sea waves were no longer noisy, but sobbing, playing funeral music for Lili, seeing her off......

"Sister Lili, you said you would be my office director, and we would open up the future together, be upright and live uprightly, why did you leave us behind?" Zheng Jianxin stared at the paper money drifting away and murmured, "You still have a family, a child, a husband, and a group of good sisters like us, how could you bear to leave us behind?"

Xu Zhuang looked at her distraught appearance, and his heart ached. "God, please let my sister Lili's soul ascend to heaven! She is a good person! I beg you to forgive her romantic sins, she has a clean heart...... I beg you...... have mercy on us, the workers who are like grass......"

In prayer, Zheng Jianxin fell to her knees and fell to the ground in grief. When she was in middle school in her hometown, Lili was the class monitor, and everyone only called her "beautiful class monitor"...... In the season when corn was ripe in her hometown, although the farm work was busy, Lili always smiled happily......

One day, she smiled and said to Zheng Jianxin: I want to work in Guangdong, make a lot of money, and then send it back home......

"Sister Lili......" Zheng Jianxin raised her head and lit the candle that was blown out by the sea breeze again. Xu Zhuangyang threw the paper money into the sea.

Achang brought midnight snacks, but Ajian and Xu Zhuang had no appetite. Several fellow villagers wanted to take turns and persuaded Zheng Jianxin to go back and rest. She held the railing and refused to leave. She hadn't talked enough with Lili, and she wanted to accompany Sister Lili.

It was late at night, and only Xu Zhuang and Zheng Jianxin were left in front of the mourning hall by the sea. The emergency light sent by a fellow villager was on, emitting a weak and pale light. Xu Zhuang replaced the incense burner with new incense and candles, and burned some paper money every hour. The candles were blown out by the wind from time to time, and he would light the candles again when the wind was light.

Zheng Jianxin sat on a stone chair next to the mourning hall. Zheng Jianxin didn't dare to look at the familiar path in front of her that brought back memories. When she looked up, she saw Lili, wearing a suspender top, a sleeveless round neck, plaid trousers, and high-heeled leather boots in different images, walking from a distance. Zheng Jianxin didn't dare to look at the rippling sea surface. When she looked up, she saw the sea reflecting Lili's different faces, some with heavy makeup, some with simple elegance, some with vitality, and some with gentleness and shyness......

She had to lean back in her chair and close her eyes. Gradually, a white seagull emerged in her mind. That was the seagull that Lili held in her arms last year.

"What's wrong, seagull?" Zheng Jianxin asked curiously at the time. Lili gently put the seagull against her chest, stroked the seagull's wings with her fingers and said, "I found it in the bushes yesterday morning. It was injured, but it's much better now." She looked up at Ajian and said, "Seagulls have a habit. When they know they are about to die, they will find a remote place to die quietly."

When Lili said that the seagull's injury was much better, the seagull seemed to understand what Lili said. It struggled and jumped up, and it gurgled in its mouth as if it wanted to speak, showing a happy look. Lili and Zheng Jianxin smiled knowingly.

Lili said, "Let it fly!"

Lili leaned against the embankment and faced the sea. When the seagull saw the sea, it fluttered and flew towards the sea and sky. Lili's eyes followed the seagulls......

Lili whispered to herself: "Where the seagulls go, there will be no smell of stinky copper coins......" Zheng Jianxin fell asleep in a daze. In the dream, Lili came. She was still wearing the sleeveless red dress and smiling as usual.

When she walked to the mourning hall, she looked at her own photos in the white candles on both sides and asked Zheng Jianxin curiously, "Why am I dead?" Then she laughed, as if Zheng Jianxin and the others were deceived, "How could I die?" Then she pointed to the sky, "Look......" Zheng Jianxin looked where her finger pointed, and saw Lili driving a red car flying back and forth in the sky, along with her parents, husband and child...... After a while, Lili, wearing a black doctoral hat, led Huihui and several children, all wearing bachelor's gowns, holding graduation certificates in their hands, and happily ran over on the clouds...... Then they flew and flew, all the way to their hometown, in the halo of gold and silver, their hometown was a brand new building......

Suddenly, the light in the sky disappeared, and she fixed her eyes in front of her mourning hall, looking at the candles and offerings with a child's clear eyes, and suddenly her face changed suddenly. When she was sure that she was dead, she asked Zheng Jianxin and the people around her in a panic: "Am I really dead?"

Everyone's face was as frosty as ice and expressionless.

At this time, a piercing laugh like thunder rang out from behind, and everyone turned around. It was Mrs. Tong's face. She laughed and her face was red. She had no neck. Her face was as thin as a piece of paper, hanging in the sky, and her bulging chin occupied half of her face.

In the laughter of Mrs. Tong, Lili seemed to have come to her senses. She did not pay special attention to Mrs. Tong's contemptuous ridicule. Not only did she endure it silently, but she also looked pitiful out of shame.

She looked around and understood: she was really dead. In an instant, a cold light flashed in her big eyes, and a cruel look appeared at the corners of her mouth. She knelt down in front of the photo in the mourning hall, and cried loudly with a "wow" sound, grief and anger.

Zheng Jianxin was also moved. She cried and held Lili's shoulders to comfort her, calling "Sister Lili", "Sister Lili"......

At this time, she could only hear someone calling "Ajian", "Ajian" and shaking herself. Zheng Jianxin opened her eyes and saw that there was no one in front of the mourning hall. Only Xu Zhuang was stroking her shoulders: "What's wrong? Are you dreaming?"

Zheng Jianxin knew that she had a dream. She raised her face and smiled sadly at Xu Zhuang, stretched her left hand across her shoulder and held Xu Zhuang's hand behind her. The portrait of Lili in front of her made her realize the impermanence of life, the fragility of life and the indifference and cruelty of the world. Holding Xu Zhuang's hand, this was the first time they had skin contact in seven years. She felt the slight trembling of Xu Zhuang's fingers -- it was a warm hand that she was familiar with.

She pulled him to sit on the chair. She held Xu Zhuang's hand and leaned against her chest, never letting go. A gust of cold wind blew, and Xu Zhuang overcame his hesitation for a moment and held Zheng Jianxin's shoulders. Zheng Jianxin's hands caressed his broad back. She couldn't suppress her inner sadness and sobbed. As she sobbed, her head pressed tightly against Xu Zhuang's shoulder. For seven years, Xu Zhuang had been in her heart, always with her, making her feel at ease. At this moment, Xu Zhuang was the person she depended on in this world.

A seagull circled in front of the mourning hall, and then landed on the lawn of the mourning hall for a while. After a while, it cried and flew towards the dark sea and sky.

Zheng Jianxin watched the seagull fly away, muttering to herself: "Sister Lili is gone!" Xu Zhuang didn't know what Zheng Jianxin had dreamed just now, and nodded as if he understood her words. Xu Zhuang put a black suit jacket he brought specially on Zheng Jianxin. He went to burn incense and paper again.

Zheng Jianxin's eyes were filled with Lili's charming and innocent smiling eyes, which floated around like teasing. She sighed to the sky, wondering if God would not accept her because she was not clean. She was still dissatisfied with Lili's debauchery in her life, but the dead were the most important, so she no longer thought about Lili's faults. "Am I a 'bad woman'?" Lili asked Zheng Jianxin nonchalantly several times, then lowered her head and whispered, "I like to make love, and do it to the fullest! I can't control myself, and there seems to be a lot of energy in my body that needs to be vented......"

Her face revealed a bold, brave and strong desire for a passionate life. She was frank and arrogant, as if to show her high IQ and her talents that she had nowhere to display...... Yes, anyone who had seen Lili would never forget her beautiful body full of vigorous youthful vitality and creativity. She often lit a cigarette. Zheng Jianxin remembered her expression clearly. She stared at the flame of the burning cigarette, she looked at the sparks hopefully, as if the sparks would bring her a golden world, but her eyes became dull, and she stared at the remaining ash for a long time.

Zheng Jianxin laughed at her: "What kind of cigarettes are you smoking? I think you are smoking loneliness and emptiness."

Lili replied: "Once I have something serious to do, I will quit." She kept her word, and as soon as she entered the fruit girl company, she immediately took out the cigarette from her handbag and threw it into the trash can.

Thinking of this, Zheng Jianxin asked Xu Zhuang for a cigarette and lit it herself. Although it was choking, she still took two puffs and presented it to Lili's statue: "Sister Lili, you smoke, take two puffs happily!" Strangely enough, although there was a constant breeze, the cigarette presented to Lili did not dissipate until it burned out, leaving a whole pale ash.

Zheng Jianxin walked to the dark seaside, facing the sea, she was filled with grief: "East, West, South, North, and Center, go to Guangdong to make a fortune. Sister Lili, this is what you said most before you came out. We all dreamed of Guangdong. But when you came here, you fell into a nightmare. The good dream didn't start, and you died in the nightmare. The red camellia was like a flash in the pan......"

The wind was howling, the waves were roaring, and the dark clouds were surging, as if responding to the suffering of Zheng Jianxin and Xu Zhuang, and adding a bit of sadness to Zheng Jianxin's words. "Oh sea,

sea, she came for you, she loved you so much, loved your broad mind, loved your deepness, but you, you are ruthlessly swallowing her; oh sea, she was originally as beautiful as the morning glow, but as soon as she surfaced and had not yet shone, she was submerged by you, forever submerged...... People saw her cynical smile, but that was a smile of enduring humiliation, a smile of losing dignity, a smile of using dignity to fight against injustice!...... Heaven, earth, did you see it? If you can't even distinguish this, then you are unworthy of being heaven, unworthy of being earth, unworthy of being the sea!...... Sister Lili, where are you? Where are you?!"

Her narration finally turned into a hoarse cry, filling the sea and sky, making the dark clouds chaotic, tearing them into cotton wool and slowly swimming across the sky; making the sea chaotic, the waves angrily knocked against the rocks in the dead of night, and wailed to the sky......

46

Ajian was suspected of bigamy
and was locked up by the police

Lili's death hit Zheng Jianxin hard. She lost the only person she could talk to, the one who understood her, and the feeling of loneliness spread over her body, as if she were dead too.

She sat dully on the beach for three days after Lili's cremation, sitting on the bench where they often sat, staring at the sky in a daze. Her eyes, which had not closed for several days, were full of bloodshot, and everything around her was bloodshot. But what was rising in her mind was a black fog, spinning and trying to swallow her. She had cried dry and had no tears left.

Although Zhuhai in December was warm under the sun, most pedestrians wore long clothes and long pants. Zheng Jianxin had been wearing a tight black short-sleeved shirt and sweatpants these days. The sea breeze messed up her long hair, but she ignored it.

Xu Zhuang returned to Shenzhen on the day after Lili's cremation. Two years before, Xu Zhuang resolutely resigned from his high-paying job in a shipping company, rented an office in a hotel in Luohu, Shenzhen, and used 100,000 yuan to register an investment consulting company called "Shanlihong". He planned two real estate projects, and at the same time the company also provided real estate agency services. He made some money and became a boss!

After he got the money, the first thing he did was to realize his long-cherished wish: he registered a "skill training center for migrant workers" under his company. He provided free three to five months of skills training for migrant workers and young people who had just entered the city, from machining, electrician, to marketing, cashier, etc. Xu Zhuang said: "If migrant workers have been in the city for two years but have no skills, they will just mess around. If they don't mix well, they will become thieves and prostitutes!"

In the past six months, he had printed out all the projects that could be developed and thought of in his hometown into exquisite business plans, looking for foreign investment and cooperation. He was busy "talking" every day, and his lips were worn out. Xu Zhuang believed that if his hometown wanted to change its poverty, it must "borrow a boat to go to sea and borrow a hen to lay eggs" and cooperate in development.

Xu Zhuang had embarked on the right path, which was more important to Zheng Jianxin than herself. Her heart suddenly became much younger. In particular, he attracted investment for his hometown, which made her feel gratified. She owed Xu Zhuang too much, and she could never repay it in this life. She prayed for Xu Zhuang's success and happiness. Lili died, and Xu Zhuang left. Zheng Jianxin felt more lonely than ever before.

Afang and her friends came to the beach and saw Zheng Jianxin's expression. They were afraid that she could not stand the shock and something would happen, so they went to a newly opened psychological clinic and invited a counselor to talk to Zheng Jianxin for a long time.

A week later, Zheng Jianxin gradually calmed down. She tried to eliminate various obstacles in her heart and said to the sisters who were full of expectations for her: "The company still needs to be run! Lili was my sister. Only by cheering up can we live up to her. She is a member of our working class group!"

In the newly painted office, the workers were busy arranging the company's opening ceremony tomorrow, placing flower baskets and flower pots, and hanging the business license that had just been received.

Zheng Jianxin went to the company's newly established e-commerce department to learn about the situation. Aju said that many customers have visited their website, some to shop, and some to cooperate. Zheng Jianxin nodded with satisfaction. At this time, Xu Zhuang came hurriedly and asked Zheng Jianxin to stop her work at hand.

Xu Zhuang was wearing a navy blue suit, and his every move showed his handsomeness and elegance. He looked around the office with admiration, and turned his sincere admiration for Zheng Jianxin into a self-indulgent sense of achievement: "Ajian, congratulations!"

Zheng Jianxin said in a sweet and innocent voice: "I was inspired by you and followed your footsteps......" Looking at the photo of Zheng Jianxin, himself and Lili on her desk, Xu Zhuang sighed and said: "Ajian, I want to go back to my hometown."

"When, so urgent, what to do?"

"Tomorrow." Xu Zhuang picked up the photo and carefully examined it and put it in place, "I told you that the executive of the multinational investment company I met in the Hong Kong prison did not forget the favor I protected him after he was released from prison, and recently introduced me to several large companies."

"Oh," Zheng Jianxin finally understood what he meant and handed him the water.

Xu Zhuang smiled again, took the water and continued: "After hearing me talk about the situation in my hometown, the bosses of those companies were interested and trusted me. They agreed to go together tomorrow and let me take them to investigate and plan to invest in building a hydropower station." He paused and said softly: "I will take Sister Lili back."

Zheng Jianxin nodded silently, "You go to handle the procedures for taking the ashes first, and we will have lunch together at noon. I will see Sister Lili off."

Xu Zhuang knew that if he wanted to comfort Sister Lili, he had to do something great. He said: "The water in the valley of my hometown has been flowing for thousands of years. Now it will bring great benefits to the villagers! I also bought a closed cement factory in the mainland and planned to rebuild it in our village. With electricity, factories and roads, it won't take a few years for my hometown to change its appearance and become as wealthy as the people here! People in the village don't have to travel thousands of miles to work!"

Zheng Jianxin looked at him and nodded vigorously. This was her Xu Zhuang, who did things in a big way. He gave up his comfortable life of more than 20,000 yuan a month. He went out to work hard. After making money, he thought about his hometown and how so many people in his hometown could get out of poverty. She heard from Lili that Xu Zhuang had been looking for information and reading professional books all day and night for the past six months, just to master more knowledge and realize this dream. In contrast, Zheng Jianxin felt that she was just looking at the tip of her nose and making a living.

Seeing that those fruit girls were busy and never stopped, interrupting the conversation from time to time and asking Zheng Jianxin for instructions on various matters, Xu Zhuang felt embarrassed to affect her again and had to leave.

"Wait," Zheng Jianxin turned around and took out a mobile phone from the desk, "This is for my dad. Tell him that I will take the child back to see them after the company is sorted out in a few months." Then she took out a cowboy hat and a pair of jeans, "Specially for you, you will look handsome with them!"

Xu Zhuang was stunned at first, looked at Zheng Jianxin's face, and then looked at this seemingly mocking but meaningful gift, clapped his hands and laughed: "Okay, okay!" He took them. Zheng Jianxin walked him two steps, then suddenly stopped and pulled him aside, whispering, "Remember one thing, so you don't forget it. I want to ask you to take care of my Sister Chahua's affairs, and go to the court to ask why they haven't been divorced for two years? It is said that the defendant never showed up. Your project is about to be completed, can you arrange a job for her?"

Xu Zhuang said he would definitely do it, and told Zheng Jianxin not to worry. When Xu Zhuang turned around to leave, his eyes caught sight of the small checkered handbag on Zheng Jianxin's table that had been washed almost white. Xu Zhuang smiled to himself, "Now that you are a boss, you have to change your handbag to a new one!" Zheng Jianxin glanced at him affectionately, and said insincerely but seriously: "This is a branded product, I can't bear to part with it!"

Xu Zhuang nodded knowingly, and said in a straightforward tone: "When I'm back from my hometown, I'll give you a new one!" Zheng Jianxin didn't decline and responded straightforwardly: "Okay, someone is giving me a gift, why don't I take it?"

The two of them spoke with underlined meaning, and their hearts were warm. The others present didn't understand, but they were infected by their friendly mood and looked at them with a smile.

Although Zheng Jianxin was reluctant, she knew that now was not the time to chat, so she had to take Xu Zhuang's hand and said softly: "Brother Zhuang, I'll wait for your good news!"

Xu Zhuang nodded, grinning: "When the hydropower station is completed, I will ask Boss Zheng to cut the ribbon!" He couldn't help but hug her gently and whispered in her ear: "Take care of yourself!" Xu Zhuang's broad chest was still so warm, and the strong masculine breath made Zheng Jianxin a little dazzled, and she was even more reluctant to let him leave.

The fruit girls passing by them all covered their mouths and laughed, and moved lightly so that the two could enjoy this sweet moment. They all knew Zheng Jianxin's experience, and they had great sympathy and regret for this pair of lovers who were destined to be together.

As Zheng Jianxin was walking Xu Zhuang to the stairs, she heard someone downstairs ask, "Who is Zheng Jianxin?" Zheng Jianxin thought that someone was looking for business, so she shook hands with Xu Zhuang and replied, "I am, please come up!"

The two people who came up were actually policemen! One of them showed his police officer ID and said seriously, "We are policemen. You are being summoned according to law for suspected bigamy!"

Everyone was stunned, even Xu Zhuang was at a loss for a moment. "Liang Xiangyun?!" Zheng Jianxin's face turned pale and she whispered in hatred. She originally thought that "bigamy" and "imprisonment" were Liang Xiangyun's blackmail and intimidation. When Ahua sent the message, she was a little flustered, but after thinking calmly, she thought that this kind of thing would not happen easily. At this moment, the sudden appearance of the policemen made her feel dizzy like a thunderbolt, and she realized that the situation was serious.

"If it is a blessing, you can't escape it, and if it is a disaster, you can't avoid it." (a Chinese idiom). In the past two days, she had sorted out all kinds of possible things and made various psychological preparations. Zheng Jianxin quickly calmed down, without saying a word, slowly read the summons, and signed her name.

"No!" Xu Zhuang's fierceness suddenly came up, and he shouted like a volcano erupting to stop the two policemen: "No! No! You are wrong!"

"Sir, please move aside and don't interfere with our performance of official duties!" A policeman said, signaling Xu Zhuang with an electric baton.

"No!" Xu Zhuang refused flatly. He was worried that Zheng Jianxin would be bullied if she went out of his sight.

"Brother Zhuang, it's okay." Zheng Jianxin gently pushed Xu Zhuang away with her elbow and said to everyone: "Don't worry, it's okay, I will explain everything clearly!"

Looking at Zheng Jianxin's calm expression, Xu Zhuang also slowly calmed down, and then he felt that he had overreacted, and slowly moved away.

Watching the police take Ajian to the car and leave, Xu Zhuang immediately called Zhong Haicai, but the call didn't go through; he found Achang again, and then he knew that Zhong Haicai was detained when passing the customs, and he and several workers were passing the customs to help.

In a hurry, Xu Zhuang suddenly thought of Chen Xiao, although he had never met him. Xu Zhuang finally found Chen Xiao's phone number in Zheng Jianxin's small phone book and called him. After listening to Xu Zhuang's story, Chen Xiao pondered for a moment and said calmly that he had been in Guangzhou and told Xu Zhuang not to worry. He would help him for the sake of fellow villagers. He said that he knew the truth and would call his friends in the police to help deal with the matter.

After contacting Chen Xiao, Xu Zhuang rushed to the border to wait for Achang, while calling his old workers at Xiangzhou Port, renting a boat to wait for orders, and crossing the sea to the town of Yinbao Island. Achang said that he knew friends in Fujian here and was familiar with the police there, so he called him in Macau to ask for help. Now he and several workers were about to cross the border to testify at the Public Security Bureau to prove that Zhong Haicai and Zheng Jianxin were not bigamy.

Xu Zhuang took out all the 20,000 yuan travel expenses he brought with him and stuffed them into Achang's hand: "As long as they offer a price to release the person, no matter how much, I will pay!"

In the pre-trial room of the police station. The police officer in charge looked through the transcript and said to Zhong Haicai and Zheng Jianxin: "Macau resident Liang Xiangyun accused you two of bigamy in our district court. The district court transferred the case to our bureau for investigation in accordance with the law because of insufficient evidence. I have read your confessions just now."

Zhong Haicai looked confused and was at a loss. He beat his chest with his hands from time to time and stared at the ground with his head down. Zheng Jianxin was in a trance, biting her lips tightly, and her chest was filled with anger of being wronged. As soon as she was taken into the police station, she went through the "routine" procedures. She held up a sign with her address and took a photo, took fingerprints, was searched, and all her belongings were taken away.

Suddenly, there was a noise outside.

"Achang?" Zheng Jianxin just turned her head to listen, and a female police officer beside her slammed the table and said sternly: "What are you looking at? Sit down! It's all because of you mistresses, you're hanging out with rich men, and you're seducing officials. You've ruined the social atmosphere!"

"Zheng Jianxin!" The chief police officer shouted loudly, "You're extremely dishonest! You didn't know anything, you didn't know, and you only found out later! -- Look at the wall, confess and you'll be treated leniently, resist and you'll be treated severely, I'm giving you a chance! Think about it!"

Zheng Jianxin held back tears and shouted: "I really didn't know! I didn't know! I'm innocent!" "I'm not a mistress!" Zheng Jianxin stood up to argue, and the female police officer beside her held her shoulders tightly.

Zheng Jianxin's face turned purple and red, and she struggled desperately like a volcano erupting. Suddenly she stood up and shouted hoarsely, "I'm not a mistress! I'm not......" When the police didn't know how to deal with such an arrogant criminal suspect, there was a louder noise from the office next door.

Achang was excitedly explaining the facts to the two policemen: "Zhong Haicai and Liang Xiangyun have been separated in Macau for ten years, how could they commit bigamy?"

"Who can prove it!"

"Me!"

"Me!"

"And me!" Zhong Haicai's co-workers raised their hands one after another.

Policeman B: "Take out your ID cards! Take notes one by one!" The policeman waved his hand majestically. In the evening, Zhong Haicai and Zheng Jianxin were locked up in the detention room. Zheng Jianxin leaned against the wall, feeling hopeless. Although she was extremely tired, her heavy eyelids closed and opened, opened and closed, and she wanted to sleep for a while but couldn't. Mosquitoes kept buzzing around her face and biting her legs and feet. At first she tried to drive them away, but in the end she didn't even have the strength to do so.

She remembered her childhood, playing on the hillside, and she remembered walking on the way to school with a basket of mushrooms on her back. It was already very cold in winter. She had no cotton pants and only wore a pair of patched pants and cloth shoes with barefoot, but she didn't know that this was poverty. She was happy in her heart.

She remembered the topic of the composition class written by the teacher on the blackboard in the middle school: "My Ideal"...... At that time, she thought the outside world was so good and the future was so good.

She remembered saying goodbye to her hometown, the old bus ran on the rugged mountain road, crossing the big and small bridges, and raising dust. She and her fellow countrymen in the bus were happy that they finally got out, walked out of poverty, and went to Guangdong, "there will be bread, everything will be there."

She remembered the workshop of the electronics factory, holding a lunch box with only a few pieces of meat and a few green vegetables and dozing off in front of the workbench. At that time, the biggest wish was to stop working overtime and have a good sleep. She remembered that when she first came to Zhuhai, she and Xu Zhuang timidly walked into the magnificent Yindu Hotel, standing outside the western restaurant with inferiority and dared not move.

She recalled that after she and Zhong Haicai received their marriage certificate at the Foreign Marriage Registration Office in her hometown, she breathed a sigh of relief. She was a woman recognized by society and a married woman. Even though he was more than 20 years older than she, it didn't matter. What she wanted was to be a decent person and a decent woman.

Zheng Jianxin thought: What are people running around for? Isn't it just to live like a human being? My expectations are not high. I just want to have enough food, clothes and live a decent life. For me, this bottom line of being a human being is so difficult to achieve.

Two contrasting scenes overlapped in her mind: the brightly lit night scene of Macau and the low thatched houses in the mountains; the sumptuous seafood on the dining table of the luxuriously decorated restaurant and the bowl of potatoes with the lid off the stove in Zheng Jianxin's hometown; the high heals and exposed thighs under the miniskirts of the fashionable girls on Lianhua Road in Gongbei, and the patched pants and cracked old military rubber shoes of Zheng Jianxin when picking mushrooms in the woods. Thinking about it, Zheng Jianxin still missed her grandfather the most. A photo of her grandfather in those days floated in front of her eyes, the photo of her grandfather as a model militiaman and as majestic as the police just now, as well as her grandfather's expectant face, and the villagers behind her grandfather, pointing and poking with contempt......

Thinking of this, she was full of feeling injustice and bitterness. At dawn, the mosquitoes gradually became fewer. She was really unable to support herself, wiped the hot sweat on her face, and dozed off in a daze. According to regulations, the time for public security summons and detention shall not exceed twelve hours. The next day, the police station asked the superior for instructions. The case could not be decided for a while, so the two were transferred to detention.

Zheng Jianxin and Zhong Haicai signed the criminal detention order and were sent to the detention center. A few days later, the chief police officer came to interrogate Zheng Jianxin and Zhong Haicai. The chief police officer asked, "What are your thoughts?" Zhong Haicai stood there blankly with swollen eyes, and habitually slapped his cheek with his palm every once in a while, without saying a word.

Zheng Jianxin glanced at the police officer in charge with weak and absent-minded eyes, trying to figure out what would happen next from the expressions on their faces. The police officer in charge tapped the table with his fingers, signaling Zheng Jianxin to speak. Zheng Jianxin spoke out the ideas she had thought about in the past few days. She faced the police officer in charge and put on a helpless smile: "We divorce, do you think the problem can be solved?"

The police officer in charge nodded and said nothing. After a while, he said: "Zheng Jianxin, your cousin Xu Zhuang applied for bail for you, and we have agreed." He paused, "In fact, your case is a headache for us. I personally sympathize with you. But I have to say that Zhong Haicai and Liang Xiangyun are in a de facto marriage and have not dissolved it, so you are committing bigamy."

The chief police officer explained in detail, "According to the judicial interpretation of my country's Marriage Law, before the promulgation of the new marriage registration regulations in 1994, those who did not register their marriage but lived together as husband and wife are considered de facto marriages. Liang Xiangyun and Zhong Haicai are in a de facto marriage. Their de facto marriage was not dissolved according to the law, and they did not go through the procedures for dissolving the marriage relationship in Macau. So we cannot say it is wrong for Liang Xiangyun to sue you. Zhong Haicai thought that he was unmarried because he had never received a marriage certificate. This is a lack of understanding of the law, and you, Zheng Jianxin, married him without clarifying their relationship. Liang Xiangyun and Zhong Haicai are residents of Macau. Whatever they do, getting married, divorced, or committing bigamy in Macau, we cannot control it according to Macau law. But Liang Xiangyun went to the mainland. Even if Liang Xiangyun's marriage certificate was forged, it is difficult to overturn the factual marriage between them during their stay in the mainland. Of course, this is just our understanding, and it has not been judged by the court. We took into account the actual situation of this case, and Zhong Haicai is a compatriot from Macau, so we will give you a chance......"

Hearing the word "bigamy" from the police officer's mouth, Zheng Jianxin almost couldn't stand steadily. Hearing the "chance" to correct her mistakes, she confirmed the meaning of divorce, tried to calm herself down, and said: "We divorce!"

Zhong Haicai lowered his head in confusion. The chief police officer said: "Okay, I'll give you ten days!" The chief police officer asked them to sign and fingerprint the transcript.

Before letting them go, the police officer in charge said seriously: "I hope you can solve it as soon as possible. We can catch you back at any time! Remember!"

We women can also stand here decently

Zheng Jianxin and Zhong Haicai returned home with disheveled hair and sweat all over their bodies. Zheng Jianxin drank several large glasses of cold water in one breath, and without taking a shower or washing her hair, she took down the frame on the wall and took out the marriage certificate.

The marriage certificate was not dusty and was still brand new. After looking at Zhong Haicai, Zheng Jianxin threw the marriage certificate fiercely in Zhong Haicai's face: "I don't want anything except my son!"

Zhong Haicai usually talked a lot, but when something happened, he was scared and lost his soul. He was still in shock when he returned home. His eyes were dull, the corners of his mouth twitched, and he lowered his head and dared not to speak. In order to fulfill his promise of divorce, Zheng Jianxin moved to the collective dormitory of Fruit Girl with Huihui that afternoon. All the belongings were left to Zhong Haicai.

The next day, the two rushed to Guangzhou and took a flight to Guizhou. At the place where they had registered their marriage, they went through the procedures for a voluntary divorce agreement. When they returned to Zhuhai and walked out of Gongbei Bus Station, when they were about to break up, Zhong Haicai staggered forward two steps, staring at Zheng Jianxin with round eyes, breathing heavily, and trembling. He wanted to say something, but he didn't know where to start.

Zheng Jianxin let out a long breath and said to Zhong Haicai: "Okay, the problem is solved!" Facing the port square, she said to herself, I can finally be a truly upright person and stand in the sun! Zhong Haicai seemed to have had a dream, an illusion, and when he woke up, he had nothing and was at a loss. Although he was clumsy and awkward, he finally mustered up the courage to whisper to Zheng Jianxin what he had been saying in his heart for the past few days: "Whether in Macau or in the mainland, I will soon find Liang Xiangyun to divorce......"

At this point, he looked at Zheng Jianxin, "I will find you to marry again!"

Zheng Jianxin looked at him, raised a tolerant smile at the corner of her mouth, but shook her head firmly. The sky was clear in the port square, and pedestrians were coming and going on the street. In the green belt beside the road, red bauhinia, yellow acacia, and kapok were in full bloom, with bright colors; white and yellow orchids were wafting with fragrance. Zheng Jianxin took a deep breath of the air full of floral fragrance, trying to calm herself down, and she was going to start a new life again. She subconsciously stretched out her arms, as if to welcome it!

She was going to break up with Zhong Haicai. Zheng Jianxin saw that his eyes were filled with desolate tears, and she couldn't help raising her hand to help him wipe away the tears from the corners of his eyes.

"Brother Zhong, I will take care of you when you are old!" Zhong Haicai nodded with dull eyes. Xu Zhuang stood quietly not far away, with an indifferent look; Ahua supported Zhong Haicai and slowly left.

In just ten days, Xu Zhuang went through purgatory twice. Now Zheng Jianxin was divorced and a free woman again, and life had returned to the starting point. He not only mustered up the courage to ignite the flame of love, but more importantly, he had a responsibility to Zheng Jianxin, a responsibility that no one could replace: to protect her well and cherish her.

Xu Zhuang saw Zheng Jianxin coming over and looking at him with eyes wide open and eyebrows relaxed. He couldn't help but feel his heart pounding. He whispered: "Ajian, why don't we hand over the company to Afang and the others, and take Huihui back to the countryside. We can live together and work on projects together. We can do a lot of things!"

"Brother Zhuang, I know you love me as deeply as the sea......" Zheng Jianxin looked straight at his face, looking at his eyes shining with desire, with mixed feelings, a trace of tenderness flashed in her eyes, and she became resolute in an instant, "But I plan to stay, for Huihui, for myself, and for Sister Lili to watch me fulfill my dream......"

"Ajian, we have suffered too much grievance here, don't you think it's not enough?" Xu Zhuang begged bitterly.

A wave of passion surged uncontrollably in Zheng Jianxin's heart. She raised her eyebrows and looked at him with a sharp gaze: "We workers here have been working hard day and night, and have paid too much. Building buildings, working in factories...... We are under the sky and on the ground. Since we have built this city, we can stand here; I am a woman, I can stand here decently without relying on men!"

As she spoke, those sad past events came to her mind, and Zheng Jianxin choked up and couldn't continue. She leaned on Xu Zhuang's shoulder and cried sadly. When she stopped crying, she raised her head and looked at Xu Zhuang: "We should live like human beings, not just for money, but for a spirit. Brother Zhuang, this world is also our world!"

Xu Zhuang stared at Ajian for a long time with a pair of scorching eyes. He sighed: "I listen to you!" He knew Zheng Jianxin's personality, and it was difficult to change once she made a decision. He could only gently stroke her shoulders and say: "Take care! Take care of yourself and the child! I......will be back!"

Zheng Jianxin smiled and licked her trembling lips. A pool of tears on her eyelashes was sparkling. She nodded vigorously, and the tears fell on her face and Xu Zhuang's chest......

48

Fruit Girl's Company is finally open,
and the pearl is found

Zheng Jianxin said goodbye to Xu Zhuang and went straight to the Fruit Girl's main store. In the morning, when Zheng Jianxin and Zhong Haicai just flew back to Guangzhou from Guizhou, they received a call from Afang. The person on the other end of the phone was flustered and just said that the store could not get any goods and asked her to come back quickly. Zheng Jianxin walked into the stall and was stunned. The shelves were almost empty. Aju and others were sitting on the side with their heads down. When they saw Zheng Jianxin coming in, they all surrounded her.

"Sister Jianxin, you are back, you are back, it's good that you are back!" The fruit girls chattered. Zheng Jianxin pointed at the shelf in confusion: "What's wrong? Didn't you go to buy goods? How can you do business like this?" Everyone looked at each other, bowed their heads and said nothing, like eggplants withered in the hot days of summer.

Afang said: "A few bad guys asked us to buy goods from their Fruit Alliance. When we refused, they threatened the bosses of the wholesale market not to give us goods."

"It's really an unprovoked disaster!" Zheng Jianxin jumped on the four-wheeled small truck after hearing it, "Afang, drive, go find them! Are they ghosts? Are they wolves?" Zheng Jianxin brought a few girls to the fruit stall where she bought goods in the fruit wholesale market angrily. The boss was talking to a few people.

"Uncle Guang, why don't you sell fruits to us?" Zheng Jianxin asked. The boss called Uncle Guang turned his head and looked at Zheng Jianxin, hesitant to speak, as if he had something to hide, and cast his eyes on the people around him.

A scoundrel came up, grinning, and looked at Zheng Jianxin: "Oh, you are the fruit girl Ajian, right? I've heard of you for a long time!"

Zheng Jianxin looked at the scoundrel, stared at him without any fear and asked: "Who are you?"

"It doesn't matter who I am, unless you plan to cooperate with us......" The scoundrel lit a cigarette and sprayed smoke to Zheng Jianxin, "Brother Guang will only cooperate with our Fruit Alliance company in the future, how about it? Or you can join our company too?"

Zheng Jianxin was stunned, looking at the owner of the fruit shop, the owner turned his head away and didn't dare to look at her, lowered his head and said nothing. Zheng Jianxin turned around and left angrily. The rascal said loudly behind her: "Don't say I didn't tell you. Our company has bought all the fruits sold by the pile in all the markets nearby. If you don't accept it, you can go buy those sold by kilograms. This is called keeping out of each other's way!"

Zheng Jianxin stopped, turned around, and shouted coldly: "I don't believe you can cover the sky with one hand!" The group returned to the fruit shop. Afang distributed lunch boxes to everyone, but everyone was dejected and had no appetite. Zheng Jianxin frowned. There were villains in all walks of life who bullied the market and bullied small business owners. She must find a way to deal with them.

Afang picked up the lunch box and cursed: "While eating melon seeds, we got a bug. (There are all kinds of people!)" She put the lunch box in front of Zheng Jianxin: "Sister Jianxin, let's eat first."

Zheng Jianxin shook her head and said nothing. Aju hesitated for a moment and said, "Sister JianXin, how about...... let's talk to that 'fruit alliance'?" Afang pouted and retorted disdainfully, "Aju, you are crying at the wrong grave. Those people are just hooligans, scumbags, and dung beetles who want to sting people. What is there to talk about? They don't work hard, but they still want to peel our skin!"

"What should we do now? We can't stop doing business!" A girl named Ahong said, "Otherwise, let's call the police and report those people for bullying us and arrest them all!"

Several girls looked at Ahong and didn't know whether to laugh or cry. Aling, who was sitting in the corner, suddenly sighed, "It would be great if it were in our hometown. There are orange trees and apple trees all over the mountain there. No one cares if you pick them at will......"

Zheng Jianxin suddenly turned her head and looked at Aling. Aling didn't know if she said anything wrong, and quickly covered her mouth with her hand.

"Yes, find the farm. How could I forget about him!" Zheng Jianxin slapped her thigh and whispered, "Aling, you are really the hero in the Water Margin (a Chinese classic novel), the Timely Rain (a character in the novel)!"

Afang reacted quickly: "'Glasses', Lin Weihua?!"

Zheng Jianxin nodded vigorously: "Snakes have their ways, and rats have their own ways. Let's give it a try!" She hurriedly found Lin Weihua's business card, called him, and told him about the bullying in the fruit market, and asked if it was possible to purchase large quantities of goods from their company? After hearing what was going on, Lin Weihua said that he would immediately ask the chairman for instructions.

Zheng Jianxin's eyes were a little bright: "Once we sign a contract with the farm and have a supply channel, the piles of goods in the fruit market will be ours sooner or later! Otherwise, the piles of goods will rot and they won't get a penny! I don't believe that those lazy bastards will pick fruits and sell them like us!"

The fruit girls were also very excited and clapped their hands. Soon Lin Weihua called back: "Our chairman fully supports you. He expressed his admiration for you after hearing about your story and said that he would supply you with the most favorable price. Come to our company to sign the contract tomorrow morning!" After a round of cheers, the girls picked up their lunch boxes and ate with big mouthfuls, eating with relish.

The worry of being at the end of their rope just now instantly evaporated like the mist after sunrise. Zheng Jianxin's tenacity infected each of them, and everyone immediately raised their heads and raised their eyebrows.

Early in the morning, Zheng Jianxin brought Afang and Aju to Zhengshun Farm in a small four-wheeled truck.

Chairman Wang of Zhengshun Farm was a fruit wholesaler in Tainan, Taiwan. Coincidentally, he was brought to the mainland by Bai Lang seven years before. He knew about Bai Lang. As soon as he saw Zheng Jianxin, he felt like an old friend. He asked her to sit down and said, "I know Bai Lang cheated you, but I didn't expect a girl to stand up so strongly. Where there is a will, there is a way. I admire you! Your arrival has made the farm glorious!"

Chairman Wang stood up and bowed deeply to Zheng Jianxin, saying that he was apologizing on behalf of the Taiwanese businessmen.

Zheng Jianxin waved her hands repeatedly: "No, no!"

Chairman Wang said that he had just returned from Taiwan and brought a catalog of Tainan fruit and agricultural products. "Please support me in the future!" Then he learned about the situation of the Fruit Girl Company in detail. What surprised him was that the online sales that Bai Lang had planned for him were actually started by Zheng Jianxin and her group of girls!

He clapped his hands and applauded, admiring Zheng Jianxin's ambition! Lin Weihua prepared a product price list based on Chairman Wang's instruction. Zheng Jianxin looked at the unit prices one by one, which were 20% lower than the price in the wholesale market. After discussing with Afang and Aju for a while, she chose the products they liked and signed the contract. She thought, we can make a lot of money!

Lin Weihua smiled and said, "Once the contract is signed, our farm will be your powerful source of goods!" "I begged for water but got wine (got more than I wanted), thank you!"

Zheng Jianxin held his hand, "I want to let all the fruit markets here see your farm's trademark. In one or two years, we will sign the second and third contracts with you! Our company will charter planes to sell your fruits and fruits from other farms in the Pearl River Delta to the whole country, like seafood sellers through airlines!"

"Hahaha!" Chairman Wang said with a smile, "General Manager Zheng is really ambitious! It's not you who should thank me, but I should thank you very much! Fish helps water, water helps fish. The fruits we grow will have no worries about the market, and Tainan's fruits will also have a market, my company should thank you! Come, let's drink a toast to our joint efforts to develop the market!"

The farm lady brought out a few glasses of bright red fruit wine brewed from farm fruits. When Zheng Jianxin raised the glass, she felt that the glass was very heavy, but her face was smiling happily, and her face was the same as the color of the wine.

Chairman Wang also patted his chest and said that he was willing to provide funds to support the development of Fruit Girl Company, and said that he would have a good talk with General Manager Zheng to let Fruit Girl Company be the exclusive online agent for the sales of Zhengshun Company's products. In the future, Zhengshun Company would also develop deep processing and fruit health products. The prospects for cooperation were broad and it would definitely be a win-win situation!

The sky and the farm fields outside the window were connected into a green one, setting off Zheng Jianxin's indescribable joy.

The Fruit Girl Company was finally open.

Zheng Jianxin was unwilling to spend extra money, and for the sake of environmental protection, she did not set off firecrackers. She only hang a string of electric firecrackers left over from the New Year by a shop owner on the door of the office, which emits red light and firecrackers from time to time, showing a festive atmosphere.

Regarding the opening ceremony, Zheng Jianxin meant to be happy within the scope of the sisters, and of course related business friends. The opening of a company was like a happy event in the neighborhood, and there would definitely be familiar and unfamiliar people who came to congratulate after hearing the news. There were flower baskets from several units delivered by the flower shop at the door of the company.

Zheng Jianxin was lightly dressed in a green Western suit with a white collar turned outward. There was a confident light in her eyes, like a lotus. She put her arm around Ahua's shoulders and laughed with Chairman Wang and Lin Weihua who came to attend the opening ceremony.

Achang came in wearing a suit and bowed to Zheng Jianxin as soon as he entered the door, congratulating her: "Congratulations! Congratulations! Business is booming and money is coming in!" He looked around the office, "Ajian, I'm so happy to be here!"

Zheng Jianxin and her colleagues were very polite. The gift sent by Achang and his colleagues was a painting of the scenery of Zhuhai and Macao. Achang saw Lin Weihua and knew that Zhengshun Farm also participated in the fruit company. He raised his thumb and said: "This is a phoenix wearing a peony on its head -- double the beauty!"

Lin Weihua said: "Yes! Our business scope is wide. We not only sell Taiwanese fruit pearl guava, soft-branch carambola, passion fruit, but also develop organic liquid fertilizer series, and promote excellent seeds, seedlings, cultivation technology......"

Ahua took out a small red notebook and knocked on Lin Weihua's head: "Alright, alright! Don't advertise your farm as soon as you open your mouth!"

Ahua was about to say something when a person suddenly appeared from the gap. Zheng Jianxin looked closely and saw that it was Chen Xiao!

She hurried over and asked him in surprise: "Mr. Chen, why are you here?"

Chen Xiao shrugged his shoulders cheerfully, rubbed his hands and said: "How can I not come to your big event, Zheng Jianxin? I came to congratulate! Let me have a drink!"

Then he said that he was conducting a survey of private enterprises in a research institute, and Fruit Girl Company was the best object for his research. The purpose was to write a research report to help the development of private enterprises and strive for a fair social environment for private enterprises to survive and compete. Everyone present happily said that this was "timely rain". There was a sound of leather shoes, and Afang welcomed two guests: a man and a woman.

The man was tall and thin, in his fifties, with neatly combed hair and a coffee-colored tie on his white short-sleeved shirt. The woman was in her sixties, elegant and graceful, with a very well-maintained figure, and the diamond pearls on her chest sparkled. Chairman Wang saw this and hurried over to the tall and thin man, nodded enthusiastically and shook his hand: "Director Zhan, you are really here, thank you so much!" He turned and greeted Zheng Jianxin: "This is Director Zhan from the Municipal Investment Promotion Office!"

"Hello! Welcome, welcome! Welcome to the leadership's guidance!"

"How dare I say guidance, I am here to learn!" Director Zhan turned and introduced the woman with him: "This is Kuang Zhenzhu, the boss of Macau Nan Guo Pearl Company, Boss Kuang!"

Chairman Wang and Zheng Jianxin hurriedly shook hands with Kuang Zhenzhu. Kuang held Zheng Jianxin's hand with one hand and adjusted her gold-rimmed glasses with the other hand. She carefully looked at Zheng Jianxin's face, then stroked her shoulder and said softly, "I saw your introduction in a magazine. You are ambitious! It's not easy! So I found Director Zhan and I must see you!"

Director Zhan said, "It's not easy for Boss Kuang to come this far. Now you have a big business. You have a factory in Zhuhai and do European trade in Macau!"

Kuang Zhenzhu's eyes were full of emotion and perseverance, which made her face have a special charm and made people imagine the charm of her smile when she was young. She looked around at Zheng Jianxin, Afang and a group of migrant workers, and said unexpectedly and with mixed feelings, "I was also a migrant worker! When I was young, I came to Macau with nothing and worked for more than 20 years. The world cannot do without us migrant workers!"

Zheng Jianxin stretched out her hands and was about to say something to Boss Kuang, but was interrupted by the loud and harsh sound of Chen Xiao's mobile phone. Chen Xiao heard that it was his wife

Jiaojiao's call. "What? What? You want me to go over and discuss it right away?...... What's the matter? Tell me clearly, I'm busy and can't leave!...... What chin fell off?" Chen Xiao hung up the phone with a "hmm" and "ah", with a look of not knowing whether to laugh or cry.

He pulled Zheng Jianxin aside: "Mrs. Tong's husband was placed under 'double regulation' by the Commission for Discipline Inspection this morning. Mrs. Tong was so anxious that the fake chin she had for plastic surgery broke through the skin and fell off. Jiaojiao is going to the hospital and is anxious for me to help. Sorry, I have to go......" After saying that, he pushed through the crowd and left.

Everyone heard what Chen Xiao said. "How funny!" Afang and a group of girls laughed so hard that they fell backwards and covered their stomachs. Zheng Jianxin shook her head and sneered twice at the arrogant face of Mrs. Tong that appeared in his mind.

"Be quiet! Be quiet!" Ahua still had something else to do. As she spoke, she opened the little red booklet in her hand and showed it to everyone: "Look what this is?" Everyone saw that it was Zheng Jianxin's university diploma in e-commerce, and they immediately congratulated her in unison.

"There is more good news!" Zheng Jianxin said, walking to the table and taking out two pink admission letters from the drawer, "Afang and Aju have been admitted to the provincial business school's on-the-job undergraduate class after more than a year of studying!"

Achang touched his forehead and shouted a sentence: "This is called the mountains need greening and people need education!" This made everyone applaud and laugh.

After the applause and laughter, Zheng Jianxin said confidently: "In our era of reform and change, no matter how difficult the environment each of us is in, I still believe in the saying that knowledge changes destiny!"

All of these people had witnessed Zheng Jianxin's journey. They respected Zheng Jianxin's experience and strong enterprising spirit from the bottom of their hearts, and applauded excitedly for a long time. After a while, Achang pulled Zheng Jianxin aside and whispered, "Is it okay for me to open a fruit supermarket in Macau? You teach me how to do business. What do you think I should sell? I'll place an order today!"

Zheng Jianxin said half seriously and half jokingly, "Great! That will be the first business transaction of our new company!" Ahua and the others heard their conversation and applauded again.

Zheng Jianxin's eyes were full of fire and she looked at everyone and said, "Just as everyone discussed, we, the working sisters, started by opening stalls and selling fruits on the street, and later opened chain stores in the factory area. In the future, we will sell online and expand our business to the mainland!"

She paused, and she didn't know whether she should say something in her heart. She was calm and confident, and expressed her true feelings. She said: "We are all shareholders and bosses. No one will bully anyone. If the business loses money, we don't complain; if we fall, we get up and work again. Don't we all have the dream of special economic zones and gold rush? Since we have dreams, we are eager to succeed, never retreat, and move forward courageously. As long as we don't kneel, we will never feel inferior to others!"

Her words were powerful. She also said: "How to distribute the money we make will be discussed by the shareholders. The employees we recruit in the future will all be our brothers and sisters. We should treat them as human beings! We will not lose our ambitions when we are poor, and we will not go crazy when we are rich. As the saying goes, everyone has a sky above their heads, and we must support our own world!"

Her heartfelt words touched the hearts of the workers. Everyone saw the future and felt at ease. Boss Kuang, who was drinking tea on the side, admired her ideals. There was another round of thunderous applause. The fruit girls all opened their eyes and relaxed their brows, and the venue was filled with joy. There was a figure swaying outside the office door. Following behind the figure was a tall, suited elder.

The figure came in timidly. He was Zeng Sheng. Because he had invested, Zheng Jianxin asked Afang to notify him to attend the opening ceremony and give him his official share certificate. Zheng Jianxin smiled and said, "Mr. Zeng, please come in! You are a shareholder, one of us, so there is no need to say welcome!"

"That's right, that's right." Although Zeng Sheng was worldly-wise, he was clumsy and could not say congratulatory words in front of the people who knew him best. Some fine beads of sweat oozed out of his bright head. The elder behind followed in.

Director Zhan immediately greeted him: "Ah! Mr. Zeng! It's you!" He turned around and introduced to everyone, "This is Dr. Zeng who came back from the United States. He came back to his hometown to invest in high-tech holographic imaging projects!"

Dr. Zeng's thick white hair was combed neatly and shiny, and he bowed deeply to everyone. Everyone applauded to welcome him.

Boss Kuang, who was standing by, stood up when she heard the words "return to hometown to invest", staring at the elder with surprised eyes.

Dr. Zeng looked kind, waved his hand slightly, and said: "Thank you all. I am Zeng Tianpeng, please forgive me for coming here uninvited. I come back every few years, and Zhuhai has changed a lot. This time my son told me to invest in the company run by a migrant worker. Great! I want to see a promising migrant worker, I come to congratulate! For a society to be better, we must not forget the enthusiasm and creativity of the vast majority of people at the bottom......"

Zheng Jianxin didn't expect Dr. Zeng to speak Mandarin fluently. At this time, Boss Kuang involuntarily moved forward a few steps, her body trembling a little. Her focused eyes lit up, and her throat couldn't help but make "oh", "oh" sounds. "Chen Tianpeng, could it be you?" Boss Kuang's surprised expression attracted Zeng Tianpeng's attention. He stopped talking. Instantly, a magical attraction pushed him towards Boss Kuang: This woman looks so familiar!

Director Zhan introduced Zeng Tianpeng: "This is Macau Kuang Zhengzhu, Boss Kuang!"

"Zhengzhu, Zhengzhu?!" Zeng Tianpeng murmured. His eyes

actually swept over Boss Kuang's face and body.

Zeng Tianpeng's forearms trembled a little. He wanted to exclude the dead Zhengzhu and confirm that this Zhengzhu was his Zhengzhu. In front of the crowd who mostly spoke Mandarin, he did not speak dialect alone with others out of courtesy, so he still used Mandarin: "Miss Kuang, may I ask if your family......"

Kuang Zhengzhu (Pearl) had confirmed that Zeng Tianpeng in front of her was her lover from 47 years before. Her heart was pounding, and she stroked her cheek with her hand, trying to calm herself down. Boss Kuang's slightly trembling fingers adjusted her gray velvety hair, and before he finished asking, she answered clearly: "This place, Xianglu Bay!"

"Ah!" He took a breath, her graceful demeanor and sweet voice told him that she was Zhengzhu of that year! Zeng Tianpeng got excited, and his beard trembled. He beat his chest and shouted, "I am Chen Tianpeng, Chen Tianpeng!"

When the facial features of the handsome Chen Tianpeng back then were restored to the facial features of the old man in front of her, Boss Kuang's face turned pale in an instant, and she opened her mouth but couldn't speak. She controlled her emotions, her eyes were moist, and she raised her trembling hands, as if she wanted to touch his face. She smiled at Zeng Tianpeng: "I recognized you, Brother Apeng, you haven't changed......"

Everyone was attracted by this sudden scene. A warm current rushed into Chen Tianpeng's chest and rushed to his mind. He shouted to Director Zhan in a hoarse voice: "She is Zhengzhu of the year, Zhengzhu! Zhengzhu I'm looking for!"

Surprise ran through Zeng Tianpeng's body like an electric wave. She, the beautiful girl 47 years ago, flashed before his eyes in an instant: the reluctance to leave, the shy closing of her bright almond eyes......

Boss Kuang's nostrils flared rapidly, and the sound of gunshots and shouts of catching an adulterer rang in her ears...... The scene of life and death separation appeared in her mind again: at the seaside in the dark, Apeng jumped into the water, someone wanted to shoot him, she rushed over and held up the gun with one hand, and the bullet shot into the sky......

Director Zhan blushed and adjusted his deep myopia glasses, and asked Boss Kuang stutteringly: "You are not...... dead?" Then, he added, "Dr. Zeng asked us to find out your whereabouts when he returned to Zhuhai for the first time 20 years ago......"

"I am not dead, I was rescued by Macau fishermen in the Hengqin Sea." She turned and whispered to Zeng Tianpeng, "I went to Hong Kong to look for you, but I couldn't find you, so I returned to Macau to work, set up a factory, and open a company......"

Director Zhan said loudly with emotion: "Today is a happy day!"

Zeng Tianpeng pulled Zheng Jianxin over and said to everyone with nostalgia: "For thousands of years, people have been looking for happiness and pearls. Today, in the hot land of Zhuhai Special Economic Zone with reform and opening up, all of you working here are pearls, and the Fruit Girl Company is the pearl. It depends on all of our hands to hold up the pearl of the South China Sea! I wish the Fruit Girl Company success!"

Zheng Jianxin waved her arms: "Thank you, Dr. Zeng, thank you Boss Kuang, and thank you everyone! "

Afang and a group of working girls were in high spirits, and the sound of applause and electronic firecrackers filled the air. In front of the spacious fruit shop, boxes of fresh fruits were golden and red, and the soft light was overflowing in the sun......

End: Life has to go on, life goes on

Zheng Jianxin was busy with company affairs for a while. When she was free, she thought of Mingming's coffee shop and the afternoon tea there. One afternoon, she took time to come to the coffee shop.

It was still a group of women, some familiar and some unfamiliar, sitting together for afternoon tea, still talking and laughing.

Zheng Jianxin wore a light green Western suit and smiled at them.

Some woman shouted at the door: "Ajian is here!"

"Ah, it's Ajian!" Everyone looked at the door, surprised and happy.

Zheng Jianxin's arrival caused a commotion. Someone said: "Isn't this the bride?" They all clapped their hands to welcome this "successful person".

Everyone laughed knowingly.

The small checkered handbag on the right shoulder of this "successful person" was washed white and looked a little old, but it was very coordinated with her noble temperament and elegant dress.

Zheng Jianxin smiled and sat in the middle of them.

She raised her glass and clinked glasses with them.

Everyone said that "Boss Zheng" was more beautiful. Zheng Jianxin accidentally saw a copy of Computer People stacked on several Mark Six lottery tabloids on the table. She looked up and asked the brown-haired girl next to her: "Yours?"

The brown-haired girl nodded: "I signed up for a secretarial class at the training center. It's unreliable to rely on others. I learn from you and rely on myself. "

"That's right! "Zheng Jianxin patted her shoulder.

"That's right," several girls shouted and laughed in dialect.

......

Through the large glass window, there was a noisy street scene, pedestrians hurried by, and Macau in the distance. Zheng Jianxin took a sip of coffee, and the scene reminded her of Lili. Lili said that here was a place where magpies chirped on the branches even without joy, which was quite tempting.

But the atmosphere here was so depressing that she could no longer breathe and could not sit still.

She looked over their heads, and outside the house was the vast sea and sky.

She got up and walked out to the port square, watching the people entering and leaving the country under the majestic building for a long time, with infinite feelings in her heart.

Around her were tall and graceful coconut trees, with handsome leaves on the tops of the trees gently waving. There were also kapok trees with upright branches, and the flowers on the branches were as red as fire and as bright as clouds. Especially the big banyan trees, the roots not only live in the ground, but also grow thick and thin roots, like countless fingers stretched out, firmly grasping the surface.

She finally worked hard like these trees to support her own sky. At this moment, she thought of her grandfather, she wanted to comfort her grandfather, and her heart was filled with complex emotions.

She looked up at the sky, across the Lovers' Road and looked at the sea......

In the sea stood the full-body statue of the Zhuhai Fisher Girl: the pearls she held high in her hands were shining, intertwined with the sun's rays......

Zheng Jianxin stroked the small checkered handbag and stared at her for a long, long time.

In the era of reform, people who have made fortunes, wealthy people, and people who have made rapid progress in their careers are admired and followed by the media. They are dazzling pearls; migrant workers are like grains of sand, but sand is also dazzling and reflects the brilliance of the sun. When grains of sand become pearls, how brilliant this society and this world will be. It will be really brilliant!

The sea is surging......

Written in January 2009
Finalized during the Spring Festival of 2012

POSTSCRIPT

Time flies. Many scenes in life, especially the social life scenes of ordinary people and small potatoes, flash by and will soon be forgotten and fade into oblivion.

In 1980, China implemented the "reform and opening up" policy. Millions of farmers walked out of the countryside, broke free from the land that bound them, and flocked to the special economic zones and cities, forming a wave of migrant workers.

The inspiration for this novel came when, while driving, I heard a news broadcast on the radio about several female workers in Shenzhen who had gone from buying fruit for their coworkers to successfully starting a fruit company and becoming the queens of the wholesale market. This inspiring news story quickly connected the many stories of struggle and hardship of migrant workers I had heard and witnessed. I recorded them in the form of a novel, presenting readers with a glimpse into life during the early days of the migrant worker boom in the Guangdong Special Economic Zone.

Behind the GDP figures of the special economic zone in those years, there were the hands of migrant workers. Miracles were created by them. They sustained the sufferings of pioneers of an era: hard work and extremely mismatched poor material life and social discrimination.

In people's impression, migrant workers are dirty living tools who move bricks at construction sites all day long. It's totally wrong. They were just born in the wrong place.

They have their own rich spiritual world, mourning their misfortune and angry at the injustice of society. Their fathers also participated in the "revolution" to seize power, and then they volunteered to serve the people, and became "second-class citizens"--farmers--with their children.

The migrant workers in this book are not illiterate, and most of them have high school education. In the process of seeking survival, development, and changing the fate of the people at the bottom of society, they have a tenacious spirit of motivation in their hearts. Just as the protagonist Zheng Jianxin in the novel represents: forbearing and moving forward, never retreating in silence, holding up the sky above their heads, longing to live with dignity, and radiating the light of reason in their thoughts.

Man is the summation of social relations. In the intersection of "one country, two systems" and two social systems, this typical environment that can more fully display the desires of people from all walks of life, it more deeply reveals different destinies and their complex mental journeys.

To record them truthfully is to record an era from one angle.

After writing the first draft of the novel, I experimented with making a minimally funded film of the same name to gauge its response. Unexpectedly, it was selected as one of the 11 films for the 2011 Cologne Film Festival in Germany, with the official commentary hailing it as "a rare glimpse into Chinese film culture." This novel in Chinese was published by China Pictorial Publishing House in 2012. I am still grateful for the concern of President Tian Hui at the time.

More than ten years have passed. Fortunately, there are still friends who remember it and love it. I hope that more readers outside China will see it and historians and humanities scholars will study it. With the support of friends from Remembering Publishing, this English version is published. I am grateful to Dr. Qiao Xihua, who enthusiastically planned and presided over the translation. My relatives and friends, especially my niece Zhang Xiaoyu and her husband who live far away in Guangzhou, have always encouraged me. I would like to express my sincere gratitude here.

August 23, 2025
New York, USA